PRAISE FOR THE WORK OF JULIE KAEWERT AND THE BOOKLOVER'S MYSTERIES!

"Publishing can get pretty deadly in England, as evidenced in Julie Kaewert's engaging and complex thriller, *Unsolicited. Unsolicited* appeals on several levels, not the least of which is the character of Alex, a protagonist directly from the Dick Francis school of strong yet vulnerable, self-reliant young men. . . . Adding to the pleasure here are the vicious rivalries between various publishers in London, giving the novel an air of authenticity unusual in mysteries."
—*San Francisco Chronicle*

"An action-packed, suspenseful thriller, with a mystery that grows downright spooky before it is all very satisfactorily wrapped up in an exciting man-against-the-sea climax. There's never a dull page in this international page-turner. We hope to hear from Kaewert again. She is good!"
—*The Denver Post*

"With its complicated plot, unassuming amateur sleuth and low-key love story, *Unsolicited* is very much an old-fashioned, classical English mystery that, but for a few modern t[ouches] [could have been written in] the days of [. . .]e."
—[. . .] [Denv]*er Post*

"I was th[. . .] [. . .]. As I read, I was remi[nded of . . .] Dick Francis novels. [. . .] [w]rites about a milieu with which she is familiar, and this adds to the realism of the novel. I recommend this new mystery highly!"
—*Mystery News*

"A roller-coaster ride of thrills."
—*Ocala Star-Banner*

UNBOUND
Julie Kaewert

BANTAM BOOKS

NEW YORK TORONTO LONDON SYDNEY AUCKLAND

UNBOUND

A Bantam Crime Line Book / December 1997

ISBN 0-553-57715-8
Published simultaneously in the United States and Canada

PRINTED IN THE UNITED STATES OF AMERICA

OPM   10   9   8   7   6   5

With love and thanks to
Wilma Ann Wallin Sagers
and
William, Sarah and Allie

ACKNOWLEDGMENTS

First, warm thanks to Krysha Niblett, who for more than a year delighted my children while I wrote and rewrote. I'll always be indebted to my writing group and dedicated reviewers: Karen Albright Lin, Janet Fogg, Renee Sprik, Jim Hester, Amy Beringer, Roxane Perruso, and my mother, Wilma Ann Wallin Sagers. Thanks for the countless hours of reading, discussing, and encouraging.

Also, thanks to Laura Blake and Mitchell Waters of Curtis Brown, calm, encouraging and ever-pleasant agents, for making me one of the happiest people in the world. And equal thanks to Kate Miciak of Bantam for welcoming me into her amazing group of authors, and for being an immensely talented, fun, and encouraging editor. I will always be grateful to Johanna Tani for her masterful copyedit.

My heartfelt thanks always to the divine Diane Mott Davidson (bestselling culinary mystery author, Bantam), who twice, at length, cheerfully sat down to talk to a virtual stranger about editors and other publishing issues. Since then she has offered encouragement and kind words at every turn. Thanks, too, to her husband Jim Davidson, who was good enough to read a stranger's first novel and offer similar encouragement.

Huge thanks also to rare book experts John Yates (San Rafael, California), John Windle, Antiquarian Bookseller (San Francisco), and Gyngr and Michael Schon (Old London Bookshop, Bellingham, Washington) who cheerfully endured long interviews and fact-checking sessions, and provided books, catalogues, and other resources.

Some sort of rare privilege in heaven is due Timothy and Kathryn Beecroft of St. Albans, England, who have dared to be friends, book experts and long-suffering editors for an American author writing in British English. The same is true for Sally Jackson Freeman, Tracy and Johnny Jackson, Lizzy Jackson, and their parents, Pat and John Jackson of Heronsgate, near Chorleywood. They gathered us into their family nearly fifteen years ago and have offered friendship, tea and education on all things English ever since. Thanks, too, to Moira Prakash, Rachel Knoedler, and Gwynn Lawrence for foreign language advice, and to Julia Garza for medical expertise.

Enormous gratitude to Tom and Enid Schantz of the Rue Morgue Mystery Bookstore in Boulder for generously providing information, encouragement, and help of all kinds. And many thanks to Nancy Missbach, bookwoman extraordinaire (printer, binder, and book restoration expert, Dancing Horse Studios, Denver), for sharing her expertise and patiently answering endless questions.

Sincere thanks also to David R. Godine, of David R. Godine, Publisher, Boston, for inspiring a fascination with printing, publishing and rare books long ago. Belated but fervent thanks to Jeanne Douglass and Dave Brower for introducing me to one of Dave's favorite authors, who helped inspire the Alex Plumtree series. Also belated thanks to Ned Perrin, author and professor at Dartmouth College, for encouraging persistence.

UNBOUND

PRESS RELEASE • PRESS RELEASE

FOR IMMEDIATE RELEASE

Publication date: 1 September 1997

Contact: Claire Dunham

0171-449-6753

The Stonecypher Saga
by Angela Mayfield

Bizarre and heretofore undisclosed secrets about one of Britain's favourite authors, Marcus Stonecypher, are revealed today in Angela Mayfield's suspenseful first novel, *The Stonecypher Saga*, published by Plumtree Press (ISBN 0-812-11089-Z, £14.99). Mayfield's novel based on fact not only stuns with its revelations bout Stonecypher's secret life of political fanaticism, but also reveals a secret code that Stonecypher used to embed treasonable political statements in his books.

Author Mayfield has cleverly used the findings of her doctoral thesis in English literature to construct a page-turner that will change the world of literature forever. As *The Stonecypher Saga* begins, literary scholar Anna Harrington is delighted to have discovered a code within Stonecypher's novels. Astounded at the number of typographical errors in his four books, printed by Plumtree Press between 1900 and 1914, Anna writes down each word in which a misprint is found. Curiously, all the misprints are complete words on their own—"friend," for instance, instead of "fried." When she is finished, to her astonishment, her pad of paper holds an unmistakably deliberate, radical sentence pertaining to the abolition of monarchies everywhere, and the desirability of a single world government.

Plumtree Press•54 Bedford Square•London WC1B 3NA
Phone 0171-449-7798•Fax 0171-449-7799

From the time her university professor begins to share her discovery with his colleagues, Anna is threatened, then pursued. She begins to understand that a secret political society to which Stonecypher belonged is very much alive—and very much wishes her dead.

Author Angela Mayfield's expertise on Stonecypher brings vivid detail and a remarkable intensity to her debut novel. Mayfield received her Ph.D. in English literature last year from Cambridge University.

—END—

Note: Plumtree Press's association with the author Marcus Stonecypher extends over the better part of a century. The famed writer resided in our building in Bedford Square for the twenty or so years before we acquired the building in 1915, and to this day we provide tours for Stonecypher enthusiasts on the first Friday of each month at ten a.m. in cooperation with the Stonecypher Society. Plumtree Press published those four classics in which Angela Mayfield found so many misprints: The Figure in the Library, The Engraving on the Desk, The Symbol by the Door, *and* The Room of the Maiden. *Finally, Stonecypher himself was fond of pointing out that his protagonists bore a remarkable similarity to his good friend Edward Plumtree, or "Plum." We are proud to publish this work of fiction based on fact to commemorate the one hundred and twentieth anniversary of Stonecypher's birth.*

Plumtree Press•54 Bedford Square•London WC1B 3NA
Phone 0171-449-7798•Fax 0171-449-7799

CHAPTER 1

These are not books, lumps of lifeless paper, but minds alive on the shelves. From each of them goes out its own voice . . . and just as the touch of a button on our set will fill the room with music, so by taking down one of these volumes and opening it, one can call into range the voice of a man far distant in time and space, and hear him speaking to us, mind to mind, heart to heart.

—GILBERT HIGHET

When I entered Armand Beasley's library that night for what would be the first and last time, it inspired the awe I always felt in the presence of a great mass of books. The myriad shelves held a wealth of volumes, each with its own subtle secrets and echoes of the past, and I was humbled to realise that I would only ever know a minute fraction of them in my lifetime.

But on that night I also got an inkling of the horrors books can hold, the spine-tingling evil of any truly good thing gone bad. For under Beasley's gilded morocco spines and original dust jackets lurked deadly secrets—one of which nearly sent me to the great library in the sky.

The door of Armand Beasley's seventeenth-century manor house, Watersmeet, swung open with a groan to reveal a gaunt, thin-nosed man of roughly my own age—thirty-two—wearing round wire-rimmed glasses and a shoulder-length ponytail. The ponytail was shiny, dark, and clean, and the man was striking in a male-model sort of way. I had the vague feeling I'd seen him somewhere before.

"Hello," I said, attempting friendliness in the face of his unsmiling silence. He regarded us seriously as cool air from the big old house wafted into the warm late-August evening, sweeping over us like a gentle breeze. "I'm Alex Plumtree, and this is my friend, Angela Mayfield."

My companion, the tiny, blond-bobbed, athletic woman who was first my friend from university and now an author for Plumtree Press, shot me a resentful glance and drew herself up to her full height of five feet and one inch. Peevish and intense, Angela was dressed to stun in a fuchsia knit dress that contrasted dramatically with her tan, and ended well above her golden knees. Angela, who was a fairly tough nut, was on the difficult side of a bad case of unrequited love—and I was the object of her affections. She didn't like it when I broadcast signals indicating that she wasn't my girlfriend.

As the man at the door silently assessed us, I reflected irritably that Angela was nothing if not persistent. In fact, she had been camped at the Plumtree ancestral home, the Orchard, all summer, ever since I'd asked her to come down to London in late May for author publicity photos in front of the plum trees. She had simply never left, and never offered an explanation. Tonight she had spotted on my desk the invitation to Armand's party, addressed to Alex Plumtree and Friend, and had invited herself along.

So I'd had to develop a new art form, the art of communicating in subtle ways that Angela and I were not "together." I introduced her casually; I stood at a slight distance; I rarely touched her. Angela knew all too well that the woman I wanted to be with that night, and every night, was Sarah Townsend. But Sarah was, as usual, remote in mind as well as body at the moment, halfway through a six-month secondment to her investment bank's Paris office.

The pony-tailed man nodded formally, and gestured to indicate that we were to step inside. "Giles Rutherford," he said with measured cordiality and utmost seriousness, stepping back as he swung open the door. "I'm pleased to meet you. The party's this way."

Giles. The name snapped into place; I had heard about him via the Bedford Square grapevine, a surprisingly accurate communications network for those of us involved in the incestuous world of book publishing in London. The walls of the buildings in Bedford Square, where our small family publishing firm had its offices, had been privy to the most cherished secrets of Bloomsbury's writers, book publishers, and collectors for centuries. More temporary occupants of the square, like me, heard them too. According to the grapevine, there was some doubt as to whether Giles merely assisted Armand with his library, or had duties of a more personal nature.

I told myself it was none of my business and did as he instructed, following Angela through the entry and into the great hall, treading on Turkish carpets that covered creaky wooden floors. A waiter approached us, offering a tray of heavy crystal champagne flutes, and I took one, sipping my champagne as I looked about.

Watersmeet was a beautiful old pile of ancient bricks, timbers, and leaded glass. The interior was elegant and simple, furnished with eclectic antiques, seventeenth-century French tapestries, and original oil paintings, all on a background of creamy walls interspersed with dark timbers.

As we traversed the great hall, I could see directly into the library, a huge room at the far end of the hall that could be closed off with massive oak doors. There was a hushed atmosphere in that room, and I could see a dozen or so people chatting quietly inside.

Even Angela couldn't be blasé at first sight of Armand's library. As we walked through the doorway she turned briefly to me and mouthed, "Wow," with a lift of her eyebrows. I nodded, smiled, and raised my own eyebrows in response.

Armand's library was magnificent. The ceiling was at least eighteen feet high, and most of the walls were covered in books. Where the walls weren't hidden by well-preserved volumes, they were covered in dark cherry wainscotting and framed pages of illuminated manuscripts—nothing later than sixteenth century, of course. And, unusual for a library, it wasn't a gloomy room; a huge, leaded-glass bay window with diamond-shaped panes admitted light that was filtered by the towering and ancient trees outside. The perfect light for a world-class library; enough to be practical, but never enough to fade the spines of resident books.

Armand, deep in conversation with an elderly man across the room, smiled and held up a hand in a greeting that signalled "I'll be right over." I smiled back, waving in return as we continued to follow Giles to a polished walnut library table. A number of books were lying as if on display there, tantalising between matching black tôle lamps that had not yet been lit for the evening.

As I approached I could see that these were not just any old books. They were the works of sought-after authors, all in nearly perfect condition, dust jackets and all. Even from a distance I thought I could pick out a Vesalius, an atlas-sized volume of the first drawing of a human dissection from Renaissance days, worth at least 50,000 pounds. Copies of this rare book came into circulation only every few years or so, and then usually at Christie's or Sotheby's. Angela, who I'd discovered was a very tactile person, was already fingering it. I followed her slowly, in awe, toward the table and turned my attention to the books with undisguised delight.

It was only when Giles hurried past us to someone at the far end of the table and said "Excuse me, sir" rather opprobriously that I noticed who was standing in the shadows. Rupert Soames, bear-like as ever, was handling a volume that I thought I recognised, bending back the binding as if cracking open a new schoolbook. Soames was a neighbouring, and competing, publisher in Bedford Square, plagued with a pathological, overweening hatred of Plumtrees. Before I'd become involved in our small family publishing house, he had loathed my father for his success and happiness. Now I had inherited his raw vitriol, and it didn't help that I had just managed to recruit a history book author who'd rejected Rupert's bid for his talents.

Giles's voice exuded disapproval and alarm. "Mr. Soames, sir, please—" He moved toward Rupert urgently, hands outstretched. "I'm sorry, but that book's reserved."

Soames looked up, and all my memories of him and his enmity for the Plumtree clan flooded back in a pungent wave. There was the time he'd stuck a banana in the exhaust pipe of my father's car, attempting to eliminate his most significant competitor in academic publishing through asphyxiation. Then there was the time that he'd thrown a brick through the window of the Plumtree Press building, which was all too close to his, out of frustration at the success of our anthologies of English literature.

The last time I'd been at a party with Rupert, he'd swung at me for speaking to his daughter, then kicked me when I was down. I'd long since learned to laugh at the situation, internally, at least, but all the same I intended to keep my distance.

Giles was heading into battle, rushing over to rescue the book as Rupert looked up at him, irritation simmering into full-blown fury. I wondered if Giles knew what he was letting himself in for. Sighing, I followed his dark ponytail. He would need my help.

Rupert slapped the book shut and glared menacingly at Giles. His lifelong inferiority complex gave rise to defensiveness. "Armand Beasley personally invited me to this party," he blustered. "I have as much right to look at these books as anyone else."

At that moment he caught sight of me, and the embers burst forth into a full conflagration. Pointing an angry forefinger in my direction, he seethed more than said, *"You!"* He positively squinted in his rage. "Plumtree! What are *you* doing here?" I might have asked him the same thing; it was surprising to me that Armand had invited him. It was the first I'd seen of Rupert since he'd lost the battle over the history author.

He headed for me, head down, face red, brushing past Giles roughly. Giles did exactly what I would have done, and attempted to grab the book from Rupert before the fireworks started.

Unfortunately for Giles, and all of us, his attempt to save the book backfired. Rupert, furious at what he perceived as an attack on his person, latched on to the volume the way a dog bares his teeth and bites onto a bone.

"Rrrmph!" Rupert's giant paws surrounded the book, pulling it back toward his ample belly.

"Gaaaah! Would you *please*—" Giles spoke through his teeth, pulling on the book with all his might, his face contorted angrily, when suddenly there was a horrible noise—a combination of a crackle and a rip.

Appalled, Angela and I watched as Rupert and Giles, wide-eyed, looked down at what they each held in their hands. Rupert had ended up with the dust jacket, Giles with the book.

"Good God, man! Do you realise what you've done?!" The fury and incredulousness in Giles's voice gave even Rupert pause for a moment, and silenced the rest of the party.

Remarkably, it took Rupert a moment to respond. He seemed to realise that his transgression had been serious. Then as his sandy brows furrowed into a giant, angry V, he said, "What *I've* done! If you hadn't come barging in here and *ripped* it out of my hands . . ."

I felt sorry for Rupert. Despite his bluster, he stood looking like a chastened bully, now the center of attention in Armand's beautiful library. Rupert simply didn't know the rules. I wouldn't have either on my first visit here, except that from childhood on my father had told me all about Armand's parties. I could still hear him explaining to me: "You see, Alex, he's too tasteful to call it a book sale—it's a party where there happen to be some books on display. And of course no one mentions money, although his parties do happen to coincide with the need for repairs on that mammoth old house of his."

My father would smile charitably and continue. "Here's how it works: one of his guests picks up a book and comments on its binding, or its typeface, or its rarity. Armand replies, 'Ah, Plumtree, never knew you were a Pepys fan. If you're really interested, I could bear to part with it.' Money, of course, is never discussed. The lucky collector slips a large bill or two into Armand's hand and walks away with a national treasure."

In the midst of these thoughts I watched Armand cross the room, coming to see what the fracas was about. Rupert was protesting indignantly. "It's only the dust wrapper, for God's sake. It's not as if—"

"My God." Giles tragically lifted the jacket from Rupert's now-limp fingers and studied the torn paper. Despite the fact that the jacket had been protected in a plastic cover, the force of Rupert pulling it off the book had ripped a jagged two-inch tear into the heavy old paper.

By now everyone present at that extraordinary scene understood that Rupert knew nothing about book collecting. If he had, he'd have known that an intact and well-preserved dust jacket was one of the more important criteria for fine old collectible books. A book in perfect condition is worth only one-tenth the value it will bring *with* its original dust jacket.

The book they'd been fighting over was one with which I was quite familiar. Angela was, too, for that matter. We could tell from the jacket that it was *The Figure in the Library*, by Marcus Stonecypher, first state, first UK edition, 1912, worth about 150 pounds *with* its intact dust jacket. As the small plum tree hanging ripe with fruit on the spine signified, Plumtree Press, then under the direction of my great-grandfather Edward, had published the book.

Angela knew the book even better than I; she had written her doctoral thesis, and then her novel for Plumtree, on Stonecypher. Stonecypher was the reason I had met Angela at Cambridge; we'd attended lectures together on the great Bloomsbury authors, or "Bloomsberries"—Virginia Woolf, Marcus Stonecypher, Maynard Keynes, Lytton Strachey.

"Ah, gentlemen." Armand's gentle, fruity voice flowed like soothing balm into the sizzling air between the two angry men. "I see you feel as much passion for Stonecypher as I do." I admired him tremendously for handling the situation with such grace. I doubted very much whether I could have done the same. Rupert had, at the very least, cost him hundreds of pounds that evening, and yet here was Armand, smiling and discussing their common love of books.

He replaced the jacket round the book, inconspicuously handed it to Giles, and said, "Have some champagne, Rupert?" He put an arm on Rupert's burly back and moved off with him toward the buffet, quietly speaking to him of something that even as we watched made Rupert's stiff shoulders gradually relax.

"Remarkable," I murmured to Giles. He turned to me and shrugged, resettling his slubby beige linen jacket on his shoulders, then tucked a stray wisp of hair behind his ear. Again I found myself studying him, wondering where I'd seen him before.

"You'll think it's even more remarkable when you see exactly what this book is," he said, looking into my eyes. He seemed to have recovered his habitual icy calm. "Here— Armand acquired this for you," he said, and handed me the book.

Surprised, I took it from him and studied the cover. It was, as I had thought, *The Figure in the Library.* Someone had slipped a small yellow index card between the plastic cover and the dust jacket with "RESERVED" stamped on it in large black letters.

Giles watched me intently as I studied the characteristic Stonecypher dust jacket. Like many book collectors, I had one of each of the books that my favourite author had written, but was always seeking to improve my collection by finding a first edition to replace a second, or a first in mint condition to replace a faded or mildewed one. Stonecyphers were becoming harder to find as his books became more popular; fortunately for Angela's novel, there had been a resurgence of interest in them, much as there had been a renewal of fortunes for the heirs of Stonecypher's friend, E. M. Forster, of late.

Giles continued to watch as I turned the book over, slipping the injured dust jacket off to inspect the cloth-over-boards cover beneath. I didn't want Giles or anybody else to know, but I was struggling a bit with my eyesight. In certain lights, such as that evening in Armand's library when it was a bit dim but not dark enough to turn on the lamps, I had grave difficulty seeing. I squinted at the book, trying desperately to see through the dark haze that enveloped it.

At such moments it was as if someone had turned a dimmer switch too low and no one else noticed. It took considerable effort to fight down the panic that I felt, as a man who makes his living from books, at going blind. I'd always had wretched eyesight, so much so that I'd been a case study for a German plastics firm. They had condensed two inches worth of prescription lenses into an eighth of an inch and inserted it into my horn-rimmed frames. But this was different; this was a frightening fading out of the books and the world around me, and it seemed to be getting worse with ever-increasing rapidity. To my immense relief, Giles mumbled, "Getting dark earlier now," and reached over to flip the switch on one of the tôle lamps.

I heard myself exhale as the gold leaf–filled indentation of a fruit-bearing plum tree in the center of the front cover jumped out at me in the light. Vowing to see the ophthalmologist that very week, I shoved my fears about the future into the background; I turned my full attention to the Stonecypher. Except for the torn dust jacket, the book's condition was perfect; no fading, no damaged edges—almost as if the volume had never been in circulation at all.

Giles seemed impatient for me to open the book, studying me as I studied it. Like him, I knew that the true test of the book's worth came with checking the date of copyright—an additional component of the bibliophile's ritual of touching, smelling, and looking that applied to the inspection of old books. A collector of Armand's caliber would have nothing other than first printings, because they were the only books with any real value, and besides, I could tell immediately from the jacket that it was the first printing. Great-grandfather Edward had changed it on the second. But it was unthinkable not to check.

Gently, I lifted the cover and turned to the copyright page, but before I could check the date, my eyes were brought up short by an inscription on the title page. Suddenly I understood Giles's interest. Inscribed in the graceful hand of a gentleman of the turn of the century, in ink that had been applied with a calligraphic nib, were the words: *To my good friend Plum. Always, Marcus.*

Marcus Stonecypher himself had inscribed it to greatgrandfather Edward—known to his friends as Plum, or Plummers. That made this an "association copy" in the book trade, an association between people via an inscription, in which at least one of them was famous, preferably by virtue of being the author. If both people were known, as in this case, the book was quite valuable.

"An association copy!" I exclaimed, delighted, and turned to look at Giles. In the spirit of a true book-lover, and despite his recent tussle with Rupert, he was smiling at my good fortune. "Where on earth did he find this?" Angela was there in an instant, silent with awe, leaning over the book in her intense way, fingers all over the book.

Giles began to answer but was distracted by Armand appearing in the flesh, portly of paunch and florid of face. "Ah. Armand returns," Giles said with a little hand gesture, and evaporated. Armand moved next to us, wearing a handsome lightweight jacket that smelled pungently of mothballs.

"Alex," he said warmly. "So glad you could come. I apologise for all the fuss."

"I'm afraid I'm partly responsible," I replied. "Rupert has never been particularly fond of the Plumtree clan."

"Mmm," Armand said thoughtfully. "I'd quite forgotten, but it comes back to me now. The banana incident, and so forth."

I smiled and nodded, not realising that the banana had reached legendary proportions. Armand had a way of making people feel that they were the most fascinating and important individuals on earth, and to speak with him was to feel admired and cosseted. I also realised that where Armand was concerned, I was profiting yet again from the overwhelming goodwill my father had established in his fifty-seven years on the earth. Nearly everyone who had known my father had loved him, and when they met or saw me, I suppose they saw mostly him. I had his dark hair and incongruous blue eyes— only mine were covered with tortoise-shell-rimmed glasses. I was also almost his exact height—six foot four. People were probably disconcerted by my appearance sometimes, as if Maximilian Plumtree had come back from the dead.

"It's a great privilege to visit you and your library, Armand," I said. "Thanks for inviting me."

"Pah." He waved away the thanks. "Wouldn't know what to do without a Plumtree at a book do—besides, not too many people know the difference between a devil and a dingbat anymore."

I smiled at his use of these old-fashioned publishing terms.

A printer's devil, in times gone by, was an errand boy. And hardly anyone used the decorative scrolls and symbols known as dingbats or fleurons anymore, though Edward had used plenty of them in his friend Stonecypher's books from 1898 to 1914. Too expensive now, too problematic in an age of maximum efficiency and minimum expense. But I had continued the use of the firm's own beloved dingbat as a colophon—a compact, leafy little plum tree hanging ripe with fruit—on the covers, dust jackets, and title pages of all of our books.

Armand's eyes were on Angela, who was totally absorbed in the Stonecypher book. I touched her elbow and she looked up quickly. "This is Angela Mayfield, my friend," I said again, not knowing how else to introduce her. She shot me the same rueful look, but then smiled and held out her hand to Armand, who was old-fashioned and gallant enough to kiss it.

"Very pleased to meet you, Angela." To my relief, he didn't make any comments about how lovely she was, or how lucky I was to be with her. That was the worst thing about being seen with Angela; everyone assumed that we were romantically involved.

"Angela's novel on Marcus Stonecypher is coming out on Wednesday, from the Press," I said, smiling, covering what was, for me, awkwardness. Armand and I both looked at Angela. "She's something of a Stonecypher expert, and I can tell you, the book's not only a page-turner, it's a revelation. Political intrigue, secret codes, et cetera, and it's all based on fact. Mild-mannered old Stonecypher was a bit of a renegade."

Armand stood in suspended animation for a fraction of a second. In his eyes, I thought I saw alarm, or even a glimmer of fear. Nevertheless, through a lifetime of practice, he said and did the appropriate things. "Congratulations, my dear." He beamed at Angela, bowing slightly. "I shall look forward to it." Angela smiled back at him, enjoying her first taste of public acclaim. Armand had charmed her as he had the rest of us.

"And this," I said, lifting the Stonecypher gently out of Angela's hands. "I don't know how to thank you." At the same time, I slid Armand three one-hundred-pound notes, discreetly folded. I had purposely got some large-ish notes the day before to avoid embarrassing him with a thick wad of money or, worse, the time-consuming process of writing a cheque.

"Thought you'd enjoy it." He smiled paternalistically, obviously taking genuine pleasure from my own delight. Armand, I reflected, was a kind and whimsical man, prone to acts of charity and generosity. He had been an associate member of Publishers for Literacy, a charity my grandfather had founded, though his true passion had always been for the Society for the Preservation of Rare and Antique Books—now renamed Folio B (For the Life of Old Books). And he knew all about my great-grandfather Plum's friendship with Stonecypher, and the fact that our offices had once been Stonecypher's home.

He pocketed the notes without a glance, displaying the aristocrat's true disdain for lucre. At that moment I saw Armand's expression change as his eyes flicked to someone behind me. "Excuse me for a moment, Alex, Miss Mayfield—I'll be right back. I'd like to take you round, have you meet some of the boys."

Giles was suddenly hovering behind me again, and as Armand put a friendly hand on my shoulder in leaving, I felt Giles bristle behind me. Angela had grabbed the Stonecypher again and was pawing through it, so I turned my attention back to the walnut book table where Giles stood guard, watching Angela as she flipped pages in my book.

"Look, here's the first one," she said, holding the book up so I could see where she pointed. Her index finger, with its nail bitten disturbingly to the quick, pointed at a sentence of dialogue on page fifty-five of *The Figure in the Library*. " 'Madam, from *when* have you come?' " she read.

"See?" Angela said triumphantly. "The 'when' is supposed to be 'whence.' "

"Oh—mm-hmmm," I said, peering down at the page. Out of the corner of my eye I saw Rupert drifting in our general direction, and watched him warily, as I would an animal who'd escaped its cage at the zoo.

Giles seemed to perk up at Angela's comment. "A misprint?" he asked intently. "In the Stonecypher?"

"Mmm." Angela was only too ready to explain. There wasn't a modest or shy bone in her body. "You see, the whole premise of my novel—*The Stonecypher Saga,* it's coming out on Wednesday—is based on my doctoral thesis, which is in turn based on a series of misprints in Stonecypher's books." She glanced over at me, smiling cynically. "Plumtree Press really fell down on the job around the turn of the century, because there certainly are a lot of them."

I nodded my acknowledgement of the barb and smiled as if to say, "Touché." Good thing we did, too, or you'd have no thesis, I added privately.

"And," she said to Giles, who was rapt, "if you write down every word in which a misprint occurs—"

"Hey," I interrupted. "Given the significance of your discovery about Stonecypher, I thought we were going to wait for the press conference to announce it."

She dismissed me—her publisher—with a wave of her hand, wrinkling her nose, and continued. "If you write down every misprinted word in its uncorrected version, you end up with a treasonable sentence that in early-twentieth-century England could have resulted in dire consequences for its author. The sentence from this collection of misprints, for instance," she said, pointing to the book again, "reads, 'When principalities and kingdoms fall, every man will come to power through knowledge of the written word.' In four books, Stonecypher came up with four of these sentences—all referring rather obliquely to abolishing the monarchy and creating a world government."

Angela looked at Giles through eyes half-closed with smugness, and pride at what she had discovered. A half-smile crept up one side of her mouth. Giles, for his part, looked taken aback that there should be such a dramatic political revelation about one of his favourite authors, who had seemed so tame to us all until now. I smiled too. I was proud to be the one helping her to make the strange and wonderful story of Stonecypher's political life public. Secretly, I was certain that England's—perhaps the world's—literary readership would go wild over it.

"You see," Angela, warmed up now, was saying to Giles,

"I set up the novel so that a young scholar at Cambridge, in the course of her research, discovers the sentences composed of the misprints. As she explores exactly what those sentences would have meant at the turn of the century, in that political setting, she uncovers a plot in modern English politics to achieve the same end—abolishing the monarchy—using violent means."

I continued to rummage delicately through Dickinson, Keats, Shakespeare, Waugh, Christie, and Milton—Armand was a man of diverse tastes—and was astounded to hear Giles say, in what could be described only as a stricken voice, "My God!" I looked up from the table in time to see him stagger off through the doorway, bumping into several people along the way without appearing to have noticed.

"Well," Angela said wryly, watching him go. "I guess that's one customer lost."

"Wonder what's wrong with him?" I asked, puzzled. Then, with a mental shrug, I dismissed his odd behaviour as a quirk of personal taste. Poor Angela—what a horrid reaction to her book, and from the first person she'd told too. "Don't worry," I said positively. "*The Stonecypher Saga* is fantastic. People will love it. Remember, it's my business to know."

Giles was certainly a moody sort of fellow, I thought. Turning back to the books, the Stonecypher still tucked protectively under my arm, I continued to survey the feast of literature on the library table—Maugham, Dickens, St. Francis of Assisi, Chaucer, Sayers, Cather, de Tocqueville.

"Look at this!" I exclaimed, spotting a potential find in the stacks of books. From the rubble I lifted one that had a telltale bright orange cover under its raucous jacket, hardly daring to hope, and held it up to Angela. To my delight, the jacket revealed that it was in fact another collectible favourite. It was a P. G. Wodehouse—who had also had the nickname Plum because of his first name, Pelham—with more escapades courtesy of Jeeves and Bertie Wooster.

She looked at me blankly. "Not more of that infantile Bertie and Jeeves drivel," she said, rolling her eyes to emphasise her point, and searched for material that would be more intellectually stimulating.

I was used to that response to Wodehouse, and was undaunted. It was true, I reminded myself as I flipped the book open to the date, that people who enjoyed Bertie Wooster's antics were not usually the sort who browsed at Armand Beasley's library parties. It was entirely possible that I was the only one there young enough at heart to be endlessly entertained by the dynamic duo.

But I wasn't ashamed; after all, Wodehouse immortalised a period in English history and a way of life that is gone forever, much as Stonecypher had. And all it took for a book to be eminently collectible—and therefore valuable—was a fool like me who couldn't resist it.

Indiscretions of Archie was the title of this particular escapade; the character Archie was actually a variation on the more famous Bertie Wooster, but was equally enjoyable. Under the pristine plastic-covered jacket, on the orange cloth spine, was a drawing of Archie in his boxer shorts, looking surprised. I chuckled to myself, not only at the pleasing inanity of Wodehouse's humour, but at the coincidence that one of this book's points was a misprint—also like a Stonecypher.

Points were unusual characteristics of a book that made it more valuable, and this book's point was a misprint that made the very first printing of the first American edition recognisable. The American publisher, Doran Doubleday, had corrected the mistake before beginning the second print run. Just for fun, I turned to page thirty-one, where I knew the word to be. There it was: "friend" instead of "fried" potatoes.

Turning the book over in my hands, I could hardly believe that it hadn't been snatched by the first person in the room, and looked around me as if someone might swoop down at any moment and wrench it from my grasp. It was very scarce.

Leafing through the book, I stopped again at the copyright page: 1921. This specimen was definitely coming home with me. It was in wonderful condition, like the Stonecypher under my arm, as if it had been purchased and locked up in a library for the last fifty years. I had a first edition of this at home, but its dust jacket was dog-eared and faded. This one was bright and pristine. I turned back to the inside cover, where I thought I'd seen a bookplate. Yes, there it was: *Ex libris Virginia Wilde, Wilde Hall, Yardley, Yorkshire.*

Hmm, I thought. I knew of the previous owner, or, rather,

had known of her. Indeed, I'd read her obituary in *The Tempus* several weeks before. Virginia Wilde had been the heiress to a publishing business up in Yorkshire, Wilde Publishing, and she had married a man named Frank Holdsworthy, who'd taken over her business.

Holdsworthy, one of the few book publishers remaining in the North of England, might appear at Armand's that night, I thought. He was a long-time member of Folio B, I knew, and he and Armand were good friends. I squirmed a bit at the thought; I had recently lured one of Holdsworthy's most successful authors away from him in an effort to expand Plumtree Press.

"What?" Angela asked, looking at me, sensing something. "What is it?"

"Oh," I said. "It's this bookplate. The last owner was Virginia Wilde Holdsworthy. I read recently that she passed away."

"Mmm," she said, coming to look at the bookplate. "Isn't Frank Holdsworthy the textbook publisher whose author you're stealing?"

Struck again by a pang of guilt, I nodded. At the Farmer's Arms with Angela one night—she'd invited me, but I'd paid for the dinner and drinks—I had told her of my victory. My acquisition of Wilde Press's best-selling history book author—the one I'd snatched out of Rupert Soames's grasp too—was going to vault Plumtree Press's academic division into the stratosphere, I'd told her. But at the moment I felt it wasn't a particularly appropriate time for me to be taking the lifeblood of Frank Holdsworthy's business out of a desire to expand Plumtree Press.

"Oh, for God's sake, Alex," Angela was saying, having seen the expression on my face. "Business is business. You won, he lost. *And* that obnoxious Soames fellow lost. Just enjoy your success—enjoy the moment."

I sighed and, looking at the Wodehouse, wondered if perhaps Frank had wanted to clear things out of the library that particularly reminded him of his wife. Perhaps he had sold her collection of books, lock, stock, and bookplate, to Armand. The intricate scrolls on her bookplate surrounded a miniature colour portrait of Wilde Hall, a vaguely Gothic old place. This was part of the fascination of old books; thinking of the people who had owned them before, and what things had been like when the first owner had read them, and the odd path that the books took to you.

Out of habit I conducted a test for mildew, riffling the pages close to my nose so both eyes and nose could judge. The pages stopped fluttering about halfway through, stopped by what looked like a letter—not in an envelope, just a couple of pages folded in half with writing on them.

I put both books down on the table and lifted out the papers, relishing the moment. Angela, ever alert, ever inquisitive, set down a red leather-bound special edition of Virginia Woolf's speech, "A Room of One's Own," and came to see what I'd found.

This was an occasional bonus—a sad one, in this case— that came with book collecting. One often got a glimpse into the lives of previous owners through letters, postcards, and other pieces of memorabilia that they had stuck in their books and forgotten. The book trade, which seemed to have a name for everything, in order to be able to charge more, called such things ephemera.

I could see at once that it wasn't old; the white paper wasn't yellowed and dry. As I unfolded it, I noticed that it had been written on fine rag paper with a fountain pen, in the looping script of a woman—perhaps Virginia herself— roughly my own mother's age. Odd, I thought, how handwriting styles are a dead giveaway of age. The penmanship of people my mother's age was unmistakable, as was that of my grandparents.

For one scrupulous moment I felt that perhaps it was inappropriate for me to read Frank Holdsworthy's wife's private correspondence, but in the end, curiosity got the better of me. I assuaged my conscience by telling myself that, after all, as I would be purchasing the book, the letter would soon belong to me. The letter read:

Virginia Holdsworthy
Wilde Hall
Yardley
Yorkshire

Saturday, 15 August 1997

Dearest Marjorie,

I am writing to you with very disturbing news, but am burdening you with it because you are the only person I know who will know what to do. I'll get right to the point because, quite frankly, I don't know how much longer I have.

I have become aware that Frank is involved in something frightfully sinister, and I believe he knows that I know. As my sister, you know that Frank's and my relationship has always been one of convenience, my money and the family business for his—well, whatever it was I thought he would be for me. A handsome escort, I suppose. I'm beginning to wonder why I thought marriage to someone handsome, well educated, and good at parties was so important. At any rate, lately I have been convinced that he would stop at nothing—not even dispensing with me, though I can't imagine he would bother, considering that the cancer's almost got me anyway—to protect a secret I have stumbled upon. It has to do with, of all things, his membership of the board of the Society for the Preservation of Rare and Antique Books—or, rather, Folio B, as they now call it. I'll hurry, because I'd like to be done with this by the time he comes back from his ride.

You might think I've lost a marble or two, but I promise you this is the truth. Frank and his cronies on the Folio B board—and I always thought they were such good, decent men—have a nasty little secret about their restoration of rare and historic books in university libraries. It seems that the author Stonecypher put some sort of coded sentences in his books, and established a

Here the letter ended with an accidental flourish of ink coming down from the "a" as if Virginia had finished up in a hurry.

Angela looked up at me, eyes wide, and snatched the letter out of my hand to reread it. I shivered, though the room was growing warmer by the minute. Picking up the Wodehouse, I turned back to the bookplate. Virginia Wilde Holdsworthy had died at roughly the time this letter had been written. Had Frank Holdsworthy indeed "stopped at nothing," as Virginia had suggested in her letter he might, or had she died a sad but natural death of cancer?

My hands felt cold and sweaty at the same time as Angela slowly handed me the refolded letter. I took it with shaking fingers, feeling as if I had just stumbled on Virginia's corpse, and was attempting to stuff the letter back into the book, when I was jostled from behind. I bumped against Angela and the pages fell from my fingers, fluttering to the floor.

She bent over quickly to pick them up. I started to turn to see who had bumped me, but on the way caught a horrifying glimpse of the outline of Angela's spine through her clingy knit dress. Disturbed, I stared as the thin fabric revealed each vertebra as a small mountain in the landscape of her back, and realised that there was almost nothing to her—a fact normally hidden, I supposed, by her usual attire of sloppy sweats and baggy T-shirts, and not apparent when she was standing upright.

Feeling shaken, and guilty about my perpetual irritation with her, I saw her through new eyes. She was slender, yes, and as she handed me the letter again, I saw that there were hollows around her eyes. But she was muscular from perpetual exercise, and glowing with a healthy tan. She certainly didn't look ill. I considered asking her if everything was all right as she peered round irritably to see who'd bumped into me, but, wary as I was of deepening our relationship in any way, I avoided the personal encounter entirely.

Instead, I stuffed the letter back into the book, shaken not only by my glimpse of Angela, but stunned at the fact that Stonecypher and Angela's information about him was mentioned . . . that is, if one read Virginia's letter that way. *It seems that the author Stonecypher put some sort of coded sentences in his books. . . .* Angela's theory about the misprints had not yet been published, and her careful research had determined that the misprints had never before been discovered—or at least written about—as the buildings blocks of sentences with political meaning.

Now Angela said exactly what was on my mind—in her own inimitable manner. "How in God's name did Virginia Wilde Holdsworthy know about *my* misprints?"

It was enough for one night; I was ready to go home. But I hadn't even spoken to Armand yet, nor had I been introduced to all the Folio B personalities he had specially invited me to meet. As it turned out, the evening's surprises had only begun to unfold.

CHAPTER 2

You two are book-men.
—SHAKESPEARE, *TWO GENTLEMEN OF VERONA*

I gathered up the Stonecypher and the Wodehouse and tried to act normally, feeling a desperate urge to get out of the mainstream of the party, almost to hide while I digested the startling information in Virginia's letter. Angela stuck close, if anything, affected more than I by the disaster of learning that her doctoral thesis had not been groundbreaking work.

"Over here . . ." I guided Angela away from the library table to a tall row of freestanding bookcases behind which we could linger while thinking things over. I told myself that my overactive imagination was getting the better of me; that I always saw sinister plots in the everyday. It was too incredible, and after all, the newspaper article had said that Virginia Holdsworthy died of cancer.

As we spun round the corner of the end bookcase, we walked straight into a heated argument.

"I can't and I *won't*," Armand's plummy accent exploded in an emphatic whisper. "Besides, you were supposed to arrive at tea-time to discuss this. I've got a full party of guests here. . . ."

Armand's back was to us; it was Frank Holdsworthy who fixed me with an angry stare as I rounded the corner. My eyes locked onto his, and I froze. It was too late to go away again and pretend I hadn't seen and heard them. Armand turned, frowning, then put on a worried smile when our presence registered with him. Meanwhile, Frank modified his glare to something like curiosity as I took my arm off Angela's, ever wary of giving the wrong impression. Angela, who knew perfectly well why I'd disengaged my arm, exhaled quickly in a sound of disgust and folded her arms.

Disregarding her, I was already in the process of muttering "Excuse me" to Armand and backtracking as swiftly as possible, when Armand said, "No, no, excuse us, please. Imagine us trying to do business here tonight, of all times." He cleared his throat and ran a hand through his hair, looking flushed. "Alex, Angela—I'd like you to meet Frank Holdsworthy— perhaps you already know each other through the publishing business?"

Angela merely smiled tactfully and murmured, "Pleasure." She was still furious with me—and probably more hurt than angry if her rejection in love felt anything like mine.

My own reaction was more hesitant. I would have preferred not to have run into Holdsworthy at all, particularly not in the middle of an argument with Armand. But I was learning that publishing, like life in general, consisted of running into the same people again and again. Overcoming differences was a necessity, not a nicety. If I was stealing the author who had made him his millions, I would now have to pretend that that was a perfectly decent and respectable thing to do.

Holdsworthy responded first with good grace, and I had the feeling that my smile was sheepish. "I know of Alex, of course, but I don't believe we've met before. It's a pleasure." He shook hands civilly, as if to please Armand, but without warmth.

I responded in kind, at a loss for words in the awkward situation, but remembered myself in time. "I was very sorry to hear of your wife's death," I said, looking him in the eye. He seemed a cold and businesslike fellow, but I sincerely

felt for him. I couldn't imagine losing the woman I loved—
especially if I'd succeeded in persuading her to marry me.

Frank nodded and murmured, "Thank you," and Armand
mercifully relieved us by accosting someone and practically
dragging her into our little group.

"Diana—over here," he said, ushering her into our uncomfortable circle. "Someone I'd like you to meet." I blinked at
the woman Holdsworthy moved aside to admit. Diana looked
surprisingly like a fox, with bright red hair flowing over
her shoulders and a tiny, turned-up nose in the center of an
alert little face. She was petite, and exquisitely dressed in a
pea-soup-colored silk skirt and blouse with matching suede
three-inch heels.

She fairly glared at Angela, then at me as Armand con-
tinued, "Diana, this is Angela Mayfield, an author with
Plumtree Press, and Alex Plumtree—he'll be speaking at the
Folio B conference outside Paris next week." She gave
Angela and then me a curt little nod.

Armand, turning back to me, said, "Angela, Alex—Diana
Boillot. Frank and Diana run Folio B's library book restoration operation. And very fine restoration work it is too," he
said, giving a slight bow to Diana. Armand seemed to be
slightly intimidated by the two of them, though I couldn't
think why. He was the king of London's rare book world, in
my mind.

When Armand had mentioned Diana's name, my mental
Rolodex started spinning until I had the association: Diana
was the daughter of two famous art restorers, François and
Isabelle Boillot. At some point Diana had been featured in
one of the book-collecting magazines for some work she'd
done for the British Library, defoxing.

Foxing, a term of unknown origin but which referred to
the gradual defacement of printed pages with myriad small
dark spots, was a sad plague that affected books published
after 1840, when book manufacturers had started using paper
containing sodium nitrate. The problem could be corrected by
carefully baking the pages, but the British Library only hired
the best for that sort of thing.

Something else clicked in my mind: there was an electricity between Holdsworthy and Diana Boillot that was

obvious, and would have been even if Holdsworthy hadn't been stroking her back with one hand. Despite his well-made summer-weight suit and regimental tie, he looked not unlike an animal staking his claim, announcing to one and all that she was his. There was overt sexual tension in the air— surprising for such a recent widower. But I reminded myself that I had no idea what the poor man had been through during his wife's illness, or after her death.

"Delighted to meet you, Diana," I said. "I'd be interested in seeing your restoration work . . . pay you a visit sometime, if you do that sort of thing." If I was going to become a more active member of Folio B—at the moment I gave financial support, but not much more—I would have to learn something about restoration. My father had had strong feelings on the subject, and felt that books should be left to themselves for the most part. All too often unscrupulous booksellers misrepresented restored books as originals to command outrageous prices, and my grandfather had passed down remarkable stories of forgeries—completely fabricated pages—committed in the name of restoration. Diana, of course, judging by her acceptance by the extremely fussy British Library authorities, was a highly respectable, legitimate, and professional restorer. Even my father had admitted that on occasion very old books did need a little mending.

Diana and Holdsworthy looked decidedly unenthusiastic about the idea of a visit, but somehow my interest seemed to have pleased Armand. He blurted out, "Splendid! We don't often find people who are interested in the details of restoration. I don't believe you're really set up for visitors, are you?" he asked them rhetorically. "Diana does the work in the small, private workshop of our Folio B president, and Frank's contribution is to pay the rent for the facility. But part of our purpose in Folio B is to defend careful, ethical restoration work. Your father, Alex, helped steer us in that direction. In fact, if you can believe it, we have some fairly militant opponents." Armand raised his eyebrows and tucked into his champagne.

"Opponents?" I wondered aloud. "To careful restoration?"

Diana and Holdsworthy looked at each other as if gauging

how much they should say. Interesting, I thought; there was some secret there.

It was Holdsworthy who handled the situation in the end. "Oh, you know." He laughed, rolling his eyes. "There are a few oddballs who will object no matter what you do. Some people think that old books shouldn't be restored, that they should be left in their original state. The 'just let them fall apart' school. You'd be surprised—they can get quite up in arms about it."

He took a sip of champagne and eyed me appraisingly. "Some things never change. We'll keep doing what we feel is right. But enough of that . . . I saw the articles in the trade rags about you and the anonymous best seller you published last year—amazing story, really. I understand we're going to hear from you this year at the Folio B conference outside Paris."

"Mmm," I mumbled, thinking with shame of the speech I hadn't yet begun to write. "Hope I can come up to your standard; I understand Lord Pillinghurst spoke last year."

He muttered something encouraging, and conversation faltered awkwardly.

Compelled by the universal human instinct to cover such moments with pleasant chatter, I said, "I've read about your restoration work for the British Library, Diana, and I understand that Folio B has undertaken quite a lot of restoration as a gift to the university and national libraries. Noble work, preserving the nation's literature."

Diana couldn't seem to be bothered to answer. She gave me a bored look before she leaned her head well back for a long swig of champagne.

Holdsworthy said, "Actually, we do consider it a privilege. When you think of the nation's treasures, rotting away in those damp old . . ."

He continued with what I perceived to be his stock statement of outrage on the condition of publicly-owned antique books in England as Armand steered us all toward the buffet. The room had continued to fill in earnest as we'd been talking, and I was interested to note that I recognised a number of book dealers from the small shops that filled the several streets south of the British Museum, round the corner from Bedford Square. I was surprised at how many people I knew—friends of the family, fellow publishers, familiar booksellers, and local gentry.

Armand and I stocked small plates with miniature quiches and sausage rolls, and he graciously disengaged us from Holdsworthy and Diana to move us on to a wiry little old man with a startling shock of white hair. Angela excused herself along the way; I wasn't sure whether it was out of necessity or some infinitesimal remnant of tact she chose to exercise. I couldn't help but notice that the gentleman we were approaching had eight gigantic prawns on his plate, and one in his mouth.

"Pilly, what a pleasure to have you in my library, eating my prawns," Armand chortled with obvious pleasure. "I'd like to introduce you to young Alex Plumtree; he's giving the address at our conference next week, you know, on the Plumtree Collection and so forth." Turning to me, he said, "Lord Pillinghurst taught me everything I know about books—let's see now, what would that have been—nearly thirty years ago."

"Very pleased to meet you," I said to the famous and eccentric Edward Pillinghurst, who did not deign to look at me until he'd wiped his cocktail-sauce-stained hand with a serviette.

There was a pause as he riveted me with ice-blue eyes that had the intensity of laser beams. "Look like your father," he said rather grimly. "Knew him well. Fine man." He scooped up another prawn, dipped it in the seafood sauce on his plate, and said, "Pity he's gone."

I nodded and took a bite of quiche myself, waiting while he chewed. The longer I lived, the more I realised that people enjoy hearing themselves talk best of all. Besides, I'd found that I could learn more and get into less trouble if I just listened.

Armand had been distracted momentarily by someone clapping him on the back, so there was no rescue imminent from that quarter. I was wondering if I should wander off somewhere else and let Pilly get on with his prawns, when the old gent turned the laser beams on me again and bit off the words, "Perhaps you'll learn a lesson from it." He abruptly turned and walked away.

Stunned at his sour tone and puzzled as to his meaning, I was left with the impression that there was something just a bit off about the man, but I knew better than to underestimate him.

Armand turned back to see me looking after Pillinghurst and sized up the situation rapidly and accurately. "Did old Pilly pull a stunt?" He leaned close and said in a low voice, "Don't pay too much attention, he's not all there, if you know what I mean. But he knows his books—never slips there. Lots more people for you to meet; ah, here's Henry."

Armand continued to conduct a tour for me of who's who in British book collecting, and where I didn't know the faces, I recognised the names. It was for the most part, a well-educated and tasteful, if eccentric, crowd—apart from Rupert Soames, of course, who was merely eccentric. I'd been fortunate enough to not run into him again so far.

Some of the booksellers from Bloomsbury—Denny "the Dealer" Minkins, for instance—were a bit rough around the edges, with grimy used paperbacks sitting cheek by jowl with first editions in their shops, and accents that I suspected did not often gain entry to this room. But they were some of my favourite people, and I had spent a good deal of time in their shops on my lunchtime walks. I looked forward to chatting with them when Armand was finished with me.

My host steered me to the president of Folio B, William Farquhart, the owner of the workshop in which Diana Boillot performed her restoration miracles, and the proprietor of a respected book dealership in Sackville Street. "Alex, you know William Farquhart, don't you?" I vaguely remembered meeting him a couple of decades ago, on a book delivery errand with my father. I'd been overwhelmed by the splendour of his Mayfair house, I remembered, with its matching stone lions guarding the front door. "Nice to see you again," I said, and took his proffered hand.

"Looking forward to your speech," he said warmly. "Always hoped your father would have a party like this at your house, with at least part of the Plumtree Collection up for grabs. You've got some gems over there at the Orchard. Any interest in selling?"

I shook my head modestly and smiled. "No, I'm afraid not. Sentimental value. It's hard to even think of them as collector's items—they're part of the family. No doubt you have some books like that yourself."

He nodded thoughtfully. "Indeed I do, Alex, indeed I do. You'll do your father proud." I might have imagined it, but his eyes seemed to grow moist and he, like Pillinghurst, abruptly left me, but with a kind clap on the back. "I look forward to seeing more of you," he said, and was gone. It was astounding to me that these people had all had such close connections to my father, but then, this had been his world, and he'd been a star in it.

Armand was scouting for the next victim, and found him by the mullioned windows in the alcove. "Ah—Alex, you must meet Michel Menceau, the host of this year's Folio B conference. You haven't lived until you've tasted Michel's chardonnay—he makes a special few hundred cases each year himself, for his own personal use. His winery, of course, makes hundreds of thousands. But his are really special; he even designs his own labels for them, for specific occasions. I shouldn't be surprised to see the 'Folio B chardonnay' brought up from his cellar next Saturday night. Ah, Angela, join us. You must meet Michel."

Menceau was of medium height, dark, and intensely stylish in a way that only the French know how to be. He wore a deep blue silk shirt with a paisley cravat, and had long raven-black hair which he'd swept back with some sort of gel. Vital and fiftyish, he was talking animatedly to a delicate, birdlike man who seemed almost unhealthily excited. He was so startled when we came into his peripheral vision that he jumped and spilled his champagne on his threadbare serge jacket.

"Sorry, Martin—didn't mean to startle you. Angela, Alex, I'd like you to meet Michel Menceau and Martin Applebaum." Looking at the two men, he said, "Angela Mayfield is an author—a Stonecypher expert—with Plumtree Press, and Alex Plumtree is our speaker for this year's conference. I've told him about your special vintage, Michel."

Hands were offered and shaken, with pleasantries all round. "I look forward to being your host," Menceau told me with a strong French accent. "Armand has, of course, told you that we will all stay at the château for the conference, yes?"

Armand nodded and smiled like the Cheshire cat while also managing to raise his eyebrows.

"Yes, I've been planning on it," I said. "Thank you very much. I'm looking forward to staying with you immensely."

Armand said, "Alex has some plans of his own for next week—a little holiday mixed with business, if I'm not mistaken, and with a very beautiful woman." Menceau's eyes flicked to Angela, and he smiled at her as Armand continued. "You're cycling to Alsace for a wine fair, isn't that right, Alex?"

"That's right." To my horror, I saw that Menceau and Applebaum thought that Angela was to be the companion Armand had mentioned. Armand, who knew about Sarah, was aware of his gaffe, but it was too late.

Angela said, "Excuse me," and slipped away again, looking almost ill. She could take only so much talk about Sarah and our holiday plans.

Menceau shrugged in a typically Gallic gesture as he watched her go. "Well, then, the château will be perfect. I assure you, Alex, it is quite romantic. I know just which room I will give you. There are, how should I say it, some rather suggestive tapestries on the walls in what we call 'the Creation room.' "

He beamed in a rather suggestive way himself; I suddenly felt uncomfortable with both Armand and Menceau leering about my holiday with Sarah.

Sarah Townsend was the woman I loved. But I seemed destined to admire her from afar. I'd gone to college with her in America, and she'd married my best friend, only to be made a widow eighteen months later. Since then she'd been a friend, but unreachable romantically . . . although instinct told me the tide was turning. I sensed that my chance to win her heart had come at last; Sarah was doing a six-month-long Parisian stint for her London investment bank, and I had arranged the most romantic one week possible at country inns between Menceauville and Alsace. But in some way I felt that our holiday was my affair, not theirs.

Rather briskly, I said, "Thanks very much, Michel; I know we'll enjoy it."

Perhaps sensing my discomfort, Menceau moved the conversation to more neutral ground. "Which route will you take to Alsace?"

I described the network of small roads to him, and he nodded approvingly. "Magnificent. You will see some fine countryside."

Applebaum had been somewhat slighted in the conversation, I thought, but he seemed relieved when we moved off again in the fulfillment of Armand's duties as host. I hoped it wasn't obvious that I was slightly relieved myself. And I was flattered that Armand had taken it upon himself to shepherd me through the crowd.

"What sort of work does Martin Applebaum do?" I asked as Armand scouted the party for other potential introductions.

"Lecturer, University of London. Turn-of-the-century British lit. Specialises in the political angle, I believe . . ."

We found ourselves standing at one end of the buffet now. Armand chattered on about being peckish and wasn't it true that one never got to enjoy one's own food when one entertained. As he loaded yet another plate with crackers, pâté, caviar, and cheese, I considered mentioning Virginia's letter to him; it was, after all, a startling discovery, and Armand was a respected friend. I felt a strong urge to confide in him.

Even stronger, however, was natural reticence. It reminded me that most things are best left unsaid. Besides, the letter would implicate Frank Holdsworthy, with whom Armand appeared to have business dealings—though apparently not very enjoyable ones. In the end I decided I could ask an innocent question without impugning Holdsworthy or saying anything about a letter.

Pretending to be fully absorbed by the challenge presented by a knifeful of Brie and slice of French bread, I said in as casual a voice as I could manage, "You know, Armand, it's quite a coincidence that you found that inscribed Stonecypher for me. I mentioned Angela's novel to you—" He nodded.

"Well, there's actually quite a revelation in it. Something that will significantly bump up the price of his books, I'll wager."

Armand and I and everyone in the room knew that any insignificant—or significant—piece of information about an author or a particular book could have the effect of hooking potential buyers and extracting more money from them. Much of a bookseller's work involved researching inscriptions to find out whether the person to whom a book had been inscribed was famous, or had at one point been in love with the author—married to the binder, even. It didn't matter; any scrap of trivia would do.

Armand looked at me quizzically as he bit into a water biscuit laden with pâté. It was not difficult to see how he had acquired his portliness. "Mmm—what's that?" Several crumbs escaped onto the front of his navy blue jacket.

I glanced round the room to see if Holdsworthy was safely occupied before speaking. He was standing halfway across the library, leaning his head close to Diana's. "It's extraordinary, Armand. Evidently Stonecypher used misprints and dingbats to communicate his political beliefs in a sort of code . . . ."

I stopped when Armand sucked in a huge breath of air and proceeded to choke on his biscuit. He coughed violently and began to turn purple, at which point I realised it was serious and clapped him on the back sharply. The cough was less violent after that, and I hurriedly handed him my champagne.

"Here, have a drink." While he was taking a sip and composing himself, I continued. "Sorry, Armand. All right?" He nodded, still speechless, looking not at all all right. I heard myself go on, somehow thinking that if I kept talking calmly, it would be less embarrassing for him. Most of the room was looking in our direction.

"Speaking of Stonecypher—I know this sounds crazy, but I do have a reason for asking—does Folio B have a special interest in his works?"

Armand's eyes bulged disastrously, and I had a feeling that he was going to choke again. He did, this time on the champagne. I suspected that he knew exactly what Virginia Holdsworthy had referred to in her letter, given his reaction. Rather ineffectually I patted him on the back, but I could tell it wasn't serious this time, just a case of the bubbly going down the wrong way.

Poor Armand was still recovering when he was greeted loudly by a new arrival. "Armand, darling," a throaty female voice trilled. I saw a look of despair and resignation on my host's face before he held up a finger to excuse himself and said, "I'd love to chat more about this later, Alex, all right?" He then put on a martyred smile and went to meet her as if marching into battle.

A tired-looking man with greying hair and a paunch moved up to the serving table, standing near me, and addressed his companion under his breath. "Iris Pennington, his widowed sister-in-law. They say she's pulling out all the stops to catch him. Poor fellow."

I allowed myself to observe Armand and his guests while I dealt with the chewy French bread. Rupert Soames, Holdsworthy, and Diana stood stiffly, speaking in rapid, almost angry snippets, about something that must have been of intense interest to them. I hadn't realised until that night that Rupert was a part of this crowd; he certainly seemed to know Holdsworthy and Diana Boillot well. Of course, he had tried to recruit the history author from Holdsworthy's stable of writers, but evidently the effort hadn't caused bad blood between them.

I cast about for Angela, but couldn't spot her anywhere. Knowing her, she was probably in Armand's bedroom, inspecting what he read before bed.

As I chewed and watched Iris Pennington flirt loudly and publicly with Armand, who continued to look in imminent danger of a heart attack, it occurred to me that Armand appeared to have a lot on his plate—figuratively speaking—just at the moment. Presumably there was at least a minor financial crisis, or he wouldn't be parting with a newly acquired libraryful of books in almost perfect condition, and his romantic life was obviously rather eventful just now. Between Giles and Iris . . .

Iris Pennington's powerful laugh, almost masculine in its aggressive boldness, permeated the library. And there was the whispered confrontation with Holdsworthy behind the bookcase, whatever that was about. "Business," Armand had called it when I'd stumbled onto them.

It was fascinating to stand at the entrance to this new—and yet oddly familiar—social and business world. As a Plumtree, I was supposed to be an authority on rare and antique books, but I was becoming nervous that the rather casual and anecdotal knowledge passed on by my parents and grandfather might not be enough. I hadn't the least idea what I would say in my lecture to Folio B, and it was barely more than a week away. I promised myself that I would get started on it that night, or at least begin to think about it as I was drifting off to sleep.

Some of the joy of the party faded when I imagined standing before the assembled members of Folio B International at Menceau's château with nothing at all to say. I drained the last of my champagne and decided that this was as good a time as any to get to work on the speech, while there was some weekend left. Besides, Armand had dedicated quite a lot of time to escorting me through the crowd, and I didn't want to appear greedy. I'd had my share of books, champagne, and introductions for one night.

Still no sign of Angela anywhere. I'd have to go in search of her. I deposited my glass on a waiter's tray and, on my way out of the library, glanced toward the corner where Soames, Holdsworthy, and the Fox held forth. Interesting. I was sure I would hear more about that threesome. As I passed Armand, I sketched a wave and mouthed a thanks behind Iris's mound of grey, ratted hair. I would write him a note to thank him for the party, the book, and the introductions, including a healthy cheque for the Wodehouse.

To my surprise, and Iris's obvious displeasure, Armand immediately detached himself from her with profuse apologies and guided me to one side of the room. His hand heavy on my shoulder, he said, "Alex, I wonder if you'd mind hanging about a bit—stay for a brandy with a few of us after the crowd clears?"

No one in his right mind would refuse to stay for a brandy with Armand Beasley and his closest friends. I'd been honoured just to be included tonight, not to mention being personally introduced to England's finest. All I could do was nod.

"Good. That's the spirit. Shouldn't be much longer now. Oh," he continued distractedly, almost as an afterthought, "Giles has taken Angela home; she didn't admit it, but he thought she wasn't feeling well and offered to drive her. Hope you don't mind."

"Not at all—it was very good of him." The conversation about Sarah had bothered Angela more than I'd realised.

Armand nodded kindly and rolled off in Iris's direction again, and I surveyed the crowd. Denny Minkins appeared to be at a loose end, looking slightly tipsy and leaning against the walnut book table. Perhaps he could answer a few questions for me about this restoration business, which seemed to be stirring up so much ill will in the book world.

"Denny," I said, half-sitting on the table next to him. "Replenishing your stock tonight?"

He raised a glass in greeting. "Replenishing my appetite for fine wine, more like." Smiling naughtily, he added, "I see you've picked up a couple of winners."

"Mmm." I held up the books, showing him the spines. "Yes, it's been a good evening. Denny, you're the book expert; is there some sort of controversy at the moment about restoration?"

He nodded slowly, and with his shaggy haircut and baggy jacket reminded me for a moment of a mongrel dog— loveable, but untidy. "Yes. The Americans have just done something rather unusual with the Ellesmere Chaucer. It's sort of brought the whole thing to a head."

The Ellesmere Chaucer . . . I had heard of it. The volume was revered world-wide as a fine example of illumination. The Americans had it in some library in California, as I recalled.

Denny took a long drink of champagne, spied a waiter approaching, and deftly exchanged his empty glass for a full one.

"Really? What did they do?"

Denny focussed on my eyes for a moment before answering. "Well, they went and un-bloody-bound the whole thing, didn't they? Took the nineteenth-century binding off, which was so tight it was eroding the illumination, and rebound it in a reconstruction of a contemporary binding." He glanced at me to see if I understood what he meant by contemporary, and I nodded. In the rare book trade, a contemporary binding is one from the period contemporary with the book. That meant that the Americans had rebound the Ellesmere Chaucer in actual oak boards, as it would have been done the first time round in the sixteenth century.

"They claimed it was for the sake of the book—that the glue made from animal parts was eating away at it, and so forth—but you can imagine what the purists had to say about that." He returned to his drink, and I followed suit. Yes, I could see how people might be upset about anyone tampering with a book that had somehow survived nearly five centuries, though I thought I sided with the preservationists.

"They had the very best people working on it, even one of the experts from Trinity College, Dublin." Denny shrugged. "I can't find fault with it. They were able to get the pages flat enough to make photographic facsimiles, which they bound authentically and sent out to libraries for display. So they not only saved the original book, they made it available for more people to enjoy. Speaking of which . . . did you hear about the new Nicholas Blake series from WalrusBooks?" and proceeded to describe the reissuing of a series of classic out-of-print Nicholas Blake mysteries, which I loved, as one of them, *End of Chapter,* was set in the publishing industry.

We carried on along those lines for some time, with Denny attempting to persuade me to reissue the works of some obscure author to whom he was devoted. When I next looked round, the room had cleared. Only Armand, Farquhart, Menceau, Pillinghurst, and Holdsworthy remained. They were looking at us, and even in his relatively sodden state it didn't take long for Denny to get the message. Time for him to leave. Smiling with casual acceptance of the fact that he was not a part of the rest of the evening, he winked and twiddled his fingers in an amused "ta-ta" to me, and went to pay more formal respects to Armand.

I checked my watch; nearly ten o'clock. Drifting over to the four remaining guests, I found them discussing the British Book Fair Association, or BBFA, book fair to begin on Monday at the Hotel Russell. Anyone who isn't a book dealer simply calls it the book fair.

"*Merde,* I don't know why they don't find another venue for the damn thing," Menceau was saying with Gallic disdain. "Last year I was so hot in that miserable old hotel, I thought I might die."

"Oh, come on, Michel." It was Farquhart, good-naturedly offended at this criticism of one of the great institutions of his country. "You know as well as I do that without the BBFA fair, the book-collecting public wouldn't be able to buy old books anymore. The Antiquarian Booksellers' Association sale at the Grosvenor House has become all dealers and snobs. Ninety per cent sales to dealers last year—it was in their literature.

"Besides, I think the old Hotel Russell setting is rather charming—what better place to sell old books than literary Bloomsbury? You know, as if old Stonecypher and Virginia Woolf might come walking in at any moment."

Farquhart, in his friendly, avuncular manner, turned to include me in the conversation. "What do you say, Plumtree? Rather nice to have a book fair practically in your back garden, isn't it?"

I nodded. "It's the only one I bother to go to. I can't afford to buy those one-offs at the ABA fair anyway. Book-collecting's no fun when it gets that serious." Smiling, I thought of Farquhart's prestigious bookshop and added, "You're the only one of us who's really in this business—will you be selling books at both fairs?"

"Almost have to, you know, to keep up appearances," Farquhart replied, inclining his head towards me confidentially. "But personally, I prefer selling to the people rather than to dealers from every corner of the world—bit sad, anyway, watching all the most valuable books leave the country. Mind you, a good deal more money comes in from the dealers, but some of the joy goes out of a book when it's purely a business proposition."

As Giles escorted Denny to the door, Armand came over to our group. "Shall we?" Our host held out walrus-like arms to shepherd us towards a round table with seven captain's chairs around it, nestled near the mullioned windows in the alcove. Opening a small, low cupboard he lifted out crystal decanters of what I could see were brandy, Scotch, and port, and deposited them on the table. As we sat down, he went back to the cupboard for cut-crystal glasses.

There were only six of us, so, out of an instinct derived from my mother's insistence on proper table etiquette, I edged the extra chair aside and made ready to push mine in. "Empty chairs at a table remind people of those who aren't there," she would have said. Especially with Holdsworthy on my immediate left, so recently bereaved, I felt it was important.

To my surprise, Holdsworthy said, "No." I looked at him, taken aback, and he said distinctly, "Put it back, please. We need one more." I looked at him, surprised at the apparent seriousness of the matter of the chair, but shrugged mentally and put it back under the assumption that perhaps Giles was to join us. Feeling chastened, and approximately seven years of age, I got myself seated between Holdsworthy and the empty chair without further mishap.

"Please," Armand said, waving a hand as he himself finally plopped down in a chair, severely stressing its structure. I heard an ominous crack, but the chair survived. "Whew!" he said. "It always feels good to sit down after these things." The glasses drifted round the table, followed by the decanters, and I chose to have some port.

"Was it a *good* evening, Armand?" Pillinghurst asked the question wryly.

Armand seemed unprovoked. "Yes, Pilly. Quite. Yes, a very pleasant evening all round. And perhaps the best is yet to come."

To my discomfort, at this everyone looked at me—with the exception of Armand, who looked down. All wore serious expressions, and I was left with the odd feeling that I'd walked into something I shouldn't have.

My discomfort grew as I swept the table with my eyes. Menceau swirled his brandy low in his glass, warming it as he eyed me with an almost sinister gaze. Holdsworthy now refused to look up from his whiskey. Farquhart looked vaguely uncomfortable; Pillinghurst was the first to break what was for me a very strained atmosphere.

"Oh, for God's sake, Beasley—let's get on with it. It's late."

Armand ignored his hostility and gave me a smile which I

found disturbing. It reminded me of the smile the dentist gives just before he goes in with the drill. Brave and cheerful, with a touch of pity thrown in.

The tension in the air had assumed such ridiculous proportions that I felt it had to be defused in some way. "What?" I said with a nervous laugh, again glancing round at them. "What is it?"

"Alex, we have an invitation for you," Armand said in a deliberate voice. Again he stopped, and they all looked at me. The air hung heavy with drama, as if they all knew something that I did not. I could not imagine what this was all leading up to, but felt the hair on the back of my neck stand up despite the warm evening. My fingers felt cold and clammy on the crystal wineglass.

"You have been nominated to the board of Folio B." Armand said this with the utmost seriousness, and the group looked as grave as if they had just chosen the next prime minister. I was tremendously honoured, but the atmosphere in the group was baffling. They all looked at me again, clearly expecting a response.

"I don't know what to say," I laughed, only partially relieved to know what they'd been leading up to. "I'm honoured. Thank you."

"You should know that there are serious responsibilities associated with the position," said Armand, "and—"

"It's not just a stroke for your ego, Plumtree," Pillinghurst put in venomously. "God!" He rolled his eyes heavenward, then shook his head with disgust and took a stiff swallow of Scotch.

"We really do see ourselves as the protectors of the nation's finest books," Armand continued, switching his gaze back to me once Pillinghurst's outburst was over. "There is a tremendous amount of work to be done. Not to mention our fund-raising activities as consultants and appraisers."

I shrugged. "If you're trying to scare me off, I'm not afraid of hard work."

"No, we know." It was Farquhart. I looked at him, hoping to find some normality in his reaction, at least. But he gazed back at me with the same sort of eerie seriousness I saw in the others.

"We know about your work with Publishers for Literacy, and your own literacy tutoring," he continued. "We also know what you've done already to expand Plumtree Press, and what direction you're going with it." Here, to my mortification, his gaze flicked to Holdsworthy, who merely looked down at his drink. "No, you're not afraid of hard work."

Armand spoke up again. "You should know, Alex, that we do take our work quite seriously, and there are traditions that we like to uphold as a group. Over time you will come to know these, and I trust that they will be acceptable to you."

What traditions? Exactly what hard work? I wanted to laugh and say: Dear Lord, why are you all behaving so strangely?

Instead, I found myself nodding seriously at Armand, as if to reassure him that I would meet his unspoken expectations, whatever they might be. It was all too strange for even me to respond normally. After all, I already knew what Folio B stood for—the responsible restoration of old books that might otherwise be lost to rot or other ruin. Were they trying to tell me something else?

There was silence for a moment. The darkened library assumed an oppressive air, and I had a belated flash of common sense. *Before you agree to something, Alex, you'd better make sure exactly what it is.* I thought I'd start with the work, and move on to the traditions.

When I spoke, my voice sounded oddly formal. "What, precisely, would my responsibilities be?"

Pillinghurst laughed—a shrill, lunatic laugh that sent goose flesh up and down my arms. When he wound down after a second round, I wondered why no one had led him out of the meeting and taken him home. Alzheimer's, I thought, perhaps.

They all looked at Armand, again ignoring Pillinghurst, to my amazement, and he nodded.

"Yes. Quite right, Alex. Simply put, your responsibility is to do anything and everything you can to ensure the safety and preservation of England's greatest treasures—her books. You are a publisher; your family's been in publishing for generations. I know the Plumtree Collection, and I know that keeping the books responsibly is a high priority for you, as it is for the rest of us."

"Mainly in the form of projects, such as the restoration operation for the universities, I assume?" I flashed a look at Holdsworthy, knowing that it was his baby—and Diana's—then looked back at Armand. The rest of the table was perfectly still.

"Exactly," he said, nodding. "And there will be other things . . . you'll learn all about us in time." He seemed keen to reassure me without going into too much detail.

"Oh, yes. Yes, you will," Pillinghurst muttered, looking down into his glass dreamily.

"So." Armand sat up a little straighter, put a smile on his face as if nothing in the least unusual had happened, and said, "A toast to our newest board member, Alex Plumtree!" There was a chorus of "Hear, hear!" around the table, and I felt back in the real world again. The five men smiled and put down their glasses, piled good wishes on top of congratulations, shook hands with me, and clapped my back.

I told myself all was well as I said my thanks and made my way out, clutching my Stonecypher and Wodehouse, Virginia's letter still safely tucked inside. Menceau and Holdsworthy were staying the night at Armand's, and in fact the entire week of the London book fairs, I learned, so Armand's valet had brought round only the cars belonging to Pillinghurst, Farquhart, and me. The vehicles waited in the circle of gravel in front of the house, and the familiar act of climbing into my own car gave me some measure of comfort.

Then I remembered the empty chair and, unaccountably, a shiver shook me from top to bottom.

CHAPTER 3

The walls of books around him, dense with the past, formed a kind of insulation against the present world and its disasters.

—ROSS MACDONALD

Rolling down the window of my car, I took greedy breaths of the evening air on the way home. These perfect late-summer evenings were almost painfully gorgeous, given the miserable nature of our weather most of the year. It stayed light very late this far north in the world, and at one point in the summer there was still light in the sky past ten o'clock. It was, of course, dark now at eleven, but the evening was still magically beautiful.

For a moment the fear of not being able to see such evenings in the distant future gripped me, but I told myself not to jump to unpleasant conclusions. It was true that my plans to continue to develop Plumtree Press and gradually to persuade Sarah to marry me would go out the window if I were to lose my sight. And it was true that life wouldn't seem worth living if that were the case. But it was also true that I simply didn't know what the problem was with my eyes; I'd been too afraid to see a doctor to find out for certain. I put the matter firmly out of my mind. It was foolish to worry about it until I had reason to.

I enjoyed the drive home down the moist, leafy back lanes,

which seemed normal as could be despite the odd conclusion to my evening. When I reached the small wooden sign for the Orchard, I turned off the lane and navigated the narrow box-wood hedges that always threatened to scratch my metallic forest-green paint—they had been planted to accommodate carriages, not motor cars—and walked through the rose garden on the way inside.

The scents of a dozen varieties of picture-perfect specimens rose up on the evening breeze, and I slowed, then stopped, to indulge my nose. It seemed a desperate shame that there was no one else there to enjoy it all, and for the thousandth time I thought wistfully of my dream for the future.

It included Sarah, several small children, perhaps some horses, and long Sunday afternoons wandering the property's footpaths together. But I had learned that it was best not to dwell on it too much.

Sighing, I went inside, depositing my treasures from Armand's on the kitchen worktop. There was no sign of Angela, but she had a key. I was certain she'd gone on to bed; her light had been out when I'd approached the house. I briefly considered going up to knock on her door and ask if she was all right, but hesitated to create the impression that I cared too deeply. I changed into pyjamas, made tea, and retired to the library, where I turned on a switch to illuminate the sconces along the walls. I knew I wouldn't be able to sleep anytime soon, and decided to do some work on my speech; the back of my mind was revolving in an endless Folio B loop anyway.

As an afterthought, I drifted back into the kitchen and picked up the Wodehouse and the Stonecypher I'd acquired at Armand's. Back in the library, I set them upright on my father's giant desk for inspiration, sat in the leather chair behind it, and opened the notebook computer on his desk. Then I must have waited a full five minutes. Absolutely nothing came—no ideas, no hints of ideas.

Taking a swig of tea, I retreated to mere contemplation of the name of the file that would contain the Folio B lecture. *Paris?* No, that would be admitting that I was going just because it was in Paris and I could see Sarah. It was true, but I hated to be so obvious about it. *Folio B?* Boring. No, how about something appropriate to antiquarian books, something attractive, like—

I never completed the thought because the fax machine beeped and then began to mumble, sending forth a slow paper stream.

Sarah?

I raced over to the machine. To my delight, the first two inches of paper proved that the fax was exactly what I had hoped: a letter from Paris. Sarah and I enjoyed writing letters almost more than speaking over the phone; we'd found that very different, and good, things were expressed in letters— things that were somehow harder to say over the phone. The only problem with written missives was the time delay between writing and receiving them, and the fax machine solved that nicely.

Like a child anticipating a favourite sweet, I forced myself to wait until it was all out of the machine before reading it. As the machine droned on, I let my mind wander to the plans I had made for the two of us for the week following the Folio B conference. The truth was that I had said yes to the invitation to speak only because of Sarah's presence in Paris. Any credible excuse to be near her was good enough for me, and less threatening for her. She was wary of getting too close to anyone, even old friends from college like me, since the death of her husband—and my best college friend—Peter, several years ago. So I spent my days thinking of her, and dreaming up ways to gradually build a bridge to her that wouldn't frighten her away.

To my great joy, Sarah had agreed to take a week's holiday after the conference and accompany me on a cycling trip through France. We would start from Menceau's château in Champagne, where the Folio B conference was to be held before the Paris book fair began on Monday, and finish up in Alsace-Lorraine for one of the renowned grape harvest festivals there. In the two weeks I'd known about the trip, I'd been on the phone stretching the limits of my French to arrange for the most romantic lodgings available. I wasn't about to let an entire week with Sarah slip through my fingers without doing my best to make it memorable. And, though no one knew it, I had made an expensive trip to Garrard, the

Queen's jeweller, on Regent Street, and picked up a very
small box covered in blue velvet.

At last the fax beeped again, indicating that the transmis-
sion was complete. I ripped the paper off on the serrated edge
and smoothed the rolling paper straight as I sat down again at
the desk.

Dear Alex,

*At last—less than a week before our trip. Jacques
asked me to postpone it so I could see a client next
week, but I told him no flatly. Probably not the best
thing for my career, but even Jacques must agree that
everyone has a private life. He had the gall to question
my commitment to the company, but I explained to him
that it was precisely because I respected commitments
that I wasn't going to break this one to you.* [Hurrah! I
thought.] *I also reminded him that this was the first
vacation I will have had in my two years with the
company, and he was so appalled at the thought that
he simply left my office in silence.*

*Anyway, enough of Jacques. I have definitely fallen
in love with Paris* [How about me?! I thought], *and am
thinking of keeping a* pied à terre *here, preferably this
very flat if I could manage it, on the Île St. Louis.* [This
made me slightly nervous; I wondered if we would end
up living in different cities after all, like American
television news anchors.]

*Mom and Dad called; they're planning to come over
from Massachusetts the second week in October for
a visit. They wanted to know if you would be free for a
weekend to come again to see them.* [Sure!] *You know
they're nuts about you. Let me know, okay?*

*I've kept my promise; my wine course is completed.
At least I'll know roughly what I'm tasting at the
festival in Alsace.* [That reminded me; the next night
was the last installment of my wine-tasting course in
London.] *And on Monday, a day off since I'll have
worked on a project for Jacques all weekend, I'm*

going on a long bicycle ride. I'll take the train into the country and go on from there. Hope I can keep up with you on the tandem!

By the way, I've got a Severe Mercy *question for you.* [Oh-oh, here it came: we'd been reading a book called *A Severe Mercy* simultaneously, the true story of a couple deeply in love making a philosophical journey together. I had a feeling Sarah was using the contents of the book to find out where I stood on a number of issues—a sort of test.] *I'm struck by the fact that Davy* [the heroine] *follows Van* [the hero] *to Oxford, and doesn't seem to care that her academic and professional life has come to a standstill. Do you think that her love for him could overwhelm her concern for her own well-being, and that she could be truly happy centring her life around him? Or will she grow to resent him later for her missed opportunities, although it was her own choice?*

See you soon,
Sarah

I would have been more pleased with "Most affectionately yours," or "Counting the moments," or anything else that wouldn't have made it sound as if I were a distant cousin. Still, I could sense the enthusiasm in her letter. I would take a healthy friendship with strong potential for future growth over nothing any day.

I sighed and read the letter again, sensing a sort of plea for help in the last paragraph. It seemed to me that Sarah felt she was facing a similar choice between career and love, though I couldn't think why. If she had any leanings toward centring her life around mine, I was unaware of them. Besides, she conveniently neglected to mention, in all her missives about Van and Davy and *A Severe Mercy*, that they had married. Marriage, I was sure, made a big difference in how much trust there was between people, and therefore in their willingness to sacrifice for each other. It seemed inevitable that at one point or other in married life, each partner would give up something irretrievable for the other.

It was understandable that Sarah was marriage-shy, considering how quickly her former marital bliss had ended in tragedy, but surely she would admit that marriage did fundamentally enhance a relationship.

Sitting back in the chair, I took off my glasses and rubbed the bridge of my nose. My response to her would not be easy to compose. The last thing I wanted to do was frighten her off with a diatribe on the benefits of marriage, but I could hardly answer her question without using the *M* word. Shifting uncomfortably as I put on my glasses again and sat upright, aware of the fact that I was merely postponing the inevitable, I decided to work a bit more on the speech; I'd tiptoe on the personal eggshells later.

Armand had asked that my speech describe the Plumtree Collection and the issues surrounding it. I finally decided to do what came naturally; that usually worked best. My speech would weave family history—only the interesting parts—with the story of the Collection and how it developed. That way I could explain how we'd ended up with some of Milton's original notes on *Paradise Lost*, courtesy of Great-Uncle Alexander, and a number of rare Audubon folios thanks to Cousin Charles, and so forth.

I was deep into the easy part, the description of the Plumtree Collection and the issues of preservation and valuation, when I heard the door from the garage opening into the kitchen, then footsteps creaking down the hall to the library.

"Hi," I said, not looking up, my fingers still flying over the keyboard.

"Hello," said Max pleasantly, going straight to the sofa to sit down. I finished my sentence and looked up at him, seeing a shorter, darker, more chiseled version of myself. My older brother and I enjoyed an easy companionability these days, living at the house together while he sorted out his life. Max had gone through a rough patch last year, and had even joined the Rupert Soames crowd in trying to eliminate me and Plumtree Press. But at the time he'd been in a fog of drugs and alcohol, and I told myself he hadn't known what he was doing.

Since then, he had undergone a very expensive, and evidently successful, three-month residential treatment for his problems, and had settled upon a life of herb tea, mineral water, and calm. He'd resigned from his roller-coaster job as a journalist at one of London's top newspapers, *The Watch,* to reduce general stress, and was doing some freelance writing and rare-book trading for fun and profit. Sometimes I could hardly believe that the put-together, peaceful person with whom I now lived was really my brother Max.

Not that he was utterly guileless; sometimes he seemed to act guilty, though I generally chalked that up to his scheming against me last year. As long as he wasn't drinking or using drugs again, and he wasn't, I was pleased.

Something else I'd noticed was that Max had a surprisingly adequate amount of money for someone doing freelance work and occasional book trading. In fact, sometimes I had the impression that there were books missing and shuffled about in the Plumtree Collection, but the Collection was his as much as it was mine, and he had every right to take books in for valuation or for showing off to his friends. I chose to ignore the fact that he might be selling the odd volume now and then. Whatever Max's remaining flaws, the contrast from last year and, in fact, the rest of his life, was remarkable. I wasn't complaining.

"How was Beasley's? Find anything good?" He looked over at me and I smiled back at him, pleased as ever to be with the new Max.

I nodded at the two books on the desk and said, "See what you think." I went back to typing and added casually, "Actually, a letter I found in one of them might mean that their previous owner was murdered, but it's hard to tell for sure."

He stared incredulously as he came to sit on the edge of the desk, picking up the books as if they had mystical powers. "How can you do that?" he asked, peering at me as if I were from outer space.

"Do what?"

"Sit there typing while you say . . ." He gave a snorting laugh. "I mean, *murder*? Something like that must be slightly surprising to you, at least."

I shrugged and stopped typing. Sometimes I hardly knew how to respond to Max's new brand of honesty—he'd learned it at the treatment centre. Since coming home, he was always aware of how he felt, and ready and able to express his feelings to others. It wasn't that I didn't like it; it just wasn't the way we were brought up. Plumtrees were of the stiff-upper-lip school. You didn't complain, you didn't stop to think about how you *felt*, and you certainly never risked boring others by talking about it.

I had to admit that Max's way was nicer, and more realistic—it didn't shut off or deny half of life. I could probably benefit from adopting some of his newfound touchy-feely skills, especially where communicating with Sarah was concerned. In fact, she had been pushing me gently in that direction lately. But the habit of a lifetime dies hard.

I decided I'd give it a try anyway, right there and then. "You're right, Max—I was surprised. More than surprised. I felt horrible at the party when I realised what the letter might mean." I turned from the laptop to face him more directly. "I guess my way of approaching such a horrible thing is to act as if nothing has happened, so I feel as if nothing has happened." Silence. "Thanks for keeping me honest."

He looked surprised, then delighted. Max has a beautiful smile when he uses it. For once he seemed at a loss for words. He didn't actually say, "Well done!" but his smile did.

Instead, he asked, "Where's this letter, then?" and turned his attention to the books in his hands.

"In the front of the Wodehouse," I said. He opened it, read the letter, and frowned. "Who's Virginia Wilde Holdsworthy? Quite a mouthful."

Max was not in tune with book-publishing world, having cast his lot for so long with more temporary publications. I explained who Virginia was, and that I had read of her death at roughly the same time the letter was dated, just two weeks ago.

He raised his eyebrows. "I see." He sat and considered for a moment, the stood. "The problem demands a cup of tea. Can I get you anything?"

"Yes, thanks. I'd love some more." I handed him my mug. He knew I meant my kind of tea, not his herbal stuff. I still liked my tea with a caffeine kick, unhealthful as that may be. And I needed any help I could get in putting some energy into the Folio B presentation. I'd started to run out of petrol on Great-Great-Great Grandfather Eleazar and his obsession with the relics of certain well-know saints, which served to explain why we had such an extensive—and surprisingly valuable—collection of books on the subject.

Max nodded and went to start the kettle, and I went back to dredging up ancient oral family history and typing it in. It occurred to me that it was really a very good thing to get the family book history onto disc.

But barely ten new words had appeared on the screen, when Max returned, eager for companionship and ready to chat. "So what did Armand say about this letter?"

"Not much, actually. He choked on his crudités and went on with the party."

Max shook his head. "Good God. You're incredible, you lot."

I asked Max about his evening; he'd been to the cinema with Madeline. Madeline was not unlike an angel who had come into Max's life. He'd met her at Sotheby's at an auction one day several months ago, and they'd been practically inseparable ever since. She looked like a supermodel on the outside—tall, incredibly gorgeous, long blond hair—but on the inside was an expert for Christie's on incunables, books printed during the "cradle" period of printing from 1450 to 1501. Madeline was also such a sweet, kind person that sometimes it was difficult to believe she was real.

Tonight, he said cheerfully, quite pleased with himself, he had taken her to dinner at a little French place near Covent Garden after the film. Good, I thought; he's really doing well, carving out a new life. I was a little uncomfortable knowing that if it weren't for me and Angela living here, he would have brought Madeline home with him. For the thousandth time I cringed inwardly at the thought that Angela and I were living in the same house, and how that must look to the rest of the world. But I couldn't just throw her out, and her book was almost announced. After that she'd go back to her happy niche up at Cambridge.

Max's eye fell on the Stonecypher. He picked up the book in its slightly damaged dust jacket. "This is nice," he said, slipping off the wrapper to look at the still-perfect binding.

"Check the inscription," I said.

He turned to the title page and gave a small gasp. "Wow!

Do you realise what this means? An association copy! This is worth a fortune!"

I nodded. "I suppose so." There was silence as Max inspected the book closely.

He looked up and saw the worried look on my face, and rolled his eyes. "Oh, come on, Alex, you don't think I'd want to sell it, do you? I know the value of this to our family. It could never be worth as much to anyone else as it is to us." He smiled self-deprecatingly. "Have a *little* faith in me, will you?"

I smiled back at him—we seemed to do a lot of smiling in those days, reassuring each other, I suppose—and he stood, stretching. "Good night, Alex."

" 'Night." I blinked as he left and glanced at my watch; almost eleven-thirty. My eyes burned. I allowed myself to relax back in the big chair for just a moment.

There was palpable comfort in this room, with its four walls of books, waist to ceiling, and, of course, its memories. One wall housed a set of French doors, not a good idea for climate control in a library, but during daylight hours the glass panes let in a delightful view of the garden beyond.

At this time of year the garden featured an ivied-trellis-covered pathway leading to the garden of grapefruit-sized roses, with a huge perennial and cutting garden beyond. It, in turn, was crowned with a large gazebo enclosed with glass doors—one of my mother's last additions to the house and garden of the comfortable paradise we called the Orchard.

The library was relatively large, almost thirty feet long and twenty feet across, which allowed plenty of room for my father's oversized desk and my mother's daintier version (one day Sarah's, I hoped), diagonally across from each other at opposite ends of the room. There was a fireplace, naturally, which did a lot to warm up the place in the winter, and keep the damp from the books.

I leaned back, scanning the shelves. It almost seemed that I could feel the presence of my father, mother, and grandfather; we had often settled in here on Christmas holidays and odd moments, and chatted about the books and things in general. This was a room where confidences were shared.

Sadly, Max had missed this education owing to his preference for locking himself in his room and listening to disturbingly violent rock music; though he was making up for it now that he was a part-time book dealer, taking seminars on rare books from Christie's—and from Madeline.

But I had been a willing listener. And over the years my family had passed on stories behind the acquisition of hundreds of books, over hundreds of years. They'd explained what was special about this binding, or that ink, or such-and-such a typeface. They'd shown me the methods publishers and typesetters used to make a book beautiful; the type of paper they used, end papers, and, yes, even dingbats.

In fact, my father had used an old Stonecypher to show me a perfect example of design elements that could enhance books. All of Stonecypher's books included within the text a particularly charming dingbat, an open book with very fine lines radiating from the top of it, as if it were illuminating the reader. The little symbol had always seemed tasteful and attractive to me, so much so that I had put it on the cover of Angela's novel.

But I couldn't forget that in one of Stonecypher's novels, an engraving of the dingbat had been a threat left by the villain—a death threat. Everyone who had received one in that novel had died. I picked up the new Stonecypher and leafed through it until I came upon one of the little books.

Staring at it absent-mindedly, I allowed the jumble of thoughts in my head free rein. Sarah . . . would she have met someone else more interesting by the end of her time in Paris, someone French and hopelessly romantic? Holdsworthy. Had Virginia died of cancer or something still more nefarious?

For the first time, the thought of Virginia Holdsworthy facing death and fearing her husband penetrated my thick skin. I set the book down as tears pricked my eyes, and the volumes on the wall collapsed into a watery vision. Blinking, I tried to focus again on the spines to force the tears away.

An irregularity in the pattern of the books at which I happened to be staring caught my eye. I sat up in the chair and leaned forward, squinting. Yes—right there, three-quarters of the way up the wall, to the right of the glass doors, several books were missing.

Not just any old books either; that was the Malconbury

Chronicles, a set that I knew belonged in a museum. They were hand-lettered, hand-illuminated books from the fifteenth century, records of what life had been like at the Malconbury Friary in East Anglia. They were the only ones of their kind; the monks hadn't made multiple copies.

I stood and walked over to the wall, worried now. Four were gone, with relatively unimportant books of the same colour stuck craftily in their slots. Three remained. It was possible that Max had taken them for valuation, or study, or something. I sighed. Most of my time seemed to be spent dreaming up rational explanations for Max's unusual behaviour.

The missing books really bothered me; and I couldn't even ask Max about them without making him think I suspected him. I *did* suspect him, after all. I decided that I would try to get round to the subject. Indirectly, of course.

The thought of it all—especially potential Max problems—made me feel bone-tired. I closed down the computer, flicked off the switch for the sconces, took off my glasses, and stretched out on the sofa in front of the fireplace. I liked sleeping there, in the calm and august presence of the books.

I was dreaming of Sarah on a tandem—with me fitting in quite nicely as her other half—when something intruded on my dream. Irritated, I tried to hang on to the vision of her tan back and strong shoulders in front of me in a black Lycra cycling top, keeping my eyes closed to ward off reality.

Half in the dream and half out, I was aware of noises somewhere nearby and knew in a vague way that the sounds were out of place—and not just because they intruded on the dream. Reluctantly I opened my eyes and blinked, momentarily disoriented. A few more blinks, and I realised I was in the darkened library, and that someone was there with me.

I lay motionless, aware that the someone was not Max, and should not be in my—our—library. A dark figure moved along the bookshelves, as if searching for something. A book, I presumed. My mind flew back to some of my last thoughts before sleeping—the missing books. Was it possible that someone other than Max was pilfering from the Plumtree Collection?

Without my glasses I had wretched vision; without them

in the dark I was virtually blind. I struggled to follow the vague outline of the figure as it drifted along the long wall that also accommodated the French doors. A ridiculous notion struck me. I'd seen paintings of Stonecypher, in biographies and our own Plumtree Press anthologies of literature, and this figure—what I could see of it—looked uncannily like him. I wouldn't have given it a second thought, except that the appearance of a shadowy figure like this actually occurred in Stonecypher's books . . . and then it struck me. The title of Stonecypher's first book was *The Figure in the Library*. In that first book and others, an all-knowing spiritual figure would appear at moments of crisis to impart wisdom, though he never actually spoke. And, like Alfred Hitchcock in the film world, Stonecypher had enjoyed seeing himself in his books. When he described the shadowy figure, he described it as looking like himself—like the shadowy figure in my own library. I had Stonecypher on the brain, I thought groggily, trying to decide whether I was really awake.

Psychoanalysts had explained Stonecypher's ghosts as a carryover from Victorian times, which had indeed ended only shortly before Stonecypher had started writing. During those days, late in the nineteenth century, such ghostly appearances in literature were common—in *A Christmas Carol* by Dickens, for instance, with its spirits of Christmas Past, Present, and Future. Stonecypher was most comfortable somewhere between moralistic Victorian attitudes and the avant garde Bloomsbury Circle, the psychologists and critics said, so he hid the moralising in a shadowy, supernatural figure.

Assuming the intruder—or whatever—was unaware of my presence, the best course of action seemed to be to wait there on the sofa and see what happened. If he drifted away again, fine. If he was a perfectly ordinary, modern, everyday thief looking for the perfect book to steal, I would wait until he had something in hand and had his back to me. Then I could take him by surprise.

But I had to admit to myself that the figure didn't have the bearing of a thief. Not only did he have that similarity to Stonecypher that I couldn't quite place, but he glided along in an odd, smooth gait not unlike that of a sleepwalker. He stopped and stood at the French doors, which were open to the summer night. Then he was simply gone.

It was too strange to be true. After several moments of doubting my sanity, I decided that it had been a remarkably realistic dream, and that I was still asleep after all.

I drifted off again, this time into a dreamless sleep.

CHAPTER 4

The fact that a book is in the public library brings no comfort. Books are the one element in which I am personally and nakedly acquisitive. If it weren't for the law I would steal them. If it weren't for my purse I would buy them.

—HAROLD LASKI

I awoke with a start, and found myself staring through the open French doors into the moonlit garden. The wind had come up, and one of the doors banged violently against the edge of the bookshelves. Odd, I thought; I hadn't opened them. Groggy, I stood, yawning as I put on my glasses, and crossed to the doors and closed them. Then I decided to abandon the sofa and the bizarre dreams that the library inspired, and retire to my own bed. Still half asleep, I plodded out of the library, down the hall, and up the stairs, falling into my cool bed gratefully. My last thought was to register that the glowing red extra-large numbers on my bedside clock said that it was two-eleven A.M.

At one minute past three o'clock I found myself looking at the digital numbers again, eyes wide. Something had awakened me, and after a moment of lying still, my heart pounding, I knew what it was. This time there was most certainly someone in the library, and whoever it was was making one hell of a racket. Groping for my glasses on the bedside table, I jammed them on my face as I flung myself out of bed. Racing down the stairs, my worst fear was that Max had somehow relapsed, and that I would find him lurching unsteadily across the room, knocking things over and throwing books in a frenzy of alcoholic delirium.

Lunging through the open door to the library, I was in time to see a small figure—much too small to have been Max— race at top speed out of the French doors. Thinking that there had been far too much action in this library for any one night, I flew across the room and out of the door after the intruder, barefoot, in my pyjamas, and unarmed.

He seemed to know where he was going, and headed for the drive. I followed recklessly, stumbling in the dark along the semicircular path around the side of the house, not twenty feet behind. But as I emerged from round the corner of the house onto the black macadam drive, I realised that I'd lost my prey. He wasn't running down the narrow drive in front of me; he was nowhere to be seen. I stood absolutely still and listened, trying to hear above my own breath and the pounding of the blood in my ears. Nothing. As a last resort, I made a halfhearted inspection of the shrubs he could have sheltered behind, but I knew it was no use. He had vanished.

Wandering back round to the French doors and the library, I seethed, furious at the invasion of my privacy and property. First the books switched about and missing on the shelves, and now this. Perhaps it was time to alarm the house, something I had put off out of distaste for the armed-camp feeling of it all.

I frowned, thinking, as I stepped into the house and latched the doors behind me, locking them firmly. It was, after all, the week of the London book fairs, and perhaps people were more desperate for stock than usual. I dreaded finding out what was missing this time. Then I crossed to the desk, flicked on the lamp, and wished I hadn't.

What I saw with the lights on gave me the willies. It wasn't just the books on the floor, some spilled randomly from each shelf around the room, in ghastly, unnatural positions.

Far more disturbing was a perfect reproduction, roughly six inches square on thick rag paper, of the book dingbat I'd seen in Stonecypher's books, with the rays of light shining out from it, in the middle of my father's leather desktop.

Feeling suddenly chilled, I realised that Stonecypher's

second book had been entitled *The Engraving on the Desk*. Had I become obsessed with Stonecypher? Was I going crazy?

Now, placed on my father's desk in the dark, the symbol had a sinister and disturbing appearance. In *The Engraving on the Desk*, it had presaged death.

That brought to mind Virginia Holdsworthy.

Could it mean that I was next?

My eyes scanned for the new Stonecypher; it was nowhere in sight. The Wodehouse, too, was gone, with its incriminating letter. I groaned. Whoever had it knew that *I* knew that Virginia Holdsworthy had been threatened, and also that Folio B was, in some incomprehensible way, related to the works of Marcus Stonecypher.

The clock on the mantelpiece said three-twelve. I left the light on and went out of the room, turning on lights as I went, first down the hallway, then through the large open area near the front door, then up the steps. I felt it necessary to tell Max that we'd been burgled, and discuss with him whether to call the police, and go over the damage to the books, and so forth. It was technically his house, after all.

And, to my surprise, I felt an odd sensation regarding Angela, hidden away in her room at the opposite end of the hall from Max's. Protectiveness? The feeling bordered on affection, and possibly concern, and I shook it off, not liking the intensity of it. Still, I thought, after talking to Max I'd check to see that she was all right.

But as I pushed on the light switch in Max's room with a shaking hand, I saw that his bed had never been slept in. I sat on his bed, puzzled.

"Okay," I breathed, trying not to let my imagination run away with me. "Okay." My voice sounded skeptical, even to myself. I tried to imagine Max on a walk down the lane at three-fifteen A.M., in the garden, anywhere but out getting into trouble. "Okay," I told myself again, aloud. It wasn't a crime for Max to be out late at night. Not at all. Probably a reasonable explanation. It was just that he had done so well, had gone to such lengths to avoid temptation. . . .

Avoiding Angela's end of the hall for the moment, I made another trip through the house, this time down to the garage.

Max's black BMW was gone. I stared for a moment into the empty, oil-stained space it should have occupied. All right, then, he wasn't out for an innocent walk in the lane. He could still be out for an innocent . . . well, something.

Couldn't he?

Feeling fuzzy of mind and tooth, I made my way into the bathroom. There I washed my face and brushed my teeth. I realised that I wouldn't have taken so much care over my appearance in the middle of the night if I weren't going to see Angela, but I pushed the thought away. It wasn't for Angela, I told myself; it was for me.

I stood outside her door for a moment, awkwardly, feeling embarrassed. Ready to turn and walk away, I heard the rustle of a paper inside and—could it have been—a sob? Tough-as-nails Angela, crying?

I knew then that I had to see her. Something was very wrong indeed.

Gently, I knocked. "Angela," I said. "It's me, Alex."

She took a moment to come to the door, wiping away the tears, I guessed. When the door swung open, it revealed her blotchy face, swollen eyes, and slept-on hair standing up in little tufts from her head. Beyond her, on the desk at the foot of her bed, the very edge of an identical copy of the Stonecypher dingbat I had myself received that night stuck out from beneath a stack of papers.

She regarded me in silence, eyes large.

"Are you all right?" I asked, my gaze straying unbidden to the dingbat, then back to her puffy eyes.

She nodded, and stayed silent.

"I'm sorry, I don't mean to pry, but it's important." I hesitated for just an instant. "May I ask where you got that?" I indicated the dingbat, realising that she had perhaps tried to cover it up before coming to the door. She would not, I knew, admit fear or weakness easily.

To my great surprise, she turned away from me, and her shoulders began to shake. To my even greater surprise, I felt such tenderness and pity for her that I went to her and held her shoulders as she sobbed. My hands were practically on her bones, it seemed; her body had none of the softness of other women I'd held. She cried quietly for a long time, and I stayed silently behind her.

When she finally spoke, she had composed herself. No screaming histrionics for Angela Mayfield. "I didn't want to tell you, Alex—didn't want to tell anyone. That's why I've stayed here for so long; I know I've outstayed my welcome."

"No," I protested automatically, taken aback by her bluntness, though we both knew it was the truth.

She wheeled to face me, dislodging my hands. Her face composed itself into a determined expression. "Someone is trying to frighten me, Alex—or worse. This isn't the first time; it's been going on now for weeks."

I felt my jaw drop. I had no idea.

"You know what that dingbat meant for the characters in Stonecypher's novels." She pointed at the paper on the desk, looking to me for confirmation. I nodded. "Well, tonight I've got a letter as well, pushed under my door. Someone was here, in your house." She shivered in the thin cotton nightgown. "Now I know what they want. They want me to withdraw my book."

"Withdraw it!" I was utterly astonished. "Why on earth—"

"For the sake of 'world peace,' or some such rubbish. Look." She pulled out a letter from under the dingbat, and it registered with me that she had indeed attempted to cover it up before coming to the door.

I took it from her, nonplussed. It was on the same handsome paper as the dingbat, but lighter weight so that it could be folded into an envelope. A small version of the Stonecypher dingbat served as the letterhead, the paper smooth in the area immediately surrounding it, a result of printing with an engraved plate. Whoever it was, they certainly had good taste in stationery.

The letter read:

Angela Mayfield
c/o The Orchard
Old Shire Lane
Chess
Herts.

Dear Miss Mayfield,

We must insist that you withdraw your novel based on the life and works of Marcus Stonecypher, and refrain from ever again speaking of the contents of the novel or your doctoral thesis, and further publication of them in any form.

Publication of The Stonecypher Saga *will have tremendous impact upon an international political situation of which you and the rest of the public are unaware. Though we cannot identify ourselves for security reasons, it is our hope that you will heed this urgent request and stop publication of your book.*

Please contact your publisher immediately and make it clear that you can no longer offer the book for publication; you might explain that you have used material without permission of the Stonecypher estate and therefore both you and Plumtree Press could be subject to litigation. Plumtree Press must cancel the book announcement, and have all manuscripts, proofs, and books pulped and disposed of immediately.

The international importance of keeping your book out of print is such that we will take whatever measures are necessary to stop publication. We are offering you the opportunity to do it yourself first; should you fail to comply with our request, we shall be forced to take care of the matter ourselves.

It would be to your advantage to co-operate with our effort. We do not wish to harm you, but will do what is necessary to preserve the fragile balance of world peace.

We will be watching, Miss Mayfield.

I looked up at her, horrified. One would have thought that I'd have learned, having been embroiled in a similar situation the year before. On that occasion, I had released pre-publication galleys of a forthcoming novel to a book critic for review, and the critic had wound up dead before the book was even published.

This time I had been careful not to release word of

Angela's book to anyone, and certainly no pre-publication proofs. I had mentioned the book a couple of times myself, tonight, but had given no details. And Angela had told Giles about the misprints, against my advice. But how could anyone have known for weeks? Was it someone at Plumtree Press? Only the employees knew the revelation in Angela's novel, and . . .

. . . and *The Tempus*. With horror, I saw my mistake. "The advert," I whispered. "Someone saw the advert we're putting in the paper. It won't run until Wednesday, but they wanted it in advance. They've had it for weeks."

Angela eyed me keenly, nodding once. "That has to be it," she said.

We stood for a moment, overwhelmed by the disaster that threatened to dash our high hopes. I felt that unwanted feeling again—partnership, shared adversity, a desire to take her in my arms and tell her that everything would be all right, that I would protect her.

My eyes came to rest, then, on the rays of light in the dingbat, and my mind turned to more practical things. "From now on you stay with me, or Max, if I'm at work, okay? Just until the book's out safely."

She laughed a bitter little laugh. "I don't think so, Alex. Thanks all the same." Hugging herself, she looked me up and down, then replied quietly, "I haven't so very much to lose. This book is all I've got, the only child I'll ever have. I'm not going to let anyone take it away from me."

Her words puzzled me, but I nodded, understanding her determination regarding the book. I felt the same way about not backing down, but wouldn't have allowed myself to go ahead with the book if she'd wanted to retract it.

"I understand. We'll go ahead, then. But please, be careful." I walked to the door and turned at the last minute to speak again. "I'll—um—I'll look out for you." She gazed into my eyes with the look of a woman clinging to a mast in a stormy sea, and it nearly broke my heart not to give her more.

I walked out of her room, feeling brutal, and closed the door.

Sleep, I knew, would be impossible. I wandered back down into the library and closed the rarely-used damask draperies over the French doors for an extra sense of security.

The books needed to be picked up and put in order on the shelves, which would take a good long time, but I didn't want to look at the blasted dingbat on the desk anymore. Nor did I want Max to be alarmed by it when he got home, just in case he'd read any Stonecypher novels in his brief flirt with literature at university.

I picked up the dingbat by its deckled edges and took it to a spot in the bookshelves along the wall, then pulled on the top of a section of books. It opened outward, revealing a small hidden cupboard in the wall.

It had been a decade or more since I'd been in my father's personal safe. I looked at the little box my father had used to hide his confidential papers and other valuables, hidden behind some rather handsome false fronts. He'd made it himself years ago from hopelessly damaged books with not much of interest between the covers—ancient business directories, and so forth—that still had reasonably attractive leather spines. He'd stripped off the spines and glued them to a solid piece of wood, and for all the world it looked like a section of a dozen or so old books.

The narrow shelves within the box were nearly full of files, envelopes, and loose papers. I sighed. These things really should have been gone through after my parents' death, but I'd been inundated with work ever since I'd joined Plumtree Press. The vacation with Sarah would be my first real holiday in those three years.

If I were honest with myself, as the new Max would have been, I would have admitted that leaving the papers untouched was a way of not admitting that my parents were gone.

At any rate, I dropped the elegant paper on a shelf in front of me, on top of a box labelled *Alexandra*, my mother's name. Unbidden, my father's thoughts on restoration came to me. He'd thought it a sacrilege to mess with a book, e.g., to restore it; he felt that a book should be allowed to speak for itself.

I couldn't help but wonder what Holdsworthy, Diana, and Armand had made of my father's attitude towards the restoration of old books. He would not have made a secret of his opinions.

My father's words came back to me easily, as they often

did in this room. "Once they start monkeying with the books," he'd said, "you never know exactly what you're buying." He'd claimed that unscrupulous dealers didn't always tell buyers that a book had been restored; only a real book expert would know upon inspection.

Even then, some restorers—like Diana, in fact—purchased antique paper from a dealer somewhere in London that exactly matched the vintage of the book. Ink could be matched, too, and typeface or script was not so very difficult to forge. There had been some spectacular hoaxes in the book world. It occurred to me that that would make a fascinating subject for a Folio B lecture: rare-book crimes. Perhaps I would weave it in somehow.

I rifled through papers in an open box, feeling guilty about not having dealt with them yet, and remembered other titbits my father had told me about restoration.

"The Frogs are the worst," he'd said, referring irreverently to the French. "They'll take a three-quarter leather binding, maybe a bit soiled and tatty, with a really nice book between the covers, and *rebind* it! Can you imagine? That lovely contemporary binding—and they throw it away. The card on the book will casually say, 'Rebound.' It's tragic." I thought of Menceau and wondered where he stood on the issue.

Then it struck me: perhaps all the mystery at the Folio B board meeting was because they were on the militant side of book conservation. But no; Holdsworthy himself had laughed at those who got up in arms about the subject.

I pursed my lips at the memory of the bizarre scene at Armand's house and told myself I'd have to shut myself in the library on a rainy day that autumn and come to grips with this safe of my father's, no doubt finding still more surprises about the remarkably eventful life of my parents. Swinging the false front back into place, I set to work replacing the books on the shelves.

It took well over an hour to restore the library to order; it had been a malicious attack on the books, and I counted eighty-four of them as I replaced the volumes on the shelves. Particularly tragic were two books that couldn't even be put back in their places; one was a seventeenth-century Bible that had barely managed to keep binding and text together—until the intruder had flung it upon the ground and snapped the last tenuous leather thongs anchoring the text to the boards. From now on, if this book were to be evaluated, it would have an extra notation: "Cover detached."

The other case made my blood boil. It was a book that had a painting on its fore-edge, the surface of a book that is opposite the binding and consists of page edges. It had been displayed with its fore-edge out, as that was the interesting part of the book. It was especially interesting to our family, as the painting was one of the Orchard, done by an artist friend of my grandfather's. The artist had become famous after his death, and the book was quite valuable, though of course we'd never sell it. The intruder had slashed the painting—put a big X through it—and thrown the book on the carpet.

When things looked pretty much as they had before the intruder's appearance, I wandered back upstairs to my bedroom, thinking a dozen thoughts at once.

Giles. He had left us distractedly after Angela had told him all about her novel. But why? And did Giles have anything to do with the dingbat messages, and the mess in the library?

Why hadn't I had a threatening letter as well as the dingbat, like Angela? I thought back to the dream I'd had while sleeping on the sofa, of the Stonecypher-like man drifting along the library wall, and how very realistic it had seemed. What if there had been two intruders that night—the Stonecypher ghost, and the one that had virtually disappeared into thin air after I'd chased him outside?

My thoughts flew off on wild tangents. What if the second intruder had *taken* the letter left on my desk by the ghostly figure, and that was why I hadn't had a letter with my dingbat?

Or had the intruder come because of my discovery of Virginia Holdsworthy's letter in the Wodehouse? But it couldn't be . . . Angela said that the strange goings-on had started weeks earlier. Besides, I hadn't mentioned Virginia's letter to anyone but Max.

Max. At the door to my room, I stopped. What, if anything, was he up to? My overly suspicious mind found evidence to indict him; he had been very interested indeed in the new Stonecypher from Armand's. Would he stoop so low as to take it for his own gain? Then it hit me; it was as much his as it was mine. He couldn't steal what was his own.

I forced the clamour of my thoughts to a stop. *Think, Alex, think.* Logic finally crowded out vague suspicions and doubts, and I remembered again that it was the eve of the book fair, the week that boasted the most rare-book sales of the entire year. Perhaps some dealer had been desperate for good stock . . . and yet, of all the truly superb and valuable specimens on our shelves, if I did say so myself, the intruder had taken not one.

Even if one of tonight's visitors had been a common thief, someone had left the dingbats and Angela's letter. There was no escaping the fact that the intruder had something to do with Stonecypher, and quite possibly Folio B, considering Virginia's letter. I didn't like the possibilities that presented.

I went into my room, threw my glasses on the bedside table, and fell on the bed, where I lay staring at the ceiling in the dark. I didn't like what drifted into my mind next—it was despicable. But it *was* possible. What if Angela, upset by the reference to my trip to France with Sarah, had a temper tantrum and did the damage to the library? I hadn't checked on her right away when I got home; she could have been seething with rage. And she knew all about the Stonecypher dingbat; she was also small enough to have been the intruder who eluded me outside the house.

But, sadly, she loved me, and I didn't believe she'd hurt my books. Who could possibly be threatened by Angela's novel? The Stonecypher Society? Folio B, for some unknown reason, if the letter I'd found was given the wildest possible interpretation?

The only people who knew that *I* knew about Stonecypher's little code were Angela, of course, then Giles (and whomever he may have told), Max, the trusted employees of Plumtree Press, and anyone who had access to the advertising bookings at *The Tempus*.

Whom did I know at *The Tempus* these days? I knew the ex-editor of the book review section, but he'd been demoted to sub-editing. William Farquhart wrote a monthly column on book collecting, but that wouldn't give him access to the advertising records. I knew lots of freelance book critics socially, but again, they wouldn't see the adverts. The only other person I could think of was Frances Macnamara, the head of the Stonecypher Society, who had inherited a seat on the board of *The Tempus*; her family had owned a good deal of the prestigious paper for at least a century now. But Frances was a gentle, refined elderly woman, and I gave monthly tours of the Press offices with her for Stonecypher fans. She was not remotely capable of issuing threats. Nor, I supposed, did she get involved at the level of reading the minutiae of the adverts weeks in advance, or ever.

The sound of the garage door opening roused me from my stupor; I turned my head and looked at the clock-radio glowing red by my bed. Five-thirty A.M.

Sunday morning.

I sat upright in bed as I realised that I had talked my good friend George Stoneham into rowing with me at Threepwood, the rowing club, this morning at ten. There was some comfort in thinking that I could at least talk to George about the strange occurrences of last night.

I heard Max start up the stairs. How often did he make these nocturnal trips? And what would he say if I confronted him? I decided to protect Max from any unnecessary upset by not informing him of the events of the evening; it didn't seem very stable, reasonable behaviour on his part to be gadding about at all hours of the night, and if he was having a relapse of some kind, I didn't want to exacerbate it.

Yet in the back of my mind a dark thought lurked: should I perhaps be trying to protect myself from Max? No, I couldn't bring myself to believe it, not with the sincerity that shone out of his eyes of late.

I waited until I'd heard him go into his room, fall into bed, and start snoring, then I quietly went downstairs and made coffee. There was no point lying in bed to be tortured by my thoughts. I leaned against the cool tile worktop in the morning dark until the coffeepot came to life, then held my cup under the trickle burbling through the filter. When I had a cup's worth, I slid the glass pot into place, missing only two drops that fell onto the hot plate, sizzling furiously. I carried the cup with me into the library.

I let my eyes wander the room; the carnage of earlier that

morning would be undetectable, I decided. It was a good thing that I would be gone by the time Max got up though— he slept until ten or eleven on weekends—because I was sure he would see something of the mental carnage in my eyes. He was all too skilful at that these days.

I thought of the Wodehouse and the Stonecypher that had disappeared, and involuntarily glanced at the spot from which the Malconbury Chronicles had been taken, the remaining three slumped sadly on the shelf. I did a double take, then blinked and looked again. The missing volumes were back.

The coffee suddenly tasted bitter in my mouth. Now I knew it had to be Max. He was up to something with our books.

A distasteful idea flew unbidden into my head: an insurance scam. Perhaps he wanted to get money by pretending some of the books were stolen, when he himself had taken them. But that sounded like the old Max, not the one I knew these days. He valued honesty above all else now.

Besides, the Malconburys weren't missing, they were *back*.

Shaking my head, I poured myself another cup of coffee for what comfort it could offer and went back upstairs. The only help for me at the moment was exercise, I thought, in the form of a long bike ride to Threepwood, where I was to meet George in three and a half hours. If I were going to be a zombie, I figured I might as well be a zombie on a bicycle. Besides, sometimes exercise helped to sort things out, and at the moment Max, the Folio B board, the Stonecypher spectre, the fleeing intruder or intruders, Angela and Sarah, were whirring round in my mind like a bicycle wheel at full speed.

On the way downstairs I picked up a shadow.

"Good morning." Angela greeted me as if nothing unusual had happened during the night. I turned on the stairs, surprised, and saw that she, too, was dressed for cycling. The day before I would have thought cynically, "Just my luck." Now I was glad she was coming.

"Hope you didn't mind that I left the party early last night," she said, bouncing down the stairs next to me. "Must have had a touch of something. Sorry."

It was fine with me if she wanted to cover up the embarrassment and fear of the previous evening with conversation that ignored it completely. I understood. "No, not at all," I said. "Feeling all right now?"

"Great. Looks as if we've had the same idea—mind if I join you?"

"No, not at all," I said for the second time. "But I'm biking all the way to Threepwood for a ten o'clock row with George."

"Sounds good," she said. "We'll put on a few miles this morning, shall we?"

I'd forgotten. She probably had better endurance than I did. I never understood where she got her unending energy. She would go for a run and come back in two and a half hours; I felt virtuous if I lasted forty-five minutes.

I smiled at her and saw that she was looking forward to bettering me in this impromptu race she had so deftly engineered. She took justifiable pride in her athletic prowess, and particularly enjoyed showing men how far and fast she could go. We went out to the garage together.

"So what happened at Beasley's after I left? Anything interesting?" She strapped on her helmet.

If only you knew, I thought. As I slid biking gloves onto my hands, I briefly considered whether to tell her everything about my odd experience with the Folio B board and the Stonecypher "ghost" later in the library. I quickly came to the conclusion that it would be condescending and patronising to assume that I could somehow protect her by withholding what I knew.

"Lots," I said, rolling my bike through the garage door after her. I slid it closed again, mounted the bike, and slipped my right foot into the toe clip. "It was a fascinating evening in many ways, not least because I was invited to join the board of Folio B."

"Really!" she exclaimed. "Congratulations."

"Well, sort of," I said as we drifted down the driveway. "The whole atmosphere of the meeting was very strange. More like a séance than a casual meeting of the board of a charity."

"How do you mean?" she asked, intrigued.

I frowned and shook my head. "There were intimations of duties that they didn't really want to tell me about, and—

well, the best way I can think to describe it is a peculiar *seriousness* about it all. Hard to explain, really."

Angela was silent. We pedalled easily down the drive of the Orchard and into Old Shire Lane.

"By the way, there were a few more—er—events in the wee hours last night that you should know about." Her face jerked up to look at mine, but she kept coasting next to me. "First, there is the matter of a very confusing dream that might not have been a dream." I paused, feeling ridiculous at what I was about to say. "I either dreamed that I saw Stonecypher's ghost—you know, *The Figure in the Library,* the one he describes as having his own appearance—or else I really saw someone who looks like him in the library last night."

Angela stopped suddenly, barely getting a foot out of her toe clip and on the ground in time.

"Dammit, Alex! How could you not have come and told me about this when it happened? Last night? God knows, you had the chance." There it was, her first reference to the threatening letter and dingbat. She seemed furious, glaring at me, gripping her handlebars with white knuckles.

"After what you had to say about your letter, it didn't seem very important. And then—this was the reason I came to your room in the middle of the night in the first place—the library was vandalised."

"Vandalised!"

"A number of books were damaged, and the fore-edge painting of the Orchard was slashed. More significantly, both the Stonecypher and the Wodehouse I picked up last night at Armand's are gone."

"My God!" She went pale under her tan. "Alex, what sort of a Pandora's box have we opened?"

I had to admit it looked fairly grim. There was nothing I could say to minimise it. Slowly, she turned away from me to look at the ground. Her head on one side, she digested it all for a moment. When she finally spoke, it was with that cynical, wry edge I had come to know so well. "So, in addition to everything else, someone knows that you know about Virginia's secret."

I nodded.

She seemed very calm; almost too calm. "Have you called the police?"

I shook my head. "When you've lived with a brother like mine for as long as I have, you learn to make sure it's not a family matter first."

"Oh," she said. "I see." She got back on her bike, and I followed her lead. Together we coasted down the hill. The mention of Max momentarily silenced her, and I understood why. The complexity of the situation was sometimes mind-boggling to me too.

Soon thereafter, we hit the road we needed to get to Threepwood, near Henley, via back lanes. Angela shot out ahead. Her muscle-to-fat ratio would have put me to shame. She blasted up hills ahead of me as if powered by rocket fuel, and simply didn't seem to have the normal human tendency to tire.

As for me, the endorphins kicked in beautifully thirty minutes into the ride, long before we reached the driveway to Threepwood. I stood panting on the tarmac in front of the club, where Angela had stopped, and consulted my watch. It was still just eight-thirty; an hour and a half to kill before George arrived.

"How about another loop?" she said, full of beans. She didn't even appear to be sweating.

"Mmm—wonderful," I said, trying to control my breathing.

Angela nodded once, briskly, glad that I had accepted her challenge, and led the way. She cycled these roads endlessly, and after one summer knew them at least as well as I did after a lifetime.

The exercise had cleared my mind, and had made everything seem more manageable than it had the night before.

As we coasted back out the entrance to the club's drive, my myriad problems seemed to have distilled into four simple questions: Who had left the Stonecypher dingbats, and Angela's letter? What was Max up to with the Malconbury Chronicles? Would Sarah ever marry me? What were my complicated feelings for Angela, exactly?

As I pumped feverishly down the level road to keep up with my pacesetter, I pondered each question and decided I would simply tackle each problem quietly, as best I could from day to day. It was all anyone could do.

I heard the sound of a car behind me and turned. It was travelling slowly, hanging back, always behind the last curve from me. A true Sunday driver, I thought. Then an exemplary Chiltern hill arose before me, and I threw all my energy into getting myself and my bike up it. After all, I couldn't fall too far behind Angela or I'd embarrass myself.

Angela appeared to be headed for, or beyond, the King's Standard in Beaconsfield, a favorite of tipplers for more than five hundred years. She did in fact turn in at that eminent hostelry, its car park deserted after what had no doubt been a characteristically frantic Saturday night. We both took long drinks of water from the bottles we'd removed from holders attached to our bicycle frames. I stood, panting. The row with George would have to be an easy, slow one, I thought, after this. With uncharacteristic kindness, or perhaps preoccupation, Angela was allowing me to catch my breath without rubbing it in. I mopped my brow and watched a white Ford Mondeo with dark-tinted glass pass the pub at low speed. The Sunday driver.

It was a white-sky day; perhaps it would rain later. My watch said nine-fifteen. If I rode back slowly, I would be there only a short while before George. Maybe Angela would go her own way from here.

"Are you going to go on, or turn back with me?" I asked.

"I'll go with you to the club. Need a coxswain?" Before I could respond, she had hopped back onto her saddle and was coasting out of the drive again. Replacing my water bottle, I did the same before I fell too far behind. This time, mercifully, Angela took it easy, perhaps remembering that I had an hour or so of rowing still ahead.

I marvelled at the way she had just invited herself along—not just to the club, but actually into our boat. Normally George and I took out a pair, a shell that seated two people with one oar each, and took care of our own steering. Now, if Angela had her way, we would take out a coxed pair—a shell that had space for a coxswain, preferably a small, lightweight person who would pull on some lines attached to the rudder and steer the boat. Angela, in fact.

As usual, I forgave her pushiness. It was the least I could do, considering that her very life was being threatened because of a book I had urged and paid her to write. Besides, it was just another small issue—like staying at my house, like the bike ride, like Armand's party—especially considering that I had broken her heart.

To my surprise, the white Ford overtook us, going back the way it had come just moments before. Not just a Sunday driver, I thought; a lost Sunday driver.

It was perhaps twenty minutes later when I became aware of a vehicle behind me again, keeping its distance. Our slow pace forced the car practically to crawl. Call it preoccupation, call it exhaustion, but for one reason or another it was only then that it occurred to me the car was following us.

CHAPTER 5

Books are fatal; they are the curse of the human race . . .
the greatest misfortune that ever befell man was the
invention of printing.

—BENJAMIN DISRAELI

M y first instinct was to panic and flee for the
safety of Threepwood and civilisation. I was
keenly aware that I was now involved, even if in the past
Angela had received her threats privately. But I wasn't certain if I was involved because I was Angela's publisher, or
because my suspicions about Virginia Holdsworthy's death
were all too accurate, and someone knew that I knew.

It didn't take me long to realise that not only could the car
overtake us in seconds, no matter how fast we pedalled, but
even if we abandoned the bikes and hightailed it off into the
woods, it would look suspicious. Whoever was in the car
would know then, beyond the shadow of a doubt, that we
were aware of what we had stumbled onto. So I would have
to pretend that I was blissfully ignorant of anything at all
unusual, and carry on.

As I concentrated on keeping a relaxed cadence behind
Angela, it became clear to me that the car's occupant was
doing nothing more than keeping track of us. It would have
been easy enough to abduct us, threaten us, shoot us, whatever—as we'd stood drinking in the deserted car park of the

King's Standard. Drenched in sweat, I felt suddenly clammy at the thought that this might be my life from now on; being watched, followed, talked about behind closed doors, possessing deadly knowledge—of Virginia Holdsworthy's death, and Angela's code as well—but being unable to tell.

A horrible thought occurred to me: was I to be privy, as a member of the Folio B board, to the horrible secret to which Virginia referred? Had they got me onto the board so that I would be tied to it, and therefore unable to expose them? My heart sank.

The driveway to Threepwood was ahead of us again, and as I rolled in behind Angela I saw George's Range Rover parked by the door, and his unassuming, less-than-athletic form climbing out of it. George was one of those people whose muscles didn't bulge dramatically out of his arms, legs, and chest; they were smoothly camouflaged under his skin, but were deceptively powerful. Rarely had I been so glad to see anyone in my life.

Evidently Angela had seen him, too because she pumped right up to him and said "Hello, George" in a breezy sort of way. She'd met him on several different occasions at the Orchard that summer. She'd also been to his home to sample the unforgettable French cuisine of his wife, Lisette.

George specialised in a humorous taken-aback stance and expression, which he now directed at Angela. Still grimacing, he said, "I thought you were going to run me over for a moment there." Then he smiled, leaned over, and kissed her briefly on the cheek. "How are you, my dear?"

"Mmm." She kissed him back. "You're very gallant, kissing a sweaty woman."

I pulled up behind her, panting. "Morning . . . George."

He eyed me comically. "What's happened to you? Has she already run you over?"

"As good as," I gasped.

"You do look all in, Alex," Angela said, enjoying her athletic superiority.

I didn't bother to explain that she might, too, if she knew that in addition to everything else, we were now being followed.

"That's right, pour a little salt in the wound," I replied

good-naturedly. Turning to George, I said, "Angela has agreed to join us—in a coxed pair."

George was brought up with the same manners I was. If he was less than enthusiastic about having a passenger that day, he didn't reveal it.

"Super! No offense, Alex, but Angela is much nicer to look at." He grinned at her. "Good. It's settled. I'll be stroke, then."

The stroke sat closest to the coxswain, in the stern of the boat. Safe, because he was long and happily married to Lisette, George could afford to play the role of flirt and pretend that he was dying to sit face-to-face with Angela while we rowed. I was grateful to him for his consideration; he knew of the situation between us.

We walked with him to the door of the clubhouse and parked our bikes in the rusty rack before going in. Threepwood wasn't big on appearances, but those who rowed there did know one end of an oar from the other. The club also did a nice Sunday lunch, Yorkshire pudding and the works, which we would enjoy today after our time on the river.

"Be right down," George said as we left him at the door of the locker room. I was already sweating in my rowing shorts, and Angela was in her sports gear, but George, seven-day-a-week physician that he was, still wore his doctor-on-rounds suit and tie and needed to change.

"Would you sign us in? I just want to check something," I told Angela as we went down the stairs to the boathouse. She'd been there before and knew what to do. I walked round the corner towards the oars, but instead of plucking them out of the rack immediately, I walked out of the rear of the boathouse. The smell of the Thames and the mud of the riverbank strong in my nose, I scrambled up the steep dirt hillside.

It was just as I thought: the white Ford with its unnaturally dark windows was parked discreetly toward the rear of the car park, partially hidden behind some tall shrubs. Its windows exposed nothing, and merely reflected the surrounding greenery with a disturbing blankness.

It was enough to make my skin crawl, and as I slid back down the hill, I realised that the joy had gone out of things. Even the trip with Sarah might be ruined, with someone following us all the way, if they went that far. I lifted the cumbersome aluminium oars with their blue and white chequered blades out of a large rack and carried them down to the dock, then returned to the boathouse. George was already there with Angela; he was a quick-change artist. They stood by the wall that housed the pairs.

Boats were suspended from the wall on racks, four high; some would house eight oarsmen or -women, others four, others two. All the boats hanging on the wall next to us were rigged for "sweep" oars, meaning one oar per person. In our case, George would take the starboard oar, because he was used to it, and I would take port.

In contrast, on the opposite wall hung the shells rigged for sculling, which accommodated two oars per person. There were four boats on that wall also; two doubles, which housed two scullers each, and two singles. These boats were more popular, as it didn't require companionship to take them out.

There were only two pairs rigged for a coxswain in the boathouse. "What'll it be?" George asked, smiling. "The Soames or the Wilson?"

Rupert Soames had given the newest pair in the club's fleet; we had a rule that all the boats kept at the club were available to any member at any time, unless they were previously reserved by the owner. Rupert's boat was certainly the superior shell; not a dent in the gunwale, and made of the latest fiberglass composite materials. But I much preferred the beaten-up, dark-stained, yellowed-varnished old Wilson, which had lived in the boathouse for the last forty years.

"I'll let you guess," I said, and moved over to the Wilson. George grinned as we lifted it down and carried it upside-down on our shoulders down to the dock, Angela following at a distance. We stopped at the edge of the dock, flipped the boat over, and gently set it in the water.

We got the oars arranged first, then situated ourselves in the narrow shell, leaving our shoes on the dock as we slipped our feet into the shoes attached to the footboards at the forward end of the slides. Angela climbed in and got comfortable—if you could call it that. There was a minute little seat for her, and almost no leg room.

George and I pushed off. It was a quiet day on the river,

the water still, the sky a metallic light grey, and George seemed to sense that my mood was sombre.

Angela let us take a few strokes, then said, "How far do you want to go?"

"Mmm," George said from his seat facing her. "Down to a little white bungalow—it'll be on the right bank after about forty, forty-five minutes. Then we usually drift just a bit, turn round, and come back."

"Right," she said, nodding. "Any requests?"

George glanced back at me. I shook my head. This was just a row for fun; we didn't need any sort of specially ordered workout, or drills of the kind she was used to administering for her competitive crew friends at Cambridge.

"No thanks," he told her. "We'll just paddle gently at first, maybe pick it up a bit later. We're sort of used to doing it ourselves. Nice to have someone steer though."

I saw her nod.

"Everything ready for the announcement?" he asked mildly as we paddled gently upstream. He knew that this was Angela's first book, and George had always been intrigued by the workings of the book business, even before Lisette had left the home fires to spend her days organising us at Plumtree Press.

"If I can believe the publisher, it is," she answered.

"We're ready," I said, "thanks to your wife, George. Press kits, luncheon arrangements, the works. We've had a huge response; we'll probably have about sixty people at the press conference. But you'd need to ask the author herself if she's ready."

"Of course I'm ready," Angela replied emphatically. "I've been waiting half my life to talk to a roomful of people about something—anything—I've written." The sentence ended on a wry note, and I cringed at the implication, knowing that she hadn't quite said it all. The second half of the sentence, which she hadn't shared with George, was ". . . and now I might not be able to, after all."

"Yes, that's an idea," George said thoughtfully. "Maybe I should write a novel—then perhaps someone would listen to me for a change."

I laughed out loud, knowing that George was surrounded

most days by audiences of medical students hanging on his every word.

"Seriously," I said, "the announcement's going to be great. And this book is going to be a huge success, I can feel it." *If,* I thought. For there was a definite "if" about Angela's book now.

We were quiet for a bit as we picked up the pace by mutual assent, having warmed up, and made for the landmark of a little cottage up the river, the destination of most casual rowers because of its location exactly ten miles from the club.

Angela steered competently for us. The water rippled past, nicely cut by our bow, making a gentle burbling sound. It wasn't choppy on the Thames that day, and the boat glided through the water as smoothly as if it were on a sheet of ice. And George and I slid up, pulled back, and feathered our oars with the magical, indescribable phenomenon of synchronised motion that oarsmen call 'swing.' It was as close to perfect as it gets.

"Weigh enough!" shouted Angela as we finally reached the cottage with its fresh white paint. It was the signal to lift the oars and coast, which we did gratefully until the boat slowed to a complacent drift. My legs felt like wet noodles: it is mostly legs and not arms that do the real work of rowing. She let us recover for a while, then said conversationally, "Alex and I have actually had some small amount of excitement lately—haven't we, Alex?"

"Mmm," I grunted.

"Oh? What's that?" George sounded intrigued. His mind leapt to a romantic association; I knew him well.

"We've got dingbats," she said, intending it to sound humorous.

He took the bait. "Bats? In the Orchard? Not surprising, really, all sorts of old houses have—"

Her laughter stopped him. "No, no, no. Stonecypher dingbats. You know the little symbols in his books that look like books being illuminated by rays of light?"

"Yes . . ."

"Well, Alex and I have begun receiving the symbols, enlarged, as some sort of messages."

George looked puzzled. "What exactly are these dingbats supposed to mean?"

She looked round. "Better take a couple of strokes, George. We're drifting too close over here."

He did, and the boat turned a bit, moving away from the riverbank.

Angela glanced at me. To George she said, "Obviously, you haven't read *The Figure in the Library* or *The Engraving on the Desk.*"

George gave another humorous grimace and mumbled, "Sorry. Guess I was busy with *Gray's Anatomy.* I mean, I know *of* Stonecypher and his little symbol, of course, but—"

"Well, in Stonecypher's later books, anyone who received the symbol was marked for death. The dingbat is a threat."

George turned to me, saw the grim acknowledgement on my face, frowned, and looked back at Angela. "You're serious, aren't you?"

She nodded. "Mine even came with a letter, which none of Stonecypher's ever did. It said that I'm to cease and desist on *The Stonecypher Saga*; cancel the announcement, scrap the book—actually, I'm to have Alex scrap it—and not say any more to anyone about it. It's a matter of national importance—or national security, something like that. They can't let the information come out, and if I don't stop, they'll stop me."

"But that's an outright threat!" George sputtered, indignant.

"It certainly is," I agreed.

"Well, it doesn't bother me," she said. "I don't care what they think they're going to do. I've a right to write what I like, and you've a right to publish it, Alex. Besides, it was anonymous. A letter doesn't mean anything unless someone has the courage to sign it, if you ask me."

I agreed with her in theory, but I tended to worry about the consequences of not complying with the letter's demands. Before I could respond, she said, "Want to start back before we drift too far?"

George nodded, taking a few strokes on his own to turn us around. As the boat turned, I caught a glimpse of a car parked along the road that ran alongside the river. The white Ford Mondeo. Evidently it was to be my companion—and Angela's—until all of this ended, which might happen in a way that would shorten our lifespans considerably.

George had started us in a slow paddle. Without giving

signs of noticing the Mondeo, I said calmly, "Angela. George. Don't look up; just carry on with what you're doing, all right?"

"Okay," Angela said.

"Right," George said, sounding confused.

"A car followed us this morning, Angela, while we were cycling; I didn't want to worry you about it. It was parked behind us in the car park at the club when we met George. It's on the riverside road now, upstream." This news was received in silence, but the cadence of our rowing didn't break.

"Okay," she said again, still facing me.

George took a couple of strokes in silence. "This is outrageous. You really ought to report this to the police. After all—"

If I hadn't been trying so hard to keep from looking at the car, I might have seen the boat sooner. But by the time I realised what was happening, it was too late. A fast launch with a severely pointed prow roared towards us, aimed squarely at our shell as if to cut it in half. My stomach turned somersaults when I saw that it was driven by someone in a black balaclava, and I thought of the shadowy figure which had disappeared through the library door at the Orchard.

"Jump! Get out! Go!" I yelled at top volume, but already the loud whine of the speedboat competed with my voice. Angela was staring at the boat in horror, and I yelled, "Angela! Jump! *Now!*" But still she sat motionless. In front of me, I saw George doing battle with the blasted laces that lashed our feet to the shoes attached to the shell.

Panicking, I tore at my own set of shoelaces and eventually ripped my feet free. George finally managed to do the same, and before everything dissolved into watery confusion, I saw him dive at Angela.

The shell capsized as they left the boat, and I fell more than jumped out, swimming down, down, down as far as I could to get away from the grinding and slashing of the speedboat's propeller. As I struggled for depth, I felt the pull of the water against my glasses and the elastic sports strap that held them firmly on my head, and was grateful for the precaution. I'd lost too many pairs of glasses in rivers over the years before learning.

From underwater I could hear the propeller blades singing, and then heard and felt a great crash as our shell was cleaved in two, and its halves were driven down into the water. After the impact, the noise receded and I dared to surface. Astounded by the violence of the moment, I watched in awe as the two halves of the delicate shell popped back up and bobbed on the water, the jagged edges of the wood as disturbing as open wounds

I saw George and Angela in the water, fifteen feet or so away, spluttering but evidently unharmed. Making my way towards them, I saw to my horror that the speedboat had turned round. It was coming back for another pass.

"Watch out!" I shouted, and their heads swivelled in the direction I pointed. Filling their lungs with air, they dived downward, out of the propeller's reach. I followed suit, and heard the boat pass over me at high speed, then recede again.

Surfacing, I saw that a launch was speeding toward us. Evidently its skipper had made the decision to rescue us instead of following the speedboat operator, and I can't say that I was ungrateful. The Thames is chilly even in late August, and not terrifically clean.

"Who on earth was that?" the driver of the boat asked, incredulous. He was a middle-aged man in rowing shorts himself, and I speculated that he'd seen what was going on and hopped in the boat to rescue us. "He might have killed you!"

"Indeed," I said, accepting his hand and hoisting myself into his launch. As I flopped onto one of the blue vinyl-covered seats, I said, panting, "I'm afraid that's precisely what was intended."

He stared at me in disbelief, then abruptly remembered what he was about and made for George and Angela. They were treading water next to an overturned half-hull of the shell, which the launch's rubber bumpers knocked against gently as we approached. I reached out a hand and pulled Angela in, noticing how the wet shirt clung to her bones, and hugged her—partly because I was glad she was all right, and partly because she looked as if she needed warmth. She was shaking uncontrollably, cold and scared, possibly even in shock, I thought. I felt a surge of—exactly what, I couldn't say, but something akin to pity, or perhaps affection.

The launch driver hauled George over the side, and when everyone was solidly in the boat, he said, "My God! Are you all right?"

In the next moment I saw what he was talking about, and staring at. George had a nasty gash on his right thigh, probably from scraping against a bolt or nut on the rigging of the shell as he went overboard. The wound was bleeding profusely.

"Yes, all right, thanks," George panted. I'd never seen him in a situation like this before; usually I was the one getting carved up and sewn back together by him. "Nothing that a good stiff Scotch won't cure back at the clubhouse."

"Would you be willing to take us down to Threepwood?" I asked the man who had rescued us. The poor man still seemed to be rather in awe of the situation. He nodded, and I thanked him as he turned back to the wheel. I was worried about Angela; her entire body was racked with tremors. Holding her tightly, I said, "It'll be all right. Everything's all right now," and continued with variations on that theme until we arrived at the boathouse.

George cast a glance our way every now and then, and I realised he was recognising a new brand of intimacy between Angela and me. I couldn't help it; it was simply the way things were. She needed help, and I was responsible. I had to protect her.

I walked her to the women's locker room and suggested that she might like to sit under a hot shower for a while. Before she could go in, I nobbled a female member exiting the locker room and asked her if she could possibly help Angela find some dry clothes. She agreed readily, and Angela smiled weakly and went through the door under her own power. Next I went up to see how George was doing in the men's locker room. He assured me that he was all right, and that his wound didn't require stitches.

"A simple cut, that's all," he pronounced blithely through the steam of the shower. "A sticking plaster will do the trick." He hesitated. "But we do have a bigger problem."

"What's that?" I asked with dread, leaving my drenched

clothes in a sodden pile on the floor and stepping under my own stream of blissfully warm water. Fortunately, I had dry clothes in my locker.

"Your dingbat people appear to be deadly serious."

I didn't answer. We both knew he was right.

Angela agreed to lunch with us. The only noticeable after-effects of her ordeal were a shaking hand as she brought her wineglass to her lips, and a sort of wild look about her blue-green eyes. The tremors had stopped, and I admired once again how strong and calm she could be in the face of disaster.

At Threepwood they still did Sunday lunch the old-fashioned way, and we'd be having three courses, complete with roast joint. Attacking the soup, I asked Angela to run through the coded Stonecypher sentences again, to see what could possibly be so frightening to whoever was leaving engravings on our desks.

She recited them in a quiet voice, and although I knew them well, I thought they had somehow acquired a rather sinister quality.

" 'When principalities and kingdoms fall, every man will come to power through the written word.'

" 'In books is to be found the greatest power to enlighten, to introduce ideas and enable them to flourish for all time.'

" 'True power comes from the diversity of many united—not in the several, but in the one.'

" 'Thrones, principalities, dominions, all shall fall when mankind achieves enlightenment.' "

" 'When principalities and kingdoms fall every man will come to power through the written word,' " I repeated quietly. "Can't think why that should have anyone's knickers in a twist."

Angela took a large sip of wine, looking somewhere into mid-space, leaving the deliberations to us for the moment.

"No," George said, shaking his head. "Nothing comes to mind."

"Sorry, Angela—what are the others again?"

She ran through them effortlessly as we listened for

something—anything—significant. When she was done, we looked at each other and shook our heads. Nothing there that seemed even remotely threatening to anyone in twentieth-century England.

Angela looked from me to George and back again. "Odd little puzzle, isn't it?" she asked, raising her eyebrows. She had put on her wry mask, probably an effective way of dealing with the events that threatened to destroy her life.

I sighed and ran my fingers through my hair. At the same time, the waiter came and removed my plate, and I sat back to give him room. "Thanks," I said. When he'd gone I leaned over the table and said quietly to Angela, grasping at straws, "Maybe we're looking at it the wrong way. Could there be a code within the code? A word that means something else?"

"I can't believe this is happening to you." George spoke as if he hadn't heard me, shaking his head slowly. "I just can't. I really think you should call the police and let them know—especially about the car and the motorboat. The anonymous letter and the dingbats might be harder to explain, I'll grant you."

"George, as I said earlier, they'd have a good laugh. There's nothing to go on. There are reckless launch drivers, and white Fords are free to go wherever they please." I sipped at my pint of bitter as George nodded grudgingly, then looked up at Angela, who was picking at her food as usual. I didn't understand how she could exercise so maniacally on the meagre meals she ate. "I'm really sorry, Angela. This shouldn't have to happen with your first novel."

She looked up at me briefly and raised her eyebrows again, as if to say "Too true," then went back to stirring her soup, evidently not intending to ever actually taste it.

We ate in silence for several moments, then George put down his soup spoon punctiliously. He folded his hands into the lecturer's characteristic steeple, and I knew he was going to impart his view of things.

"So someone's trying to get you to stop Angela's book from being published, and you don't really know why. But, as I understand it, you do know that all this started after you took out the ad for the book in *The Tempus*. Then it accelerated after you mentioned the discovery of the Stonecypher code to Armand Beasley and Giles Rutherford. So that's significant. One of the two of them could be responsible."

Or Max, I thought; but that was a private worry.

George continued. "And this Beasley is one of the kingpins of Folio B, right?" I nodded. "And he's a friend of Frank Holdsworthy's right?" I nodded again. "Well, there you are." He opened his hands in a little *"voilà"* gesture. "Maybe Folio B doesn't want you to publish the novel, for whatever reason Virginia Holdsworthy's letter said that Stonecypher and Folio B are related."

He frowned and sat forward with characteristic vigour, then had to apologise to the waiter, who had been attempting to deposit a huge plate of potatoes, vegetables, Yorkshire pudding, and roast beef on the table in front of him.

"Sorry, sorry," he said kindly to the waiter, then continued, frowning again. "You said they've invited you to sit on the board of Folio B, right, Alex?"

I nodded.

"How about a quiet word in the right places?" George suggested conspiratorially. "There must be someone in that group you can talk to."

Angela watched me closely for my answer, sipping at her wine.

"Actually, that was another strange thing." I took another sip of bitter, giving myself time to think. "When they brought me onto the board, after Armand's party, they all looked at me extremely oddly. Armand almost gave the impression that he was sorry to get me into it. And Frank Holdsworthy seemed really strange, insisting that I keep an empty chair next to me." I shook my head at the memory.

They both spoke at once.

"An empty chair?" Angela demanded, intrigued.

"That's it!" George's face was alight with discovery. "Of course!"

"What? What?" I asked them both.

"It's just that in *The Engraving on the Desk*, the second Stonecypher novel, there's a character who always leaves a chair at the table for the spirit—you know, the ghost, the one in your library," Angela said.

George and I looked at each other as if we'd just seen one.

"The ghost in your library?" he asked with exaggerated good diction.

I sighed. "It's a long story, but it seems that something actually was there. A flesh-and-blood ghost, most likely."

"How ghoulish," he said. "And they performed that—er— chair ritual at your board meeting?"

I nodded. "There are some rather eccentric characters involved," I said, competing for the understatement of the century.

Angela was fascinated by all of this, I could see; she wore a slightly dreamy expression, as if lost in her thoughts—or lost in half a glass of white burgundy on an empty stomach. Stonecypher was such a part of her by now that to her, it probably seemed that people were playing games with her mind. But if that was the case, she was certainly on firm ground. She had a mind that rivalled a steel trap.

I wondered again if Angela could possibly have anything to do with the dingbats and threats. It was inconceivable to me that anyone could be any more obsessed with Stone-cypher and his little symbols than she. But I strongly doubted that she would have tried to engineer her own demise on the Thames. Besides, her reactions seemed far too normal for her to have orchestrated all of it as either a publicity stunt, or a shortcut to my heart, or the aimless product of a sick mind.

Belatedly, I remembered that George had been eager to speak as well. Turning to him, I said, "George, what were you going to say a moment ago?"

He leaned over the table, as if to relate something in the deepest confidence. He wore a look of epiphany, his eyes aglow. "Frank Holdsworthy. Didn't you tell me last week that you were stealing his top author? That historian?"

I nodded, feeling a moment's relief as I considered George's explanation. Of course. Industrial rivalry; a Rupert Soames in Holdsworthy's clothing. Blackmail to keep me from taking his prize author. Or, perhaps, characteristically violent sour grapes on Rupert's part over losing the author.

"That would explain the malicious break-in, with the books thrown about." He beamed at me. "And maybe even trying to scare you with the Stonecypher dingbat—that's a clever one. Leaving them as the villain in Stonecypher's books did, as a threat, to keep you from going on with your lucrative trade publishing division. Holdsworthy probably knows that the trade books help fund your first-rate academic acquisitions. Same with the white car, even the boat; give you a bit of a fright." George chuckled and shook his head. "What wit, what intelligence! You're in with a fascinating crowd there, Alex."

I smiled back at him, intrigued with the thought of Holdsworthy using the dingbat as a threat. "It's tempting to dismiss it as professional jealousy, even blackmail. It might even explain Angela's letter; Holdsworthy might be trying to cast a long shadow over all our publishing operations, including your book, Angela, until we capitulate and give him back his author." I shared with them the possibility of Rupert's retaliation, as well; he was always a wild card. George rolled his eyes at the mention of Soames, but I found myself rejecting the idea in the next breath. "It still doesn't explain Virginia Holdsworthy's letter though, or her death."

His face grew serious. "Damn. You're right."

Our food sat untouched on the table before us. I took another long drink from my pint glass, and George followed suit. Then I sat back and said, "Here's an idea. Well, more a feeling than an idea. Last night—I'm not sure if you were with me at this point, Angela—Frank Holdsworthy and Diana Boillot were anything but enthusiastic about me visiting the Folio B restoration workshop when I brought it up."

I paused, looking deep into the amber of my glass. "Virginia's letter said that Folio B—or Holdsworthy—had a nasty little secret about the book restoration. Perhaps that's the key to it all. Holdsworthy and Diana even exchanged a rather meaningful look at the mention of certain people opposing restoration, and I remembered thinking that they knew something the rest of us didn't. So . . . I think a little discreet snooping would be in order at the Folio B restoration workshop."

Judging from Angela's reaction, the idea of action was comforting to her. It was one thing to sit and wait for bad things to happen; it was quite another to do everything in your power to make things happen the way you wanted them to.

George gave me his "You're going to get into trouble again" look, but I knew he'd do the very same thing in my shoes.

We indulged in the main course at last—at least George and I did. The food was excellent—reviving, comforting, wonderfully familiar in the face of the bizarre events of the recent past. George brought up the venomous personal battle waged by Rupert Soames to fight my proposal to admit female members to Threepwood, thinking it would be of interest to Angela, and we had a good laugh over it. It even took our minds off our current problems until Angela said, as an afterthought, "Maybe that's what this is all about. Rupert Soames is running about placing dingbats in the Orchard, trying to scare you into abandoning your battle to desegregate this monument to amateur male athleticism."

We laughed, but sobered again at the thought of the threats against us. When we'd had jam roly-poly—Threepwood could always be trusted for a good nursery pudding—and coffee, we retreated from the dining room, saying hello and good-bye to various members of the club who passed us on their way in to lunch. Many wished us well after our motor-boat ordeal, which had apparently over the last hour passed into the realm of club lore. Many also, to my mortification, looked with meaning and even winks at Angela and me as we walked together through the room, and that reminded me that I had never responded to Sarah's fax. It was the first time I hadn't responded immediately upon receiving a letter from her; I hardly knew how to write to her without referring to the odd occurrences of the past twenty-four hours, let alone the *M* word.

Having run the gauntlet, we retrieved our kit bags from some cubbyholes along the wall and stepped out into weak sunlight. There was a fine film of white cloud between us and the sun, giving the day a sultry, depressing air.

George stopped short outside the heavy wooden door of the club, with its bull's-eye window. "Anyone know how to get to this restoration building, then?"

I caught his drift, but didn't want to pull him into criminal charges of breaking and entering into the workshop, even if I was willing to risk them myself. "Don't you want to go and play football with your boys?" I said, looking at him askance. "And Lisette? We're not going to be doing anything terribly legal."

"Can't," he said flatly. "They've gone to visit her sister in Kent for the day." He smiled. "I'm going with you," he said mildly. "In fact," he added, looking round the car park, "I think I'm driving."

He was right. Angela and I had only bicycles; not the logical choice of transportation for a trip into London, even on a Sunday. He, on the other hand, had a Range Rover.

"Good," Angela said firmly. "That's three of us, then."

I hesitated. I hadn't intended it to be a group outing, or even necessarily something that happened that very day. But I couldn't think of a reason to put them off; actually, it would be nice to have some companionship—perhaps even a bit of help.

"Oh, come on, Alex," George said, heading for the bicycle rack. "Here, let's put your bikes in the back of my car."

"All right, then," I said. "But remember about the car following us. We can't let them know where we're going."

"Trust me," George said.

Knowing what I know now, even then we could have turned things around, had I not been so pig-headed.

CHAPTER 6

. . . Of making many books there is no end.
—ECCLESIASTES 12:12

Instead, we buzzed southeast on the motorway in George's Range Rover, after losing the white car in a remarkable show of bravery at a large roundabout outside Henley. We were a merry little band, cheerfully nattering on about everything but Stonecypher and threats and motorboats. When we got to Marble Arch, I got George's *A-Z* street guide out of the glove compartment and flicked through the pages, searching for Farquhart's street in the index.

"What street does he live on?" George asked. "We're in my neck of the woods now—my office in Harley Street isn't far from here, you know."

"Balfour Place," I said, abandoning the book. "I know I'll recognise the house—it made quite an impression on me when I was a twelve-year-old. My father and I came to pick up a book that Farquhart was selling us—it was on a weekend, and Farquhart's shop was closed. Stone lions and the works. And from what Armand said, the workshop is just behind the house, in Balfour Mews."

"Ah!" George exclaimed, pleased. "I know just where that

is—driven past it hundreds of times. Worry no more, my good man."

I was, in fact, feeling increasingly worried. It didn't seem at all right to simply sneak into the restoration workshop; we would be on Farquhart's property, after all, even if Holdsworthy paid for Folio B to use it.

"George, may I use your phone?"

"Of course."

"I think I should call Farquhart first. We can't go skulking about like common criminals." He nodded grudgingly; I think he'd been looking forward to the surreptitious part. After first ringing directory enquiries for the number, I let Farquhart's number ring at least twenty times. Meanwhile, George pulled into Balfour Place and glided to a stop across from number 79. I recognised it instantly. The area was quiet and luxurious. He eyed Farquhart's large three-storey house of brick and stucco, mere streets away from the mansions that had been transformed into embassies near Grosvenor Square. The snarling grey stone lions seated either side of the front door had something to guard, indeed. "The book business must be fairly profitable," George said, raising his eyebrows.

"One of Farquhart's ancestors invented the stock cube."

"Ah," George replied crisply.

"But a more recent Farquhart tired of the business and sold it, so William chose to make his book-collecting hobby a business, just for the fun of it. He was an only child, and lives alone in the house now. He and his wife are divorced, and his children are grown."

As George nodded in response, I took the receiver from my ear, disconnected, and tried again, in case I'd misdialled. No answer. Farquhart was probably at his shop in tony Sackville Street, preparing for the book fair starting Tuesday. As I knew all too well, Saturdays and Sundays were often work-days for those of us who owned our own businesses.

"Not home," I told George. "I've no idea how to reach Frank Holdsworthy, or Diana Boillot, so I imagine we're in the clear—sort of—to go have a look round. I'll knock at Farquhart's door anyway, just in case." In the back of my mind I was well aware that I could—and should—ring Farquhart at his shop. But I ignored this pricking of my conscience; the fact was, I wanted to snoop in privacy.

Angela had dozed on the way down from Threepwood, with George's suit jacket thrown over her. In sleep she looked deeply tired and worn, and so thin, it was almost frightening. Glancing back at her occasionally along the way, I had reflected that she seemed to have only two speeds: high and off.

I gently woke Angela. "We're here," I said.

"Oh?" she said, sitting up quickly.

Nearly bursting with curiosity to find out what "nasty little secret," in Virginia Holdsworthy's words, Frank Holdsworthy and Diana were keeping about the Folio B restoration operation, I unfastened my seat belt and hopped out of the car. As I opened Angela's door for her, I reflected that they surely wouldn't have left evidence of it lying about, but perhaps it could be pieced together with a bit of imagination.

Angela had no reaction to the imposing house as we mounted the steps to the elegantly raised front door, other than to glance with disdain at the stone beasts. She had, I thought, almost no regard for material things. I remembered presenting her with a contract for *The Stonecypher Saga*; she had flipped to the last page and signed, and had never even asked about the advance on royalties. I'd been somewhat disappointed, as I'd given her roughly twice the usual money for a first novel, certain that the British public would be fascinated by anything to do with Stonecypher—especially with a film about him underway at Pinewood Studios, and another slated for Elstree the next year. "Aren't you going to ask how much I'm giving for an advance?" I'd asked. She'd responded, "No, that's not why I'm writing this book. You don't have to give me money, Alex." Feeling deflated, I'd handed her the cheque anyway, remarking that it was a first in the publishing business.

When at last we stood in front of Farquhart's door—no doubt an odd-looking crew with Angela still in her borrowed, too-large clothes, George in his straight-from-rounds suit, and I in my jeans and polo shirt—I pressed the bell. "Perhaps the faithful family retainer will answer. We can leave a friendly little message that we stopped by to see the restoration workshop." Angela merely yawned, but George smiled.

"Yes, I should think Jeeves might pop out any moment now," he said. "Looks just the sort of area."

But Jeeves never came, nor Bertie, nor Gussie Fink-Nottle—not even William Farquhart. After ringing again and waiting for several moments, I shrugged. "Well. No one at home." With a confidence I didn't feel, I said, "I trust Farquhart and Holdsworthy won't mind my taking a peek into the restoration workshop now that I'm a member of the board."

George said, "That's the stuff," and started back down the stairs to a path that led to the mews behind. Balfour Mews was a separate street behind Balfour Place, and in days gone by the more modest buildings there had housed servants, animals, and carriages. Now the houses on Balfour Mews were separate residences of their own, and fairly nice ones too. Farquhart's little mews house was made of the same materials as the main house, and was joined to it by a path lined with manicured shrubs but, I noticed, no flowers. The lawn and shrubs looked a bit run-down, I thought as we strolled down the paving stones, but attributed it to very-late-summer, early-autumn gardener's slump. Before too long anyway, everything would go dormant for the winter.

In comfortable silence we approached the mews house, which bore neither sign nor number. Out of habit I knocked on the varnished wooden door, but again there was no answer. Next, we tried to peer into the two windows on the wall facing us, but not only were they screened with heavy iron bars, as if to prevent theft, they were heavily curtained—perhaps to prevent peeping Toms while Diana slaved away alone at night on the books. All in all, a very secure facility. But, I reminded myself, Diana probably restored some very valuable books inside; she had to have a secure place to leave them.

Angela looked at me and raised her eyebrows.

"Looks pretty secure for a place to restore books," George said, putting our thoughts into words.

"Mmm," I agreed, reaching for the doorknob. "I'll bet some very valuable books come through here. No harm in checking the door, I suppose."

But as I took hold of the knob, we heard the noise of a small van blasting into the quiet square, and screeching to a stop in front of Farquhart's.

"Visitors!" I hissed, wheeling and practically pushing George in front of me in my panic to get round the back of the small building. I didn't know why I was being so furtive—after all, I could have simply explained to the newcomers that I was on the board of Folio B and wanted to see where the restoration was done. But I suppose I expected that the building held Frank Holdsworthy's "nasty little secret," and imagined that surely someone would want to keep that secret from us.

Angela, quick to react as usual, had already flown ahead of us. There were no windows into the rear of the building, making a secure barrier for us. We leaned against the rear wall, listening.

There were footsteps on the stone path up to the workshop, more than one set, then the rattle of keys.

"Wonder what they've got for us this time, then." The speaker, who had a pronounced cockney accent and a bad attitude, got a grunt for a response. There was the sound of an opening lock, then more rattling of keys, the sound of another lock protesting and then turning, still more key-rattling, then the creak of a door opening.

I suppose the number of locks was justified, and consistent with an authentic restoration operation. If they kept the nation's most treasured books in there, they had to be careful.

At last they stepped inside, and their noises became muffled. We waited, still listening. There was no more conversation, but in a moment they came shuffling out.

"Easy does it," a voice said. "Don't want to drop this lot."

The quiet one snorted in answer this time, and the two men grunted and panted their way toward the street from the door. From the sound of it, their load was extremely heavy, and we advanced carefully to the corner of the building, peeking round to follow their progress. Two men were carrying a cardboard box, roughly two feet square. Both wore workmen's uniforms. One was sixtyish, with a giant beer belly, and the other was a balding but otherwise nondescript man. The quiet one, I judged.

The door to the workshop stood open behind them, but we

couldn't go in because the men were obviously going to come back. We waited, and finally heard them coming slowly across the car park, Beer Belly complaining loudly about the weight of the boxes.

"Oy, a box of bleedin' bricks." The men reentered and hoisted another box between them, then shuffled out through the door as before. "Reckon the boss won't mind if we have a smoke after this one. It's hard work for the day of rest, i'n it, even on triple time." We waited until they were behind the van, loading their burden into the back of it. The back of the van was screened from our view by some overgrown columnar Irish yews, and when the pair didn't reappear, we assumed that they were sitting on the tailgate of the open van to take their break. Then, certain that their smoke would take a good ten minutes at least, and hidden by the cooperative yews, we slid quietly through the open door.

It was every bit a printer's paradise. Towards the front of the room was a trestle table, with what I recognised as rebinding gear on it—a loom, a press, a hot glue pot, and a small knife for paring leather, with its sharpening stone nearby. Along one side wall, two rows of shelving ran the length of the room, the top shelf just above waist level. The shelves held what looked like jars of paint and ink, along with stoppered glass bottles of clear liquid—solvents for removing glue and heaven knew what else.

Lining the rear wall were rows of old printer's chests that I recognised from our barn at the Orchard. We had all sorts of old typefaces that we kept as souvenirs, and I didn't doubt that Diana had the same ones, for completely reconstructing missing sections of the books. A debatable practice, unless one could be absolutely certain that anyone who ever purchased those books in the future knew they'd been tampered with. And with human nature as predictable and fallible as it was, that was highly unlikely.

Angela trod gently on the bare wooden floor over to the trestle table. She delicately fingered the loom, which was strung with thread like a weaver's loom, but with the strings attached at the bottom, in the spine of a book. I moved over to explore a row of locked cupboards along the other side of the room. The cupboards looked like the ones used by art supply stores for storing oversized watercolour paper. That, too, was in keeping with the restoration business—there were dealers who sold old paper for the purpose, some from as far back as the seventeenth century. Next to the cabinets were a large, vaguely disturbing paper-cutting guillotine which I wouldn't want to put my hand under, and a stove surrounded by hand tools.

All in all, it was what I had expected. A hideaway in which to restore books, a sort of artistic haven. I turned my attention to the centrepiece of the room, Farquhart's letter press. Farquhart was known to be something of an amateur printer and designer. This was the sort of old treadle press used for small, fussy artistic jobs—not the kind of thing that would be used for mass copies.

There was even a big, dusty blue corduroy loose-slipcovered chair in one corner; the lined curtains were made of the same well-worn fabric. I found myself thinking that before this had become Diana's studio, it had obviously been a man's workshop, and presumably Farquhart still used it. The room had the sort of untidy feeling, with its wood shavings and paper bits on the rug-covered floor and the industrial smell of an active home printing shop. I knew what that smelled like; my father had kept his in the barn, and when I was young I'd gone out and helped him. He'd enjoyed printing invitations from time to time, and the odd poem. The old press stood gathering dust there to this day.

Feeling nostalgic, I turned away from the press to eye several more boxes near the door, similar to the one the men had carried out.

Books? Of course. Few things are as heavy as a box of books. They were taking books out of there, buy why? Had Diana finished restoring this many at one go? And why was she moving the books on a Sunday afternoon—during triple time hours for the workmen?

I knelt and looked at the box closest to me. An address label read, *M. Michel Menceau, Château Menceau, Menceau-ville, France*. Not much chance of a missed delivery here, I thought. The Wilde Publishing logo, a scrolly, William-and-Mary-looking W, was printed majestically on all sides of the box in deep green ink.

George, who was looking at the instruments on the table with Angela, went to the door and peered out after the men. "I'll keep watch while you snoop," he whispered to me.

"Thanks," I whispered, and moved to the tall cabinets at the rear of the room, trying the door of the first of four. It was locked. Perhaps Diana's gold leaf and morocco leather for replacing and restoring covers were kept there. I walked quickly round the room, trying doors and thinking about what I saw. Cabinets and more locked cabinets. The printer's chests were locked as well, but when I shook one, it rattled with tiny pieces of type.

"They're still sitting and smoking—I can hear the one with the gut chattering on," George whispered over his shoulder, his head out the door.

"Okay, thanks." I moved to the boxes the men were removing, followed by Angela, and wondered if I could get one open and somehow close it up again before the men got back. There were two cartons left; I focussed on the one farthest from the door, hoping they'd pick it up last. It was sealed with transparent packing tape at every seam. Taking a pen out of my coat pocket, I quickly slit the tape along the sides of the top of the box and down its middle. I flipped the box flaps open. Inside, I saw a dozen heavily bubble-wrapped parcels floating in polystyrene chippings.

With urgency, George said, "They're getting up! Come on," and motioned wildly that I should hurry. Hurriedly I pressed the lid down, hoping the box would still appear to be sealed, and saw Angela slip out the door past George. Then I followed him out the door and ducked round the corner of the building just as we heard their boots on the path. He looked at me and smiled; he was enjoying this. It was a far cry, I supposed, from his usual work.

This time the men wordlessly hefted their load, sweating a bit, and shuffled out again. George pretended to wipe his brow, and moved back to the front of the building to keep a lookout. Angela and I returned to the box, reopened it, and ripped open one of the bubble-wrapped packages.

I pulled out a marbled manuscript box two inches deep, and about ten by fourteen inches. When I opened the lid, my breath caught in my throat. Inside lay Bunyan's *Pilgrim's*

Progress in a contemporary binding—that is, contemporary with the author's time—in this case, 1678. Even I knew what this was . . . this volume had been on display at the Bodleian at Oxford as one of the most valuable and sought-after books in the world. The value of a book this rare was almost inestimable. I wasn't sure if Angela knew how important it was, but she stared at it in awe. There was just one problem with it—a tragedy, really—except that one took what one could get in ancient books. Aside from the one complete copy that was displayed at the Bodleian, the only known remaining copy of the book was not complete; it was missing large sections at the beginning and the end.

Quickly I found a calligraphed card inside the box, bearing the Wilde Hall engraving in the upper-right-hand corner. *John Bunyan's Pilgrim's Progress, 1678. Extremely rare, fine condition, part of recently discovered collection of Virginia Wilde Holdsworthy, now deceased. In Wilde family for two hundred years. Second of two complete copies known to exist.*

In that moment the full understanding of what Holdsworthy and Boillot were doing with the books came to me, and it was so outrageous, so evil, I shuddered. I knew what we must do.

"I don't believe this," George said incredulously from the door. "They're opening soft drink cans—another break."

"The boss isn't getting his money's worth today," Angela said wryly.

I thought for a moment. "I need to see what's in those cabinets. Anyone agreeable to coming back in after they leave?"

Angela nodded her assent. She wasn't afraid of anything.

"Sure," George said. "This is great fun. I haven't enjoyed myself this much since—" He stopped, and his smile faded when he noticed the look on my face. "Alex, what is it?"

"They're selling the books." I felt slightly sick at the thought.

He looked nonplussed. "*Selling* them . . ."

I swallowed and began rewrapping *Pilgrim's Progress.* "They take the good books from the national libraries, remove the library markings, and patch them up a bit to make them seem like perfect versions, then claim that they're newly discovered books from Virginia Holdsworthy's collection."

Kneeling, I nestled the package back down in the box reverently, and picked up a second book, larger then the first. Gently, I unwrapped the bubble packing and found a Kelmscott Chaucer, again one of the world's rarest and most beautiful books, bound by William Morris. The card inside repeated the statement that the volume had long been part of the Virginia Wilde Holdsworthy collection, fine condition, 40,000 pounds. I checked; her bookplate was inside the cover, though not adhered. It would be unthinkable to paste anything on a Kelmscott Chaucer, and Holdsworthy and Boillot knew enough not to try it.

I exhaled slowly, shaking my head, and began rewrapping the white leather-bound book. Then I tucked it back into its nest of packing material. "He's selling off parts of her library, so the story won't look totally implausible. Then—and this is what we've got to find proof of—they find less perfect copies of the same book and patch them up to look like the library's version. New covers can be made and aged, if necessary—it's called 'remboitage.' Sangorsky and Sutcliffe, here in London, are famous for it—though, of course, *they* do it ethically. It's amazing what a really good restorer—or forger—can do." I remembered a story my father had told me about a man who'd become famous for mixing glue and wood filings and rubbing them on new covers and pages to make them look as if they had dry rot.

George looked astounded, but automatically glanced out to check on the men. "Still there," he reported from the door.

"Good. Maybe I can get this taped up." A roll of the wide sticky tape that had been used to package the box sat on the trestle table behind me. I picked it up and Angela took it from me, pulling tape off the roll slowly, so it wouldn't screech. She handed me the end, fed me what I needed, then cut the appropriate length. We started again on a different seam.

Once again, reluctantly, I recognised a feeling of camaraderie with her—closeness, even. We were so often in these extraordinary situations together, and she was always so calm, so competent, so . . .

Unaware of my thoughts, she cocked her head to one side,

frowning as she studied the address on the box. "Alex—isn't this the Frenchman we met at Armand's party?"

"A Folio B friend of Armand Beasley's," I explained. "Sarah and I—" Angela's stricken look at the mention of Sarah's name reminded me to be more careful in future. "Er, we've been invited to stay there for the weekend during the Folio B conference. Menceau is actually hosting the conference at his château, treating it as a big house party. I'll bet they're going to sell these books at the Paris book fair."

We had safely re-sealed the sides of the top, but not the middle, when George reported, "I hear them rousing themselves. We'd better move."

"Damn," I said. I abandoned the project, hurriedly patting the tape down as best I could, and Angela put the roll back on the table. There was nothing I could do about the cut layer of tape showing through the new one, except to hope that they wouldn't notice. Once again we scooted out of the workshop and round the back.

"Blimey." The talkative one strode in, his big work boots clomping on the wooden floor. "Glad this is the last of it, I'll tell you that much." He'd tell a lot more too, I thought, if he ever got more than half a raised eyelid in response. He was obviously one of those rare individuals who had elevated complaining to an art form, and I hoped that he would keep right on with it if it would help him to ignore the irregularities of the last box.

They stood and looked at it for a moment before lifting it. "Had a bit of trouble with this one, didn't he?"

If he noticed the unsealed top of the box, he must have decided it wasn't his job to worry about it. With a responding grunt, his partner took his half of the box and they carried it just outside the door, then set it down.

"He said to lock 'er up tight, and that's what he'll get." The talkative one closed the wooden door and locked it—one lock, then the next. Finally they lifted the remaining box and made their last trip to the truck.

As they retreated, Angela lifted her T-shirt and unzipped the nearly microscopic runner's pack she wore around her waist. "There we are," she said quietly, holding up a narrow strip of metal. George and I squinted at it, trying to figure out what it was. "A part from my bicycle lock." She was nonchalant. "It comes in handy now and again." Smiling, she walked round to the front of the building as we heard the van roll away and began fiddling with the metal scrap in the lock.

"Angela," I said in astonishment, watching over her shoulder. "I had no idea."

She raised her eyebrows and continued working on the first of the locks. "I wasn't always a good girl at school. Don't worry—I don't make a habit of it anymore."

George and I looked at each other, impressed with the hidden talents of Angela Mayfield.

She had the locks open in a matter of minutes, something I was sure Holdsworthy would be furious to know, and as she swung open the door, I made for the tall locked wooden cabinets. "I'm afraid I'll have to prevail upon you again for these," I said.

"A pleasure," she said.

I held my breath as she finally turned the latch on the first one. "Paints," I said, disappointed. "Terribly innocent. But that's all right. Lots more cupboards to go."

She opened eight in all, with both of us leaning over her shoulder, watching. Six contained disappointingly legitimate materials for restoring old books, and a seventh seemed to be a storage place for some of Holdsworthy's wife's memorabilia—the memorabilia that was making it possible for them to pass off partially forged books as complete copies. It contained a stack of her beautiful bookplates, engraved cards of the sort that Holdsworthy had stuck in the Chaucer and Bunyan with descriptions on them, and engraving plates for both.

But it was the very last one that made Angela's eyes sparkle as she opened the door.

"Bingo," she said.

"Bingo indeed." I reached in and took out a crumbling stack of pages, virtually unbound but for a few yellowed threads. "Part of Shakespeare's poems, 1640, including the title page. The sonnets, 1609. Good God! I mean, sorry. Here's a good chunk of the Tyndale New Testament! The British Library only recently bought the first copy on the market this *century* for one and a half million pounds."

Placing the stack on the work-table, I lifted out unbound

fragment after fragment of famous or at least valuable literature—valuable, that is, in its entirety, but not as a fragment or
"cripple," as incomplete copies of books are called in the
trade. They had purchased all these partial manuscripts,
nothing more than interesting junk in the book world, to help
them cobble together complete copies. The partials could
then be bound in a fitting manner, along with any forged
pages required, aged appropriately, and sold at a vast profit.

"Complete copies of these would sell for hundreds of
thousands—millions—of pounds, in some cases," I mumbled.

George frowned. "Surely people would be suspicious of so
much exceptional stuff coming onto the market, and all at
once."

"Mmm. Maybe. But remember, Holdsworthy has his
wife's library to fall back on. He could always say she had a
secret stash of these valuable books somewhere. Things like
this are always happening in the rare book world. And, unfortunately, Holdsworthy and Boillot are two of the few people
who know their way around books enough to pull it off. They
know all the right people too."

"It's diabolical," he said, personally offended by such a
breach of decency.

"Diabolically clever," Angela said with a naughty smile.
Her ethics were a bit underdeveloped, but she knew clever
people when she saw them.

George looked at her askance, then asked me, "What are
you going to do?"

I couldn't keep a vindictive little smile from creeping
across my face. "I'm going to let them think they're safe, then
nobble them when they least expect it."

"Oooh, I love it." Angela's face lit up wickedly. "Really,
Alex! I wouldn't have thought you'd be capable of such
deceit."

"That man Holdsworthy deserves what he gets," George
said. He was indignant. "Boillot too. What a betrayal of
trust—and in more ways than one," he finished with meaning.

We didn't stay much longer; Angela locked up the cupboards again with her scrap, and we took a final look round
before going out the door. I shook my head as I regarded the
comfortable yet purposeful room. "Doesn't exactly look like

the centre of a book-stealing and forgery ring." George snorted in agreement and led the way off down the path to his car.

Late afternoon shadows followed us as we half-sneaked down the path, chattering with animation about Frank Holdsworthy's plot to sell the books he and Diana were supposed to be restoring.

But I found myself silent as George sped us homeward. These seemed to be layers of evil here; I had figured out what Frank and Diana were up to, but still didn't understand what could be so threatening about Angela's book.

It was a bad feeling. Nasty little surprises were cropping up all over, and I couldn't help but wonder what was coming next.

CHAPTER 7

Never were the plane trees loftier, leafier
the planes of Bedford Square,
and of all that summer foliage motionless
not one leaf
had fallen yet . . ."

—LLOYD PLOMER

"Alex." I thought I'd heard my name, but couldn't be bothered to answer. A car door closed, and then I heard a door click open. Something was dragged out, amid shuffling on the gravel, and the door closed again.

"Alex." It was George. I opened my eyes and found that I was in George's Range Rover, outside the Orchard. He stood on the gravel drive, holding Angela's and my bicycles upright. "All change," he said in a stage cockney accent, imitating a bus driver telling all passengers to disembark at the end of the route.

"Mmm. Sorry." I rubbed my eyes. "I can't imagine—must have fallen asleep." I jumped out of the car, feeling flushed, noting that Angela was still sleeping in the back seat.

"Yes." George peered in at her childlike form. "I notice that both of you have a great deal of trouble sleeping. You should take more exercise," he said, unable to suppress a smile.

"Thanks, George," I said, taking the bicycles from him. "I always appreciate your sound advice. Still on for Tuesday?" I yawned.

He grinned. "Wouldn't miss Lisette's promotion lunch for anything. I haven't breathed a word—she'll be thrilled." Then he grew serious. "You'll ring me if you need help with any of this, won't you?" He waved his hand vaguely.

I nodded. "And you ring me, too, if your superior mind figures out what's going on here."

"Want me to wake Angela?" George asked.

"Thanks."

He got in the back seat and gently spoke her name, touching her shoulder, and she sat up and followed him out of the car, her short hair standing up in little spikes. She took her bike from me.

"Thanks for driving us, George," she said sleepily, and gave him a kiss and a hug, which he returned. "Bye."

"Not at all. Be careful, both of you," he said, and got into his car as Angela and I walked toward the garage. I waved, yawning, as he drove round the circular drive and out into the lane. It was only tea-time, I thought—probably six at the latest. The crickets chirped riotously in the warmth, and I longed for early bed—probably a result of the long bicycle ride and row, not to mention the motorboat incident.

As Angela and I wordlessly stowed the bicycles in the garage, I noticed that Max's BMW was home for the night. I wondered if it would stay that way, or creep out again for some late-night rendezvous. Shaking my head at the perpetual confusion my life represented, I ushered Angela into the quiet house, returned her "good night" as she plodded upstairs, and went into the kitchen to make a cup of tea.

I had no sooner set the kettle to boil than my eyes flew wide open. "Sarah!" I said aloud, and headed for the library at a run. Her fax had gone unanswered for twenty-four hours, an unprecedented occurrence, and she would wonder at the change. Glancing over at the fax machine, I noticed that its tray was empty. She hadn't written again.

"Alex, Alex, Alex," I chastised myself angrily as I sat down at the laptop on the desk. "You idiot." Of all times, this was not the week to disappoint Sarah, just before our holiday. And after she had so delicately broached the subject of marriage—in a way.

I picked up her fax of the day before, which had been left undisturbed on the desktop, and reread it.

Dear Alex,

At last—less than a week until our trip. Jacques asked me to postpone it so I could see a client next week, but I told him no flatly. Probably not the best thing for my career, but even he must agree that everyone has a private life. He had the gall to question my commitment to the company, but I explained to him that it was precisely because I respected commitments that I wasn't going to break this one to you. I also reminded him that this was the first vacation I will have had in my two years with the company, and he was so appalled at the thought that he simply left my office in silence.

Anyway, enough of Jacques. I have definitely fallen in love with Paris, and am thinking of keeping a pied à terre here, preferably this very flat if I could manage it, on the Île St. Louis.

Mom and Dad called; they're planning to come over from Massachusetts the second week in October for a visit. They wanted to know if you would be free for a weekend to come again to see them. You know they're nuts about you. Let me know, okay?

I've kept my promise; my wine course is completed. At least I'll know roughly what I'm tasting at the festival in Alsace. And on Monday, a day off since I've have worked on a project for Jacques all weekend, I'm going on a long bicycle ride. I'll take the train into the country and go on from there. Hope I can keep up with you on the tandem!

By the way, I've got a Severe Mercy *question for you. I'm struck by the fact that Davy follows Van to Oxford, and doesn't seem to care that her academic and professional life has come to a standstill. Do you think that her love for him could overwhelm her concern for her own well-being, and that she could be truly happy centring her life around him? Or will she*

> *grow to resent him later for her missed opportunities,*
> *though it was her own choice?*
>
> > *See you soon,*
> > *Sarah*

At least I wouldn't fail the *Severe Mercy* part of the test; I had kept up on my reading. I had loved the book; it was beautifully written, extremely romantic, and deeply moving, not to mention inspiring. An excellent book for two young lovers to read . . . how I wished Sarah and I could be called that.

Dear Sarah,

> *I'm glad to hear that you gave Jacques a piece of your mind! Wasn't he the one you told me jetted off to New Zealand for the entire month of July?* [I always resented her bosses, no matter who they were; it must have been some form of jealousy for the amount of time they spent with her. Jacques was no exception.]
>
> *My wine course is coming along as well, though I still haven't acquired a nose for some of the more unusual aromas. I have yet to be able to detect "petrol" and "straw" in any of the wines. I do, however, now have an infallible procedure for recognising Sauvignon Blanc (I don't know if that's produced in Alsace, but this is useful anyway): "cat's piddle on a gooseberry bush." Memorable, isn't it? I've enjoyed Mr. Falke at the Cask immensely; enjoyed the wine, too. My last session is Tuesday night.*
>
> *I'd be delighted to come to Paris again in October. I really enjoy spending time with your parents, and am glad they won't mind having me around. Consider me there.*
>
> *As for Davy and Van, I think that it's entirely possible for one person to be willing to sacrifice, at least temporarily, his or her professional pursuits for the other.* [I took a deep breath.] *This would be especially true, of course, of a married couple who had already pledged before God to stand by each other*

*"for better, for worse," et cetera, in marriage vows, as
Davy and Van had.*

*At the same time, I think it would have been a
terrible thing for Davy to have had to sacrifice her
career for Van if she hadn't wanted to. But—and
here's the key—Van cared too much about her to allow
her to suffer for him anyway. (Ironically, as we know
from the ending of the book, she did suffer to save him
in another sense, but you know what I mean—he would
not willingly have allowed her to suffer.) I think that
real love and concern between two people takes care
of those problems; they would never want to make
each other miserable.*

*So, for instance, applying this to our situation, I
would never ask you to leave a career or a place that
you love, because I want you to be happy. I would,
however, consider such things for you because, as you
know, I love you. I love you far more than old Plumtree
Press, and much, much more than any place.*

Yes—I will see you soon!"

Love,
Alex

I printed the letter, pressed the button on the fax machine
that would automatically dial her home machine, and hoped I
wouldn't frighten her off with it as I watched the paper disappear into the paper feed. We were certainly discussing more
weighty subjects, and I was saying more about my feelings in
our written correspondence, than we would have verbally if
she were here. No doubt it was better that way. But putting
everything in writing was so permanent, so definite. My
words stood out starkly on the white paper, and there was no
refuting them. I could only hope she liked what she saw.

I had some tea and toast and went to bed early. Unbelievably, the entire night passed without excitement. There were
no intruders, ghosts, or speeding vehicles. I didn't even dream.

The next morning, Monday, I awoke early. Six o'clock was
early for me, at any rate. For some incomprehensible reason I
felt invigorated, though of course there was still a small personal storm cloud far overhead. By nature I was an optimist,

though admittedly a worrying optimist, and I suppose it was a basic character flaw that even at that point I expected the best of nearly everyone and everything. I was out of the door by six-thirty, thermal coffee cup in hand, and something about the remarkably blue sky, a full cup of Sumatra blend, and the beauty of an English summer morning made me feel surprisingly content.

It wasn't until the white Ford joined me as I passed Chorleywood tube station, not half a mile from the Orchard, that the cloud descended again. I frowned as the car followed me at a respectful distance, realising that he had known exactly which route I would take. I couldn't make out a thing behind the tinted windscreen.

Who on earth was doing this, and why?

Driving into the West End, watching the white car in my rear-view mirror along the way, I catalogued all the reasons I had to feel discouraged. There was the whole mess surrounding Angela's book, threats and all, to be dealt with, which in turn was wrapped up with the Folio B board. Then, of course, there was the continuing process of signing Holdsworthy's author, not to mention working out how to deal with Frank and Diana, and the books apparently stolen through their restoration work.

Finally, there were the Historic Buildings Society people coming for a visit later that morning. I was undertaking a restoration and expansion project that would link our offices at 54 Bedford Square with the building behind, a run-down but historic hotel. The Historic Buildings people would be eager to find any part of our restoration project out of compliance with regulations so they could put a stop to the whole thing.

Still, I tried to reassure myself, things were going quite well at the Press. We were about to capture Holdsworthy's future share of the history market through his prize-winning author, and I was still confident that Angela's book was going to be a sensation if we could get it published.

And at the top of list of pluses was Sarah; I would have the entire next week with her to myself. If things turned out the way I hoped, by the end of the trip my life might be entirely different.

Pulling into Bedford Square, I circled, sharklike, for a parking spot and found one several doors down from the brass door plate of Plumtree Press. It was another perfect day, the leafy plane trees in the center of the square in all their glory, the sky blue, and the air warm, with just the slightest scent of impending autumn. As I got out of the Golf, I caught a glimpse of the white car gliding into a parking spot across the square. Would someone sit in it all day, waiting to see if I came out of the door?

I felt a bit more calm at the prospect of being followed continuously than I had the day before, if only because I'd survived a whole day of it. Whoever it was, he was not out to kill me—not yet, anyway. Apparently he merely wanted to frighten me, and Angela, for any one of the reasons George and Angela and I had discussed at lunch the day before. The motorboat had been most successful in that respect.

Still, I couldn't live in dread of their next appearance; I had a life to live, a business to run. I loved the place, loved what I did, and felt a flush of proprietary pride and well-being as I walked down the row to Number 54 and up the five steps to its door. The door was deep forest green with a huge brass knocker in the centre of it. Derek, our post-room and everything person, kept the door plate, door handle, lock, and knocker nicely polished. I would have to remember to tell him that I appreciated his good work.

Opening the door, I stepped in and smelled the fine old building—floor polish and old wood—marred temporarily by construction dust and generator fumes. The builders started early; I was tempted to stop and chat to check on their progress, but decided to let them get on with their work until I took the building people round to see them.

I ran up the three flights of stairs two steps at a time, my daily exercise, and nearly crashed into Lisette as she flew out of the tiny storeroom we used as a canteen and coffee-brewing grotto.

"Mon Dieu!" she exclaimed, trying in vain to hold her coffee mug away from her clothing. The thick black stew she called coffee dribbled down the side of her skirt, one-half of what I speculated was a very special birthday present from George: a brand-new, touchably soft peach knit suit.

"Oh, no," I groaned. "I'm so sorry, Lisette. Here, let me . . ." I went with her, dripping mug in hand, back into the storeroom, where there was a sink and clean towels.

Fortunately for me, Lisette replied with her own highly individual brand of humour, which always relieved the awkwardness of things.

"You pig!" She winked and smiled a pouty smile as she continued. "Look what you 'ave done to my new suit. George will 'ave your 'ead."

I wet a clean cloth with warm water and started mopping gently at the fine knit. "Oh, go on," she said, grabbing it from me. "You won't do it right. Take your coffee and get out of 'ere." She said these angry words with cheerful nonchalance, and I thought for the thousandth time that George was a lucky so-and-so, as Lisette would put it, to have found her.

As I poured a cup and made it palatable with a healthy portion of cream, Lisette pointed with the towel to a small box of pastries and buns. "We must keep our energy up," she said. "It's going to be one 'ell of a week, *n'est-ce pas?*"

I nodded humbly and left, knowing that if I said I was sorry again she would merely hurl another cheerful insult at me. Standing over my desk, I checked my watch and sipped the coffee, imagining the caffeine jolt travelling through my body. Lisette's coffee was a powerful drug, indeed.

Seven-thirty—the earliest I'd been to the office in months. The first thing I had to do was call our printer in Singapore about the advance copies of Angela's novel—which we hadn't yet received. Two days before an announcement was far too late *not* to have advance copies. I couldn't introduce the book without at least the advance copies in hand—and it would be the first time I would have introduced a book without bulk copies. The journalists would receive book proofs anyway—relatively inexpensive photocopied, paper-bound copies of the book. They were used to receiving them instead of finished books, but it simply wasn't done to launch a book without copies available in the shops. If all went well, the British public would rush to the bookshops to buy *The Stonecypher Saga*—only to find that it wasn't available. And book buyers were a fickle lot; if it wasn't in the shop when they were desperate for it—immediately after reading a review, for instance—it could be forgotten by the next day.

I dialled the number of my contact at the printers, Kei-King Lee. It didn't matter what the hour was there—they had to operate round the clock because of their world-wide clientele.

"Lee here." I marvelled. Whenever I called, he was there. Perhaps he survived on two-minute catnaps next to his phone.

"Kei-King, it's Alex Plumtree. How are you?"

"Great, great, everything's fine." Not only was Kei-King always awake and at work, he was consistently upbeat. On top of it all, he had a remarkable grasp of colloquial English. "How are things at Plumtree Press? I thought *The Stone-cypher Saga* came out looking very nice."

"Well, that's just the problem. We haven't seen it yet, and we're getting a bit anxious. Our press announcement is on Wednesday."

There was a pause. "You mean you don't have your advance copies yet? The bulk shipments went out long ago to the big wholesalers; I'm expecting confirmation of their receipt any minute. But I can't imagine—"

"No—we haven't seen anything yet."

"Ah! This is bad. Hang on, let me check with a couple of people."

He put me on hold, and I imagined him running out of his office. Kei-King had never slipped up before, and I was sure he took this as a personal humiliation.

In a moment he was back, sounding dejected and apologetic. "Alex, I have bad news. Your advance copies were supposed to go out via overnight air, but they went by sea instead." His voice lowered. "We have a new boy in shipping. I am so sorry." I heard motion, and realised he was checking the time. "I can send them out right away though—I'll do it personally. You'll have them tomorrow."

The day before the announcement. It was far too close, but I could always have some bulk copies sent from the big wholesalers if they didn't arrive. It would be highly unusual, but it could probably be done. "All right, Kei-King, thanks for seeing to it."

"Please accept my apologies, Alex. I will personally

ensure that it does not happen again." He sounded heart-broken; I felt sorry enough for him to bite back the words that naturally came to mind.

"Please—don't give it another thought. You're the best in the business, Kei-King." We said our good-byes, and I hoped that we wouldn't have more availability problems with the book; we had plenty of other problems to contend with.

I looked at my watch; seven forty-five. Still time enough to make a few notes on the historical novel written by Dr. Angus MacDougal, Holdsworthy's history book author, which I had agreed to publish in exchange for his move to Plumtree Press. I opened the lid of my notebook computer and started typing.

Wincing on behalf of Rachel Sigridsson, our senior editor, I recalled that MacDougal was coming in to meet her first thing in the morning the next day. Rachel could handle anything, I knew—even an angry redheaded author with a God complex who was volatile at the best of times—but I felt sorry for her anyway. I decided to write them with enough tact that she could show my notes to him and say that her boss insisted that these changes be made, if he gave her trouble. After reviewing my scrawls, liberally scattered throughout the disastrous manuscript, I began:

Date: Monday
To: Rachel
From: Alex

Re: The Storms of Time

Rachel,

Storms *needs, in my opinion, considerable rewriting. In general, things need to be shown and not told, and we need much more dialogue among the main characters. If the author can think of ways to communicate the background narrated by the omniscient narrator through action rather than narrative, we'll be much better off.*
    First let's start with the opening. Something needs

*to happen here; an event, not a lengthy exploration of
the protagonist's thoughts. Perhaps at least the author
can put Angus the Great together with the other
warriors as a foil for revealing information through
dialogue.*

*Also, on page 5, let's eliminate the description of
certain aspects of Edwina's physique; he's not writing
a romance, and I don't think their encounter could
have taken place in the midst of the army saddling up
for battle.*

*Besides, I suspect it was fairly parky out there on
the blasted heath in January; he wouldn't have been
able to see the parts of her anatomy that he claims to
beneath her bearskin coat.*

*I deeply disagree with the decision to focus on the
gore of the battle; some incidental description would
not be amiss, but two chapters of it is not only
offensive, it derails the plot. The battle needs to take
place, I know; but perhaps it can fill one chapter or
less rather than two. It is a*

I heard a knock outside my open door, and Lisette stuck her head round the corner.

"Frances Macnamara and the building people," she said. I looked at my watch: it was five past nine already. "I've put them in the large conference room with the pastries and sticky buns."

I saved the MacDougal file, put the Mac to sleep, and walked down the hall to the conference room after her. Her scent lingered in the air. What a fascinating phenomenon it was, I thought, that women always seemed to choose perfume that described them perfectly. Or perhaps it only seemed that way because I associated the scent with the person I already knew. Lisette's scent was voluptuous, flowery, overtly feminine, whereas Sarah's was more subtle and complex, spicy rather than floral. Angela's, on the other hand, was deep, dark, and intense.

I noted with satisfaction that the construction work seemed to be well under way; the portable generators hummed intermittently, powering their tools and machines. Today was the day they would take down the wall at the rear of our building, and I had no doubt whatsoever that it would take them the entire day to do it. When the inspectors from the historical buildings organisation had finished grilling me on the plans and how closely we would be sticking to them, I was supposed to give them a brief tour. I could show them the site of the proposed opening and how carefully we were preserving the existing building during the project.

A bushy white head popped out of a door just outside the conference room as I walked past. "Morning, Alex. Still on for our Monday chat?"

I nodded. "Morning, Ian. Eleven o'clock, right?"

Ian Higginbotham *was* Plumtree Press, to all intents and purposes; even after my three years with the company, Ian knew things that no one else did, including me. He took care of the academic side of the business, and when I'd joined the company after my father's death, he'd handed over all administrative responsibility to me, preferring to stay close to the books in an editorial capacity. We specialised in literary anthologies, and under Ian's excellent leadership had recently branched into history texts as well. Meanwhile, besides generally managing the Press, I saw to the trade division, or the books for mass consumption. Angela Mayfield's novel about Stonecypher and better-quality versions of MacDougal's historical novel were typical of the sort of book I tried to acquire.

Ian had been my father's right-hand man all through the years; they had begun at the company together forty-five years ago as young men, working for my grandfather. My father had enormous respect for Ian, as a friend and a publisher, and on my father's death he had become a sort of surrogate father to me. We frequently had meals together after late nights at work, and our conversations consisted of shared confidences as much as publishing business.

An almost mystical quality surrounded Ian and his spartan, solitary lifestyle. He had lost his wife and daughter before coming to work at the Press, and he had a wisdom that seemed to apply to every facet of life. He was surrogate father, spiritual guru, mentor, and business genius rolled into one.

He was also, I suspected, the mysterious anonymous author

who had become our trade division's first bestseller two years ago. That little episode had nearly resulted in the premature end of both of our publishing careers. I liked to think that he was the author of the unsolicited, anonymous manuscript—the world knew the author only as "Arthur"—but he wouldn't say. The royalties were all paid directly to charity at "Arthur's" instruction, so I would never be entirely sure.

Last but not least, Ian had the distinction of being Sarah's grandfather, which only increased the awe and respect I felt for him.

Ian, who was usually serious and invariably sparing with words, said, "Bang on the wall if the Historic Buildings people get dangerous," and disappeared back into his room. This was as close as he came to a joke—in person anyway. In writing, I suspected he had another personality—that of our witty anonymous author. I smiled and opened the door to the conference room.

I always had the sense of walking into a drama when entering a conference room full of people; in the first place, the setting was right. My forebears had outfitted this room with a massive round cherry table with a patina to end all patinas. Plenty of sweaty palms and tweed jacket elbows had done their parts on its polished surface. On the walls were folios from illuminated manuscripts, and old leather chairs crackled and squeaked as their occupants shifted.

Secondly, meetings were unpredictable things; one never knew when injured feelings might turn a meeting nasty, and in fact I feared precisely that unpleasant prospect with Mac-Dougal the next day. These historic building preservation people were sticklers for detail, and spared no expense to make us live up to their (grossly unrealistic) expectations for the rejuvenation of old buildings. On the one hand, they wanted us to restore them, but they didn't approve of us making the buildings really useful. I believed in preserving beautiful old buildings, certainly, but they preferred an almost museum-like mentality, something few businesses could afford.

Standing in the doorway, I smiled across the room at Frances Macnamara, the president of the Stonecypher Society. She, at any rate, wasn't about to bite my head off. Frances was as kind and mild a woman as I ever hoped to meet. She was nearing seventy, had white hair and piercing blue eyes, and possessed an undying enthusiasm for all matters related to Marcus Stonecypher. I had invited her along today as a courtesy; I knew she would be interested in what we were doing to the historical home of her favourite author. Besides, in her role as tour guide she would need to be familiar with the new structure of the building. Also, as with the building people, I wanted Frances to know that we were taking great care not to destroy what I knew she viewed as a shrine to one of the country's best-known authors.

"Good morning," I said, stepping into the room and closing the door. The visitors—Frances, two men, and a woman, all past fifty-five—already had coffee and buns in front of them. Lisette knew her business.

"Hello, Frances," I said, nodding. She beamed back at me, obviously pleased to have been included.

Lisette took over with introductions; she'd been working with these people for months, to my immense gratitude. "Alex, I'd like you to meet Margaret Turner, secretary of the local 'Istoric Buildings Society. Mrs. Turner, Alex Plumtree." Still standing, I reached out a hand to Margaret, who looked remarkably like the Queen Mother, and who seemed more interested in returning to her cinnamon bun than in dealing with me. Ignoring my hand, she gave me a brisk nod with her mouth full.

"And Neville 'Eppelthwaite," Lisette continued. "Mr. 'Eppelthwaite is the society's architectural authority. No doubt you've heard of 'Eppelthwaite and 'Eppelthwaite, Architects."

"Yes, yes, of course. Very pleased to meet you, Mr. Heppelthwaite." The old man looked at me with sensitive, sparkling eyes. He had rosy cheeks and seemed likeable in a sweet, absent-minded sort of way, though something in his half-smile said he saw this meeting as a drama himself.

"Enjoyed studying your proposal," he said quietly. "I could see you'd really put some thought into it. Brilliant idea, making it useful for your business with no damage to the historic aspects of your building."

"Thank you," I said, nodding. I had in fact put a great deal of work into it before ever having the plan professionally drawn up on paper.

"And this is . . ."

"Fred Craggins. I run this show." Craggins nodded sharply as he looked me over. I could see that he was the type who thought, because he ran a quasi-charitable, quasi-governmental society, that he sat at the right hand of the almighty. In reality, he was a sixtyish stuffed shirt—the boldly striped shirt in question clashing wildly with his checked suit and diagonally striped tie.

"Thank you for coming, Mr. Craggins."

Craggins picked up the conversational ball and ran with it. He drank Lisette's coffee and pontificated on past projects and historic building renovation in general with grand, sweeping gestures.

"Of course, you can imagine," he said nearly ten minutes later, "how horrified we were when those people wanted to renovate the Duke's Theatre in Covent Garden. Even worse than your project—I mean, wanting to connect two very special buildings, nearly ruining them both—only in their case it was *three* buildings. They wanted to take the buildings either side of their theatre, and both were national treasures. Wanted to knock the walls clean through! A crime, really.

"Mind you," he continued, enjoying the sound of his voice, "the protestors nearly got to them—used some fairly creative threats to the owners' family. You know—Save Our Buildings and that lot." He paused, eyeing me. "I shouldn't be surprised if they give you a run for your money yet, Plumtree."

I moaned internally. Save Our Buildings, also known as S.O.B., was a miserable group of what could only be called radically conservative building conservationists. Not only was their acronym slightly over the top, they were by and large a wealthy group of would-be social activists in need of a cause. Not being fruitfully occupied in the running of businesses themselves, they had little or no idea what it took to really keep old buildings in good repair. They were lucky anyone bothered with the damp, crumbling old things at all.

The owners of the Duke's Theatre, the Burket-Joneses, were friends of mine. They had been terrified by the thinly veiled threat, uttered by one protester outside their home, that something unfortunate might befall one of their two young daughters.

Craggins stopped momentarily for a bite of danish and continued with his mouth full. "We had to approve the Duke's Theatre amendments too, for political reasons. Tragic." He shook his head, looking at us imploringly as he chewed.

Trying to keep my expression neutral, I raised my coffee cup and said, "Wasn't that the project on which the Burket-Joneses spent a hundred thousand extra pounds, just to keep the buildings looking as they always had on the outside?"

Craggins puffed himself up and responded. "Yes, and it was only a drop in the bucket in terms of what needed to be done. I mean, if these outrageous projects are to be suggested, people should bloody well be prepared to—"

"Fortunately," Lisette broke in, "this discussion is academic, because we already have the permit for the work in progress downstairs. We wanted to invite you 'ere today out of gratitude for your cooperation, and to—"

"Remember," the Queen-Mother double interjected frostily, "*your* permit is conditional upon *our* approval. If you want to get down to business, young lady, we shall." She focussed a withering gaze on Lisette. "What exactly is your plan for following the protective restrictions we have specified for your project?"

Her beady eyes reminded me of those of my piano teacher when I was young; terrifying to one of inferior strength, and all too ready to rap a ruler across my knuckles if I made a mistake. Fortunately, I knew Lisette had inner reserves of monumental proportions, and she was addressing Lisette. They all knew she'd done the work on the permit.

Sweet Mr. Heppelthwaite looked uncomfortable at the aggressiveness of his colleagues' tongues, but merely squirmed briefly in his chair and continued to watch the drama as if from afar. Frances seemed appalled at the venomous nature of the exchange. She looked from one speaker to the next with wide eyes.

Unfortunately Lisette replied, "I know that Alex 'as every intention of complying with your specifications—'e will be in charge of the project from this point on, now that the actual construction has begun."

She could see immediately that she had made a mistake.

Craggins rolled his eyes, sat forward angrily, and snorted,

"Oh, God. It won't do, you know, to keep switching the project back and forth. One person has *got* to have *complete* accountability . . ."

It was at this point that I saw a truly amazing sight. Something in Lisette must have snapped; after the months of work she had done for this permit, and knowing how much the project meant to me, she wasn't about to watch it go up in smoke. I saw her wink at Craggins, send him an unbelievably bedroomy smile while the others were still looking at him, and rise to go to him. She put her hand on his back and leaned down, saying, "More coffee?"

Then, though I wasn't certain, I thought that as her mouth was close to his ear she whispered, "You *promised,* Freddy." She rose again, smiling, bearing his coffee cup, and for an instant I wondered just how far she had gone to get that permit.

Trying to respond normally despite what I had just seen, I said, "Yes, of course I can see that," to a very much placated Freddy. "I assure you, Lisette and I work quite closely together."

The Queen Mother, who had missed the tête-à-tête between Lisette and Craggins, raised her eyebrows and cast a dark glance at Lisette. "Yes, I don't doubt that you do," she said caustically.

"Um, Frances? Mrs. Turner, Mr. Heppelthwaite? More coffee for you?" I offered.

"Mmm, yes, please," said the Queen Mother.

Heppelthwaite merely nodded as she continued, taking over now that Craggins had been defused. Frances, who seemed a little overwhelmed, shook her head.

"It's just that we've seen projects before where responsibility gets shuffled from person to person, and the understanding of how delicate the buildings really are, and how carefully the restrictions must be adhered to, never seems to be passed on from one to the next. Really, this is a very serious issue. The history of England is in our hands. No one else seems to care about our historic buildings."

"On the contrary, Mrs. Turner." I recrossed my legs, my rising anger camouflaged, I hoped, by a casual and relaxed bearing. How dared she insult us, and our ever-so-cautious-

and-respectful effort with the building, when we were the ones who had kept it up so carefully over nearly a century, spending thousands of pounds to keep our yearly maintenance up to their ridiculously arbitrary standards?

"Perhaps you are forgetting that the Plumtree family history is tied up in this building, and has been for some one hundred years. No one cares more about this building than I do, I assure you." I smiled at her calmly and continued.

"In addition, the Plumtree family history, and that of this building, is closely tied to that of the Bloomsbury Group through the literary giant Stonecypher. Frances and I guide monthly tours through the building for Stonecypher enthusiasts, and it should be encouraging to you that we plan to publish a book in the coming year on Stonecypher's life and works. I'd say we have a very strong reverence for history."

My reassurance stopped her tirade, and she sought refuge in her coffee. Frances nodded in my support; she knew how I felt about the building and more than once had expressed her gratitude on behalf of the Stonecypher Society. Experience told me that I needed to seal the moment with a further act of goodwill toward Margaret Turner.

"You know, Lisette, in view of the fact that our guests have an interest in the building, would you please have invitations sent to them for the book announcement on Wednesday?"

Lisette looked horrified but quickly hid her feelings, nodded with an overly bright smile, and departed, saying, "I'll get them right now."

"We're announcing a novel based on Stonecypher's life over luncheon during the BBFA book fair, here at the Press. Should make a nice break from trudging round the stands at the book fair, and we're only a few minutes from the Hotel Russell, where the fair is held. Tasty lunch, good wine, that sort of thing. I hope you'll all come."

Frances already knew of the event and had accepted the week before; the others looked flattered and pleased. I decided that the next act for this particular drama should be the tour, before they lost their feeling of goodwill.

Rolling up the building plans Lisette had had open on the table in a not-so-subtle hint that the meeting was over, I said jovially, "Fancy a tour?"

Craggins pointedly looked at his watch and back at me again to communicate that he felt I was rushing them—no doubt he wanted more time to stare at Lisette's captivating contours beneath the coffee-stained peach suit—but the others nodded enthusiastically.

The Queen Mother even said, quite decently, "That would be lovely, thank you."

As far as I could tell, Mr. Heppelthwaite was the only one who cared more about architecture and the building than posturing. He alone had spoken knowledgeably about the renovation plans earlier in the meeting, and it was clear that he'd studied them carefully. Now, as he rose, he said, "I commend you on the way you've designed the joining of the buildings so that it has minimal impact on the existing structures."

"Thank you, Mr. Heppelthwaite," I said gratefully. That meant a lot to me, coming from him.

As they took final sips of coffee and the Queen Mother gathered up her handbag, Lisette returned and briefly widened her eyes at me in exasperation before handing the announcement invitation cards round. I smirked in silent agreement and decided that the best defence was to be chatty and keep them moving. I stood and started toward the hallway, mentally donning my tour guide hat and gambling that they would all be cheered by a little-known piece of information to share at their next drinks party.

I led them into my office at the very back of the building and said as we went, "Frances, pipe up if I forget something, all right?" They all squeezed into my office, at my urging, and I said, "This was the room that Stonecypher's lover, Marie-Louise, occupied. She was the upstairs maid, you know, until she died under somewhat mysterious circumstances."

Frances looked distinctly uncomfortable, and I regretted not being more respectful of Stonecypher's memory in her presence. Margaret Turner barely suppressed a gossipy smile. All were clearly fascinated by this titbit of historical scandal. After all, Stonecypher was easily as famous as Forster, Waugh, or Maugham. I pointed towards the wall to one side of my desk, the rear-most wall of the building. "The third-floor bridge will go right through here. As you saw in the plans, there is also a first-floor bridge. The gap between the two buildings—what was the alley—is being enclosed, making one long, narrow room on each floor to house photocopiers, coffee machines and so forth. I can show you from a window, downstairs."

They filed behind me obediently, down the creaky narrow hallway with its comfortably threadbare plum-colored carpeting, to the top of the stairs. I pointed into the room immediately to our left; it was the large, sunny area shared by Lisette and Shuna, her assistant. Shuna, on the phone, looked up with a smile and a wave. The room overlooked Bedford Square through two large windows decorated with wrought-iron railings and geranium-filled flowerpots.

"This was the room of Stonecypher's invalid wife, Marissa Godwin Stonecypher," I said, continuing the tour. "No one really knows why she was confined to her bedroom, but we know from his diaries that he set her up in here because of the cheerful aspect of the room." They glanced about appreciatively, and I ducked back out of the room again, standing just at the edge of the stairway.

"I'm afraid we'll have to take the stairs; they're using the lift to bring up construction materials. Please do be careful," I said. "These were the servants' stairs, and as you can see, they are quite steep and narrow." I held on to the polished cherry banister and hoped they would do the same; I didn't need to be sued for negligence on top of the expensive renovations.

I went first, both to lead the way and to block a potential fall; if one of them did miss a step, they wouldn't roll all the way down onto the marble on the ground floor. We made it safely to the first landing; one flight down, two to go. I pointed out the ballroom at the rear of the building. Now it was far from Stonecypher's cosily arranged room with multiple groupings of chairs and tables to encourage discussion; it was filled with six desks, all belonging to our growing production department. Sub-editors, designers, and those who arranged for printing and binding populated the paper-strewn desks.

"This is the room in which Stonecypher and Marissa, in her wheelchair, entertained the Bloomsbury Group—Virginia Stephen, later Woolf, her sister Vanessa Bell, Lady Ottoline

Morrell, their next-door neighbour, her friend, Nijinsky, Maynard Keynes, E. M. Forster, Lytton Strachey, and so forth." I could see that this glimpse into the lives of the famous literary and artistic personalities intrigued them. Like me, they enjoyed imagining the informal gatherings of those larger-than-life figures, having their "cocoa and buns," as Virginia Woolf had recorded for posterity.

I let them linger there for a moment, as I sometimes did when I thought of the past life of this grand old building. Then we began our descent of the last flight of stairs. I prattled on about how convenient it would be for us to have the use of the other building as well, twice the space for both the academic and the trade divisions.

"Of course," I continued earnestly, "we are very keen to do it without disturbing the character of the buildings from the outside. Or the inside, for that matter." At last we were standing before the four-by-seven-foot space that would become the ground floor's doorway to the other building.

"Morning, Harry," I said, grinning at the construction foreman. Harry specialised in delicate renovation and expansion projects such as ours that involved historical buildings. He was the best of his crowd, and I'd been lucky to get him. In our hallway chats over the summer we had struck up a casual friendship, and he had shared some of his jokes with me—some sexual, some political, and all unrepeatable in present company. He was a short, mischievous, elfin-looking man about my own age, and I liked him a great deal.

He winked. "Morning, sir. How are we today?"

"Fine, fine, thanks. Harry, I'd like you meet . . ." and I proceeded to introduce our guests with all due respect. Harry knew what nightmares these people had dealt Lisette, and in fact anyone who proposed the renovation of an old building.

But he nodded to each deferentially, then said, "You're just in time. We've got her about ready to go—been at it since early this morning. Mike, here, and Rich are about to punch the wall through—we've got the doorway roughly cut so it should go right out—and of course we've got the supports for the existing structure ready, as you can see."

He was laying it on a bit thick, but the committee of three nodded authoritatively at a simple structure of wood that

Harry and his colleagues had built. It braced the original structure for the rectangular hole they were about to make for the door. This was one of the specific precautions on which the society had insisted; I was secretly delighted that they were seeing how carefully we were following their instructions.

I'd seen Harry and Mike in the building for months, but it was the first time I'd seen Rich. He wouldn't meet my eyes.

Harry said, "Hang on a minute. This is your building, Mr. Plumtree. You want to have a go?" He held up a sledgehammer, and I smiled as I reached out and took it from him. I loved demolition.

"Right, then." The foreman spoke to Mike and Rich. "Ready with those extra supporting beams." Obviously, Harry was taking no chances; the two men stood at the ready with two more eight-foot-tall four-by-four pieces of wood, already pointing at the spot where the top of the doorway would be. When I had knocked the wall out there, they would immediately place the beams where the wall had adjoined the ceiling for additional support.

"Mr. Plumtree, sir?"

I accepted the invitation and swung the hammer well back, then forward into the wall with a satisfying thunk.

What happened next is still somewhat confusing, but just as I hit the bricks where the doorway was supposed to be, one of the sturdy four-by-four beams of Rich's brace seemed to separate from the structure. It came crashing down, hitting me on the side of the head. I saw stars and stumbled, groping about for something to help me regain my balance, and finally fell to my knees.

Then I heard a terrific groaning and creaking, and while I knelt stunned on the floor, Harry latched on to me with meaty arms and half-threw, half-dragged me away from the wall. Before I had figured out what was happening, a large-ish section of the ceiling of Plumtree Press collapsed onto the floor in front of me with an ominous, earthquake-like roar, exposing the structure beneath the old floor above.

There was a moment of silence, then I heard Harry swearing with creativity and enthusiasm. He was standing over me, pulling bits of wood and plaster off my hair and clothing.

"Everybody all right?" He had taken charge, and got a

grunt from Mike, who had been the only one of us actually hit full-force by any of the plaster-wood-brick mess. I saw through the settling dust that he had a nasty cut on his head.

Frances came forward to help immediately, expressing concern for my welfare. I heard nothing from the Queen Mother and her companions, but I needn't have worried. They had been standing well back, and had also escaped the falling plaster dust and old wood. They did not look pleased, however, and I imagined that they would return immediately to their office, where they would file some sort of noncompliance report.

What incredibly stinking rotten luck. I hated to think what Lisette would have to do to placate Freddy Craggins this time.

"I'm sorry," I said to the buildings people. "This should never have—"

"Damned right it never should have fallen." I'd expected it to be Craggins who got shirty first, but it was Harry.

Harry was looking daggers at Rich, who had somehow managed to stay out of harm's way himself.

"You go back to the office and collect your pay for this morning. Then I never want to see you again. Someone could have been killed here. Now, get out."

Rich sneered and complied, rather smugly, I thought, swaggering off down the hall without apology.

"I'm sorry, Alex," Harry said, reverting to our usual friendly way of addressing each other. "Honestly, I can't imagine how this happened. As you can see, we had adequate support, and we investigated the strength of the structure before ever starting. That Rich was a bad egg, been driving me barmy all morning. He was a substitute for Martin— Martin went and got in a fight at the pub last night. But this bloke—he sneaked off for a while earlier, then was careless when he finally got back." He shook his head in disgust. "We'll get this cleaned up in no time. I'll let you know what's going on with the building."

"Thanks, Harry. I know you'll put it right." I looked at my guests, who, apart from Frances, seemed to be growing more indignant all the time as the shock of the near-miss wore off. "Shall we?" I opened my arms towards them to gently suggest that they turn round and make for the door, which they had the good manners to do without further comment. I followed them, brushing debris and dust off my suit coat. Looking at my watch, I saw that I was already keeping Ian waiting.

I apologised profusely as we clattered down the black and white marble-floored hall, and was about to say good-bye, when something on the floor mat just inside the door caught my eye. It was a duplicate of the rag-paper folio that had been left on my father's desk, and in Angela's room, complete with black book dingbat pressed into the soft paper.

I stooped quickly to pick it up before my guests saw it, and heard Heppelthwaite say gently, "You know, if it wouldn't be too much trouble, might I have a copy of your original plan? There's something rather intriguing about the design of your building, Plumtree."

I tucked the paper behind my back and said, "Of course, of course. Lisette, would you please?" I would have gone myself, ordinarily, but my equilibrium still felt a bit off from the beam incident, and there was a sort of buzzing in my ears.

Frances patted me on the back. "I'll say good-bye, dear. Take care of yourself, now—you should put some ice on that head, you know," she advised, and was gone.

As Lisette ran upstairs for the plan, and I half-listened to our guests chattering indignantly about their near-miss, exaggerating their proximity to danger, it all became clear—or mostly clear. Martin's "fight" at the pub may not have been an accident. Then Rich, employed by the mysterious manufacturer of dingbats—the people who wanted to stop Angela's book—had arranged for things to go as they did this morning. A troubling new thought presented itself: what if Rich was just the first in a long line of S.O.B. activists, eager to forestall any change to Stonecypher's historic former abode? They were a well-educated group; they knew all about Stonecypher's novels and his threatening dingbats.

My head ached as I ran a hand through my hair, feeling mildly desperate—not to mention confused—at the sudden profusion of people determined to stop the very projects that meant most to me. I could see why S.O.B. wanted us to leave the building as it was, if I tried very hard to view the world through their warped lens. But why would S.O.B. or anyone else want to stop Angela's book being published? And exactly how far would they go to get what they wanted?

Unfortunately, it wasn't long before that, too, became clear.

CHAPTER 8

It is a riddle wrapped in a mystery inside an enigma.
                                    —SIR WINSTON CHURCHILL

I walked into Ian's office, shut the door, and tossed the dingbat onto his desk. He froze, and the blood seemed to drain from his face. I sank into a chair across from him, a little surprised to have evoked such a response. I had never seen Ian, who is even more stoical than I am, react so strongly to anything. After a moment he said through clenched teeth, "Where did you get this?"

"I've received two now, and Angela one. She's had a letter as well, on letterhead carrying out the same theme." I trusted Ian with my life, but wasn't sure how far I wanted to involve him in this, for his sake. "Whoever it is, they desperately want us to stop publication of *The Stonecypher Saga*."

"Good God, Alex, you don't want anything to do with this. You have no idea what you're involved in." He looked at me with eyes that had gone hollow. "Tell me exactly what happened."

I could see that he knew there was more to the story than I was telling. Deciding to reveal part of the truth, I explained that there had been an intruder or two in the library the night before, and that a duplicate of this dingbat—a copy of the ones in Stonecypher's book, as far as I could tell—had been left on the desk. I also told him that I had acquired a Stone-cypher at Armand Beasley's, along with another book, which had coincidentally contained a letter revealing some very un-flattering news about Folio B's book restoration work. Both books, letter included, had been stolen in the library break-in.

"Oh, my God," Ian said quietly, as if in a daze. "You know . . . and they know it."

He looked so stricken that I dared not say anything more. We sat for some time in silence as he stared down at the design on the fine paper. I waited. Finally he raised his eyes to meet mine.

"Alex, this is a very bad business. My worst fears about this Angela Mayfield novel are coming to pass. You'll re-member that I tried to discourage you from publishing the book, using rather unconvincing arguments, I'm afraid, be-cause I couldn't tell you the real ones."

He looked directly into my eyes with such intensity that I was tempted to look away, as if from a very bright light. "I strongly advise you to put out a press release saying you won't be publishing the Stonecypher-based Mayfield novel after all. Think of a reason—any reason." He rubbed his face with his hands and let a burst of air out through his teeth. "Even that might not satisfy them."

He didn't have to say what the consequences would be if "they" weren't satisfied; I could read that between the lines.

"Ian," I said quietly. "I'm into this so deeply now that you might as well tell me who 'they' are, and what this is all about."

He looked at me with a mixture of sadness and apprehen-sion. Suddenly he looked much older than his sixty-eight years, his eyelids drooping and paper-thin, blue eyes watery underneath. "I knew you'd want to know. . . . Let me think, Alex. We must tread softly. I'll see if I can think of a way to get you through this." He looked at me with sad eyes. "In the meantime, be very, very careful."

"Right." I tried to smile encouragingly. "Now on to real business."

Ian looked down as if he knew what was coming. This was

the first real conflict we'd ever had, and it was awkward for both of us.

"You know Holdsworthy's history author, Angus Mac-Dougal, is coming here for a meeting tomorrow. He's verbally agreed to leave Wilde Publishing and come to us. I'd like to offer him a contract while he's happy about our publishing his novel, which, I'll tell you in confidence, is virtually unpublishable. Rachel will need to perform major surgery. How he can be such a fine textbook author and such a shoddy novelist is beyond me."

I was chattering on to soften the fact that I was deliberately ignoring Ian's sage advice, which had been to leave MacDougal alone and either purchase a smaller academic publisher with a strong history line, or develop our own. I still couldn't understand what he had against MacDougal. The fame of the MacDougal/Wilde history texts was legendary. Unless Ian could give me a reason, and he couldn't (or wouldn't), I wasn't going to miss this chance to expand Plumtree Press—even if the academic line had always been Ian's bailiwick.

Ian didn't smile at my little joke, nor did he look up. I had the odd impression that he was ashamed—for me. True, what I was doing in overriding Ian flew in the face of my normal management philosophy, which was "every tub on its own bottom," or that Ian should acquire titles for his academic part of the company and I should manage mine, the trade list. But recently I had begun to wonder if Ian was perhaps too cautious—and maybe too old—to be a really forward-looking manager.

Finally he looked up at me, and I was humbled by the look in his eyes. It spoke of sadness, and compassion, and painful wisdom. "Alex, I can't stop you from doing this with Mac-Dougal. But you know that I have reasons for discouraging you from signing him on. If that's not enough, then I have no more to say."

"Why won't you tell me *why*?" I asked in exasperation, springing to my feet and pounding his desk hard, once, with my fist. The frustration of the past weeks, of trying to discuss the subject rationally with Ian while he clammed up and said no, had been simmering too long. Now it blew up in an ugly way—and, as it turned out, to my detriment.

"Why the secrecy, Ian? What have you got against Mac-Dougal? Why can't you *agree* that it would be good for our academic line to have the best-selling history author in the country?" I glowered at him.

His eyes never leaving mine, he shook his head slowly. "If you won't trust my opinion, Alex, I'm not going to say more."

We both knew it was wrong for me to take this out of his hands, but my ambition was not to be stifled in those heady days. It almost had a will of its own; ambition for the fiction line, ambition for the academic line, ambition for the building. Ambition, perhaps, to be as admired as my father had been.

There are very few times in my life when I have lost the ability to hide my emotions, but that morning with Ian was one of them. I laughed a short, derisive laugh, shook my head once ironically, and left his office. So upset was I, knowing I had made a horrible mistake as soon as I had done it, that I went straight down the stairs and out of the front door to find a pub that would have me for lunch.

Striding down Bloomsbury Street to Great Russell Street, I turned left and headed for the Book and Binder, a regular haunt for the publishers, rare-book dealers, and British Museum personnel in the neighbourhood. Halfway down the street, however, I remembered that I would be followed, and for lack of anything better, used the ridiculous old trick of re-tying my shoe to stop and surreptitiously look about.

A fortyish, muscular-looking man with an almost comically thick neck and meathook hands had stopped to look closely at some books in the front window of a travel book publisher's building. He had to be the one. There weren't many of us wandering about the neighbourhood at eleven-thirty in the morning, and he didn't look the type to be interested in Baedeker-type guides. I filed his size and stance away in my memory—particularly the neck and hands—and continued on.

By the time I reached the pub, my anger was mostly gone, and shame and despair had taken its place. I had insulted and offended the person I admired most—aside from Sarah, of course—and I could take back neither my words nor my attitude. My pride still wouldn't let me go back directly and apologise to Ian, but perhaps after lunch I'd feel equal to the task.

The only problem was, my stomach was in knots and I didn't feel much like eating. Perhaps a bit of book-browsing first . . .

Denny the Dealer's was in the next street, Bury Place. His was a refreshingly unpretentious shop, and he often had some unusual books—things that he liked, but which not everyone and his dog were looking for. A Michael Innes or Nicholas Blake paperback wouldn't be unwelcome either; there were still a couple I hadn't read, although if all went well, I wouldn't be reading any books on my holiday with Sarah. And if all went even better, I'd be too busy planning a wedding after I got home to read for pleasure.

I turned the corner and pushed open the door to Denny's narrow but deep shop. The first impression at Denny's was made by the paint peeling off the pale green door, and the second was the total absence of a sign identifying the owner or the nature of his business. Inside, what one noticed instantly were great stacks of books on the floor, and the smell of mustiness and dust rising from the general surroundings. Worn beige industrial carpeting covered the wood floor, but I doubted it had been cleaned in the twenty years he'd had the shop.

He was with a customer at the desk directly opposite the front door, obviously completing a sale. When the customer turned to see who'd come in the door, Denny winked at me and said, "Be right with you."

I nodded, making for the new-acquisitions shelf. It wasn't labelled as such, but Denny's regular customers knew where he put his latest finds. I carefully pushed back two books on either side of a burgundy leather spine on a chest-high shelf, and pulled out the middle book.

It was some kind of a special leather-bound edition of Somerset Maugham's *Of Human Bondage*, but "Brighton Library" was stamped all over it—fore-edge, title page, and page 30, in red ink. Good condition, but a library copy nonetheless. Not highly desirable by collectors unless one simply wanted a copy of the book, or an attractive spine on the shelf.

It made me think again of Diana Boillot, and how difficult it was to remove notorious library stamps from books; that was the whole point of the blasted things. Diana would have to be incredibly good to re-create entirely the pages that had library stamps on them, but then, I already knew that she was. The British Library didn't hire just anyone to fix up its books.

I still didn't know what I was going to do about Boillot and Holdsworthy's deceit in sending the stolen books to France for sale at the Paris book fair. First I would have to watch at the fair and see if they really were being sold; then I would have to tell the authorities.

It was at this sombre moment that Denny clapped his hand on my shoulder and the bell on the door jangled as the customer left. I jumped, and Denny laughed. "Nervous, are we?"

"It's been quite a week, Denny." I smiled ruefully. "And it's only Monday lunchtime."

He laughed. "Yeah, well, at least you stand some chance of making a few quid from it all. I go through the motions and just about manage to keep the door open." Despite this grim pronouncement, he grinned cheerfully. "Join me for some lunch? I'm eating in, doing some pricing for the book fair, but I'd love the company. Quiet day, Monday. If you don't mind my saying it, you look as if you could use a bit of companionship."

He practically pushed me out of the door before I could say a word, and I found myself walking with him to the sandwich shop at the end of the street. I was keenly aware of the faithful Neck following us, and confirmed it with a glance, but didn't worry Denny about it.

On the way he told me about the amazing sale he'd just made; he'd got two hundred pounds for a book he'd bought last week for forty-five. "Now I can almost pay the rent," he said, satisfied. He ordered two ham and cheese sandwiches on granary, two packets of crisps, and two fizzy orange drinks. He insisted on paying for them himself, then we left again.

As we walked back to his shop, I had an idea. My bookselling friend knew a great deal about a great many things. "Denny, you're a member of Folio B, right?"

"Mmm. Why?" He glanced up at me briefly, then surveyed the increasingly gentrified Bury Street as we walked.

"Have you ever noticed anything odd about the organisation?"

He looked at me askance, then laughed cynically. "Have you ever known an organisation that wasn't odd? Honestly?"

I laughed in spite of myself. "No, I suppose not."

He shrugged. "Folio B does an all-right job of encouraging ethical bookselling, and I don't know of any fiddles on the consulting side. And we are helping the large public collections restore their books. Boillot's one of the best. I saw her at Beasley's the other night. Nuzzling right up to Frank Holdsworthy, I notice, and not losing too much time about it."

I realised I'd be better off not commenting on that. "Well," I said, "this is a strange sort of question, but the something odd I'm thinking of would have to do with the works of Stonecypher."

"My God." I thought I heard him mutter under his breath, but wasn't sure, as he was fishing for his key in his pocket. Then he spoke clearly, almost abruptly. "Say no more." I looked at him, but he was transferring the lunch bag to his left hand in readiness to open the door of his shop, and didn't meet my eyes. He pushed the door open, holding it for me as I came inside behind him.

"Back here," he said. I noticed that he left the grubby pencilled "back in 10 minutes" sign on the door, and locked the door again from the inside. I followed him into the back of his shop, where I knew from past visits there were more stacks of books, and a desk piled high with papers that looked as if they'd been read once and never touched again. He closed the door on the front room, handed me our lunch, and then to my surprise, peeled back a section of the carpeting to reveal a small cut-out square in the floor.

I stared in amazement as he put his finger through a small metal ring in the square of floorboards and pulled. A small wooden door roughly two feet square rose out of the floor. Denny motioned for me to follow him down as he descended into the nether darkness. I could see the top three rungs of a ladder; inky blackness consumed the rest.

Feeling I had suddenly walked *into* a Michael Innes novel—specifically one in which a visitor in a shop is ushered into an underground chamber, and in fact an entire underground world—I started to ask Denny what on earth was happening when something about his seriousness made me stop.

Meekly, I watched him disappear, then saw a light flick on as he said, "Here, toss those down." I dropped the lunch things down to him and bent my ridiculously large frame through the hole as I climbed down the worn, creaky ladder. Looking round in amazement, I saw three chairs, a folding bed covered with a worn duvet in a dingy brown floral pattern, and a simple wooden table with a lamp on it, all in a room of about ten by twelve feet. The floor was covered with an old rag rug, and the lamp on the table wore a red fringed lampshade. I might have just dropped into the forties.

I stared at Denny as he pulled on a string, which brought the trapdoor slamming back down, then dropped into a straight-back chair and sighed. "This was useful, I understand, during air raids in the last war. Sit down, Alex." He passed me my sandwich in its thin white paper bag and I found a chair and sat. "This is not good."

"What isn't good?"

"This." He let out another sigh, somewhere between anger and frustration, took out his sandwich, and bit into it, hard. I merely sat and watched, not at all interested in lunch.

I wanted to say, "What do you mean? What are we doing here? Why are you being so secretive?" But even as the questions flashed through my mind, I knew that I had the answers to them.

Denny knew about Folio B and Stonecypher; he knew what Virginia had known, what Ian knew. And by bringing it up, I had endangered him.

Oh, no, I thought, guilt wrenching my gut. The man with the bull neck. I had brought him here. It was too late.

"Bloody hell," Denny said, his mouth full of ham, cheese, and pickle. "Sorry," he added, looking up at me. There was silence for a moment as he finished chewing. "How much do you know?"

I swallowed the hard lump in my throat. "I know that Frank Holdsworthy may have had his wife killed for knowing that the Folio B book restoration operation was not completely above board, and I know that there is some connection between Stonecypher and Folio B. What that connection is, I have no idea. I also know that an author of mine, who has written a novel based on Stonecypher's life, has been told to stop the book—which we're publishing—or *be* stopped."

"Just what does he know about Stonecypher?" Denny asked, leaning forward in his chair, frowning.

"She." He blinked once. "That Stonecypher's political beliefs were encoded in his books in strings of misprints. One world government, idealistic claptrap. No monarchies, no national patriots, knowledge via books for all, and therefore freedom for the masses."

Denny sank back in his chair. "That's it," he said with resignation.

"And I keep receiving large-print versions of the book dingbats"—here Denny nodded knowingly—"every time I turn round. Very elegantly printed, I might add."

"You're in trouble, my friend." He looked at me in much the same way Ian had. "So's your author. If I could tell you anything, I'd tell you to leave your business, leave your house, and disappear from the face of the earth. Go find some unpopulated island and go native—though there's no guarantee that'll save you either. Didn't help your mum and dad."

The blood rushed to my head as what he was saying registered. "My parents?" I whispered.

Denny nodded and reached forward, grasping my arm above the elbow. "I'm sorry. I hate to be the one to tell you, but it seems only right that you of all people should know."

I struggled for control. White-hot anger blazed in me, blanking out my vision and all thoughts except of anger, and retaliation, and revenge. After several moments the fire went out, leaving me feeling dangerously calm. They wouldn't get away with this. I wouldn't let them. They wouldn't get Angela, me, or Max, and they wouldn't be allowed to go unpunished for my parents' death.

So my father had known; had been trying to expose them, I was sure. And, remembering his comment at Armand's party, Edward Pillinghurst had had something to do with it. And now I was a board member of the group that had killed my father.

"All right," I said finally. "What is it?"

Denny took his hand away. He sat back, looking at me with worry under his characteristic bluster, and shook his head ever so slightly. "Alex, you don't understand. If you don't know, I'm not going to tell you. You're better off not knowing."

"Damn it!" I stood, and the little chair I'd been sitting in fell over backwards. It hit the table, and the fringe of the lampshade swung wildly, casting eerie shadows around the tiny room. "This is bizarre! Look at us, sitting down here in the dark. What could these people be doing that is so awful? And what's so cataclysmic about publishing a novel based on Stonecypher's political life? You've got to tell me, Denny!"

It took me a moment to realise that it must have looked to Denny as if I were about to beat him to a pulp; I was standing in front of him aggressively, ready to throw the first punch. I'd been yelling; now I took a step backwards and let my arms fall to my sides, slumping a bit in my shame. "Please."

"No. You don't understand. If you know, they kill you. I've been more careful than most. They're such toffs, they think someone with a cockney accent who hasn't been to university isn't smart enough to give them any trouble. They haven't bothered with me." The cockney accent to which he owed his life made the words come out "bovvered wif me."

I picked up the chair I'd knocked over and sat on it. Elbows on knees, I rubbed my hands over my face and left them there for a moment. It had been the second time that day I'd lost my self-control, though if I said so myself, I'd good reason to. "How did you work it out, then, whatever it is?" I asked Denny. My voice sounded weary.

He eyed me, then said, "You know, I just might tell you that, if you'll promise not to go chasing around asking anyone else on the street if Folio B has a link with the works of Stonecypher."

I sighed and nodded, thinking again of the Neck. I would have to be more careful.

"All right, then." Popping the top of his orange drink, he raised it toward me with a questioning look, asking me if I wanted mine. I shook my head.

"Part of this you can't help but see," he began. "I'm a bookseller. When I walk into a bookshop, I notice things.

You can't be in this business and walk round dozens of bookshops a year and not spot something as strange as this.

"Some shops I'd walk into had that dingbat you mentioned—the Stonecypher one—round their doorway somewhere. For years I thought it was just a coincidence; it is an attractive little device, perfect for a bookshop. One time I complimented the bookseller on it—he actually had it carved into the wood of his doorway—and I thought he was going to have a heart attack. He looked terrified; turned round and knocked a whole pile of new stock off his sales desk."

"The Symbol by the Door," I said softly, astounded. It was the name of the third Stonecypher book. With some dread, I wondered when and how the title of the fourth—*The Room of the Maiden*—would enter my life.

"Very good," Denny said, pointing at me with his orange drink. "You do know your Stonecypher." He put his drink on the floor and ripped open his bag of crisps. Again he offered some to me. The smell of salt and vinegar travelled quickly across the tiny room and seemed revolting under the circumstances.

"I never said anything about it to anyone." When Denny said "anything" it came out as "anyfink." "Then I noticed one year at the Antiquarian Booksellers' Association book fair, you know, the ritzy one, that all the ones that had it in their doorways put it in their catalogues somewhere as well; hidden—buried, like—but there. Then it stopped seeming like a coincidence. I thought about it some more, more as a curiosity than anything sinister, of course, at that point, and realised they were all in Folio B."

He crunched several crisps, chewing thoughtfully, then punctuated his words by jabbing a greasy forefinger in my direction. "All the booksellers who had that symbol in their doorways were members of Folio B, but not all members of Folio B had that symbol in their doorways."

He looked at me as if he'd said something significant. So far, I thought I understood; it was some sort of a bookexchange scam, like Diana Boillot's. And the booksellers were in on it; some sort of a crime ring.

Denny continued. "At the end of the week I was sitting in reception at the Grosvenor House fair a few years ago, worn out from standing there behind my books, having just made a satisfying sale to some rich Saudi bloke. I spotted one of the 'symbol' booksellers walking through the lobby. Then two more of them came walking together, and one by one, mostly, in the next ten minutes all the booksellers who had the symbol in their stores came through that lobby. That was when it occurred to me that they were having some sort of meeting; that it was an actual organisation."

He looked me in the eye. "That's as much as I'd tell you. Now we'd better get up there before things look suspicious. You can't imagine who's watching when you think they aren't." He stood and handed me my crisps and drink can.

I took them woodenly. "Denny, I'm so sorry."

"What?" He frowned.

"I—I was followed here today. It was before—well, I didn't think that it would endanger you if I came in." I felt sick as I watched the blood drain from his face.

He stood still a moment, then spoke grimly. "It can't be helped. I don't blame you, Alex. Just be careful from now on, right? And take care of yourself." Stunned at what he had told me, and what I had done, I merely stared as he started up the stairs to open the trapdoor again. Turning, he said over his shoulder, "Switch off that light after I open the door, all right, and wait for a moment after you hear me get out into the main room. Then close the door behind you, replace the rug, and go out the back way. Right?"

I nodded, still stunned, and watched his slightly threadbare polyester-blend trousers disappear up the stairs. But he stopped again before reaching the top. "One more thing. Did Beasley get you onto the board?"

I nodded again in silence.

He shook his head quickly, once, and climbed up and out of the room.

The whoosh of warmer air from above that flooded into the tiny, chilly space roused me from my stupor. I followed Denny's instructions, turning out the lamp, closing the trapdoor, and replacing the rug on top of it. I checked to see that it was all in order, no tell-tale bumps in the rug, then wandered out of the back door into the alley, passing the rubbish bins of the other shops as I made my way through the narrow passage. The Neck wouldn't expect me to come out the back, I thought.

I'd decided to go in the direction that would bring me out on a quieter street, rather than on busy Great Russell Street, where someone might see me. Denny's shop was on Bury Place, the least prestigious of the three streets that ran south from the facade of the British Museum, but popular nonetheless. By travelling in the opposite direction to the Museum, I would come out on Bloomsbury Way, where it was less likely that I would be encountered by anyone I knew from the publishing or collecting world.

I walked east quickly on Bloomsbury Way, heading back to the office in round-about fashion, feeling as if I had lost my way and ended up in a science fiction film or a nightmare. Nothing looked the same. The late summer day, with its tinge of autumn in the bright light, familiar old Bloomsbury, even the trees, seemed poised with sinister intent instead of standing as benevolent guardians.

Then I saw St. George's Church, with its odd pyramidal structure and statue of George II, and was unaccountably moved to go up the steps and into its cool, dark interior. I sat down in a pew, intending to ask for help—for my parents, for Angela, for Denny, for myself—and ended up crying as I hadn't since I was a child.

I cried for my mother and father, for myself, for all the time we had lost together. I cried for the painful rift with Ian. I cried for Sarah, and the pall that the secret and sinister part of Folio B was casting over our future. And I cried, too, out of pure, childlike fear of the unknown.

When I'd picked myself up and dusted myself off, wiping my eyes and rubbing my face, it was almost one o'clock. On a normal day I would just be leaving to get lunch, or sitting down to eat whatever Lisette or someone had offered to pick up.

Sighing, I walked out of the church resigned to do what must be done to keep Plumtree Press afloat, mundane as those duties might seem. In an odd way, when earthshaking disaster struck—as it seemed to do so frequently in the publishing business—taking care of the Press was comforting. It was still my father's, and my grandfather's, and his father's before him, and so on. If I could carry on for them, then I was doing something worthwhile. I decided to head for the solicitor's office and ask him to draw up a special contract for Angus MacDougal to sign at our meeting tomorrow, making the acceptance of his novel conditional on our receipt of satisfactory history texts from him. It would be more efficient to phone, of course, but I wasn't ready to go back to the office yet.

The bright sun mocked me as I strolled eastward toward Gray's Inn Road. It seemed all wrong; a nasty contradiction of the deep darkness of the day. I tried to focus on what the unusual contract with MacDougal would need to specify. It would have to include the normal clause of his novel being of acceptable quality, just in case Rachel and I couldn't make it work. I also wanted to specify a deadline of one year for him to complete the first history text written for Plumtree Press. . . .

My thoughts drifted from the issues of the contract back to the more basic idea of signing MacDougal. Though I felt bad about the way I'd treated Ian, it seemed necessary to add MacDougal to our stable of authors.

It was the responsible thing to do, I thought; if our prize-winning and hugely successful anthologies of English literature ever faded, which things do unaccountably over time, we would have a strong performer in history to fall back on. It was unimaginable to me that a man of Ian's intelligence and experience was unable to see it.

The solicitor was surprised to see me, and offered me a cup of coffee as we did our business. When that errand was done, I strolled back to Bedford Square and more or less braced myself for whatever would befall me. The Neck picked up my scent as I approached the square; I saw him watching me from across the street, where he stood by the hot dog vendor in front of the British Museum. There was something chilling about the fact that he knew that I knew he was there, and that he didn't try very hard to keep it a secret anymore. It was as if they wanted me to know that they were watching; nothing more.

I entered the Press, feeling safe for the time being. Lisette smiled as I came into her office, stopping by to say hello and find out what, if anything, had happened in my absence before we spent the rest of the afternoon working on Angela's press announcement.

Earthy, vivacious, sweet-smelling Lisette always brought me right back to reality when things seemed too awful to be real. At that moment I was tremendously grateful for her, and sank down in one of the worn chairs she kept in front of her desk for potential chats.

" 'Ello," she said, taking her hands off her keyboard and leaning back in her chair. She had never mastered the art of the "h." " 'Ow is your 'ead?" She frowned in concern, searching for a mark or bump with her eyes.

"Oh, fine. Rotten luck though, wasn't it, that happening just while they were here."

"I think they bring it with them," she said cynically.

"By the way, thank you for saving the day. I won't even ask what you did to pacify Fred Craggins." I looked at her knowingly, and she busied herself with the mail on her desk. Lisette was fun to tease. We both knew she was completely loyal to her husband, but we both also knew that she had a certain sexual presence about her which she knew how to use to maximum advantage.

"Yes. I guess that's that," she said brightly, and looked up with a quick smile before returning to the post. "Oh." She picked up an A4-sized envelope, eyed it, and handed it to me. "This came for you while you were out. Marked Private and Confidential. By courier. And Rachel stopped in. She said to ask you, and I quote, 'How are we going to dispose of that wretched disaster of a MacDougal manuscript?!' " She smiled mischievously. "That bad, is it?"

I groaned. "Yes. And we *have* to publish it. MacDougal is signing with us only on the condition that we publish *The Storms of Time*." I stared at the envelope in my lap without really seeing it.

Lisette was looking at me closely. "Are you feeling all right, Alex? Are you sure you don't need George to look at your 'ead?"

"No, no, not at all," I mumbled, waving off her concern. The little episode in the church had probably left me with swollen red eyes. I was too discouraged even to be embarrassed. No doubt the discussion with Denny had left its mark on my face too.

Smiling was too much of a stretch, so I tried merely to present a relatively pleasant facade to Lisette. After all, none of this was her fault. "Oh. By the way. I had a little chat with Kei-King first thing this morning; the advance copies were sent by sea instead of by air. He's sending more today by overnight mail."

Lisette rolled her eyes. "Just what we needed." She sighed. "Still, I guess we'll 'ave them for the announcement."

I nodded. There was comfort in the details of things. "Where do we stand with the press conference? We were going to deal with the final bits and pieces this afternoon, weren't we?"

The question was academic; I knew she would have everything, from the press releases to the pâté, well in hand. Still, it was just a few days off, and any time we invited the press to anything, I worried. Disaster was only a misquote away.

"I know 'ow you worry about these things," she was saying. Sometimes I was certain she could read my thoughts. "I've asked Claire to come over and go through everything with us, just to be sure." She looked at her watch, the face of which was encircled with diamonds, thanks to George's generosity. "She should be 'ere any minute now."

Claire was an ex–editorial assistant of ours who had gone to work for a pricey public relations firm to bump up her salary, found she had a knack for it, and started her own firm, all in the remarkable space of a year. We knew she was good, and we liked her first-year prices; very reasonable for an inspired job.

Lisette's phone rang and she picked it up. "Send 'er up to the conference room, please. Thanks." She stood and looked at me. "Let me get you a cup of coffee. Yes?" There was pity in her sympathetic pout. "She's 'ere, right on time."

"Mmm. Thanks, Lisette." I stood to make the move down the hall to the conference room.

"Whatever 'as 'appened to you today, I am sorry," she said gently, speaking over her shoulder as she walked to the door. "You know George and I are always ready to 'elp, if you need us."

"Thanks," I said, putting a hand on her shoulder from behind, safe in the knowledge that our friendship was too strong for her to misinterpret the gesture. She reached up and patted my hand.

Claire flew up the last three steps, flushed and pleased to be doing business with us, as Lisette and I were walking into the conference room, coffee mugs in hand. "Hello, Alex! Lisette! Great day, isn't it?"

We didn't seem to drag her down too much as she put her briefcase on the table, took a chair, and agreed to a cup of Lisette's master blend. Her youth and irrepressible enthusiasm overwhelmed me. It was depressing. At thirty-two, I had already missed ten years that I could have been married to Sarah—ten years during which we could have been producing the future publishers of Plumtree Press.

I pushed the thought aside, and Claire and I chatted about her new firm until Lisette returned with cup in hand. Then Claire handed us copies of the agenda she'd drawn up for our little meeting.

"First," she said, smiling with barely controlled excitement, "I think this is a masterstroke, announcing on Stonecypher's birthday, and here at the Press where he lived. He's so popular now, with the film *The Figure in the Library* coming out, that it's perfect for your book. Have you got those advance copies yet?"

I shook my head. "No. Makes me nervous. But the printer claims they'll be here tomorrow—I just spoke with him this morning. He's sending more by overnight mail today."

"I'll call them later today, just to make sure they've overnighted them," Lisette said, making a note in her diary.

Claire nodded. "Good. Okay. First, the invitation list. We've had responses from . . ." She proceeded to list the names of some of the country's finest journalists and literary critics. We'd chosen carefully, because the rooms at the Press were none too large. By specially arranging Stonecypher's wife's retreat, the area Lisette now shared with her assistant, sixty-five people could be accommodated—albeit in a slightly cramped fashion. We already had sixty acceptances.

These things were always feats of last-minute planning because journalists consider themselves above responding to invitations until the day before, but we had a fairly good crop of responses, considering that it was still two whole days before the event.

"We have to leave room for Angela and the two of you," Claire said, running a finger down her list. "I'll ask my assistant to call two others and check to see if they're coming; if not, we'll start on the reserve list." She sent a blazing smile, framed in bright pink lipstick, across the table. "It seems everyone wants to come to your party, Alex!"

She and Lisette did cheer me up a good deal in the course of the next hour as we reviewed the menu, the comments I was to deliver, the first few pages of Chapter One that Angela was going to read, and potential problems. Claire even asked me a few truly nasty questions as practice, in case it happened on the day. It was remarkable how badly behaved print journalists could be.

"So, Plumtree," Claire sneered, impersonating one of the nastiest of the familiar lot of them. This particular journalist was likely to be drunk by the time the party reached the stand-around-and-chat-about-the-announcement stage after lunch. "Don't you feel Stonecypher is becoming rather hackneyed, now that both Hollywood and the British film industry are making him a legend?"

I smiled benignly back at her. "Well, I know what you mean. Subtle little Stonecypher has become a world star overnight. But actually, I feel that the movie has played into our hands quite nicely. Now that the great unwashed have heard of the man, they'll be interested to read about his secret—even dangerous—political life."

"Yes," Claire said, herself again, nodding approvingly. "That's it. You acknowledged his comment, so he can't feel you reacted negatively to him, then you went on to make your point in a tantalising way. He'll go straight home to read the book, after sleeping off the burgundy."

We had a chuckle at the notorious journalist's idiosyncrasies and, having completed the agenda, Claire stood to leave. "Angela's all ready, right?"

"Yes, she'll be fine," I replied. "She's going to keep it

simple, as you suggested; do a reading, then answer questions with us there to help in case anyone makes trouble."

"Good." Claire stopped at the door to say, "Don't worry. It's going to be smashing on Wednesday."

Her enthusiasm was contagious, and I felt almost cheerful as she left. Buoyed by her reassurance, Lisette and I went down the hall to our respective offices. As I sat down in my desk chair, I thought I'd better open the envelope someone had cared enough to deliver by courier.

The sunlight Claire had brought into my day vanished in an instant. The fine, cream-coloured piece of paper I pulled from the envelope was engraved stationery that bore the Stonecypher dingbat elegantly centred at just the right distance from the top. It was similar to what Angela had received the night before last. The smoothly word-processed letter read:

Mr. Alex Plumtree
Plumtree Press
54 Bedford Square
London WC1

Dear Alex,

We regret that you have chosen to ignore our first letter, as well as our letter to Angela Mayfield. [What first letter? I thought.] *We have tried to be subtle, but to no avail. Surely by now you realise that it would be best if you did not publish* The Stonecypher Saga? *We regret that there must be so much secrecy about our request, but it is a matter of great international importance.*

By the end of the business day tomorrow, please contact the book distributors stocking your book, and tell them the book must be destroyed for legal reasons. They have complied with such requests before, as you well know.

Also contact those you have invited to your press conference and inform them that the announcement is off; tell them that the book cannot be published for

*legal reasons, the result of an unfortunate dispute with
the Stonecypher estate.*

*We urge your complete cooperation, as we will do
what is necessary to prevent publication of this book.
We will know when you have complied with our
requests, and will not trouble you further. Should you
ignore our request, you will be most displeased with
what we shall be forced to do, and you will know of the
seriousness of our intentions—if you do not already—
by tomorrow night.*

The letter was unsigned, and its audacity made my blood boil.
They didn't know me very well if they thought that I would
cave in to pressure to scratch a book from our list. In the first
place, it was a moral challenge; I would publish and be
damned—or killed—rather than let anyone dictate what
should receive the Plumtree Press logo.

I couldn't help but think back to what my father would
have done in my situation, as I so often did. Had he come up
against something like this? Was that really why he—and my
mother—had died in the yachting accident?

I jumped up and started pacing my tiny office, fuming. If
there had been anything convenient to hit, I would have sur-
rendered to temptation. In the first place, they were trying to
censor us. That had gone out in the Dark Ages. Second, they
wanted us to dump tens of thousands of pounds worth of
books into the incinerator. Small publishing houses simply
couldn't throw money away like that. But that wasn't their
concern.

Third, *I* had suggested that Angela write the book. It was
one of the best things that would ever happen to her career as
a scholar and a writer. I wasn't about to turn round and tell
her that I wouldn't publish it, despite the fact that we'd both
been threatened. I'd felt a commitment on her part to go
ahead with the book on Sunday, despite the letter and despite
the boating disaster.

Half of me wanted to go outside, find the Neck, and tell
him directly that he and his friends would never get me to stop
publication of this or any other book. The other half said that
it would be much smarter to play my cards close to my vest.

Furious but determined, I stuffed the letter into my jacket pocket and banged out the rest of the MacDougal memo to Rachel, then wrote her a private memo to explain that she should feel free to use the other document when discussing the book with MacDougal. I fired them both off to her on our primitive electronic mail system, then stood and went to tell Lisette I was leaving for the day.

"Cheer up," she said, smiling at me sadly. "It is not the end of the world." She cocked her head to one side and narrowed her eyes. "You know, we 'ave not seen much of you lately. At least I 'aven't; I know that you and George were up to no good yesterday. 'Ow about coming over tonight for a bit of duck and tarte tatin?"

I was tempted; but I wasn't sure I'd be very good company.

"Oh, come on. I know you—left on your own, you'll have a frozen pizza or some such disgusting thing." She grimaced. "Say yes."

In the end, I did follow her home, enjoyed her usual feast of a home-cooked dinner and some excellent wine, and caught up with George and Lisette and their boys. Michael and Edward loved it when I came to their house. I was willing to wrestle with them, for one thing, and that was something their father got enough of from breaking up their fights, and so declined to do during playtime. Their parents usually let them stay up later when I came than on normal evenings, and that didn't hurt my standing either. They were delightful boys, Michael more introverted and thoughtful than his younger sibling, and Edward a clown.

Playing with the boys was bittersweet, and I suspected that George and Lisette knew it; when I was with the children, the prospect of ever having offspring of my own seemed more distant than ever.

When George finally forced the issue and got the boys to bed around nine, Lisette sat back on the sofa in the long, brightly-patterned caftan she wore in the evenings. She curled her legs up beneath her, an after-dinner lollipop in her hand to ward off the temptation of a cigarette, and said, "All right. Now, what is making the long face I saw at work today?" She looked at me with genuine concern.

I sighed. "Ian and I disagree over signing MacDougal as a

history author for the academic division. He won't tell me why he wants to stay away from the whole thing, and I see it as a way to vastly expand our academic business with almost no risk."

George came back in after bedding down Edward, who always stalled longer, with some light blue toothpaste drying on his cheek. Lisette motioned to him, pointing to and rubbing her own cheek.

"Sorry to interrupt. More coffee, anyone? Brandy? Port?"

"Thanks, George. Just coffee, please." I held out my cup on its saucer to him in the easy familiarity of a long friendship. Lisette made her thumb and forefinger into the space of about half an inch, the amount of brandy she wanted. George wandered off into the kitchen.

"So today I was rather short with him," I told Lisette. "To be honest, I was horrible. I feel awful about it. But worst of all, I still think I'm right about going ahead with MacDougal, and tomorrow morning, when he comes, we'll sign the contracts."

"I always miss the good stuff," George said good-naturedly, rejoining us. "You always get into the meat of things right when I'm putting the boys to bed. So what is it?" He handed me my coffee and Lisette her brandy, keeping a snifter in his hand for himself. He frowned in concentration as he sat next to his wife, putting an arm around her shoulders.

George and I had an understanding without ever actually saying it; Lisette was not to be brought into the Stonecypher trouble unless it became absolutely necessary. He wouldn't have worried her with the boating incident, and I hadn't told her about the "requests" to stifle Angela's book. I wondered how he'd explained the cut on his leg.

"Oh." I waved a hand to minimise the seriousness of it all. "I've got a case of the guilts. Ian and I had a disagreement, and I finally blew up at him today." Sipping the coffee, which had some sort of chocolate liqueur flavour to it, I shook my head. "It's just isn't like him to be unreasonable."

"Yes," Lisette said, nodding and looking into my eyes intently. "That's right. It's not like 'im."

"Well, darling, what do you mean?" George asked Lisette. "Do you think there's something wrong with Ian?"

Lisette, snifter in hand, cocked her head to one side. "No."
She paused for effect. "Knowing Ian, I suspect he knows
something that we don't."

On that disturbing note, which I already knew to be true
after my morning's discussion with him, I turned the conversation back to more cheerful matters—Lisette's birthday the
following day.

But the sense of disaster never left me. The threat I felt cir-
cumscribed every moment, began and ended everything, just
as the anonymous letter had crackled when I'd taken off my
jacket at their house, and did so again when I put it on to
leave.

I was not surprised when the white Mondeo followed
me home.

CHAPTER 9

Unless he has a genuine sympathy with the author's problems, no one can hope to make an enduring success of publishing.

—MICHAEL JOSEPH

I derived very little pleasure from the meeting with MacDougal the next morning, which might, under ordinary circumstances, have brought me much satisfaction.

He stood peacock-like in the reception area when I ran down to meet him. Spot on time at nine o'clock, he actually checked his watch when he saw me coming. I groaned internally and prepared myself for the worst.

"Dr. MacDougal," I said, using his title out of courtesy. Somehow my instinct said he was one of those Ph.D.'s who actually expected to be called doctor. "So pleased to meet you. Alex Plumtree."

"A pleasure," he said formally, not looking at me, and frowning as if it really weren't much of a pleasure at all. He was a smallish man with a barrel-like chest and very short legs. He had shoulder-length red hair, scraggly, with a matching beard—also worn long. His face was flushed, and his red nose was so bulbous as to appear swollen. Short dark hairs stuck straight out from a number of large pores in his nose, and his black eyes flashed out of narrow lids. He was not a person I found myself attracted to immediately, but he did write a remarkable history book. Nearly one hundred thousand copies had sold in the last year alone, and it was due for a revision.

"Shall we?" I indicated the hallway and the staircase, which we could see from where we stood, just inside reception. He picked up a black suitcase-style briefcase and passed in front of me into the hallway. Behind him, one of the builder's air compressors roared to life and he started, then covered his ears against the deafening noise.

"I must apologise," I shouted, leaning close to him to be heard, "for the construction mess. We're doing some renovation. A bit of adding-on, in fact, for the academic division. You see, I have high hopes for your books." I smiled at him, and he broke into a self-conscious grin. I found myself thinking that here was a man who probably didn't engage in smiles very often.

"Normally we'd take the lift, but I've promised the contractors they'd have the use of it for the duration of the project." As I spoke, I could hear it humming down to the main floor behind us. Harry had told me that morning in our daily chat that his people were hauling supplies up to the third floor, where my office was, to begin work on opening up the third-floor passageway to the other building. The rubble and dust and hanging plastic sheets were clearly visible from where we stood.

"Mmph," he panted, badly out of shape, his balding pate glistening as we started up the second flight of stairs. I let him endure the rest of the hike in silence, and focussed my thoughts on the shape of the meeting before us. Rachel, the master editor, had assured me she would be ready for him when I was done. What I needed to do was, first, reassure him that we would throw massive marketing support behind him to launch his new history series, leaning heavily on Plumtree's undisputed reputation as the finest publisher of English literature anthologies in England.

Then I would remind him of our commitment to publish *The Storms of Time*, and that would be a good opportunity to pull out the contract and show him the specific language in it about his novel. He would want to look at the contract, and then I hoped he would want to sign it. I had a feeling he was eager to move forward with us, and could only guess that he'd been looking for a way to leave Wilde Publishing when I'd called.

By the time we reached the third level he was huffing and puffing, and I wondered if the danger we'd avoided by not taking the lift in the construction area would have been as bad as MacDougal having a heart attack. Perhaps I'd have to retract my offer to Harry of exclusive use of the lift.

I showed the poor perspiring man into the conference room and, to give him a chance to catch his breath, said, "Would you like some coffee?" He nodded an enthusiastic yes. "White?" I guessed, and again he nodded.

Lisette was in the coffee grotto, stoking her cup, when I entered. " 'Ow's it going?" she asked. Earlier in the morning I had wished her happy birthday, thanked her again for the dinner and conversation of the night before, and she had waved it off with the airy disregard she saved for her own good deeds.

"Don't forget your birthday lunch," I'd said. "We're leaving here promptly at noon."

"I 'ave not forgotten," she said. "But I am not sitting next to you." When I looked at her quizzically, she said, "I cannot afford to 'ave another suit ruined," and winked. Then she leaned towards me conspiratorially. "Did you resolve your problem with Ian?" she whispered, knowing that he was just down the hall.

"No," I'd answered, frustrated at the thought. "But, damn it all, I'm going ahead anyway. I can't see why not, and I can't let the opportunity pass." Now, an hour later, the opportunity was almost a reality—I hoped. Like Angela's book was almost a reality . . . "By the way, have those advance copies arrived yet?"

She shook her head mournfully. "But it's only just after nine o'clock," she soothed. "The overnight courier often doesn't come till ten."

I knew she was right, but didn't like it. If there had been another mix-up, and we didn't receive the books in time, we might have to delay the announcement. Then we would miss the convenience of announcing during the week of the book fair at the Hotel Russell, and on Stonecypher's birthday. . . .

"I know what you are thinking," Lisette said. "Stop it. I'll get the bloody books 'ere, come 'ell or 'igh water."

I actually smiled, recalling Lisette's tactics with Freddy Craggins. She had a way of getting things done, all right. She was an absolute marvel, and had never let me down yet. George was a lucky man.

"I'll bet you will," I told her.

"I'm 'aving some sent from Blackwood's," she said matter-of-factly, "just in case. If I 'ave to, I'll drive to Oxford to get them on Wednesday morning."

I knew she would, too. Blackwood's was the giant wholesaler of books that supplied most of England's bookshops, and their huge warehouse was just outside of Oxford in the countryside. Then I thought of the author sitting in the conference room and sighed. "At least MacDougal's here, so that's progressing," I said, filling two mugs and adding cream. "So far. Wish me luck."

"Good luck," she said. "I'll stop in and see 'im on my way past. Oh—by the way," she said as an afterthought, shooting me a meaningful look as she started out the door. " 'Ave you seen our friends outside this morning?"

"Oh, no," I groaned. "Don't tell me Save Our Buildings has swung into action."

She smiled sarcastically. "I saw them through the window, putting their signs and things together, just after you went down to get MacDougal."

Shaking my head, I picked up my mugs of coffee and followed her as she adeptly balanced on her high heels down the hall to the conference room, trailing her floral scent. As I watched her enter the room, I wondered how I could hide the impending protest from MacDougal. There would be shouts, jeers, placards—the works. I sighed and went through the door into the conference room. MacDougal had seated himself with his back to the door, so he didn't realise that I was there, and saw only Lisette when she moved in front of him.

"Good morning," she said, smiling angelically as she stuck out her right hand, transferring her coffee cup to the left. "Welcome to Plumtree Press. I am—"

"Just put it down there," MacDougal growled.

It took Lisette a moment to accept the fact that to Mac-Dougal, a woman appearing with a cup of coffee meant that she was serving it to him. She responded with the sincere goodwill that she presented to all mankind—up to a point.

"I'm afraid you are confused, Mr. MacDougal," she said with a smile. "This is my coffee. Alex, 'ere, 'as yours. I am Lisette Stoneham; I work closely with Alex and Ian and wanted to welcome you to Plumtree Press."

MacDougal grunted a response and glanced at her briefly before averting his gaze to the papers he'd spread on the table before him, which I noticed with dread were additional chapters to *The Storms of Time*.

"Well, I'll let you get on with it, then," Lisette murmured, widening her eyes at me as she passed out of the room.

I deposited MacDougal's coffee in front of him and said cheerfully, "She doesn't know it yet, but Lisette is to be promoted to deputy managing director today. She practically runs this place."

"Where is—um—you know, that Higginbotham fellow?" MacDougal shuffled his papers. He had got the point about Lisette, but wasn't about to acknowledge it. "I thought *he* headed your academic division." He looked up, disgruntled, as if he disapproved of how I was handling the situation.

His words stung like shot. "Yes, Ian Higginbotham is the head of our academic division." I had told Ian via an electronic mail memo first thing that morning what I intended to do with MacDougal, and I still felt awful about it. Ian should have been at the meeting, in charge, and I knew it; I also felt that MacDougal knew it. As if to torture me further, the first round of chants began outside. Perhaps if I kept talking he wouldn't hear them. . . .

"I wanted to meet with you too, as head of Plumtree Press. You're very important to us." I smiled as best I could. "You'll be meeting Ian one day soon."

"Hmph."

He seemed suspicious, and I thought he cocked his head at one point as if to listen for the noise outside, but I moved on to the first item on my agenda: a small sales presentation on what a great sales and marketing job we were going to do for him.

"You know, Angus," I said, hoping he agreed it was time for first names, "Plumtree Press now has eighty per cent of the world-wide market for literary anthologies. That jumped considerably last year as a result of our agreement with the American firm, Megatext."

I paused as the unmistakable sound of raised voices drifted into my hearing, *"Historic homes should be left alone! Plumtree Press, Bloomsbury's distress!"*

Gulping, I continued. "Their foreign sales divisions have taken our books to the far corners of the world, and I want you to know that the same will be true of your—"

"Pish-tosh. I don't care about all that, Plumtree." He drank half his cup of coffee in one gulp, leaving a milky residue on his long mustache, which he then wiped with the back of a freckled hand. Scowling, he looked at me and said distractedly, "What's that god-awful noise out there?" As I attempted to frame an answer, he continued. "I had phenomenal sales with Wilde, as you well know."

He seemed to think of something then that disturbed him, and he fumbled a bit with the array of chapters before him. "Yes. Well. As I was saying, it's not the sales. Let's just say that I, er, have a new career in mind. Yes. A new career."

I looked at him, silenced, waiting, unable to do anything about the *"Stonecypher's home, leave it alone!"* outside. I envisioned half a dozen middle-aged men and woman clad in their best upper-class down-at-the-heel clothes, pacing in a tight circle, doing their part for the morning. It probably made a change from tennis, I thought unkindly, and allowed them to polish their London parking skills. There was no doubt one Range Rover beached in the square for each protestor. It was, after all, a beautiful day for a protest; the weather was in limbo between summer and autumn, warm but not too warm.

"And my fiction, you know," MacDougal was saying. "No one has any taste anymore, they don't seem to want historical fiction, and I know that you specialise in that kind of thing. Just ready for a change, and to get my novel published. Have you read it?"

I was used to things working out in any way but the one I expected, but he still took me by surprise. "Yes, yes, I have."

"Well?" Behind his gruff question I sensed the tender ego of every author.

"We will certainly publish it, and as I mentioned, Rachel Sigridsson, our senior editor, will be meeting with you later to go over it. I do think some changes are required, but that's routine. I don't anticipate any problems in working it out."

"Changes?" MacDougal got to his feet in one quick motion, his normally ruddy face deepening to a disturbing red. "I am the leading author of history texts in the world, and you want me to make *changes*?"

"I assure you, Angus, most of our authors have to make some changes." I spoke in the most soothing voice I could muster. "You do want the book to be well received, don't you?" I had arrived at this technique for handling recalcitrant authors the year before. After all, sometimes authors and I had only that in common and nothing more: we wanted people to like the books.

My approach seemed to work. At the thought of the possibility that the book might not be well received, he appeared to be slightly humbled. I was certain that for a moment there, he earnestly desired to cooperate.

"Mmph. Well. Hmm." He sat down in a bit of a fluster, patting the piles of paper in front of him. Another round of *"Plumtree Press, Bloomsbury's distress!"* wafted into the room, and MacDougal squinted at me. "Is that someone yelling at you out there? I thought I heard your name."

"Mmm . . ." I waved it off vaguely. "Nothing to worry about. Now," I said in my most matter-of-fact manner, opening the folder in which I had stowed his contract and sliding a stack of four copies of the twenty-four-page document towards him. "Shall we get this out of the way? The clause about the publication of your novel has been inserted— section four B." I thought it best to try to get him to sign the contracts, since he didn't seem to be interested in discussing our business arrangement, and there was no point in idly passing time with sharks circling outside if he would agree to sign.

In that very awkward moment I also wanted to ask him what he meant about starting a new career, but didn't want to risk any more scenes. Given his volatility, and the protestors, I figured I'd just better get on with it.

The odd little man had another surprise for me. He gave me an incredulous look and grew quite indignant. "Good God, man, you don't think I've been in this business this long for nothing. I've my own clauses to insert."

This was a first for me. Usually our authors, and academic authors in particular, were quite meek when it came to the contracts—even embarrassed to admit that publishing a book was in some way a business arrangement, and not merely for the sake of art or science. They simply signed on the dotted line. Even our nonacademic trade authors, like Angela, who were often represented by agents, didn't attempt to add clauses.

Yet another surprise was coming. "I don't see any reason, though, why we couldn't do the contracts today if you don't mind me amending them myself."

"Amending them . . . in what way exactly?"

He fiddled nervously with the corner of the first page of one of his chapters, bending it into a curl. I heard a rousing chorus of *"Keep your wrecking ball out of Stonecypher's hall!"* but MacDougal, distracted, seemed not to notice. For some reason, he was embarrassed or nervous about this amendment, I thought.

"I want a clause inserted specifying that amateurs, either within your publishing house or hired by you, will not be allowed to review and change my history books, that only a board of qualified historians and professional educators, specified by me, may review my work before publication."

Now I could see why he had reacted so negatively to my mention of the need for changes in his novel. He was worse than most with regard to the infallibility of his work.

Nodding slowly, I said, "I don't see any problem with that, provided that Ian and I approve the members of the board and agree they are qualified to do the review."

This was a part of publishing unique to the academic side of the business; before any textbook is published, professors at universities are asked to review several chapters for a fee and comment on the work. It is the only way we publishers can be sure of the accuracy and quality of the work of authors in highly specialised areas.

MacDougal, frowning, sent another broadside across the table. "Doesn't Ian Higginbotham want to publish my novel? Is that why he's not here?"

My mouth must have hung open for a moment before I could respond. How could he possibly have known? What was going on here? Why did he even care about Ian?

"Please, Dr. MacDougal," I felt myself slipping back into titles to distance myself from the man. "You needn't worry about Ian's involvement in the project. It just happens to be that *I* am meeting with you today, and I would ask you please not to attach any particular significance to that. I assure you, I have full authority to take care of any issues that might arise pertaining to your project with us."

I was tempted to add that I owned the company and Ian Higginbotham worked for me, but fortunately realised the childishness of it before it left my mouth.

He glowered at me for a moment, then nodded.

"Do you have the wording of your amendment in writing?" I asked.

"Yes," he snapped, and reached down for his briefcase. He clicked the clasps open, lifted the lid, pulled out a word-processed sheet of paper that had obviously been carefully prepared in advance, and handed it to me. I was fascinated by his behaviour. He had obviously come hoping to finalise our arrangement today, just as I had.

"Thank you," I said. Glancing at the document, I could see that it repeated his earlier words about reviews and changes almost verbatim. "I'll just have this inserted in the contracts as an addendum, then, if that's all right."

He nodded brusquely and tucked into his now cold coffee, apparently relieved. I shook my head as I left the little conference room and took the four copies of the contract and MacDougal's paper to Shuna, who handled our document preparations, photocopying, and filing. She shared the large front office on the third floor with Lisette. Shuna received my instructions and the papers in a business-like manner and immediately got into MacDougal's file on the computer, agreeing to produce one more sheet for each contract with the addendum on it, and then to bring all the papers back to us in the conference room.

"Thanks," I said, then walked over to the window behind Lisette's desk to glare at the protestors. "I'm glad to see they're having a good day out," I mumbled. I couldn't help but smirk when I saw that there were, in fact, six Range Rovers parked in and around the square that weren't usually there. And five protestors, each carrying a placard and half a sheet of paper with the words of the chants on them. I was willing to bet that one of the group had already gone off to get take-away cups of herb tea for the others. Heaven forbid that their sacred duty to England's buildings should cause them any discomfort or sacrifice, I thought unkindly.

Lisette shook her head in disgust. "Can't we *do* something?"

"I think I'll have a word with them, after I show Mac-Dougal out the back door. Obviously they have no idea what we're doing with the building."

"Mmmph," she huffed in agreement, typing with gusto at her keyboard. "Oh—still no books from Kei-King, but Black-wood's are sending some down."

"Good. Thanks."

Returning to the conference room, I offered MacDougal more coffee, which he declined with a grimace, and firmly closed the door. Then I endured a detailed description from him of the way in which he intended to greatly expand the scope of *The Storms of Time* with the chapters on the table before him. For the first time since he'd arrived, his eyes were alight. This was clearly his true passion.

"You see, with my in-depth knowledge of Scotland going back to the tenth century, I can actually make the novel span *ten centuries*. When I was a boy, I reenacted the ancient battles with my mates, all in authentic costume and with the appropriate weapons. And the other day I recalled one particularly poignant episode near Stirling in the year 1244 in which—"

I was truly grateful when Shuna knocked on the door and entered with the papers. "Thank you," I said rather too fervently as MacDougal stopped his reminiscences long enough to glance round at the interruption. Shuna seemed to grasp the situation, or at least hear the relief in my voice. She smiled with genuine humour as she closed the door behind her.

"Well." I was all breezy and cheerful. "Shall we?"

I put the contracts on top of his precious chapters and he flicked to the end of each document, checking that the addendum had been attached to each. Satisfied, he signed and initialled in all the places Shuna had circled, and put the pen down. I picked it up again and signed on the line above the words "for Plumtree Press" on all copies, then handed the top copy to him.

"Great." I was slightly nonplussed as to how to deal with him; I for one had nothing more to say. It had all gone relatively quickly and easily, and Rupert Soames hadn't even stormed the building in a final attempt to wrench MacDougal from my grasp. "Is there anything else you would like to discuss before you talk to Rachel about your novel?"

"No." He didn't look at me. "Let's get on with it, then." He stood and packed his copy of the contract into the briefcase with his other papers.

"Right," I said, smiling and standing. It was good that one really excellent thing had happened that day, when so many dark clouds were hanging overhead. "Rachel is just down the hall, this way."

We processed through the hallway to Rachel's sanctum sanctorum, a tiny room lined with shelves holding the piles of paper that represented book manuscripts, manuals of style, and reference books of all kinds, including encyclopaedias and dictionaries. She even had the complete, giant-sized, unabridged *Oxford English Dictionary*—all twenty volumes, of course. Fortunately, her office was at the rear of the building and was well insulated from the sounds of the protestors outside.

I knocked on her door, and she stood briskly to greet us. "Mr. Plumtree, thank you, I received your memo." Then she turned to MacDougal, her very bearing communicating to him that she was no pushover. I introduced them and left, feeling that I had bequeathed Rachel a truly miserable task.

An odd man, I pondered as I retreated down the hall. It always amazed me that some people seemed to escape, somehow, the norms of human behaviour. Through the years

I hadn't been able to figure out whether these people knew about the norms and just didn't bother to conform to them, or simply didn't perceive them. I had come to know a number of people in my life who had such an unusual way of dealing with people and situations that they might have just dropped in from another planet.

If only I had realised then what sort of figurative aliens were invading, and that MacDougal was indeed one of them.

CHAPTER 10

There died a myriad,
And of the best, among them,
. . . For a botched civilization . . .
For a few thousand battered books.

—EZRA POUND

Whenever they burn books they will also, in the end,
burn human beings.

—HEINRICH HEINE

My office felt like a positive sanctuary when I returned to it. Sinking into the old leather chair behind my desk, I blew out a pent-up breath and checked my watch. Ten past ten. A good chunk of time to work on the presentation I wanted to include in my Folio B lecture on sensational book crimes—initially intended as a boredom-stopper, but all the more appropriate now that I suspected a book fiddle within Folio B, emanating from Diana Boillot's restoration work.

Actually chuckling as I opened the file on my computer, I anticipated the looks on the faces of those involved in the book-stealing and switching operation when they heard my speech. This was more family lore than anything else, stories of book crimes passed down from one Plumtree to another. It would be good to record them on paper, I thought, though some had now been publicised widely. It was a topic that came up every so often in the book trade, but it never ceased to fascinate.

The real authorities in the field were John Carter and Graham Pollard, who had published the definitive work on forgeries in rare and antique books entitled *An Inquiry into the Nature of Some Nineteenth-Century Pamphlets*. This book, published in the mid-twentieth century, revealed that some very valuable works purported to have been printed in the nineteenth century—Thomas Paine's "Common Sense," for instance—had actually been produced in a typeface created *after* the supposed date of publication. I would relate some of their discoveries, duly referenced, of course, to my listeners. Some of the younger members of Folio B may not have heard of the famous work.

But they also deserved to hear of the less frequently quoted examples of bibliocrime, such as the Larrovitch saga. In this hilarious instance of academic horseplay, some academicians got together and decided to create a famous author. They made up some poems, published numerous books under the fictitious name of Vladimir Larrovitch, and before long university professors were teaching serious courses on the nonexistent author's works. The hoax went on for years, and Larrovitch's books are still highly collectible today as a result.

A less humorous instance of crime with books was the fairly recent American episode, in 1992, concerning one Stephen Blumberg, a bibliophile who simply could not resist collecting his favourite books—by stealing them. Masquerading as a professor, he spent time at some of the best libraries in the nation, sometimes removing an entire lorry full of special-collections books in a single evening. Eventually the day would come when he could nick the librarian's keys to a locked treasure room from a desk drawer. Blumberg would copy the keys and replace them the next day, so that they were rarely missed. It was months before anyone noticed that the books were gone; they would be missed only when they were requested. Blumberg stole some of the most valuable books in the United States to simply store them away. He didn't want to sell the volumes; he simply needed to possess them. When one of his friends finally told the FBI, the books were discovered to fill an entire warehouse. Unbelievably, some pundits argued that he should be let off lightly because, after all, his was only a crime of bibliophily. Blumberg simply couldn't help himself when it came to books, they said. Fortunately, in my opinion, the judge disagreed and called him "nothing more than a common criminal."

When I next checked my watch, it was eleven fifty-two. Time to begin collecting myself and others for Lisette's birthday lunch. I had summarised the Carter/Pollard and Larrovitch stories briefly, but the Blumberg case would have to wait for another day. The exact title for my speech had not yet presented itself, but I thought something like "A Bibliophile's Guide to Book Frauds, Forgeries, and Fantastic Stories" would work. I bashed in the first few words as the file name and closed down my Mac, then grabbed a large carrier bag containing Lisette's promotion present.

Despite the storm clouds swirling round Plumtree Press and, more particularly, Angela and me at the moment, I felt a strong sense of anticipation and pleasure at the thought of the next two hours—except for the act of passing the protesters between me and the taxis.

I stopped by Lisette's office to say that I would be outside, dealing with our little obstacle, and trotted down the stairs. On the way out I mentioned to Dee, our receptionist, that if the protesters were still there when Rachel brought Mac-Dougal down, she should nab them and have him go out the back way, construction or no construction. "Right, Mr. P," Dee said, and winked at me. I didn't want our leading academic author to think he was associated with a publishing house of no social or architectural responsibility, nor did I want him to be accosted by a hostile group.

I took a deep breath and stepped out the front door. Interestingly enough, not one of the six protesters looked up at me, or made any move to intercept me. The proceedings had roughly the feel of a sporting event; they were serious enough to be there on a weekday morning, but it didn't dominate their lives. Looking past the circle of four women and two men, I saw the taxis that would take our party to lunch waiting in a line at the kerb, and the Neck parked in the white Ford. Or, more accurately, I saw the Ford and not the Neck, and figured he must be inside. I couldn't help myself; I was just irritated enough that I waved.

Then I walked over to the little circle of protesters and approached a friendly-looking woman my own age. "Hello. I'm Alex Plumtree. This is my building. May I speak with you for a moment?"

"Of course," she said cheerfully, thereby missing the next rendition of *"Stonecypher's home, leave it alone!"* She kept walking, though, and so as I fell in line, I found myself part of the circle protesting my own building.

"Do you realise," I began, "that I'm not changing Stone-cypher's home at all, except to shore up the rear exterior for another few hundred years, and to put two doors where there are now two windows?"

"I wouldn't know," the woman said unconcernedly. "We've just got the morning shift." She lifted her wrist to check her watch, the brushed gold band of which glistened in the bright early-autumn sun, and smiled. "Mmm—almost lunchtime."

In exasperation I blurted out. "Well—then why are you here?"

"We care about London's historic buildings," she replied promptly, as if perhaps I were a bit dull to even ask the question. "We want them to be preserved."

"Plumtree Press, Bloomsbury's distress!" the group shouted, obviously not overly distressed themselves.

"Well, since you're out here disrupting my business, and since I, the owner of the building, am not disrupting Stone-cypher's home but am busy preserving it for posterity, I thought you might like to know. You see, you don't really have to be here at all."

She stopped to look at me. "Well, you don't have to get shirty about it," she said, looking me up and down. "We're just obeying our consciences. This isn't against the law."

"Keep your wrecking ball out of Stonecypher's hall!"

I shook my head in disbelief, and left them marching, obviously relishing their bit of activism. As I waited by the taxis, having had a word with the drivers to let them know we were leaving momentarily, George arrived.

"Your lucky day, I see, Alex. Did you see that squib in *The Tempus* this morning about the new president of Save Our Buildings?"

"No," I said sourly. "You'd better tell me."

"Brace yourself." His eyes were dancing with private amusement. "Rupert Soames."

"No!"

"Would I lie about something like this?"

At that moment the door of the Press opened and Lisette, accompanied by all the editors from the Press, joined us—except for poor Rachel, who was stuck in the meeting with MacDougal. My colleagues gaped at the complacent protesters as they walked past, and seemed as surprised as I not to receive any catcalls or rotten tomatoes in the face. We piled into the waiting cars, and at last several taxis full of us proceeded to the Ivy.

I'd chosen the Ivy as a special treat for Lisette; there is little glamour in our business, but at this restaurant one is likely to run into a movie star or famous politician or two while enjoying a really first-class meal.

It had been a stressful month for all of us, preparing for the announcement of Angela's book, and this was a well-earned reward for everyone. It was the first time I'd seen Ian since I was rude to him, and I uttered a contrite apology as we climbed into the taxi. As far as I could tell, he had already forgiven me, as one forgives a child for a temper tantrum, and to Ian's credit, he didn't let our discussion cast a pall over Lisette's celebration.

I ordered champagne, and when everyone had a glass, I raised mine. "I would like to purpose a toast to a woman who will do almost anything to get an Historic Buildings Society permit." There was a chorus of laughter and "Hear, hear," and everyone raised a glass. "And," I continued, "to a woman who can do everything better than I can, whom I admire tremendously."

George scowled good-naturedly. "Hang on, Plumtree. Are you trying to tell me something?" He couldn't have given me a better segue.

"Well, yes, George, I guess I am," I said, nodding with exaggerated seriousness.

Even Lisette looked a little worried at this. "I'm trying to tell you that your wife, as of this very moment, is the deputy managing director of Plumtree Press."

I'd caught Lisette totally off guard, and she raised a shaking hand to her lips as she swore softly, her usual response to embarrassment. Before things got too awkward for her, I pulled out the brown bag. "This is from all of us."

Blushing as she tore off the wrapping, when she saw what it was, she held it up, laughing. "You so-and-sos. You don't want to drink my coffee anymore!" It was a super-deluxe, gourmet coffee machine, equipped with a timer that would allow her to walk in in the morning and find it already brewed, saving the irritable banging, clanging, and swearing associated with Lisette making her first cup of coffee. "Thank you. Thank you very much," she said proudly.

"And see if I ever offer you a cup of coffee again," she ended cheerily.

We laughed and went back to our champagne. It felt a bit odd to go on with normal life while dire threats were appearing in increasing numbers.

After the meal I leaned over to George, on my right, and said, "I'm becoming more and more popular. Didn't want to tell you last night in front of Lisette. Not only did I get another dingbat yesterday, but an honest-to-goodness letter. It said to pulp the book or find out tonight that they're serious."

George lifted his eyebrows. "Really," he commented. "That does sound dire." He allowed a waiter to fill his cup with coffee, then picked it up. "What are you going to do?"

"No one is going to tell me what to publish. I'm going ahead with it, as long as Angela agrees. I'm to meet her in half an hour at the Hotel Russell for the book fair; I'll ask her then."

George nodded. "That's what I thought you'd say." He gave me a brief, mirthless smile. "Publish and be damned, eh?"

I didn't reply.

Lisette, on the other side of George, stood up and said, "Right, you lot. If I'm the new deputy managing director, I say it's time to go back to work. Shuna called the taxis ten minutes ago; they should be here now." There was assorted mumbling and grumbling around the large table, mostly with good-natured insults for Lisette, whom everyone loved.

"Slave driver."

"Promote a woman, and she thinks she's God."

"Watch out, Lisette's in charge."

George put the icing on the cake with, "Now, you all know that Rumpole is really referring to Lisette when he speaks of 'she who must be obeyed.' "

Everyone laughed and started to their feet as Lisette hit George over the head affectionately with a serviette.

"Watch out! She's dangerous," he said, then stood and kissed her on the lips. "It's back to the office, my dear," he said with devotion. "Happy birthday. I'll see you tonight." Then, as everyone began to move toward the door, he leaned toward me and said quietly, "Ring if you need me." I nodded my thanks.

It was two-thirty when we got back to the office; the white Ford was the last in the Plumtree Press caravan, and the "afternoon shift" of Rupert's storm troopers was doing its part in front of the building. Together, the two intrusions were enough to make me laugh; a virtual circus seemed to follow me about these days.

Rachel Sigridsson called to me as I climbed out of the taxi in front of the Press.

"Alex! Oh, Mr. Plumtree!" She had never got used to addressing me by my first name, though I was roughly half her age, and seemed to be more comfortable calling me the same thing she had called my father, and my grandfather.

I made my way across the street and met her on the kerb by the gate of the private garden. "Rachel. How did you make out with our friend?"

She was obviously agitated, most unusual for the icy, school-marmish Rachel I knew, and seemed to have been walking in the garden to calm down. I'd never even known her to lunch outside the building before. Her dark, shapeless floral print dress hung straight down over her fireplug shape. I noticed that several hairs had actually slipped out of her severe grey bun, an unprecedented occurrence.

"I'm afraid we've had a bit of a row, Mr. Plumtree." Her eyes were red, but I couldn't tell if she'd been crying. It was, after all, hay fever season. "In all my years in the book trade, I've never seen such behaviour. We started discussing the changes, and he was—well, so *disrespectful*!"

She was too well-mannered a person to detail his transgressions to me, but I could imagine the treatment MacDougal had given her, considering the way he'd dealt with Lisette that morning.

"I'm sorry, sir, but he walked out on me." She twisted her hands in agony. "And before he left, he . . . he . . ." Her agonised eyes finally lifted to meet mine. "He wished you ill, sir. He said that bad things happen to people who go back on their word."

Great, I thought. Tot up one more black mark against Alex Plumtree. Mentally, I counted three separate causes that would prefer I ceased to exist: the people with the fine dingbat stationery, who claimed "international importance"; Save Our Buildings; and now Angus MacDougal.

It angered me that MacDougal—a weak, pompous, petty man—had reduced the fine woman before me to shuddering tears. I could tell she felt she'd failed Plumtree Press in some way.

"Rachel, he behaves very badly. I saw it this morning. I'm sure it's not your fault; please don't worry. I'll find a way to work it out with him. He can't expect us to publish a book that won't sell. And I don't want you to have to go through that again. Why don't we do what we did with the Treminnick manuscript?"

Relief flooded over her face. Noel Treminnick was an author who lived in the West Country. He was so introverted that it had obviously been painful for him to come and meet with us in London. We had met once at the Press, and from then on he posted us chapters, which we sent back to him for his approval of Rachel's extensive edits. It had been a very satisfactory arrangement, and it seemed to be the perfect solution to our current problem. If we were to have arguments with MacDougal, we would simply have them the easy way: by post.

"Oh, yes. Yes, sir. That would be wonderful." Rachel actually smiled, then caught herself. "Well, I'd best be getting back. Thank you, Mr. Plumtree."

I walked back over the road with her, making small talk about Lisette's birthday lunch, expressing regret that she couldn't come (though she never attended such events anyway), and informing her of the promotion. She went upstairs to her office, and I stopped in at reception briefly before leaving to meet Angela at the Hotel Russell for the book fair lecture.

Dee, our cheerful operator and receptionist, had an earful for me. "Ah, Mr. P. These just came by courier; haven't even sent them upstairs yet." She handed me a padded mailer from the printer in Singapore; I knew it was the advance copies of *The Stonecypher Saga*, and ripped it open, spilling messy paper packing material all over Dee's desk.

It looked great; absolutely first-class. The book dingbat glowed in a sort of ghostly way in the background, with mist emanating from it, and the outline of a solitary woman drifted through the haze. It was powerful, and frightening. We'd approved the design months before, but it was different seeing it on an actual book. The book itself was three hundred and sixty-eight pages long, and had a nice heft to it. Grinning, I handed Dee one of the five copies.

"Oooh. Gorgeous, isn't it?" She stroked the smooth dust jacket with her fingers. "Looks spooky. Don't suppose I can have one, can I?"

"Of course you can. Have to wait, though, until we get the bulk copies." My eyes feasted on the cover; this was one of the best moments of being a book publisher. I was glad that the books had come now; I could take one to show Angela.

"You wouldn't have believed that MacDougal bloke, Mr. P. I could hear him yelling all the way down here." Though she had clearly enjoyed the scene, she shook her head in mock disapproval. "Walked out on Rachel an hour ago, called her a name she'd probably never heard except in breeding dogs, if you know what I mean, with a couple of adjectives attached. Then he told her she could put her suggestions in a physically improbable location."

I groaned at the thought of Rachel, of all people, enduring that sort of abuse. Had authors always been this difficult? I wondered.

"Poor Rachel. Okay. I'll deal with him later. I'll be at the book fair the rest of the day, Dee, but I'll see you in the morning."

"Ta, then, Mr. P. Congrats on the book!"

"Thanks." As I ran down the steps, late for my rendezvous with Angela, I felt as if I were playing hooky. I told myself it was work, in a way; it wasn't my fault if what I did for work was so pleasant that it seemed like play. This was the first year that the British Book Fair Association was hosting panels of expert speakers at its yearly rare and antiquarian book fair at the Hotel Russell. I was going partly to gather fodder for my speech to Folio B, partly just to be a part of the book world and enjoy the fair, and partly to scratch the backs of Armand Beasley and William Farquhart, as both were on the panel.

I ran across Gower Street and turned into Montague Place, passing a solid block of University of London buildings on my way to Russell Square. My lack of specific knowledge on the subject of rare books made me nervous; I had spent my entire life in the comfortable presence of old and valuable books, but had never bothered to learn their exacting code for the condition of books, for instance. The words were familiar, but not their precise meanings—very fine, fine, as new, good, poor, crippled, and so on. The first panel of the day had been advertised as "Rare Book Collecting for Beginners," and I planned to make the most of it.

I was twelve minutes late. The Hotel Russell loomed ahead of me across Russell Square; the grand old building was the very heart of Bloomsbury, and beloved as a relic of Victorian splendour.

I saw Angela standing at the entrance and ran up the stairs, calling out an apology as I leapt up the last three steps in a bound. "Sorry I'm late, Angela." I'd run most of the way and was out of breath.

She responded as I knew she would, not letting me off the hook and not looking me in the eye, ignoring my apology. I was struck by the fact that she seemed to have dressed for the occasion; she was wearing a white linen suit that was practically luminescent against her tan skin. The jacket plunged to a thought-provoking V in the front, and she appeared to be wearing nothing underneath. I found myself noticing that she was really very attractive.

When I finally reached the top of the stairs and was standing face-to-face with her, she turned to go in with a irritated whirl of her short pleated skirt.

"Just a sec," I said, panting. "What do you want first—good news or bad?"

"Oh, God," she said, rolling her eyes in exasperation. "What now? You'd better give me the good first."

I brought her book out from behind my back and held it out in front of her. For a reaction, from Angela, it was dramatic. She stared at it for a moment, then reached out for it tentatively, as if not certain she should really have it. Her eyes flicked up to mine, and I could see how much it meant to her to have the real thing at last in her hand. Then she seemed to realise she was revealing too much. Recovering somewhat, she gave a grudging half-grimace. "Not bad, is it?"

"It looks fantastic," I assured her. "Ready to climb the best seller lists."

"Now," she said grimly, slipping the book into her leather tote bag as if it were a newspaper, then standing with her hands on her hips. "What's the bad news?"

I reached into my jacket pocket and brought out the unsigned letter. "I received this yesterday."

Her eyes narrowed as she quickly snatched it up, scanning. "Mmm. More of the same."

"And still more, I'm afraid."

"What now?" she asked a little incredulously, with a weary lift of her eyebrows.

"Sorry," I said. "Both a bookseller friend of mine and Ian say that we've fallen into something that's way beyond us. They say we should move away, lose our identities, and forget about Stonecypher. They claim that there is a group"—I glanced around as we stood in the sunny entry—"that might kill us for publishing your book."

"A group?"

"Some sort of subset of Folio B. Mostly booksellers, evidently. They won't tell me much; they say the more I know, the more dangerous it is." I studied her. She looked a little worried, and was silent as a talkative group of four men passed us on their way into the hotel. They reeked of beer, and I reckoned they had just drunk their lunch at a nearby pub.

"So," I said. "Do you still think we should publish?"

I thought she might say she was inclined not to. But instead, she said, "You know, the very fact that they want so badly to keep my book out of people's hands makes me think that it's all the more important to publish it. No matter what." Her tiny, upturned nose jutted out defiantly.

We stood there for a moment, speaking only with our eyes, acknowledging with our seriousness exactly what we were saying. She handed the letter back to me. Then Angela, ever impatient, looked at her watch. It was a not-so-subtle reminder that we were missing Armand's panel, the first ever panel provided for the public on rare books by the British Book Fair Association.

"Yes, sorry," I stammered, amazed at her ability to recover, and followed her into the lobby. For all the effect our conversation had had on her, we might have been discussing the weather.

"I wouldn't mind so much," she said, picking up what was evidently a former train of thought, "if you weren't late every time, Alex. *Every* time. You know what it tells me? It fairly shouts 'I don't care about you.' And since I already know that's true, the constant reinforcement is hard to take."

"Angela," I murmured, embarrassed. At that opportune moment we arrived at the admission desk. "Two, please," I said, perhaps a bit more loudly than necessary, relieved at the distraction. I paid and handed Angela a ticket and catalogue, then saw the sign for the BBFA lectures behind the desk. "Oh, look. Here we are."

Still blinking as my eyes adjusted to the low light, we rounded the edge of the table, and I squinted at the sign that had been placed to one side of the hotel reception area. It listed the various rooms in which book fair events were taking place. "Panel dicussions" was listed opposite the Virginia Woolf Conference Room.

The misprint jumped out at me immediately—I had a sort of sense about them, and it was one of my missions in life to call them to the attention of their perpetrators.

"Oops," I said, pointing at the transgression as we gazed at the small black sign with its moveable white plastic letters. "I must do something about that. It's vital to the survival of the English language. I'll be just a moment."

Angela let out a "Rmmmph!" of irritation, but she knew of my obsession with misspellings, and my habit of correcting them. She said, defeated, "Oh, for goodness' sake. Go ahead, then." She of all people, I thought, should understand the significance of misprints; her thesis and novel on Stonecypher revolved entirely around them.

Walking hurriedly up to the registration desk, I caught the eye of a young woman apparently ready to be of assistance. Angela stayed behind, staring at the ceiling and tapping her foot in high dudgeon.

"Good afternoon," I said, prepared to be pleasant about my little errand.

"Good afternoon, sir," the young woman responded with equal cheerfulness. "Can I help you?"

With an effort I refrained from correcting her grammar to "*may* I help you," since I was on a language errand anyway, but kept to my original purpose. I smiled nonchalantly. "Yes, I just thought you'd like to know that your sign has a spelling error. When you make your living from words, you notice." I wrinkled my nose in a self-deprecating way to let her know that I understood we book people were a weird bunch, but couldn't help it. Indicating the sign with my head, I said, "It's d-i-s-. You have it spelt d-i-cussion."

Her smile faded as she looked at me, the sign, and back again at me as if I had lost a marble or two. With exaggerated seriousness, holding my eye sarcastically, she took up pen and paper. "That was . . . what was it again, sir?" Beneath a thin veneer of courtesy, her voice had an edge to it.

"Discussion. D-i-s-c-u-s-s-i-o-n. Okay?"

"Umm . . . was that two s's the second time round, or one?"

I honestly couldn't tell if she was just trying to be difficult, or merely had no spelling ability whatsoever. I knew that the latter was frequently the case, but it was still incomprehensible to me.

"Here." As gently as I could for my level of frustration, I took the pen and wrote it out for her. She'd put two more errors in her version, something like d-i-s-u-c-s-i-o-n, which I scratched out before setting down the pen on her ivory marble counter with a snap.

"Thank you, sir," she said, briskly standing to her full five foot four inches and sweeping up the paper. Her smile was far too bright to be pleasant.

"Not at all," I replied, doubting that she would do anything more with the paper than toss it in the dustbin. When I turned away from the girl, Angela stamped off towards the Virginia Woolf Conference Room ahead of me.

"Doesn't it drive *you* barmy?" I asked. She appeared to ignore me, but I knew she was listening. "Everywhere I go, there are excruciating spelling errors. Signs, menus, adverts in the tube stations, even *The Tempus* of London. 'Avocardo,' 'nucular,' 'mischievious.' What's the point of having a common language if people can't use it properly?"

Shaking my head, I followed her off down the hall. I could get really wound up on the subject. Who would write the newspapers of the future? Who would proofread menus and other things that couldn't be spell- and grammar-checked thoroughly by computer?

Angela stopped short at the door. She turned, a wry expression on her face. "That's the pot calling the kettle black." She frowned in mock confusion, putting a delicate index finger to her chin. "Let's see now . . . whose great-grandfather was it who published books full of misprints in this very century—which, by the way, have put both of us in grave danger?" With that, she swung the door open and went in.

Just before the door slammed closed in my face, I caught it and followed her through. I carefully eased it shut behind me so it wouldn't bang and distract the speakers. Looking up, I saw we were at the back of a large banqueting room, the chairs half filled. Just inside the door sat a table with a row of brochures and dealers' catalogues on it. Like Angela, I gathered up one of each as quietly as possible, moved to a row of seats about halfway up, and sat.

Armand, William Farquhart, and someone who I soon learned was from the Rare Books Room at the British Library, sat at a long table covered in a dark green cloth and skirt, at the front of the room. Behind them on the wall was a huge logo of an open book with a fox lounging sleepily across its top, the symbol of the British Book Fair Association. A BBFA representative was introducing the panel, and I tuned out, reflecting on the fact that I had chosen to announce Angela's book during the course of this particular antiquarian book fair as opposed to the better-known, flashier but less authentic fair put on at the Grosvenor House Hotel the previous week by the Antiquarian Booksellers' Association.

In the first place, the Hotel Russell was barely a five-minute walk from the office. But the association with this audience and setting was more appropriate, I thought, for an announcement of Angela's novel. Not only was it more Bloomsbury, which was perfect for Stonecypher, but it was more—well—English. The Americans and Japanese, who descended on antiquarian book fairs in England in ever-increasing numbers, would have already flown home after attending the other, swankier London book fair. Besides, somehow, the down-at-the-heel gentility of the Hotel Russell had the right feel.

I glanced up at the panel and saw that even Armand appeared to be impatient with the lengthy introductions. Ever the student, Angela flipped through one of the vendor brochures. Sorting through my pile, I pulled out the catalogue that said, "Armand Beasley, Bookseller" across the top. I was curious to see if I'd find any of the books I'd seen there on Sunday night.

1. Chapentier, Jean de. Essai sur Les Glaciers et sur le Terrain Erratique du Bassin du Rhone. Lausanne: Marc Ducloux, 1841. £600.

First edition. *8vo, contemporary half calf gilt, marbled boards and edges, pp. x + 363, with 8 lithographed plates (1 folding), map and text illustrations; some slight edge-staining of endpapers, else a very good copy.*

2. Adams, John. An Analysis of Horsemanship, Teaching the Whole Art of Riding. *3 vol, 20 engraved plates, some soiling of margins, occasional slight spotting or dampstaining, late nineteenth-century half calf, slightly rubbed, t.e.g., others uncut, 8vo, 1805.* £150.

3. The English Hexapla Exhibiting the Six Important Translations of the New Testament Scriptures. Wicliff (1380), Tyndale (1534), Cranmer (1539), Genevan (1557), Anglo-Rehmish (1582) Authorised (1611). The Original Greek Text After Scholz Preceded by a History of English Translations and Translators. London, Samuel Bagster, 1841. *Thick folio, original blindtooled black morocco, ornate cover and spine designs, fancy inner gilt dentelles, ribbon, very ornate gauffered edges, marble eps. Greek orig. at top of each page. Below are the six translations in parallel columns. Scholarly 64pp. introduction on all translations. Fine. Very rare.* £300.

Surprised at the obscurity of the titles, I reflected that that seemed to have little to do with their value. Evidently professional collectors didn't collect anything as common as my old Wodehouse copies, or, I thought, as interesting as the volumes at home in the Plumtree Collection. There were, I noticed, no dingbats in Armand's catalogue.

Armand piped up, when his turn came as the first of the panel to speak, in a refreshingly deep and confident voice. "Good afternoon. I'm delighted to present to you Rare Book Collecting for Beginners; it is always a pleasure to see people interested in the rewarding pursuit of collecting rare books.

"I'd like to begin the panel by acquainting you with some terminology that's vitally important in this field. Without an understanding of these words you might stumble blindly through the book-collecting world."

Armand stood and began to pace about in front of the long table, evidently more comfortable speaking on his feet. "You see, an old book with no dust jacket, a binding that's falling off, and tattered or partially missing pages might be worth as much as twenty pounds. But an old book with its dust jacket in excellent condition might be worth hundreds of thousands of pounds, depending, of course, on the book."

I only hoped that Rupert Soames was listening.

Armand received sufficient "oohs" and "aahs" to be encouraged. "Yes, dust jackets are very important indeed in book collecting. In fact, an American rare-book dealer wrote a novel about a policeman-turned-book-collector, and one could say that his plot revolves around the importance of dust jackets. I encourage you to look it up for a fun read—it's called *Booked to Die*, by John Dunning.

"All right. An equally important area is that of condition. We begin with 'as new,' which is as good as it gets. This term may be used only when the book is in the same immaculate condition in which it was published. No defects, no missing pages, no library stamps, et cetera are allowed, and the dust wrapper must be perfect and untorn. 'Fine' condition is close to 'as new,' except that the book is not crisp. The term 'fine' also means that there are no defects. If the dust wrapper has some sort of defect, or is torn or worn, these faults must be called out. A 'very good' book is one that shows wear on the binding, paper or dust wrapper, but has no tears. Again, it is only ethical to note all defects to the purchaser."

I knew these basics, and again tuned out. It was an excellent opportunity to look for the book dingbat in the catalogues, embedded as Denny had mentioned in the vendors' listing. My eye scanned for anything out of the ordinary, and indeed, something caught my eye as I browsed through the catalogue from a Unicorn Booksellers, Ltd. I turned back through the last few pages, not certain exactly what I'd seen. But there it was indeed, three pages back.

Buried in the dealer's sport books list, in miniature version, and used as a sort of bullet to precede a book on football statistics, was the Stonecypher dingbat. The symbol had acquired a decidedly ominous appearance the last few times I'd seen it, and after talking to Denny I knew that it meant not only that the dealer was in the sinister group that he and Ian had told me about—the bookstealing ring, perhaps—but that there was a meeting of the group concurrent with the book fair.

I searched the catalogue for further occurrences as Armand continued, now on the subject of bindings. On a whim, I flipped to the back of the catalogue. *Printed by William Farquhart, MXMXCVII.*

I nudged Angela, and she almost seemed relieved at the interruption. Holding the catalogue over in front of her, I pointed at the dingbat, then flipped to the inside back page so she could see the credit Farquhart had given himself. She arched her eyebrows as if to say, "Interesting . . . what do you make of it?" I pulled out a pen and scrawled *"Tell you outside"* in the margin.

"Finally, " Armand continued, "it saddens me that I must touch on one rather unpleasant aspect of the rare-book trade. Because of ambiguities—some books being marked 'first edition,' for instance, and others not—some booksellers will take advantage of the novice collector and pass off a second as a first, or a doctored book as an original, or a piece of rubbish for a masterpiece. There is nothing but his conscience to prevent an unethical bookseller from fobbing off an inferior book club edition as a first edition, or one that has been repaired—perhaps with pages taken from another book—as an original in 'perfect' condition. Only the expert would be able to tell for sure." Armand regarded his audience sombrely.

"So, I would say, in conclusion, if something seems too good to be true, then it probably is. Should you encounter that situation, I would encourage you to consult an expert. As you may know, Folio B, of which I am a member, conducts such consultations, and does valuations for a small fee, which goes toward our charitable book restoration efforts. Our leaflets are on the table by the door, and on the information tables in the main room."

When Armand sat down, a number of hands shot up, but the moderator of the panel spoke into his microphone and informed us that we would have to save our questions until each of the participants had spoken.

William Farquhart stayed seated and spoke into his microphone. I thought he looked just a bit—well, rumpled, for lack of a better word. Perhaps he'd had to hurry to arrive on time. "My good friend Armand has done an admirable job of telling you all about condition." Armand, his nose stuckin a water glass, bowed his head in acknowledgement of the compliment.

Farquhart continued. "I'd like to talk to you today about first editions, and first states. It's just the slightest bit confusing, but essential to know if you want to collect books." I knew about this too, but I wanted to hear how Farquhart presented it. As I studied Farquhart, I was surprised to notice dark circles under his eyes. He looked as if he hadn't slept in a week. Perhaps it was all the printing jobs he'd taken on for his fellow dealers.

"If you remember nothing else," he was saying, "hang on to this: the first of anything is the best and most valuable, and the first of a first of a first is even better. I think of it as building a tower of firsts." Farquhart smiled at the intrigued but confused looks in his audience. "What on earth is he talking about, you ask? Well, many of you will be familiar with first editions. That is the first version of a book that comes off the presses at a publisher's behest. Now, of course there are first printings, second printings, third, and so on. So, to begin our tower of firsts, the first printing of a first edition is the one you want.

"On with the tower. Sometimes a publisher or a printer will make a mistake—a misprint or a factual error—and will go back and correct it. The correction might come after fifty books have rolled off the presses, or ten thousand, or two hundred thousand. At any rate, whenever the correction has been made and the presses started up again, the product thereafter is known to book collectors as 'second state.' So what you want is the first state of the first printing of the first edition."

I couldn't help but think of the blasted Stonecypher first editions with their misprints. My great-grandfather had evidently drawn the line at allowing the deliberate mistakes to continue beyond the first edition, despite Stonecypher's probable request to do so.

"All right?" Farquhart made a show of looking over the audience briefly to see if people comprehended. Evidently satisfied, he continued. "This business of firsts applies even to items other than books. Let's say that an author makes notes for a book, then puts the project aside for twenty years. He picks it up and decides to start again, and eventually writes the book, gets it published, and becomes famous. Even if he wrote the book based on the second set of notes, the first set is the more valuable—the more collectible.

"Do remember, however, that collecting should be done according to your personal taste. It doesn't matter if something is sought-after by collectors; if you don't like it, you shouldn't feel you ought to acquire it. Something that might be very precious to you might not have value in another's eyes at all."

"Now, as my learned friend Mr. Beasley mentioned, a word of caution. In looking for firsts—of any kind—it's *caveat emptor* in the extreme. There are first editions that are first *book club* editions. There are first editions that are first *US* editions, or first *UK* editions that are not first editions in the truest sense of the word.

"Adding to the confusion is that most first editions are not marked on the copyright page, or anywhere else, as such, and in that case the bookseller can tell you anything he damn well pleases. That's when you either need to buy from someone you know or trust, or call in an expert."

Farquhart seemed satisfied that he had finished. "That's it for firsts; thank you."

The elderly gentleman from the British Museum spoke next about incunables, or "inkies"—books from before the sixteenth century, when printing presses came onto the book-publishing scene. Since I already knew a good deal about that aspect of old books from the Malconbury Chronicles and other items in the Plumtree Collection, and since the gent was a crashingly boring speaker, I turned my attention back to the catalogues and tried not to make crackling noises as I turned the pages. Angela gave me a black look, as if I were fidgeting in church, and turned back to the lecture. I carried on cheerfully, flipping quietly through the catalogues, looking for more dingbats, knowing that it would irritate her.

I'd checked the listings of a bookseller called Butler and Sons. Finding no offending symbol among their books, I moved on through the Cs, Ds, and Es to Fyffe Ltd. Nothing there either. And none of them had been printed by Farquhart. I had begun to think that I was making too much of it all, and that it had only been some sort of odd coincidence, when I found another. This one was in the catalogue of a bookseller called Morris of Hull, and immediately preceded the listing of Dorothy Sayers's classic mystery, *Gaudy Night.* No possible relation to Stonecypher there either. Turning to the inside back cover, I noted that the small but elegant catalogue had been printed by Farquhart too.

I reached over, took the first catalogue from Angela, and compared the first entry to the one in my hand. I shook my head in frustration. Angela frowned at me, as concerned and puzzled as I was.

The incunabula expert wound down his slow torture at last, and the moderator invited questions from the audience. There was a question from the floor about bindings, and I whispered, "Let's go."

We quietly gathered our papers together and left. Once outside the door, she asked in characteristically blunt fashion, "So what does it mean?"

"I can explain part of it." I hadn't had a chance to tell her about that part of my chat with Denny yet. Speaking quietly as we walked together down the nearly empty hall towards the large room where the books were displayed, I said, "You know the bookseller friend I told you about, who's been—er—advising me."

She nodded.

"He said he worked out years ago that these symbols in the catalogues have something to do with calling together a group of booksellers. It's all extremely secretive, and"—I lowered my voice still further—"guess what they do to people who find them out?"

Her eyes narrowed. "This is unbelievable. All of this has been going on right under our noses in our green and pleasant land—all this violence." She shuddered. "I say we find out what's going on—besides the little book-exchange our friends in Folio B have set up with the libraries. What do you make of the fact that Farquhart printed both of those catalogues with dingbats in them?"

I shrugged. "He has a reputation for fine printing—small items done for friends. It's possible that he merely prints what they ask him, or . . ." We looked at each other, and I knew we were thinking the same thing: Farquhart had an engraving for the dingbat in his printshop—if only in ten-point size. "While we're here, let's start by paying some quiet visits to the stands of the two booksellers who have the symbol in their catalogues."

"Mmm."

The ballroom was reminiscent of a large sardine can, with only a slightly less pungent aroma. Scores of vendors crammed the cramped room, sweating up a storm. It was three-thirty, and it must have been at least one hundred degrees Fahrenheit in the room. I felt sorry for the vendors, including Max and Madeline; we could come and go, but they were stuck here for days on end.

As we strolled down the nearest aisle, between two rows of vendors, I searched through the directory of dealers. Individual vendors had rented ordinary hotel bedrooms to display their wares. Yet another charming characteristic of the Hotel Russell: private vendor rooms. Unicorn Booksellers had Room 328, and Butler & Sons had 521. At least that was some sort of pattern; both of the vendors with dingbats were among the fifteen that had private rooms.

I pointed out the private room business to Angela. "If you don't mind, I'd like to see if there are any more."

She nodded. "You've done A to H; I'll take I to P, you do the rest."

We skimmed the catalogues for the pesky little symbol; it wasn't easy, because in ten-point Bodoni it blended in rather well with the small type used throughout most of the catalogues. "Here," she said, thrusting hers under my nose. "G. Jacks, Travel Books. By a book entitled *My Experiences in Manipur and the Naga Hills*." She made a face, then flipped to the inside back cover, where neither of us was surprised to see Farquhart's imprint.

"It's odd that none of the listings seems to be related to Stonecypher in the least. But there's some correlation; I *know* there is—and I know it's significant that they all have Farquhart as their printer. I hope there's time to look at some books when we've finished playing detective," I said, pulling my ticket out of my pocket to see how late in the day the fair continued. "Good. Open until six." It was a quarter to four.

I thought ahead to the rest of the day. "We've got two more hours here. Then what do you say if we nab a bite at the Book and Binder? I've got the wine class at seven, but there'd be time for us to chat about the announcement and—er—everything."

"All right." She spoke unenthusiastically.

"Alex Plumtree! It's been ages! How are you?"

I must have jumped nearly a foot when I felt a stout clap on my back. It was an elderly bookseller friend of my father's, from Folio B in fact, who had been at our house several times. My father often had him in to show him some new find he'd made for the library. I assured him that it was lovely to see him again, and introduced Angela as one of the Plumtree Press authors to prevent him jumping to conclusions, which earned me yet another nasty look from Angela. We chatted on about the heat, my two best sellers from Plumtree Press's anonymous author, and the success of the man's bookshop in Knightsbridge.

I was preparing to extract myself tactfully from the conversation, when he suddenly frowned and said, "Say, you knew Denny Minkins, didn't you?"

I froze. "Knew?"

He nodded gravely, and I couldn't help but wonder if he was part of the sinister group that had threatened us. "You haven't heard, then?"

All I could do was shake my head. I felt sweat trickling in rivulets beneath my shirt, but the warm room had suddenly gone chilly. Angela took my hand, possibly to quiet the shaking of her own. I was actually glad of the comfort, and for once didn't try to distance her. I knew what he was going to say.

"A customer came in and found him in his shop on Bury

Street, just yesterday, sometime after noon. It's difficult to see how it could have happened, but evidently one of his long bookshelves fell over on him—it—er—I'm afraid it crushed his skull." He shook his head, grimacing.

Angela's grip tightened on my hand.

"Your offices are in Marcus Stonecypher's house, just over in Bedford Square, right?" he continued. I nodded like an automaton. "You'll never believe what they found on his desk—one of those big, open-book dingbats from Stone-cypher's books." Again he shook his head. "Strange, isn't it?"

No doubt he could see that we were visibly shaken. Though I suspected virtually every member of Folio B at this point, including him, my father's old friend seemed disturbed that he had caused us grief. "I'm sorry," he said, looking from me to Angela and back again with apparently genuine sincerity. "Didn't mean to ruin the fair for you; just thought you'd like to know."

Still, we didn't—couldn't—respond.

"Good-bye, then—Alex, Angela." He departed, somewhat taken aback by our reaction, or lack thereof. I think I managed to say good-bye.

Angela, with the same blotchy look she'd got on Sunday when she went pale under her tan, looked up at me. "He's the one," I said, tears stinging my eyes. "Denny Minkins is the one who told me about the booksellers with their dingbats in the catalogues." Woodenly, I went on. "I led the man to him. I killed him, Angela."

Uncomprehending, she stared at me for a moment, then seemed to almost visibly shake herself into action. "No, Alex. Don't. Of course you didn't kill him," she said in a no-nonsense voice. "Come on, let's get out of here." I let her lead me out of the ballroom and into a space sheltered by several large potted trees near reception. "Now. What man are you talking about—the man you say you led . . . ?"

"A man with an ape-sized neck, who followed me from Bedford Square to Denny's yesterday morning. The occupant of the white Mondeo."

"Ah." she understood it all, then. "I see."

I was watching the terrible knowledge register on her face,

when I caught a glimpse of Armand and Frank walking away from us, behind Angela. They hadn't seen us, and spoke in low tones as they walked down the hallway that led past the Virginia Woolf room.

"Look," I said, nodding after them. "What do you suppose they're up to?"

She turned and looked, then swung back to me. "Do you really think Armand is involved? I thought you respected him, admired him."

"I do," I lamented. "That's part of the reason I find myself so confused about all this."

Another familiar figure caught my eye behind Angela. William Farquhart trotted out of the ballroom and down the same hall Frank and Armand had travelled moments before. I caught Angela's eye and motioned with my head towards the hall again.

"Interesting," she said.

When we saw Lord Pillinghurst follow Farquhart down the same hall, I began to think I'd been left out of a Folio B board meeting. There were others turning down the same hallway, certainly, and I wondered which ones were part of the scheme. They were all so serious, so definite about where they were going. These were not men shopping for books.

I turned to the back page in my catalogue, where information on the hotel was provided, including a floor plan. Beyond the Virginia Woolf room were two smaller rooms, the Lytton Strachey and the Dorothy Sayers.

"I'll be back." I left Angela poring over her dealer catalogues with such concentration that I wasn't even sure she'd heard me. I didn't exactly want to be seen by those passing down the hallway, but I did want to be a bit closer to see if I could overhear what they said. As I wove my way towards the ballroom door, staying to the side of the lobby so as not to attract too much attention, I saw a very curious thing. For several moments afterwards I stood with my back to the hallway and the ballroom door, fiddling with my catalogue to look busy while I replayed the action in my head, hardly believing it had happened.

Rupert Soames, of all people, had come out of nowhere and was heading in the same direction as the other Folio B members. Since he always reacted to me like hot oil to water, I pressed myself back as close as I could to the wall, trying to melt into it.

A dark-haired, compact man in a navy blue suit passed Rupert, heading for the ballroom, and discreetly slid something into his palm. A note, perhaps. It happened so quickly, I couldn't be sure, and it was so odd—they didn't stop or acknowledge each other at all, and Soames quickly concealed whatever it was in the palm of his sizeable hand.

I wanted to know who the gent in the blue suit was. I went into the ballroom after him, knowing he couldn't be far ahead. The crowd had thinned a bit, as it always did late in the afternoon, and I saw his back moving down the first aisle to the left of the door, between two solid lines of booksellers' tables and temporary shelving. Following him as casually as I could, I continued walking after my peripheral vision had seen him stop at a table and sit down there. As I passed, I glanced up at the sign. *T. Docherty, Bookseller, Belfast*. Walking at the same pace, I continued to the end of the aisle and turned up the next, checking my watch more for something to do than any urgent need to know the time. Nearly four o'clock.

Angela didn't even look up when I found her in an overstuffed chair in reception and sat down next to her. She was hunched down over the low coffee table, her shoulder blades jutting disturbingly out of the back of the linen jacket, studying something. I bent over and looked. She had written down the vendors and their dingbat-preceded entries on a piece of paper, probably in much the same way she had first written down the Stonecypher sentences. They weren't even in the same format, but they looked like this:

• Sayers, Dorothy. Gaudy Night. London: Victor Gollancz 1935. First edition. Fair, slightly rubbed. Rare. £50.

• volume 29-8 of Football Facts, Chauncy Walters et al., eds. London: Edwards. 1959. Complete but worn, some torn pages. £15.

♦ Johnstone, Major-General Sir James. My Experiences in Manipur and the Naga Hills . . . £430. Sampson Low, Marston and Company, 1896. First edition. 8vo, original blind-stamped red cloth gilt; ppxxvii+[i] +286, with photogravure frontispiece . . .

Denny had said that the dingbats in the catalogue had something to do with a meeting, so I looked at the listings in that light. When I spotted the "430" in the last entry, it all fell into place.

"Angela," I said, trying to keep my excitement in check. "I've got it."

"What?" she asked, looking as if I'd just awakened her from a dream.

"It's the place, date, and time of their meeting. Look. The first item in the first listing is "Dorothy Sayers." The Dorothy Sayers room is at the end of that hall. The second item in the second listing is 29-8—the twenty-ninth of August. And look at the third—430. Half past four."

She looked at me wide-eyed. "My God. You'd have been better at this Stonecypher stuff than I was."

"By the way, I saw a man who turns out to be an Irish bookseller pass Rupert Soames a note. It was all very underhanded; they didn't even look at each other."

Narrowing her eyes, she turned her head slightly and stared into the middle distance. "What do you think it all means? What on earth are they up to?"

I knew it was a rhetorical question, coming from Angela, but I couldn't help myself. "I think it means that Folio B is up to no good, as Virginia Holdsworthy wrote. I think they murdered Denny and have similar plans for us." I shifted on the edge of my chair. "Would you be willing to go to the front desk and ask what group is meeting in the Dorothy Sayers room at four-thirty? I'm afraid I'm too recognisable round here."

"Right." She sat up, slipped her heels back on, stood, and strode away in the white suit. It seemed to me that Angela's shoulders drooped uncharacteristically. It might have been my imagination, but she seemed to be looking more and more tired lately. But then, who wouldn't spend a few sleepless nights after what had happened to her—and her first novel— in the last few days? I watched her cross the room and wondered again if she was ill. Where did her world-weary, beyond-it-all attitude come from?

Sighing, I realised I wasn't exactly in top form myself at that point. Events were taking their toll on both of us. Straightening my shoulders with resolve, I watched Angela as she completed my little errand.

Catching the attention of the same woman I'd confronted about the misspelling, Angela spoke to her briefly, then turned from the desk and walked back towards me. The skin seemed to be stretched tightly over her cheekbones as she neared my chair and said wryly, "Private party."

I don't know what I'd expected, but was disappointed nonetheless.

"Come on," she said, boosting her bag higher on her shoulder. "We can't bring Denny back now. Let's go and look at the books. There's safety in numbers."

With a start, I remembered that this was the day the letter had said something would happen if I hadn't called the distributor and told them to shred Angela's novel.

Something certainly had happened.

I stared in amazement as Angela actually proceeded to shop for books, despite what we had learned about Denny. She seemed to revive, and had a fruitful time at the book fair; she found several items that she absolutely had to have. There was a biography of Bach from the nineteenth century that had a portrait of him inside the cover, a Stonecypher in decent condition that bettered her existing copy of that particular book, and a book of Wordsworth's poems published in a sort of collector's edition, with deep green embossed leather and gold leaf.

After she'd made her purchases, gentleman that I was, I fulfilled my promise and escorted her round the corner to a dinner which she barely touched—the Book and Binder had a mild curry that night—and ordered her a glass of wine. I opted for a conservative half-pint, reflecting that it would have been a day for indulging—champagne at lunch, beer at dinner, and wine at the oenophile's class barely half an hour later.

The Neck, who'd been waiting in the Russell Square gardens across from the hotel, had followed us into the pub. As I stood at the bar watching the Watney's flow into the glass, I half-considered approaching him and asking if he fancied a tipple. In the end I merely raised my glass to him in greeting as I left the bar, but he turned away, pretending not to see.

When I returned with the drinks, I was touched to see that Angela had set the advance copy of her book on the table, and was studying the cover as if to commit every detail to memory. "Nice, isn't it?" She pushed the book away and nodded brusquely, and it took five minutes of animated chatter about cover design strategy to get another response out of her. I couldn't blame her for being discouraged; I knew how she felt. The joy had gone out of it all.

As I sat trying to make conversation about anything but *The Stonecypher Saga*, I found myself continually torn between clinging to the trappings of my once-normal life and retreating into the gloom of my new and ominous life of the past few days. Was there any point in continuing the wine class, or even in having dinner? There was, if we managed to get through the publication of Angela's book on Wednesday unscathed. Then all my plans for the holiday with Sarah would come to fruition, and life would be worthwhile again.

I sighed and left Angela at the table while I went to get her a second glass of wine. When I returned, she was studying the surroundings, presumably to avoid thinking about her book. She hadn't been to the Book and Binder before, and the tools of the trade finally captured her interest—at least momentarily—as I had hoped they might. We sat under a shadowbox frame that contained an old engraving of a binder at work behind his loom, other binding and restoration tools, and a few supplies. Nestled inside the brown-velvet-lined box were, I explained to Angela: a sheet of gold leaf, thin as tissue; a hand tool called a "line," which resembled a pizza cutter; a gouge, for impressing curves into leather bindings; and a leather paring knife next to a piece of burgundy suede. Tonight the tools looked violent to me, though I'd seen them there hundreds of times before and never given them a second thought.

I explained the uses of the various tools, but conversation faltered again after that, and Angela seemed preoccupied. We both knew we'd been avoiding the obvious. I finally asked her if she wanted to talk about it.

She looked at me with one of her all-knowing, rather bitter looks, and answered. "I've wanted so much to get this book out ever since you suggested it, at the end of the last academic year. I delayed publishing my thesis in academic circles for the sake of the novel, and now that it's finally here, and it's so beautiful . . ." She cast a wistful glance at her book. "It just seems a shame that people are working so hard to prevent it being published. It's—it's *my* book."

She tried to look unconcerned then, which told me she really had strong feelings about it. She gave a harsh little laugh. "I don't know what I'm going to do next." She took a long drink of wine, then set the glass down gently. "I've the reader's position up at Cambridge, but you won't be there, will you?" Her too-bright smile told me we were in deep waters.

"You know I'll always be your friend, Angela. No matter what."

I was aware that those words were as inadequate for her as they would have been had Sarah spoken them to me, but it was all I could do for her. Loneliness, I decided, was part of her sadness; it was a shame that she couldn't share the good news of her first book with her family. They had virtually disowned her, she'd explained one night, for pursuing a career in academia instead of "marrying appropriately." I still remembered the way she'd said those words, and knew that there was someone in her past. Her family must have wanted her to marry him, whoever he was, and when she didn't . . .

She was probably thinking of him that night too. I didn't like to leave her there, in the depths of despair at the pub, but I had to get to my wine class. It was much faster to take the underground to the City than to drive at that hour.

"Can I get you a taxi?" I asked. "You could still catch the seven-ten rocket from Marylebone."

"No, thanks. I think I'll just sit and relish the moment for a while. It's not every day your first novel comes out." She stared at her book sadly, affectionately, for a moment. Then her overbright smile flashed out at me again, a warning. "Maybe I'll have another." I didn't like the thought of her sitting there alone, drinking, but she was an adult. If she wanted to, she could.

Not a day of my life since has passed when I haven't wished I'd done something different that night. As I walked out, I looked back and saw her sitting pensively, her shoulder bones jutting out of the linen jacket, swirling the white wine slowly round in the glass, a faraway look in her eye.

CHAPTER 11

We have a natural right to make use of our pens as of our tongue, at our peril, risk and hazard.
— VOLTAIRE, *DICTIONNAIRE PHILOSOPHIQUE*

By the time I sat down in front of my row of glasses at the wine merchant's in the City, I felt I'd lived at least a week in one day. The Neck had trailed me yet again, riding in the tube car behind mine. I supposed he was having a drink in the wine bar upstairs while he waited for me to finish the class. That night, I'd decided, I would definitely be spitting out the wine after tasting it, though it always seemed a terrible waste. Especially considering the wines this gentleman served.

Mr. Falke, my instructor, ran one of the finest wine establishments in the kingdom, an institution. The Cask was known not only for its unparalleled selection of wines, running the gamut from fine old vintages worth thousands of pounds, to Beaujolais Nouveau, to California chardonnay, to Spanish plonk. The wine bar within the shop was a popular meeting place for young people listed in Debrett's Peerage, and I myself had been there on occasion, though I wasn't in the society register. I wondered if the Neck would feel that he fitted in.

The wine courses were conducted in Mr. Falke's own private office, a large suite equipped with long, well-polished old tables laid out with bottles at appropriate intervals. At both ends there were metal buckets encrusted with silver grapes for spitting in, and slices of French bread on plates to cleanse the palate between tastings.

When we'd all assembled, sitting before pads of paper and pencils at our places for note-taking, and six empty glasses each for tasting, Falke stepped to the front and wished us a good evening. He was a short man with a round face and almost no hair, and was droll in a very deadpan sort of way. "You're in for a treat tonight, you lucky devils," he said, winking at me. Several curious classmates turned to look at me. "One of our number is attending the wine festival in Alsace next week, and I thought we might as well have a taste of the very distinctive and delightful wines found there."

I beamed tired but sincere gratitude at him. We'd all filled in questionnaires on the first night of the course asking why we were studying wines, if there were any of particular interest, et cetera. Having tasted all the wines on that first night without spitting any out, I'd been a bit free with my pen and had mentioned that I was trying to impress the woman I wanted to marry with my knowledge of wines at the wine festival in Alsace. Mr. Falke was evidently quite detail-oriented, to my great good fortune.

"We'll start with a Pinot Blanc from Trimbach of Ribeauvillé, Appellation Alsace Controllée," he said. He tasted from a glass freshly poured by an assistant, and indicated that we should do the same. After a moment Falke shrugged and made a comment about its dryness, and we moved on to a Pinot Blanc from the Hugel winery, which Falke explained was still completely family-owned and had been founded in 1639. "This is the Cuvée des Amours, um, let's see, yes— 1990. I thought so." He held up his glass and indicated that we should all sniff the aroma of the wine.

We swirled it in our glasses to release the scent, and sniffed.

"Mmm. Smell that huge, flinty, fresh-scented nose?" He tasted, and we all did the same. "Excellent, ripe flavors. This approaches a great wine. Can you sense the balance of the sugar with the dryness?"

We proceeded towards the sweeter wines, trying a Gewürztraminer from the same vintner. Falke obviously loved it, breathing air in as the wine lingered on his tongue, and making a little slurping sound. "Aromas of honey, butter, with notes of peach, pineapple, and a pleasingly thick texture that helps flavours persist on the aftertaste." A smile lingered on his mouth after this pronouncement. I did my best, but couldn't catch the butter or the pineapple.

The Rieslings were next, and I found myself barely able to distinguish between them. My thoughts wandered a bit at this point—particularly as I have no great affection for Riesling—and then the hour was over. When Mr. Falke dismissed us, I went up and thanked him rather sheepishly for having given me a custom class.

"Not at all, my dear boy, not at all. One likes to be able to do some good with one's expertise, don't you know?" He gave me a quick smile, then returned to his habitual deadpan expression. "Best of luck, then, Plumtree. If I were you, I'd pop the question over the Cuvée des Amours. Almost magical quality to it, especially in 1990."

I told him I'd keep that in mind and felt quite chipper as I hiked to Bank tube station. So wrapped up in pleasant thoughts was I that I didn't do the Neck the favour of checking for him, though I felt sure he was there.

What if, I thought? Just what if I really did jack up my nerve and ask Sarah to marry me over a glass of that lovely stuff? And what if she actually said yes? I indulged in a bit of daydreaming as I rode the Underground back to Tottenham Court Road to pick up my car. I envisioned us together at the Orchard. I wondered if our children would have my eyes or hers. I almost forgot to get off the train.

I looked at my watch as I walked away from the intersection of Tottenham Court Road and Oxford Street, and up towards the quiet oval of Bedford Square. It was eight thirty-five. I wondered if Angela had got home all right, and at the thought of her I turned down Bedford Avenue and walked back in the direction of the Book and Binder. It was really very close, and it would take only a moment to check and see if she was still there, and if so, in what condition. I didn't want to worry all night if she wasn't back at the Orchard when I got there.

It was a pleasant night for a walk, and a light breeze stirred the trees overhead as I strolled the nearly deserted pavement. I crossed Bloomsbury Way and turned the corner into Great Russell Street, from where I could see the Book and Binder's gently swinging sign.

Even when I saw the police car outside the pub, lights flashing, it didn't occur to me that anything was amiss. It didn't hit me until I heard a frightened-sounding young man who was standing, pointing at the road and saying shakily, "She was just crossing the road there. As I told the police, she wasn't drunk or anything—the car came out of nowhere. Made right for her. Then just sped away. It was unbelievable."

The certainty of what had happened descended on me like a crushing weight. I broke out in a cold sweat. At that moment I knew Angela, too, had been killed, and I knew it had been the anonymous letter-writers who had killed her. Rage and guilt warred within me, and it was only the virtually unbearable weight of it—shock, perhaps—that kept me relatively calm on the outside.

I hurried over to the policeman and asked, "Could you please tell me what happened? I think it might have been my friend who was struck."

"Her name?" he asked kindly enough, but not ready to cooperate unless I produced the right name.

"Angela Mayfield," I breathed.

He nodded. "We identified her from the contents of her handbag."

"How badly . . . ?"

The policeman looked down. "I'm sorry," he said, shaking his head. "She was still alive when they took her in the ambulance, but it didn't look good. Fairly serious head injury, apparently."

My heart sank. "Where did they take her?"

"University College Hospital. But I need to ask you some questions first, please."

I spent the next twenty interminable minutes answering questions about what we had done that day, how she had seemed, did she show any tendencies to depression, was suicide a possibility, and on and on. I answered the suicide in the negative, though she had seemed down when I left. But even before the threats had begun regarding her book, she'd been fighting an internal battle of gigantic proportions. The disappointing relationship with me was no doubt part of it, but somehow I was sure there was more. At any rate, I was quite certain Angela hadn't thrown herself in front of a car the day before her book announcement.

Part of me longed to tell the police that someone had deliberately struck Angela, that she and I had received threats. But our letters were anonymous, and the dingbats couldn't necessarily be considered threats. If the investigating officer had read any of Stonecypher's novels and knew what the dingbats meant, he or she would be slightly more likely to believe me. But even if I could persuade the police that "they" had done it, I didn't know exactly who "they" were. I would sound a complete fool. Glancing round for the Neck, I saw that for once he wasn't there. And I couldn't prove who had come at us in the motorboat; there was no point in bringing it up.

The policeman eventually let me go, and I raced, on foot, back to my car in front of the office. To my utter disbelief, and extreme confusion, it was gone.

"Can't be," I mumbled, confused. Had I parked the Golf somewhere else and forgotten? It had happened before. Sometimes, when in a hurry, I took the tube and temporarily forgot where I'd left my car. I rubbed my face and wondered if I was going berserk. Maybe it was just Angela's accident that had me so badly confused.

The hospital wasn't far, and I was desperate to get there. There would be no chance of finding a taxi unless I ran back to Tottenham Court Road, and by the time I did that I could be halfway to the hospital. I set out at a run, north on Gower Street toward Euston Square.

I burst into the emergency room and enquired about Angela. A nurse behind the desk informed me that she was in intensive care, on the fourth floor, and that I wouldn't be able to see her. I thanked the nurse and went straight up to the fourth floor anyway.

Not really thinking, I headed over to the nurses' station, where there was a wall full of monitoring equipment beeping and flashing, and caught the eye of the nurse sitting down behind the desk.

"Angela Mayfield?" I enquired. Before she could help herself, her eyes flashed to one of the glass-walled rooms behind me and to the left. I looked where her eyes had been drawn, but saw only white curtains pulled and the footboard of a bed.

"Are you related to the patient?" she asked, looking businesslike.

"Yes. I'm the only family she has at the moment." This was the truth, considering the mutual abandonment of Angela by her family, and of the Mayfields by Angela. The nurse looked dubious, but something in my eyes must have persuaded her.

"All right; in that case, you'll need to complete some paperwork for us." She pulled papers from four separate cubbyholes in her desk, shuffled them deftly into a neat stack, and clipped them onto a board. She reached for a pen and handed the whole thing to me, saying, "I'll call her doctor for you; he was just here. She's in 405."

I hesitated. "Can you tell me, please—will she be all right?"

She must have seen the despair in my face, and gave me a sad little smile and a half-shake of her head.

"It's not good," she said gently. "I'm sorry. We'll know more in the morning. All right? I'll call her doctor. You can wait over there."

She indicated some chairs lined up against the wall in assorted primary colors. I nodded and moved away, peering into Angela's room as I went. The door was open, but white curtains surrounded her bed. I stepped in further, and heard the ominous sucking and wheezing sound of a respirator at the same moment that I saw her unrecognisable face, swollen and cut and completely surrounded by the white bandages that swathed her head.

Stunned, I stepped back out of the room, praying that she would live. I made my way to the ugly chairs and sat down. I tried to turn my attention to the papers the nurse had given me, but I stared at the words for a long time before they made any sense. Finally, with shaking hand, I provided the information they requested.

I completed a form with her name, address, religion and age; a form stating that I would take charge of her when she was released; and a form that said I would give permission for any emergency surgery required. The nurse brought over a plastic bag containing her jewellery, bag, leather totebag, and one severely damaged copy of *The Stonecypher Saga*, and I signed another form saying that I had received all of the above. I sat on the bright blue plastic chair against the wall, staring at the once-shiny dust jacket that now had a deep rent in the cover and was smeared with blood and grit. Perhaps I should have called the distributors and Kei-King and had them *hold* the book, at least.

But until when? And was it right to give in to pressure like that? England's stand against terrorism was firm; the country never gave in to demands, the royal family never cancelled an appearance because of threats. This had always seemed very brave and right to me, but now I was the one affected. Should I be any different? Should I have decided, for Angela's sake—and Denny's—to be a coward?

Tortured with guilt and confusion, I put the book down with the rest of her things on the red chair next to me. I leaned forward, elbows on knees, and let my head fall into my hands. I held on to great tufts of hair and tried to still my guilty, racing thoughts.

A hand fell on my shoulder. I looked up to see a man in a white coat, wearing a stethoscope round his neck.

"Are you Angela's friend?" He was Indian, and had a strong accent.

I nodded, and he sat down next to me. "Ranjan Michaels. You are . . . ?"

"Sorry." I shook my head as if that might help clear it. "Alex Plumtree." I had learned not to say that Angela lived with me, because it was so easily misunderstood. Instead, I said, "I'm Angela's publisher—and also her family. She's—um—estranged from her parents. Her book was coming out tomorrow."

He acknowledged that with a nod. "To be perfectly honest with you, Alex, I have no idea what will happen with Angela.

Her skull was fractured, and an electroencephalogram, EEG, showed some loss of brain function." My heart sank. "But at the moment we have no idea whether this loss, and of course her unconsciousness, is due to swelling from the trauma or actual brain damage. We won't know for a day or two, maybe more. There is a very slight chance that she might recover completely; then again, she might have permanent damage." He looked at me closely. "Are you willing to assume responsibility as her guardian?"

"Yes." I thought I understood where he was leading. Angela might need permanent care. Though disastrous enough in itself, providing care wouldn't be a problem—I could set her up in her own suite at the Orchard with a nurse, occupational therapists, whatever it took.

"You might have some difficult decisions to make, depending on how the next few days go; but, then, you already know the future won't be easy for either of you."

I froze. He couldn't know about Folio B. "You mean, because of her injury?"

"Well, of course, as I say, we won't know how difficult life will be for her until a few days have passed. I was referring to the leukaemia. We found it on her Medic-Alert card, in her bag."

For just a moment the bright hallway went dark as his words sank in. Then the lights came back, more cruel than ever. "Leukaemia . . ."

Suddenly her exhaustion and frailty, her almost manic drive to experience all that life held, made sense to me. I was sorry for all the resentful thoughts I'd ever had about her pushiness, her insistence on her own way. She had to get all she could from life, and quickly.

Her behaviour earlier in the evening was perfectly understandable now. She'd nearly got one book out, but might never have the chance to see another published if the issuer of threats succeeded in preventing *The Stonecypher Saga*.

Michaels looked at me in surprise. "You didn't know?"

I shook my head.

"I'm sorry. She had her doctor's number in her wallet, and we called to check for any drug allergies or other relevant history. It's possible that she's in remission now; I'd say she's putting up a good fight."

I stared at him, understanding so much that I hadn't before.

Compassionate brown eyes looked back at me, then blinked. "For now, you should go home and sleep. It will be a matter of waiting; she's not in immediate danger."

"Is there anything at all we can do to improve her chances?"

He pursed his lips and shook his head. "No. As far as the injury goes, we just wait and see. I'll be here tomorrow morning; feel free to have me paged when you come." He stood up and put his hand briefly on my shoulder again; I appreciated the small comfort.

"Thank you, doctor." As his rubber-soled running shoes squeaked off down the corridor, I fought down waves of emotion. They threatened to rise up into one disastrous tsunami and sweep me away. I had to be strong, I thought, to stay in control. I had to make this evil deed work against the people behind it, use it to prove their existence to others.

Striving for normality, I glanced at my watch. Eleven o'clock. I gathered up Angela's things and decided to walk back to the Press and sleep on my office sofa. I didn't know if I had any more clean shirts at the office; usually I kept a small stash of clothing in my office cupboard for nights when I worked late and didn't feel like making the trip home.

A hysterical laugh rose up in my throat, and I quashed it just in time. What was I doing, thinking about clothes at a time like this? Who cared what I looked like at the press conference?

On the way out of the hospital I passed a phone, and realised that I owed it to Angela and her family to let them know about her accident—estrangement or no estrangement. I dialled directory enquiries, got the number and punched it in. A young female voice answered. "May I speak to Mr. Mayfield, please? It's about his daughter, Angela."

A moment later a gruff voice came down the line. "Yes? Who is this?" When I had introduced myself and explained what had happened and where she was, there was a moment's silence. "We'll come straightaway," Mr. Mayfield said, and rang off before I could offer to book a hotel room for them or offer other help. I was glad they were coming.

As I walked down deserted Gower Street, still carrying Angela's book and bag, a debate raged within me. Should I reveal my suspicion at the press conference the next day that Angela's accident may have been a deliberate attempt to silence her? The thought of making a media circus out of her injury was despicable. But perhaps it would help bring attention to the fact that people were trying to silence her. As long as they didn't think I was doing it to sell books.

Would I be doing it to sell books?

No. I had to do it to bring public attention to the people who had done this to her. It was still incomprehensible to me that they would try to kill, or permanently maim, someone over a book-stealing ring—especially if "they" consisted of Armand Beasley, Frank Holdsworthy, Lord Pillinghurst, and William Farquhart. Oh, yes, and Rupert Soames. Aside from Rupert and Pilly, it was a rather benign crowd, and I just couldn't imagine any of those men involved in anything so violent. Either their book ring was terribly profitable, so that they had a great deal at stake, or had some deeper significance that I had not yet grasped.

The peace of Bedford Square was soothing to my soul; I almost felt I was coming home as I used my big, old-fashioned key to open the polished brass lock. The door swung open to the smells of construction, and that, too, was soothing. At least part of my life was moving along according to plan, improving ever so slowly, but surely.

I walked past the open door to reception on my way to the stairs, and was struck by a thought. When I'd been in there earlier in the day, I'd had the advance copies of Angela's book. I'd taken one to give to Angela; but were the others still there? It wouldn't make sense for them to do away with Angela but allow her book to survive.

I backtracked and went into the dark room. Flicking on the lights, I saw that Dee's desk was bare except for a catalogue of romance novels she'd evidently been perusing. I checked the bookshelves on which we displayed one of each of our wares, on the off chance that Dee had put them there. No *The Stonecypher Saga* on any shelf in the room.

I turned out the lights and bounded up the creaky stairs; it was also possible that Dee had done exactly what she should have, and taken the books up to the editorial offices. From there, Lisette might have taken one to Rachel, who had worked on the novel, put one in my office, and kept the rest in reserve to display at tomorrow's press conference.

Running into Lisette's office first, I turned on the lights and checked her desk and shelves. No books. Next I searched Rachel's office, then mine, then production; none to be found. "Damn!" I banged my fist on a desk in frustration. They'd been here, taken them.

But I smiled a vindictive little smile when I realised that they'd made one mistake: they hadn't got Angela's copy.

Exhausted, frightened, and thoroughly disillusioned, I went back down to reception, where I'd left the bag containing Angela's things, along with her ruined advance copy. Picking up the horribly scarred book off Dee's desk, I mounted the stairs once again and retreated into my office. There I allowed myself to collapse onto the soft leather sofa against the wall, and went to sleep clutching Angela's novel.

I woke up when I heard someone coming into the building. It was light, and I was blissfully unaware of my problems in the fog of residual sleep until I saw the book, which had slipped out of my hands and onto the floor during the night. It all came back in a rush, and the bright sunlight seemed inappropriate to the sense of utter disaster that had suffused the day.

And on top of it all, it was press conference day.

Thank God I was still there to tell the story, I thought. Then I wondered why they had let that happen. Why had they let *me* live to tell, if they were so deadly serious about everything? What did Angela and her book know that I didn't?

I picked up the book and was staring at it, wishing they had taken me instead of Angela, when Lisette knocked on the edge of my doorway.

"Bonjour," she said gently, perceiving that I had just awakened. Her face fell as she saw the book and my face. "My God, what is it?"

I told her, and she sank onto the sofa beside me. Lisette's

emotions were always close to the surface, and tears streamed down her cheeks as I explained that the doctor didn't know if Angela would ever be right again. I didn't mention the leukaemia; if Angela recovered, I wasn't sure I should let Angela know that I knew. She'd obviously wanted to keep it a secret.

I handed Lisette tissues from a box on my desk, and she mopped her face, sobbing quietly. "Lisette," I said. "There's more bad news." She looked up at me through watery eyes. "I don't think it was an accident. Someone is trying to stop the book being released. They've taken all the advance copies." I looked at the battered copy in my hands. "This is the only one left; she was carrying it when they—when they did it."

"No," she whispered, aghast. "Who would do such a thing?"

I explained about the threats.

Lisette in a temper was an unholy thing to witness, but in this case I was glad to see her anger flare because I knew it would give her strength.

"They won't stop us," she declared, getting to her feet as she heard the phone ring. "It's going to be business as usual around here." She picked up the phone with a vengeance. "'Ello. Plumtree Press, Lisette speaking. . . . What do you mean, cancelled? Of course not! Who told you this?"

Lisette scribbled madly on a piece of paper while she tucked the receiver between her ear and her shoulder. "Absolutely not. The press conference will be held as scheduled. Yes, noon. Uh-huh. *Au revoir,* Mr. Chelmsford."

She looked at me, furious, her cheeks a mottled red. "Someone called *The Tempus* office last night and left a message that our press conference was cancelled. Mike Chelmsford thought it was odd and phoned to double-check."

"So that's what they're doing," I said. "Ring Claire, would you, and have her call the others, let them know it's still on. No, wait," I said as a thought came to me. The decision was, somehow, clear to me now. "Tell them it's industrial sabotage; someone is trying to stop the publication of Angela's book. That'll be a real story for them. I'll get onto the book distributors."

Lisette's eyes lit up. "Right." She hurried to her office, and

I heard her dialling Claire as I went to my desk. I picked up the phone and got directory enquiries for the number of Blackwood's, the book distribution company. Dialling the number, I was relieved that someone answered; it was only eight-fifteen, still before normal working hours.

"Yes, hello. This is Alex Plumtree at Plumtree Press. We were expecting a delivery of bulk copies to your Oxford distribution center; I wonder, can you tell me if they're there, and if they're all right?"

The voice that replied sounded distracted. "I'm sorry, sir, you'll have to be patient. We've only just got the phones working again; there was a fire in the warehouse last night. Let me take your number, and I'll have someone ring you as soon as possible."

"Yes, of course. Thank you." My voice wavered slightly as I gave her our number, and I cleared my throat and told myself to pull myself together. The realisation that these people would stop at nothing shook me yet again. They had so much control, so much clout. . . .

I had to think clearly; there could be no succumbing to panic. I sat down, found the number for the printers in Singapore, and punched it in.

"Eastern Printing, may I help you?"

"Kei-King Lee, please. This is Alex Plumtree."

"Yes, one moment please." I waited only several seconds before I heard Kei-King's voice on the line.

"Alex." He sounded harried. "How did you know?"

I groaned inwardly. "How did I know what?"

A sigh came down the line. "I meant to call you earlier, but the police have only just left. I'm so sorry—I still don't see how it happened. We have watchmen here at all hours. . . ."

I tried to be patient, but in the end had to interrupt.

"What is it? What's happened?"

"Someone broke in and took the films and discs for the Mayfield book. We'd just finished the first printing the other day, a little behind schedule, as you know—so they were in the holding area, waiting to be taken to the warehouse. I'm so sorry, Alex. The hard copies and unbound sheets—or galleys—we kept here are gone too." He was miserable, I could tell, and I did my best to let him off the hook.

"Don't worry, Kei-King. It'll be all right. I'll have our one copy photocopied today, and overnight it to you. You'll have to scan it and reset it. I'm afraid we're being sabotaged by someone who doesn't want this book out. They've even burned the warehouse here in Oxford—the first printing is gone."

"My God," he exclaimed. "I've never heard of anything like this."

"Nor have I," I said. "I'll get you the copy as soon as I can." We rang off, and I dialled directory enquiries again, this time for Angela's college at Cambridge. When I got through I asked for the office of Angela's professor. "Dr. Gilding's not in yet," an embittered secretary told me. "We don't often see him before ten o'clock."

"Could you possibly give me his home number? I'm afraid it's urgent that I reach him."

I could almost hear the wheels turning in her head; she wouldn't mind if he was awakened at home. Serve him right. There he was, lying in bed, earning twice as much as she was. Sighing, she said, "Just a moment." I heard her chair squeaking, probably as she leaned over to her address file. "Here it is: (01223) 99872."

"Thank you," I said, and quickly disconnected. I dialled the number of Angela's professor and willed him to be there.

"Hello?" a fruity male voice answered, sounding a little put out at being assaulted by the phone so early in the morning.

"Hello, Dr. Gilding, my name is Alex Plumtree. I'm Angela Mayfield's publisher. I'm afraid I have some bad news for you."

"Yes?" His voice became concerned. "What is it?"

"Angela's been in a serious car accident, but I suspect that it wasn't really an accident. Someone is trying to stop her novel being published, and they've taken all the copies. The warehouse at Blackwood's had a fire last night, in fact."

"Good Lord!" There was a pause while he absorbed this news. "Is Angela all right?"

"I'm afraid it's not at all good; an injury to the head. We just don't know yet if she'll recover, or—er—how completely she'll recover." I couldn't believe I was saying those words, but there was no avoiding them. "I'm wondering if you could check your files there to see if you still have Angela's thesis, or any other papers she might have left with you."

"Yes, yes. I'll go right in to the office. Surely these people can't expect to silence a legitimate, scholarly—"

"Yes, I know, it's incredible. But they're trying. And I think there must be something she knows that we don't, or you and I would be in the same sort of shape." I realised I'd interrupted him, and apologised. "I'm sorry to be short, but we've got her press conference later this morning, and I'm trying to find out all I can before then."

"Of course," he said, sounding shaken. "I'll ring you when I get to my files."

I thanked him and rang off. Lisette appeared at my door. "I can't reach Claire anywhere," she reported, looking desperate. "Shuna's come in; I've got her calling the invitation list."

"Oh, no," I breathed. I saw my own thoughts reflected in Lisette's worried eyes. "Do you know where Claire lives?"

She nodded. "I'll drive." Good thing, I thought—I didn't know where my car was, and hadn't even reported the theft to the police yet. I'd have to get to it later, perhaps after the conference—if there was to be a conference.

Lisette drove like a bat out of hell at the best of times, and now she drove more aggressively than ever. We didn't have far to go; Claire lived in a run-down but convenient and inexpensive area just on the other side of Bloomsbury, amid down-at-the-heel bed and breakfasts and student housing for the University of London.

Screeching to a stop before one of the narrow buildings, Lisette hopped out and slammed her door. She got to the front door first, banged through it, and ran like I'd never seen her up the steep, narrow stairs to the third floor, lifting her skirt high with both hands to avoid stepping on it with the toes of her high heels. Blowing like a racehorse, she was pounding on Claire's door as I came up behind her. "Claire! Are you there?"

We looked at each other as we heard, at the same time, muffled thumps and cries. I tried the door; it was locked. This wasn't a time to be cautious, so I banged my hip against it with force, and the old, inadequate lock couldn't stand up to the abuse. We were in, and there was Claire, bound to a chair in the main room with a dishtowel tied round her mouth.

Lisette reached for the gag first, and I went to the kitchen for a knife to cut the ties round her hands and feet. "Mmffhh—ahhhh." Claire worked her mouth around a bit and exclaimed, "Am I glad to see you!" She actually smiled. I marvelled at her cheerfulness.

"Are you all *right*?" Lisette was horrified at the way we'd found her, and sounded more upset than Claire. "Did they 'urt you?"

"No." She shrugged. "Not at all. I was scared when they pushed in through the door last night—I was a fool to open it—but they kept saying they weren't going to hurt me. The one man said they had to 'keep me out of trouble for a while.' I wasn't happy about it, of course, but I'm none the worse for wear."

Suddenly she seemed to realise that it was highly unusual for her ex-bosses, now clients, to be standing in her flat, especially while she was in her pyjamas and dressing gown. Her taste ran to pink and frilly, with hearts. She frowned. "How did you know to come here?"

Lisette said, "I tried to reach you this morning and you didn't answer at your office or 'ere. I knew that was unusual, that you'd either be 'ere, or at your office or ours on the day of an announcement. And I tried to reach you because someone 'as sabotaged our press conference."

"Bloody . . . !" Again she remembered she was with clients and stopped herself. "Sorry. I mean, how could they?" She looked incredulous, and angry, and slightly comical in her ruffled slippers.

"Simple," I said. "Incredibly simple. They called everyone and said it was off. Shuna's calling everyone and telling them it's on again."

"But . . . who would want to *do* that? Why?"

"Someone," I said, "doesn't want Angela's book published. They're doing everything they can to keep it from coming out. The bulk copies were burned in a fire at Blackwood's warehouse this morning, the discs and films were stolen from the printer's in Singapore along with their unbound sheets, and all the advance copies have been stolen from the office. The only copy of the book we've got to prove that it actually exists is Angela's advance copy."

Claire's mouth hung wide open. She closed it when she realised I was watching her, and nodded with wide eyes.

"So," I continued, "I'd like to go ahead and tell the press it's a case of sabotage. The only thing I can see for us to do is to put *The Stonecypher Saga* on the bookshop shelves, get as much press for it as we can, and right whatever wrong Angela unknowingly revealed in her book."

"Right," Claire said, understanding dawning slowly on her face, along with something like determination. "We're not going to let them stop us, are we? *Illegitimi non carborundum,* as they say."

"There's just one more thing, I'm afraid. Last night Angela was injured by a hit-and-run driver. She's alive, but just. She won't be at the press conference."

She put a hand to her mouth and murmured, "Oh, no." I feared I had delivered the final blow to her equilibrium.

"I'm sorry, I know it's a shock, especially after all you've been through. But I'll do all I can to make up for it, to speak for her at the announcement."

I hated to disillusion her further, but my mind had travelled on to details. The press were unforgiving. Everything would have to be just right today, despite all of this. "Claire, where do you have the materials for the announcement?"

"Oh, my God! The press kits!" I could see her mind working. She had no doubt personally stuffed them all with the press releases and photos of Angela, not to mention promotional blurbs from other admiring authors. She'd had the unbound sheets for the journalists too. "They're at my office."

"And the caterer. We'll have to call her too—perhaps she received a call yesterday as well."

Claire's eyes went wider still, and she ran to the phone and punched in a number. "Catherine! Yes, it's me, Claire—" There was a moment's stunned hesitation, then, "Wait, no—you don't understand . . . *Catherine!!!*" The shout took us somewhat by surprise, and no doubt did the same for the caterer. "Someone *else* called you and cancelled it after you'd bought all the food. A competitor is trying to sabotage our announcement. It's still on. *Yes*—it's still on. Now, can you do it?" She listened, looking stern.

"All right, good. And next time don't take instructions from anyone but me on one of my jobs, all right?"

Wow, I thought. Claire was really a wonder at bringing people round. First she got the caterer off the offensive, and in the next sentence put her on the defensive.

"Good. See you at the Press later, then." She exhaled, somewhat encouraged by her victory with the caterer. "I'll just get dressed, then we'd better stop by my office and see what they've done with the press kits and the book proofs. Don't worry—I should be able to make more in time if they're gone."

We stood gaping at her, a bit in awe of her energy and optimism. "Why don't you let us drive you to your office?" I asked. "We can help you get things ready."

She nodded, then disappeared into the recesses of her flat, reappearing eight minutes later in a trim navy blue suit, her golden-blond hair pulled into a twist at the nape of her neck. She seemed composed enough as we walked down to Lisette's car. We didn't have far to go; for her office Claire was renting the flat in which I used to live before moving to the Orchard, the third floor of the building just two doors down from the Press. There had been a fire in the flat last year, and it had been rather minimally restored and not decorated at all beyond two fresh coats of white paint.

It was an odd feeling, being back in my old flat. I had fond memories of it, especially times I'd spent with Sarah there, but horrible ones of the fire I had barely survived. It didn't look like a particularly happy place that morning; our saboteurs had cleaned out Claire's files and knocked over or broken everything in sight except the computer. There they had settled for merely clearing the hard disc of files. Her floppies were gone.

So Lisette, Claire, and I spent the morning rewriting the press release from scratch, photocopying, and stuffing press kits. We gave up on replacing the book proofs; we'd have to post them later. I ran over to the Press offices and found a press photo of Angela; all we could do at that point was to make photocopies of it and stuff it in the packet as well.

It was eleven-thirty when we marched with determination back to the Plumtree Press office two doors down. None too early, considering that the announcement began at noon. I couldn't help but wonder where the conscientious S.O.B. marchers were; the paving stones in front of Number 54 were curiously empty. The morning shift should have begun chanting long before. Perhaps Rupert had heard about Angela through the grapevine, I thought, and had been merciful enough to call off his protestors. It was, however, unlikely.

"Well!" exclaimed Claire breathlessly. "We should be fine, as long as the caterer has done her job." She smiled up at me as we hurried across the paving stones. "As we discussed, then, Alex, you'll kick things off after they've all got coffee or whatever. You'll read the first two pages of Angela's first chapter, then open it up for questions. Then we give them lunch. Right?"

"Right. No problem." We walked up the steps at Number 54 and I opened the door for them. "I really appreciate all the work you've done on this, Claire. And I hope you never have to go through so much for a press conference again."

She waved it off. "Why do you think I'm in public relations? I love the excitement. A little danger, some sabotage, sudden changes of plan—it's made for me."

We laughed and proceeded up the stairs to check on the room. Everyone in the editorial department had pitched in to help Derek, the handyman, set up rows of chairs in the large front room normally shared by Lisette and Shuna. It overlooked the oval garden at the center of the square, and was pleasant and airy, especially with the desks and usual office clutter removed. The coral geraniums Lisette had bought in May were hanging on, and made bright splashes of colour in the wrought iron window boxes.

The longer I occupied these offices, the more difficult it became to imagine moving off into the countryside to save money the way so many London-based publishing houses had. But then, having owned the place for so many years, we had no rent to pay, and the rates didn't seem a great hardship in exchange for the privilege.

Claire put her stack of press packets on a table at the back of the room, where the journalists and other guests could pick them up along with coffee, tea, or soft drinks. Then she went off to deal with the caterer. Lisette and I plunked down our piles of shiny folders, too, but stayed and took cups of coffee from the giant urn to fortify ourselves.

" 'Ow are you doing?" Lisette eyed me shrewdly as we leaned against the table.

"Very well, thank you." I gave her the best smile I could. "I'd just like to know what's going to happen next."

"Mmm." Lisette took a large sip of coffee and grimaced. "And you? All right?"

She slid her cup back into the catering company's saucer and looked me in the eye. "I am mad as 'ell. Whoever this is, 'e is not going to get away with it."

I nodded. "Yes. The truth will out."

Shuna appeared in the doorway, looking regretful. "I hate to tell you this," she began.

"You might as well," I said, resigned to disaster.

She wrinkled her nose. "Angela's professor from Cambridge called—a Dr. Gilding. His office at the university was broken into last night. The disc containing Angela's paper, along with half a dozen various hard-copy versions of it, are gone."

I nodded. "Nothing unexpected, at this point. Thanks, Shuna." She ducked out with a rueful smile as the trickle of guests began—with the people from the Historic Buildings Society.

"Mr. Heppelthwaite," I said, putting my cup down and standing to greet him. "Good afternoon. So pleased you could come."

The old man nodded congenially, murmured a thank-you, and said, "There's something I've found in your building plans that might be of interest to you, but I won't bother you now." His eyes flicked to someone behind me, and I turned briefly to see Mike Chelmsford of *The Tempus* stride through the door. "Perhaps I'll call round on Thursday afternoon, if that's convenient; I'll return your plans then as well."

Heppelthwaite was already moving off to a chair at the

front of the room as I murmured, "Yes, of course. Thank you," then turned to deal with more challenging guests.

"What's all this about a conspiracy?" Chelmsford never beat around the bush, though I liked him. A large, athletic-looking man my own age, Mike didn't seem devious or complicated enough to have the job he did; he was an investigative reporter for the nation's top paper, *The Tempus*. He balanced a cup of coffee on his press packet, and had a BBFA book fair brochure tucked under his arm.

I shook my head. "I can hardly believe it myself, but someone, somewhere, must stand to lose a great deal if *The Stonecypher Saga* is published."

He scowled. "You honestly have no idea who?"

I hesitated for the merest fraction of a second, and he caught it.

"Ahh," he said. "So you do know." His eyes were riveted to my face. "Why on earth . . ."

"No," I said. "I don't exactly know who. But I do know something about whoever did it. They're obsessed with Marcus Stonecypher. I've got an idea, Mike. If I let you in on the story, would you help me?"

He looked interested, but didn't want to appear too eager. "It depends."

We cut the deal right then and there, and somehow I was more at ease. With *The Tempus* on my side, I had a fighting chance.

CHAPTER 12

Go, litel bok, go, litel myn tragedye.
—GEOFFREY CHAUCER, *TROILUS AND CRISEYDE*

I checked my watch; nearly twelve-thirty, time to begin the announcement. Glancing through the crowd as I walked to the front carrying the one remaining copy of *The Stonecypher Saga* known to be in existence, I noticed that nearly everyone we had invited initially had come. Besides Mike Chelmsford from *The Tempus*, representatives from *The Bloomsbury Review*, *The Watch*, and *The Nonpartisan* graced the room. Frances Macnamara from the Stonecypher Society was in the front row, and ranged about were less well-known faces from other groups and publications that were smaller but equally influential in their own ways.

Standing at the front of the room for several moments to let everyone get settled, I smiled at those I knew and watched Lisette and Claire working the crowd from the rear. Just as I opened my mouth, I saw Ian walk in and take a seat by the door. I realised with a pang of guilt that I hadn't let him know what happened to Angela, though I'm sure he'd heard the moment he walked through the door this morning. His expression was grave, but he nodded at me kindly.

"Good afternoon," I said to the assembled group, acknowledging Ian with a nod in return. "Events have turned this into a rather extraordinary press announcement." I paused for a moment to allow the seriousness of the situation to sink in. "We were going to announce the publication of Angela Mayfield's first novel today—*The Stonecypher Saga*." I held it up in front of me, with the massive great welt in the cover, through the jacket into the board. Both book and dust jacket were hideously stained, and the mangled dust jacket hung like ripped clothing on the book. I left it that way for maximum effect.

"The novel itself is extraordinary, and I'll give you a sample of it in a moment. But what has happened to Angela *because* of this novel is more extraordinary by far." I looked from eye to eye in the crowd; every one was focussed on me. "You all know that you were phoned by someone pretending to be our publicist, and told that this morning's announcement was off. By the way, our publicist, Claire Dunham, was bound and gagged through the night."

There were "oh, nos" and frowns and much looking back and forth among the audience at that. I continued.

"I'm happy to report that she survived the ordeal in fine shape." I indicated Claire with my head, and when people turned to look at her in the back of the room, she nodded and smiled, blushing.

"That sort of industrial sabotage is bad enough," I went on. "But what you may not know, and what is far worse, is that Angela Mayfield was struck by a hit-and-run driver last night, and is still unconscious. Her injuries are very serious. She may not recover."

A ripple of shocked surprise passed through the room.

I allowed them a moment to absorb this astonishing news, then continued. "It would have been possible to believe that it was an accident had Angela and I not received anonymous threats about publishing the book beforehand." They sat up a little straighter at that, now fully at attention.

"Then, last night, I realised that the unbound book proofs, the discs, and all the advance copies of *The Stonecypher Saga* had been stolen from our offices. Angela was carrying this one." Once more I held up the tragically stained and crushed volume. "This morning we learned that Blackwood's had a fire in its Oxford warehouse where our books were stored, ready to be despatched to the nation's bookshops. I also checked with Angela's professor, in Cambridge, with whom she'd done her doctoral work. All copies of her thesis have disappeared. The first edition of *The Stonecypher Saga* has been wiped out, with the exception of this copy. So, ladies and gentlemen, it would appear that we are under siege."

The great Basil Garth—by far the most obnoxious print journalist in London—couldn't help himself. He heaved his huge bulk into a standing position and wheezed, "Why in God's name should anyone give a whit whether a novel about Marcus Stonecypher is published?" There was a sneer on his spotty, mustachioed and bearded face, and clearly it was his intent to belittle.

I tried to be patient with his interruption. In a way, it helped—it was more interesting than having me stand up there and say it all myself. "Yes—well you may ask, Mr. Garth. I can tell you that there are some rather interesting political and philosophical revelations about Marcus Stonecypher in the book, but nothing that would seem to have any great significance now, since he's been dead for so many years.

"Also a rather fascinating tale, based on rumour— although now perhaps it's passed into the realm of legend— about his relationship with his housemaid, later his mistress, Marie-Louise. As you know, she died under rather suspicious circumstances here in this house, and it was after that that Stonecypher's wife's health failed rapidly. When she died, mere weeks after the maid's death, Stonecypher sold the house to his friend Edward Plumtree. Shortly afterwards, Stonecypher committed suicide. Angela's book suggests that perhaps Stonecypher's wife, Marissa Godwin Stonecypher, knew about their affair and harassed Marie-Louise with nasty notes and angry words."

Francis Macnamara sat bolt upright and went two shades paler. I didn't want to cause her distress, but I did want to tell the story. It was practically popular knowledge, after all.

I looked over the crowd and shrugged, my eyebrows raised in a question. "I'm as puzzled as you are. As Mr. Garth rightly asks, who would care enough to go to such lengths to stop this book?" Garth sat down, trying to hide his disappointment that I hadn't taken offense.

Silence reigned. I could almost hear the group thinking, except for poor Frances Macnamara; she was blushing now.

"I'd like to read you a bit of the book, give you an idea what it's like. It will probably be a couple of weeks until the printers can get more to us. But I pledge to you, and to Angela, that the full story will be told."

Opening to Angela's first chapter, I shifted gears into what I liked to think of as her loping prose—she wrote in long, ornate sentences—and began to read.

It was midnight in the library, the hour at which nothing seems real, and every object, every thought, has the ethereal glow of the distant past and the faraway future. Anna stared at the books spread before her on the table, her eyes alight, unnaturally still. A breeze blew in at the open window, ruffling her papers; still, she did not stir.

It had all begun innocently enough; her doctoral thesis on the works of Marcus Stonecypher had been a daily indulgence. Anna had revelled in the intricacies of his prose; nearly swooned over his subtle insinuations and hidden meanings. And then, one day, not two weeks ago, she had stumbled onto the ultimate hidden meaning. It was there, on the pages before her. And now, for no real reason that she could discern, her professor had forbidden her to use the fantastic discovery she had made, giving the excuse that it was "too far-fetched."

He could hardly deny that her discovery was valid, and not some fantasy of hers. No doubt she was capable of developing Stonecypher fantasies, but hadn't indulged herself that far—except perhaps in the case of Marie-Louise, and her suspicion that Stonecypher's wife had somehow been involved in the maid's untimely death. But she was quite certain that her awareness of the nature of Marie-Louise's demise was not in her imagination.

No, something in his books had hinted it to her . . .

the cruel wife who appeared in *The Figure in the
Library* and several other, later, volumes, and her overwhelming anger and desire for revenge over even the
smallest wrong or slight. . . .

But the code. It all came back to the code. Anna had
discovered it one day after finally becoming exasperated with the misprints—all of them, so many, even for
1910, and especially for a book printed by the renowned Plumtree Press. Each of Stonecypher's four
books was riddled with them, at least one per chapter,
and they drove her to distraction. She had finally decided that if she were to know everything about Stonecypher, be the greatest authority on him in the world,
she should know the misprints completely as well. So
she had written them down methodically, in order, one
misprinted word for every line on her paper, listing the
pages on which she had found them. When she sat up
from her task, at the end of one book, she had been
startled to notice that they formed a complete, perfect
sentence, reading downward in a line from the top of
her page.

"When principalities and kingdoms fall, every man
will come to power through knowledge of the written
word."

Seventeen words. An average of one misprint per
chapter. This sentence came from his first book, and
was all the more meaningful, Anna thought, because of
the dingbat used extensively throughout the book. The
dingbat, a small, decorative printer's device, took the
form of a book with rays of light radiating outward. If
one considered the dingbat, Stonecypher's use of the
word "enlightenment" had special significance.

The other sentences ranged from the mundane to the
bizarre.

"True power comes from the diversity of many
united—not in the several, but in the one."

"In books is to be found the greatest power to enlighten, to introduce ideas and enable them to flourish
for all time. . . ."

I looked up as I saw someone leaving the room. It was Ian. I knew him well enough to recognise alarm in his posture, and the way he bumped the edges of the doorway with his shoulder. He was a graceful, athletic man, and didn't normally bounce off the walls as he walked. Worried, I closed the novel and decided I'd read enough. I hoped I hadn't put still more distance between us; I couldn't seem to do anything right in his eyes lately.

"Questions?"

Juliet Quimby, from a literary magazine called *The Quill*, waved her hand briefly before asking a question. "Alex. This might be in the press kit somewhere, but what's the whole story line?"

"Right. Anna looks for the reason behind her professor's refusal to allow the misprints to be the new subject of her doctoral thesis. He also subtly suggests that she not discuss it with anyone, as it might damage her reputation. He explains that people might think she is a dreamer, not a serious student. Then she learns of a socialist group which keeps a low profile, but which is dedicated to abolishing the monarchy, and follows Stonecypher's tenets. Her professor, it seems, has been associated with them from time to time through the years.

"Anna writes a story for the university newspaper about her discovery, somewhat burning her bridges with the professor, and the editor is excited about it. But then a PPE student—politics, philosophy, and economics—tells the editor that the group Anna refers to in her article has been a fantasy of conspiracy theorists for years, that it would degrade the paper to publish such a story. The editor informs Anna of the reason her story remains unpublished, and in anger and frustration she tracks down the PPE student and follows him. She tracks him to her professor's office, and eavesdrops through the door. Their conversation makes it clear that both men are members of this group and that they are trying to silence her.

"When she goes back to her room, she finds a copy of the Stonecypher book dingbat under her door. For those of you who might be unfamiliar with the works of Stonecypher, in his first novel, whenever the symbol appeared, it meant that tragedy—usually deadly—was about to strike the recipient.

The symbol also represented an occurrence of the supernatural in his novels; a mysterious, all-knowing ghost figure appears from time to time in his books to impart wisdom, and his appearances are linked to those of the dingbat. Literary critics interpret the figure as a symbol of fear in a society moving out of the staid Victorian era into the unknown.

"At any rate, from that point on, Anna is stalked and I can't tell you more or I'll ruin the story. Needless to say, Anna is a young woman of intelligence and ability, like her creator, Angela, and she handles the situation with great originality."

Juliet smiled and nodded a thank-you.

The journalist from *The Nonpartisan*, whom I knew only by name and sight, looked round as if troubled. He stood uncertainly. "Well, Alex, I'm no political expert. But isn't it possible that the same sort of political group is now attempting to silence Angela?"

"I can see how you might think that," I replied, trying not to sound patronising. "It fits so well with the story, doesn't it? But we don't seem to have a political conspiracy theory in Britain. We leave that to the Americans and the Trilateral Commission."

There was scattered laughter at the Americans' ability to transform a think tank into a giant political conspiracy, finding evidence in anything and everything. I considered it a self-deprecating comment; my mother had been American, Sarah was American, and I had been college-educated in the States. Since I was practically half-Yank, I felt justified in a little mild colony-bashing.

"No, really," I continued when the laughter died down, "I have considered it. But I've rather got the impression there is someone out there who's slipped a cog, and believes he is Stonecypher, or is acting on his behalf—something like that." I shook my head. I wasn't about to tell the press about Stonecypher "appearing" in my library the other night; they'd think I'd invented it to publicise our annotated modern editions of *The Figure in the Library*. "If any of you knows something I don't, please . . ." I put out my hands as if to open the floor to them, feeling more like Hercule Poirot in a closing scene than a publisher announcing a book.

Basil Garth said, "Yeah." He thrust his hoary head forward in aggression. "The police should be involved in this. Don't you think you owe your author a bit more effort? I can't believe you're simply allowing this to happen."

This time his comment flew straight to its mark, having roughly the effect of an arrow to the heart. "I am confident that the authorities will be able to help us. They have been involved since Angela's accident. Unfortunately, before the accident, a decorative symbol and an unsigned letter—the forms in which our threats arrived—were not sufficient grounds to involve them."

Though I felt guilty even thinking about such things with Angela lying unconscious in a hospital bed, barely alive, the announcement was going remarkably well. This was the goal of every journalistic press conference; to get people talking, involved, interested in the subject at hand. I regretted only that it had taken tragedy to achieve it.

The questions petered out, and I said, "Thanks for coming, everyone. Lunch is served in the conference room, out of this door and to the right." As I watched people pick up their briefcases and strike up conversations among themselves, Frances Macnamara, the president of the Stonecypher Society, approached.

"Hello, Alex," she said warmly, the skin around her eyes crinkling into a smile. The blue of her eyes was stunning next to the periwinkle silk dress she wore, and against her white hair. She was a very intelligent and comely woman, I thought—very like my own mother had been. "How nice to see you again so soon," she said, looking me straight in the eye. "Thank you again for inviting me today." She held out a hand, which I kissed instead of shaking—something my mother told me I should do for women past a certain age— and she beamed.

"Good to see you again too, Frances. So glad you could come."

"I'm sorry about the situation—it doesn't sound good for your author." She looked genuinely concerned.

"No, I'm afraid it's not at all good. We'll just have to take one day at a time."

"Yes, indeed." She sighed, and seemed to make some sort

of decision. "Alex, I hesitate to mention this, because it's rather unpleasant. But I think you should know." She fixed me again in her bright blue gaze. "People who look into Stonecypher's political past, as the protagonist of Angela's novel did, really do meet with disaster—in real life."

I was silent, trying to keep my expression as normal as if she were speculating about whether it would rain later in the day. Frances was as sturdy, predictable, and firmly rooted in reason as anyone could get. She even wore sensible shoes. It was difficult not to believe her.

"How do you know?" I asked quietly. "Have people stumbled on the misprint theory before?"

She shook her head. "No—not that I know of, at any rate." She frowned again in her concern, and something akin to embarrassment, or shyness, then decided to plunge forward. "Well, it's rather awkward, you see—I don't have actual records of the events, just a vague collection of memories. From time to time an enthusiastic student comes up with a theory related to Stonecypher's politics, based on his literature. Many students contact us at the Stonecypher Society, in fact. They think *we'll* know if anyone does. But we explain that we don't have any information on that aspect of his life, and they go away disappointed. All the books published on him say it was a great unknown, you know." She paused significantly.

"At any rate," she went on, "until now I've thought it a coincidence, but two of the young men who called us at the society have met with rather nasty fates—bicycle accidents, that sort of thing."

There was fear in her eyes now, and she was speaking more softly. Leaning towards me confidentially, she said, "I've become worried we have someone in the society who's a bit—how did you put it?—who's slipped a cog."

Stunned at her revelation, I thanked her earnestly and ushered her in to lunch. As a member of the society, I had its directory of members. I mentioned this and told her I would mull it over, and wouldn't tell anyone without speaking to her again first.

I wanted to ask Frances about the stationery with the engraved dingbat on it, to see if she'd ever seen it before.

After all, the dingbat was very Stonecypheresque, appearing as it did in his books. But before we'd reached the conference room, I'd decided it was yet another of the many things best left unsaid for the moment. I didn't want to drag her into the mire the way I had Denny.

But my lunch tasted like sawdust, and I doubt I made much sense to the journalists at my table. Basil Garth was seated across from me, and after about ten minutes he was half in the bag and doing a fine job of monopolising the conversation, which was mostly with himself, about himself.

"God, it was great! Did you see my exposé of the health inspectors, with the photos of the rat-infested kitchens? *I* claimed that . . ."

In spite of him, everyone seemed to be having a jolly time, and the burgundy was excellent. This crowd didn't need to be entertained.

As I listened to Garth, I thought of how Frances's revelation changed things. Before today I'd had, unbelievably, four possibilities in mind for who could be behind Denny's death, Angela's injury, and the attempt at censorship. One suspicion was that someone certifiable who thought he was Stonecypher was trying to prevent the great author's memory from being tarnished.

Another was that a biblioklept within Folio B, probably in Diana and Frank's book-stealing ring, had a lot invested in Stonecypher first editions and didn't want the great author's popularity diminished—and therefore the value of his books—through a connection with some bizarre anti-Royal political faction. Sometimes I even thought those two culprits could be one and the same; the Stonecypher crackpot could be part of the criminal contingent of Folio B.

Finally, there were the unwelcome possibilities of Rupert Soames and Save Our Buildings behind the dramatic threats, not to mention angry Angus MacDougal—though Mac-Dougal hadn't been angry for long enough to have sent the earlier threats. I grimaced.

My other suspicion, that Angela had planted the dingbats and written the letter—admittedly obsessed as she was with Stonecypher—was now shameful to contemplate.

Frances's revelation had forced me to consider yet another

possibility: there might be a political motivation behind the threats. I took another sip of wine, noticing its slight sourness at the outer edges of my tongue thanks to Mr. Falke, whose wine class of the night before seemed a part of the distant past. I simply could not think of any political group that might be threatened by Angela's revelations.

A colossal headache built beneath my temples as Garth guffawed drunkenly at one of his own jokes. As a waiter delivered the pudding, which, appropriately, was a not-too-sweet plum tart, along with a glass of Riesling, my mind flew to Sarah.

Riesling. Alsace. In two days we were scheduled to begin our holiday. Could I—should I—leave Angela in her fragile state? *Should* I still do it? It didn't seem right to proceed with life as usual when disaster of such gigantic proportions had struck. But as quickly as that thought came to mind, others warred against it, urging me not to miss the time with Sarah. Angela's parents were probably already by her side at the hospital. Surely they could help look after her. Besides, if I didn't go to the book fair in Paris, I wouldn't find out what was going on with the books I'd seen in Holdsworthy's packing boxes, ready to go to Menceau's. I was fairly certain that Menceau's was only a way-station; that they were to be sold at the book fair in Paris.

And what about Sarah? Should I tell her—some or all?

Thanks to my brother Max, in my heart of hearts I knew I would have to tell Sarah most of my current situation. With his insistence on honesty, he had taught me that much. To an alcoholic, he said, honesty was everything. And he'd shown me that without honesty between two people, there was no hope of a relationship. If I kept this from Sarah, ugly as it might be, she would merely perceive it as distance between us. I came up with my own compromise, which was to share everything I could without endangering her.

Eventually my guests left, but none too soon. I'd been wishing for the last hour that they'd toddle off so I could visit Angela and speak to her parents. It seemed that everyone enjoyed the party—some perhaps a bit too much. It was three o'clock when I finally showed Garth out the door; there was no way he'd be able to write an article in his state, I thought. Perhaps we'd have to wait an extra day to see it in print in his paper.

When I got back upstairs, Lisette and Claire had collapsed onto the deserted chairs back in the briefing room. "That is some of the 'ardest work I 'ave ever done," Lisette said wearily, her head drooping, legs splayed in front of her.

"It went absolutely *marvellously*." Claire's eyes were sparkling as she unscrewed the top of a leftover Coke. Its effervescence was not unlike her own as it released a "ffffft!" of carbon dioxide.

"We're going to see some super articles out of this," she continued. "Did you see how they all latched on to *The Non-partisan* journalist's idea of a political conspiracy? I could practically see the wheels turning: censorship plus violence plus conspiracy equals sales." She looked up at me, a little ashamed. "Sorry to put it that way," she said, wrinkling her nose. "But it is true."

"You're right," I said, still standing by the door and the drinks table. "I understand." We were all sobered by the unsettling circumstances of the day, but there was no denying that it had been a total success. Reaching for a Coke out of the melted ice water in a large bowl on the table, I said, "I hope Angela will be able to enjoy it. I'm going to stop by the hospital and see her—then I'd like to check something out at the book fair. I doubt I'll be back before the end of the day."

Claire's eyes drooped despite her enthusiasm, no doubt from her sleepless nightmare of the night before, and Lisette slumped on the hard metal chair. "You two deserve to take off for the rest of the day—we'll take care of the rest of this tomorrow. All right?"

They issued assorted thanks and requests to give them a call from the hospital. "And you'd better take a brolly," Lisette said, glancing at the windows. Grey and white water-colour clouds hung low over the park; darker and more threatening clouds moved in from the west. "Oh!" she exclaimed ruefully. "I almost forgot."

She got up and went to her desk, which had been shoved back against the wall to accommodate the press conference. "You see? That Garth man is making me lose my mind."

Rolling her eyes and reaching into a bottom drawer, she pulled out a small wrapped package. She handed it to me with a smile. "A little something for your trip with Sarah," she said significantly. "Go on—open it."

I tore open the glossy peach-and-coffee-coloured paper and found a small box, about four inches long and one inch across. Opening it, I pulled out what felt like a rather heavy metal object, wrapped in tissue.

I looked at Lisette for enlightenment, and she winked as I pulled the tissue off. "For your after-dark picnics, just in case," she said. "Candles make all the difference." Then I understood. I was holding three stubby, pen-like tubes of bronzed metal that were fused at the top with rotating brackets. When fiddled with, the whole thing opened into a miniature tripod. A small wheel on the inside of the tripod, which resisted my turning it, was nothing more than the lighting mechanism—exactly like a cigarette lighter. I flicked the wheel, and flame burst out of the top.

"It's brilliant, Lisette," I said, pleased with the gadget. I gave her a peck on the cheek. "You're incredible. How on earth did you think of such a thing?"

"You can refill it with butane when it runs out; it's supposed to last for twelve hours," she said, modestly avoiding the question. "And"—she lifted a finger as she adopted her mother-hen persona—"I don't want to 'ear any talk of you cancelling this trip with Sarah. I won't 'ear of it. I will personally take care of Angela while you are gone. We'll set up a rota so that she is checked on every few hours."

I wasn't willing to commit to a decision about the trip yet, but I said, "You're an angel, Lisette. By the way, her parents are probably here by now too—I called them last night, and they said they would come straightaway." She nodded in acknowledgement.

I popped the tripod-candle in my inside pocket, tossed the wrapping and box into the rubbish, said thanks again, and bade them good-bye. Following Lisette's advice, I grabbed a giant dark green and white umbrella out of the corner of my office, and popped the Coke open on the way downstairs.

As I stepped out the door I realised that I hadn't communicated with Sarah in almost forty-eight hours—I hadn't even been home in the last twenty-four. It was disturbing, but there was no question that Angela's accident had changed my feelings towards Sarah and the whole idea of a holiday. Even Lisette had sensed it. I thought again about the fact that I had an obligation to Angela. I'd got her into this—invited her to write the book, got it published, mentioned it to Armand. Didn't I owe it to her to stand by until she was all right again?

And thereby hung another thought. What if she was never all right again? She would probably always battle the leukaemia, for as long as she was able to keep on fighting. Would I feel comfortable walking out on her then? I shook my head, took another sip of Coke, and kept walking, automatically glancing round for the inevitable companion. They were using the Ford; I saw it slink out of its space in the square, so it could circle round and come out on Gower Street to keep tabs on me.

I shook my head at the absurdity of it. And just exactly where was *my* car? For a moment I slowed, and considered going back to ask Lisette to report a stolen Golf. But I really couldn't be bothered; with Angela hanging in the balance, the car could wait.

The walk north on Gower Street brought back a sense of the normal rhythm of life, that some things would go on no matter what. Bread vans delivered baked goods to the tiny bed-and-breakfast establishments up and down the street, which led to thoughts of toast, fried bread, and comfort. Old women in aprons swept the grit and dust off of their steps, and matching old men polished name-plates and door fittings. The street hadn't changed much since I was a boy, a welcome relief from the current state of my life, which was utter chaos.

When I got to the fourth floor, the news at the hospital wasn't good. It wasn't exactly bad, but I had hoped for better. I walked straight up to the now-familiar nurse as she sat scribbling notes in a file. The high-powered downlights cast a halo of light on her shining auburn hair. She looked up and saw me.

"She's stable," the nurse said. "But there's been no change."

"Would you page Dr. Michaels for me, please?"

"Certainly."

I waited for twenty minutes, staring at Angela from the foot of her bed. She looked horrible, with the huge white bandage wrapped round her head, and eyes black from the impact of the car. Her face was a ghastly light yellow colour. She looked as fragile as a porcelain doll. I had to fight the impression that she was already dead and no one had noticed but me.

Dr. Michaels came in and nodded a greeting. "I'm sorry," he said. "There's been no improvement. But she's still with us. And I've spoken to her parents—I finally urged them to leave and get some rest. They're quite elderly, and they were here from the wee hours."

I nodded and rubbed my eyes briefly, as if a piece of grit were responsible for the fact that they were welling up with tears. "Thank you for coming, doctor. I need to ask you a couple of questions."

"Of course." He looked at me kindly. He knew it hadn't been grit.

"Is there a certain time during which she is more likely to improve, after which the chances grow slimmer?"

"Yes." He nodded. "After the first three days it's still possible, of course, but much less likely."

"Is there anything at all that I can do that would help her?"

"Well, some people believe that talking to patients while they're in a comatose state helps. We just don't know if it's true. It certainly can't do any harm."

Hope, and the relief of being able to do something that might conceivably help, made my eyes grow moist again. "Is it all right if I . . . ?" I indicated her bedside.

"Yes, of course. She'll be moved from intensive care later today; you can take her hand if you like. I wouldn't sit on the bed though; we don't want her to be jarred."

"Thank you. I'll be careful."

He smiled his sad smile and went away again on what were apparently perpetual rounds. I advanced towards the head of Angela's bed and gingerly pulled a chair from against the wall over to the bed.

"Hi, Angela. It's me, Alex." The thin fingers of her hand were near the edge of the bed, the golden colour of her tan looking horribly out of place. I picked her hand up carefully from underneath so as not to move her arm; it was startlingly warm and alive, in contrast with her appearance.

"Angela, I'm so sorry. But everything will be all right." I hesitated, aware that I might have just lied. "And there's good news." I watched her face, but there was no response. "We just had your book announcement at the office, and it went really well. Really, *really* well. I think we're going to have a hit on our hands."

I paused for a moment, thinking what to say next. "All of the people we wanted to come were there—Mike Chelmsford of *The Tempus*, Basil Garth—though I'm not sure if that's good or bad—*The Nonpartisan, The Watch, The Quill, Bloomsbury Review* . . . we couldn't have asked for more. And they were fascinated with the premise of your book. I read from the first chapter, through about the third page, I think." I remembered Ian walking out, and told myself I should have stopped in to see him before leaving.

Watching Angela, I had the impression that she was waiting. Was she waiting for life to resume, or for death to take her? Or . . . was she waiting to hear something from me?

"You might be thinking about your accident." I decided to head right into it. Despite her appearance, her brain might be functioning perfectly well.

"I announced at the press conference that we'd had threats, and that we didn't think your accident was really an accident." At that moment there was a twitch under her eye.

I sat up and stared, hoping I hadn't imagined it. "You heard me, didn't you, Angela?" There was no response, but I couldn't ask for everything at once. Encouraged, I continued. "And here's the really big news. Frances Macnamara—head of the Stonecypher Society, you know—had an interesting titbit for us. She told me that since your accident, she's beginning to think there's a correlation between investigating Stonecypher's political life and—um—serious accidents." I had been about to say "fatal" instead of "serious," and caught myself just in time.

There it was again: the twitch. When I spoke again, my voice squeaked out like a teenager's. "Angela, this is great. I'm convinced you can hear me." I felt myself smile for what seemed the first time in months. "We'll have you out of here in no time, and you can help me work out what's going on."

I got a nearly imperceptible squeeze on the fingers that time, which was doubly heartening because it meant that her brain was communicating with the rest of her body too. I dared not think that these small motions were involuntary muscle spasms; I needed to believe that she would be all right.

"I hope this isn't being too demanding," I said. "But if you can squeeze my hand like that again, please do." She did. I beamed, and wondered how much effort it had cost her. "Okay, you're doing wonderfully. Why don't you rest for a bit now, and I'll prattle on about other things."

I talked to her about Garth's behaviour at the announcement, about what we had to eat, the way we set up the rooms. When I had finished with everything that could be of any possible interest to her, I patted her hand and told her that I was going to go back to the book fair to sniff round a bit, and that I would be back later.

Stopping by the nurse's station, I left the good news with them about Angela's responses. They considered it very significant and said they would be certain to let the doctor and Angela's parents know.

I left feeling a tremendous relief about Angela, but curious about what would now happen to me. Everything that she knew, I knew, having read her book, but for some reason they had tried to silence her and not me. Did they think she had grasped something significant and I hadn't?

What did she know that I didn't? As I exited through the hospital's automatic door, emerging into the oppressive atmosphere of an impending thunderstorm, I had a thought that gave me goose flesh. Perhaps Angela had seen her attacker in the moment before the car had struck. The thought made me check round the hospital entrance for the white Ford; it was there, not fifty yards away. I shook my head and began to walk back towards Bloomsbury along Gower Street. It was entirely possible that she had everything worked out, but I had no way of knowing.

It still hadn't begun to rain when I mounted the steps of the Hotel Russell ten minutes later, and I began to blame the low air pressure for my increasingly irritating headache. The Ford had watched me from its parking space near the hospital until I covered most of the distance to Bedford Square. Then it had started up and followed slowly behind, turning toward Russell Square just after I did, and parking again in a convenient space to watch me.

My first stop at the book fair was Max's stand. I hadn't seen him in days—his stand had been jammed with customers the day before, when Angela and I had tried to stop by. I thought he should know about Angela from me. Besides, I wanted to encourage him in his new career of bookselling.

Not that he needed encouragement from me when he had Madeline. The supermodel-like Madeline, in skin-tight dress, and with flowing long blond hair, smiled and said she was glad to see me. I genuinely liked her, especially the kind heart and bright mind beneath the gloss, and was happy for Max.

"Hello, Madeline. How's business today?"

"Just super," she replied. "Max is very pleased. All of his Jack Londons have gone, and there seems to be a run on Wilkie Collins as well." I could see that a lot of the books my brother had told me he was taking to the fair were gone now.

"That's wonderful," I said, sharing their thrill of success. The fact that Max actually sold rare books really impressed Madeline. She was an expert on rare bindings for Christie's. It seemed to be very exciting to her to sell rare books with Max; "actually being out in the marketplace!" was one of the wide-eyed phrases she used, as if it were breaking broncos, or flying rockets to the moon.

"Where's Max?"

"In the bar with a customer." She saw my look of alarm and smiled soothingly. "You really must learn to relax, Alex—and have a little faith." She spoke gently. "I'll guarantee you he's having a Perrier with a twist of lime."

I nodded grudgingly and she went on.

"After the gentleman bought a three-hundred-pound book, Max decided he deserved a drink." We smiled and I congratulated her, asking her to please tell Max that I'd stopped by. I decided not to ruin their day with my news, and instead leaned over the little table, gave her a hug, said good-bye and began to browse. It wasn't that I was really shopping for books; it was more a case of looking at them while I thought about my predicament. I had just stopped at the stand of a vendor who I noticed had a fair stock of old books of music, and was picking up a collection of Bach's two-part inventions to inspect it as a possible get-well gift for Angela, when I heard a voice behind me.

"Alex P.," said Mike Chelmsford. "I'm glad I ran into you. A little while ago I left a message for you at your office. I had a thought that might interest you. A bit far-fetched, I'll admit, but it sounded like you were open to ideas at the press conference."

"Absolutely. Thanks. I'll take all the help I can get."

"All right if we sit down in reception for a bit? They've propped the front door open; it seems slightly less muggy in there." He steered me out to one of the conversational groupings that Angela and I had made use of the day before.

Mike had the physique of a muscular rugby player gone to seed, and his trousers and coat always seemed to be on the verge of splitting. He put down his catalogue and briefcase, then sat heavily. When he'd eased the strain on his trouser legs by pulling them up just above the knee, he leaned towards me confidentially. I moved a bit closer by sitting forward in my chair.

His ruddy face was serious, and he frowned as a trickle of sweat ran down his temple in the suffocating humidity. "Please, don't think I'm a lunatic for suggesting this, Alex, but the similarities seem too great to ignore."

His voice dropped still further in volume, and he glanced round at the surrounding tables and chairs as he asked, "Have you ever heard of a group called the Illuminati?"

I nodded. "Sure. Supposedly it's another Trilateral Commission–type of group, all sorts of powerful people invited to become members—the president, ex–prime ministers—another conspiracy to take over the world." I could hear the mocking tone in my own voice. "But no one knows if it really exists, right? I've always assumed it's another fantasy of the conspiracy-obsessed."

Mike raised his eyebrows in a look that said "Don't be so sure," and went on. "It was the light shining out from the open book in the dingbat you showed me," he said. "It made me think of illumination. Illuminati. And then when Nate from *The Nonpartisan* mentioned the political conspiracy plot, I could hardly believe it. It's as if Angela had planned to reveal a conspiracy by the Illuminati, all except the socialism business. Then again, minor variations might be insignificant."

Whatever it was he was getting at, and I had no idea at that moment what it could have been, I felt a thrill of excitement. Could this be what they thought Angela knew but I didn't?

"What exactly do you know about this group—*if* it really exists?" I asked, impatient to know.

"I hate to disappoint you, Alex, but it really does exist. Their meetings have been documented around the world. It's a group of business and political leaders that meet occasionally to discuss world events—supposedly a think-tank type of group, promoting world peace. But a rumour started somewhere that they have an ulterior motive. Supposedly they're working towards a world government."

I looked at him, astonished. A frisson of fear caused me a mental shiver, but I said merely, "Yes, I see."

He smiled a grim little smile and nodded. "The Stonecypher sentences in Angela's book. If they're for real, they hit the nail on the head. Tell me if I'm not supposed to ask this—but I have to try. I'm a journalist." I smiled. "Also, I'm lazy. I should go to the library and look it up myself. But . . . did Angela Mayfield *really*, honestly find those sentences in Stonecypher's books?"

I nodded. "The misprints are only in the first editions. They were corrected after that."

"So." He let out a big sigh. "It's just possible that her imagination was a bit too close to the mark."

I frowned. "If this Illuminati group is really a force, why haven't I heard more about it in the legitimate press? If it's all above board, it shouldn't have to be secret, right?"

"That's right. I mean, I agree with you. But it was founded as a secret society, because the Church, and the government, and the monarchs were all against it when it was founded in 1776." He shrugged. "I suppose it's still secret, but perhaps for other reasons. From what people have seen, these blokes just attend their little meetings in all corners of the globe and go on about their business. They don't issue statements, publicise themselves, or make a fuss. It's only the membership that has caused speculation—some of the most powerful people in America and Britain, ex-presidents, heads of state from all over the world, leading business people. That's why there have been only a few suspicious, half-joking articles. There are no real sources who will admit membership or talk about the meetings."

"Has the group ever been violent before now?"

He shook his head. "Certainly I've never seen any violence attributed to them. And it's not quite their style; I can't see any of the people who are supposed to be members ordering someone to run down a first-time novelist in the street."

"No."

He looked at me with something like sympathy. "If I see anything in the paper related to this, or hear anything, I'll be sure to let you know. And I'll fax you the articles I've seen on the subject; there aren't many, but they might help."

"Thanks, Mike. Remember, I might be in touch with you too."

"I'd be grateful." He stood and handed me his card; we were done. I stood as well. "Stay out of dark passages."

I returned his smile, thanked him again, and decided I'd wander through the hall one more time before heading back to the Press. At the very least I would write to Sarah, try to finalise my speech for the Folio B conference on Saturday, and possibly try to do some orderly thinking about the mess I was in before stopping by the hospital again later.

Here it was, the most appealing of the London book fairs in all its glory, and I could hardly pay attention to the thousands of books surrounding me on all sides. Ordinarily this would be a special three days, like a romp in a massive toy shop. No book collector could ask for more. But as soon as I picked up a book, I would be distracted by an unwelcome thought—Angela, the dingbat sender, the Illuminati, the figure in my library. . . .

After twenty minutes of half-hearted snooping, I called it quits and walked out into the sultry late afternoon. The sky now rumbled with thunder. I walked back to the office slowly, feeling oppressed in every way. Oppressed by the weather; oppressed by my would-be censors; oppressed by Angela's condition. As I made the brief dog-leg up Bloomsbury Way along a small stretch where no one knew if it was really Bloomsbury or Gower Street, nearly ready to cross the road to Bedford Square, I stopped for a moment. There was our new building—the conglomeration of the two buildings with the alley closed in—from the side.

Viewing it from where I stood, across the street, the old hotel we had purchased stood on the left, and our existing building on the right, with the alley in between like the filling of a giant sandwich stood on end. Harry and his colleagues had made good progress with the alley area; part of a wall had gone up, closing it off from the street, and the roof was already on, apart from the slates.

I was proud of the new development, proud in several respects. Instead of leaving Bedford Square, we had stayed and were not merely hanging on by our fingernails; we were improving the building. And we weren't merely improving our own, we were taking care of the old hotel behind us too. We were reviving the beautiful old neighbourhood instead of deserting it.

Second, when my father had died and it had fallen to me to run the business, I'd worried about keeping it afloat. That had turned out to be the least of my concerns; Plumtree Press was going from strength to strength. MacDougal would help us grow even stronger, become even more of a force in publishing—if we could stand him.

The beginnings of a grin started across my face, and something in my peripheral vision made me turn to look back at the corner. The white Ford edged to a stop at the corner of Great Russell Street and Bloomsbury Way, behind me and to my left. My grin faded.

Its sinister, dark-tinted windows never revealed who was inside, but I knew that the Neck was among them—a hireling taken on by someone with nearly limitless resources. To follow me everywhere I went, twenty-four hours a day, every day, had to be an expensive proposition. Perhaps money was a small concern compared to what was at stake—if they were the Illuminati, with illustrious members all over the world, they could easily afford such an expenditure.

On impulse, I ran into the road and across one empty lane to the car, grasping the driver's door handle and yanking at it, peering in the window all the while. I could see absolutely nothing inside. The door was locked, of course, and didn't budge.

"Open it! Come on—come out and face me. I dare you!"

I wrestled with the handle as if I could force the door open, rocking the entire vehicle back and forth with the vehemence of my effort. At some point I took to pounding on the window, and rather lost myself in the anger of the moment. The car and its occupant, or occupants, remained silent, motionless, unaffected, like a tank in enemy territory.

It wasn't until cars begin tooting behind us, and the motorist immediately behind the Ford opened his door and shouted "Oy! What're you *doing*?" that I stopped my rain of blows, but not before I delivered one last shattering smack that I saw, with satisfaction, rendered a spider-web pattern in the glass. They were not entirely invulnerable.

"You'll be sorry," I shouted into the driver's invisible face, through the spider web. "You wait and see. I'll save you the trouble of following me—I'm going back to the office," I shouted.

Turning on my heel, I walked across the street, up the steps to the office, and let myself into my sanctuary.

CHAPTER 13

Thou art a monument, without a tomb,
And art alive still, while thy book doth live,
And we have wits to read, and praise to give.
— BEN JONSON

The comfort of the old, familiar surroundings of the Press wrapped itself around me like a warm blanket. A huge thunderclap rent the air, and that, too, was a relief. Anything but the endless oppression and uncertainty.

I climbed up to my office, and unlatched and thrust open the small window that looked onto the nearly-enclosed alleyway at the back of the building, hoping for a small breeze to relieve the stuffiness. Then I rolled my desk chair over to the big Macintosh computer, where I had the notebook in its docking station, charging. The first thing I wanted to do was get into PeopleServe. It was a service through which one could purchase airline tickets, check the weather, or research obscure political groups like the Illuminati.

But as I reached for the keyboard, I noticed a piece of paper in the tray atop the fax machine. It was unlikely to be the information from Mike so soon; was it a letter from Sarah? Or a missive from the Illuminati . . .

As I rose to pick up the paper, I realised that I was quite confused about my feelings. Would it be right for me, having caused Angela irreparable damage, to blithely marry Sarah—

if she would have me—and live happily ever after? How would I live with myself? I could barely live with myself for thinking about going away and leaving Angela for a week.

Breathlessly, I snatched the paper out of the tray.

Dear Alex,

I haven't heard from you in a few days, and am wondering if our plans to meet at Orly still stand. Is everything all right?

It's rainy here today, and I'm hoping we have better weather for the trip.

No other news; just let me know if everything is still okay.

Sarah

I grimaced, noticing the relapse from "See you soon, Sarah" to the less cheerful and infinitely more reserved "Sarah."

How could I not have written to her sooner, despite everything? After all the work I'd put into the holiday, and all the time I'd spent thinking of her, I had virtually ignored her for the last few days.

I would do it, I decided, as soon as I'd researched the Illuminati. Surprised at myself for procrastinating yet again, I acknowledged that I wasn't sure exactly what I would tell Sarah had transpired, nor was I sure how I would tell her. More to the point, I was also aware that things had changed subtly between Angela and me, and therefore also between myself and Sarah, without Sarah's knowledge.

The rain began to bucket down as I thrust away that line of thought and started clicking through menus on the computer. I arrived at PeopleServe's general encyclopaedia, then entered the word "Illuminati." Another violent thunderclap shook the floor, and the screen flickered. The characters slid drunkenly sideways and downward for an instant, but remained. The following choices appeared on the next menu: Summary, Newspaper Articles, Books.

"Summary" seemed the logical first choice. I clicked, fascinated, barely breathing in my anticipation.

ILLUMINATI, il-ü-mə-'nät-ē, is a term meaning "the enlightened" in Latin. It has been used to refer to a wide variety of groups, in general, esoteric, ritualistic societies whose members claimed some special type of enlightenment either (1) as a result of mystic illumination by divine power or (2) through a natural exaltation of human intelligence. Accordingly, the philosophical views of different groups of Illuminati were sometimes theistic, sometimes rationalistic.

Eighteenth-century *philosophes*, or intellectuals, proposed to abolish whatever seemed inconsistent with man's enlightened reason. Among the many groups active during the "Age of Enlightenment," the name *Perfektibilisten* was assumed by members of a secret society founded in 1776 by Adam Weishaupt. This society hoped to liberate men from the state's authoritarianism and the church's domination so that they might regain their primordial freedom and equality. This program of "illumination" quickly incurred opposition from the Bavarian government and condemnation by the Catholic Church. Other groups, such as the Illumines, the adherents of Quietism, the Rosicrucians, and the Martinists, have also been called Illuminati.

Fascinated, I scrolled back up to the lines that had caught my attention: *"liberate men from the state's authoritarianism . . . so that they might regain their primordial freedom and equality."* But for the wording, it might have been one of Stonecypher's anti-Royal sentences.

Moving on to newspaper articles, I was struck first by how few of them there were. The most recent of them had been written several months before by someone named Richard Leiby of *The Washington Post*. It was entitled "Paranoia: Fear on the Left. Fear on the Right. Whoever they are, they're closing in." I chose it first of the five and read, scanning through a lot of quotes about people who were afraid the federal government were conspiring against them. Finally my eyes hit the word "Illuminati," and I read more carefully:

The New Order, Coming Up
    "Its object is the total destruction of all religion and
    civil order. If the plot is accomplished, the earth can
    be nothing better than a sink of impurities, a theatre
    of violence and murder, and a hell of miseries."
    —Sermon against the Illuminati conspiracy, Massa-
    chusetts, 1798

    Eventually, all evil can be traced to the New World
Order. The Eastern elites, the invisible string-pullers,
the stealth agencies, the Federal Reserve. They've been
running the nation for many years. They actually suspended the Constitution in 1933, but you don't know
it yet. They're the ones bent on establishing a world
government and implanting microchips in people's
foreheads.
    Need proof? Look on the back of a dollar bill.
What's that creepy, all-seeing eye doing there, above
the pyramid? And the slogan, *Novus Ordo Seclorum.*
The New Order of the Ages. It's a Masonic slogan. The
secret cabal . . .

It was a very long article, and I scanned the rest of it, enjoying the author's tongue-in-cheek dismissal of the Illuminati's
New World Order, and conspiracy theories in general. Looking for an English article, I came upon only one, from years
back. It had been published in *The New Statesman and Society*, and was still more tongue-in-cheek and dismissive than
The Washington Post article had been. The author, Vicky
Hutchings, had attended a conference called the First International Conference That Exposes a Global Deception, and
learned the following:

    . . . The anti-gravity technology of the flying saucer
    [was] funded by the Illuminati and developed by Hitler
    in secret underground cities, spread around the globe
    after the war. . . . The Illuminati have prevented us for
    decades from knowing the truth: "They will never
    allow us to run our own saucers on free energy."
    The Illuminati are made up of Freemasons or other

related secret societies, and are found in positions of power throughout the world. All American presidents have been Freemasons, for example, except Eisenhower, who was a Jehovah's Witness.

David Summers is an expert on the Bilderberg Group, the Trilateral Commission, the Council for Foreign Relations, the Royal Institute for International Affairs—these are some of the secretive organisations controlled by Freemasons. . . . Many speakers quoted Stephen Knight, author of *The Brotherhood,* who claimed the Freemasons "provoked" the 1917 revolution in Russia (Kerensky was a Mason).

The article went on about everything from UFOs to evil signs embedded in oil company logos, and I found myself scrolling onward. So far, I was convinced that a lot of people *thought* there was an Illuminati, and that those highly suggestible people belonged to fringe groups displaying a disturbing paranoia. I read the remaining articles, but they seemed even more hilarious and dismissive than the others.

Taking off my glasses, I sat back in the chair and rubbed my eyes. It was curious, I thought, that there was no serious article—not one over the years—that truly tackled the subject of whether the Illuminati existed. Was it because journalists were afraid of retaliation if they probed too deeply? Did the ones who probed meet with unfortunate accidents, like Angela, Denny, and my parents? Like those students who had contacted the Stonecypher Society, so that their articles were never published? Or was there really nothing to probe?

I felt badly in need of some organised thought, a way to sort through what I knew so far.

I thought, chewing on a thumbnail. I didn't see how the book-stealing ring related to anything—Illuminati or Folio B. But I did see how it related to Holdsworthy, since he seemed to be shipping the books off to be sold, and was working closely with the woman doing the forging and replacing . . . in more ways than one.

Holdsworthy, in turn, was related to me by way of industrial espionage—if I listened to George's theory—because I had just taken his star author.

Holdsworthy could be responsible for all of it, I thought, or none of it—and the same could be said to be true of both Folio B and the Illuminati.

The upshot of it all was that I still don't know who had done what, and couldn't prove a thing.

I took the notebook computer out of its docking station in the Mac, rolled the desk chair away from my desk, and sat back with the computer in my lap. I felt as if the bottom had fallen out of my world. Somehow, I couldn't dismiss the possibility that the Illuminati really did exist. An ancient and international secret society may have done its best to kill my author, and might soon have another go at me as well. If they could get American presidents elected and arrange for the European Union to become a reality—one step closer to a world government—it would certainly be child's play to eliminate us.

To stay alive, and to keep Angela alive, I would have to be terribly clever about it all. And I didn't feel particularly clever just at the moment.

I rubbed my temples. What could I possibly use to threaten them? I could post a guard for Angela, of course, but we couldn't hope to be guarded every moment for the rest of our lives.

Would we be forced to live out our lives in a self-imposed prison, with a small array of gunmen, like Salman Rushdie?

There had to be a better answer, something I could use to threaten them. Then it hit me: I would proceed with my original idea to help and be helped by Mike Chelmsford. After all, I had the ultimate weapon, the truth, and Chelmsford had a way to make it known. I sat up, feeling almost hopeful. I would write down everything I knew, send it to my solicitor, and instruct him to post it to Mike Chelmsford if anything should happen to me or Angela.

But something already *had* happened to Angela. Come right out and say it, Alex, I told myself: if Angela or you should *die*. If either of us were to die, Mike Chelmsford would have an article in *The Tempus* before they could say "revenge": names, specifics of what they'd done, the works. The Illuminati should be very solicitous indeed of our health for the remainder of our lives.

Of course I would have to let them know that I had this power against them, and I didn't know exactly whom to tell. I told myself wryly that I could always shout it out the door at the white Ford, or at the Neck.

Unless there was something I wasn't thinking of, some reason why that wouldn't stop them. It was the best I could do.

With my elbows on the desk, I rested my face in my hands, staring at the words on the monitor and marvelling at the layers of evil that seemed to be embedded within Folio B—the book-switching ring, the Illuminati . . . how had a genteel, charitable organisation dedicated to the preservation of books become involved in such corruption and political plotting?

I sighed, rubbed my face hard with my hands, and considered whether I should write to Sarah first, work on my speech, or write my life insurance letter to Mike Chelmsford. I suddenly felt incapable of doing any one of the above. I decided to look in once more on Angela and then come right back to the Press and do what I could to salvage life as Angela and I knew it—always assuming she'd be all right. Next I'd post a private security guard outside her room, then call or write to Sarah. As I stood I realised that I hadn't rung Lisette as promised from the hospital earlier in the afternoon—another broken promise. What was happening to me? I picked up the phone.

" 'Ello," she answered. Her voice was just a bit indistinct, as if her mouth weren't quite in line with the mouthpiece. I heard the clink of a lid on a pan and knew that she was speaking from her remarkably prolific kitchen, gripping the receiver between her chin and shoulder as she wielded food preparation equipment.

"Lisette, it's Alex. Sorry I didn't call you from the hospital earlier. There's been a dramatic development, I'm happy to say."

"Yes?!"

"I don't want to get your hopes up, but Angela seems to be responding. She squeezed my hand in response to a question, and her eye moved when I spoke about her accident not having been accidental."

"Alex, that's wonderful!"

"Mmm. It's a start anyway. I'm just finishing up something here and thought I'd go and see her again. I'll ring you again if anything stupendous has happened." If only I'd known what I was about to find at the hospital, I think I'd have chosen another phrase.

Lisette said an enthusiastic yes, please, and added that she'd put George on except that he was in the middle of bedding down the boys. I said not to worry, and to please tell him hello for me, and I'd see her in the morning.

I saved my file and stood, stretching. The walk up to the hospital was becoming routine. It showed how bizarre my life had been that I hadn't given another thought to finding my car. Perhaps when every moment didn't seem like a disaster waiting to happen. Perhaps after my holiday with Sarah. Better yet, maybe I would call on some brotherly goodwill and ask Max to look into it while I was away.

When I stepped outside, the rain had stopped, but the air was acrid and the pavement glistened. There was a slight breeze stirring. I could hear distant thunder as I walked past the far side of the square, where the white Ford was parked, its damaged window its only acknowledgement of me. It was quiet at seven-thirty of a Wednesday night, except for the sound of the Ford starting up to track me. I hardly cared anymore, almost expected it, in fact—especially now that I had a better understanding of what it might represent.

Roughly three-quarters of the way up Gower Street it abruptly occurred to me that I was ravenously hungry. I turned left into Torrington Place and ducked into a pub there, the George, that served evening meals. I had the only remaining thing on the menu—a chicken pie—and some chips, with a cup of coffee. The hasty meal was unexceptional but filled the void, and I marched on, turning after several streets into the drive of the hospital.

Walking through the front door of the hospital, I felt sadness settle on me like a cloak. Even if Angela recovered fully from her accident injuries, there would be the leukaemia to deal with.

The doctor had said she would have been moved, but since I didn't know where her new room would be, I took the stairs up to the fourth floor and enquired at the nurse's station.

"Yes, good news—she has been moved out of intensive care." I'd never seen this nurse before, but she seemed to recognise me. She put down a stack of documents she was holding and leafed through some sheets of paper on a clipboard on the counter. "Let me check for you . . . here she is, Room 318."

"Thank you. I know it's late, but will it be all right if I see her?"

"Family members quite often sit through the night," she replied, cheerfully picking up her papers and giving me a knowing look as she went about her business.

I darted down the stairs and over to the other side of the building, following the "300–320" sign. As I came round the corner towards rooms 312 to 320, however, a man knocked into me hard. He'd practically been running, and as he barged on past me without an apology and banged through the door to the stairway, it struck me that he looked a great deal like Rich, the carpenter who'd been fired from our job at the Press after letting the beam fall on my head.

In fact, there was no doubt in my mind that it was Rich.

With a sense of foreboding, I let him go and broke into a run towards Angela's room. There was no one in sight, nor was the nurse's station visible from this part of the hallway. Where were the Mayfields? At dinner, perhaps. I opened the closed door and ran across to the bed. A ghostly, indirect hospital light shone on her, and I didn't think it was the fluorescent light that gave her skin a bluish tint. It took only an instant to take it all in—the apparatus hooked up to her face, the machine sitting still and noiseless, the plug at the end of the electrical lead lying uselessly on the floor.

"Dear God," I exclaimed, and lunged at the plug, fingers fumbling in the effort to get the prongs in the outlet. The machine lit up and came to life again. I grabbed the nurse-call button at the side of the bed, punched it hard a few times. Then I ran out the door to get help. A stout nurse hoved into view, looking irritated.

"Hurry!" I cried. "She's not breathing!" She broke into a trot at that, and hurried into Angela's room. Knowing that the nurse would take care of her, I took off down the hall and down the stairs in hope of finding Rich to give him what he deserved. Flying round the stairwells, floor after floor, I wondered if he had been the one driving the car which had struck Angela. I wouldn't have been surprised. But when I got down to the ground level, there was no one in sight, inside or out, except for the white Ford.

I was sick and tired of Angela being used by these people, and swore that they weren't going to get away with it. I stood panting outside the hospital, feeling horribly guilty that I was alive and well, while she was inside fighting desperately for a temporary reprieve. Why hadn't I called for a guard while I was still at the Press? Once again I'd managed to fail her.

It was clear that something had to be done to protect Angela immediately. Her elderly parents couldn't possibly stay by her side every moment, nor should they be put in the position of dealing with thugs like Rich. Hurrying to hospital reception, I dialled the number of a trusted security guard who, with his brother, had done some work with us at the Press last year.

He answered quickly and quietly. "Kent here." I told him what had happened and arranged for him to post himself or his brother outside Angela's room for the foreseeable future. Then I took the lift back up and found the nurse frowning over Angela, though her colour was already improving. Angela was stable again, she told me: the breathing apparatus couldn't have been unplugged for long. I explained to the nurse what had happened, and told her that one or the other of the Kent brothers would be coming. I would be staying until he arrived.

"Lucky for Miss Mayfield she has you," she said, thinking she was comforting me as her ample hips swayed out of the room.

"Thanks." I turned away and hung my head as I went to the head of Angela's bed. The nurse couldn't have known that I was responsible for Angela's accident in the first place.

When John Kent arrived half an hour later—a remarkable journey time from Ealing—I went over again what had happened that evening. John, who looked exactly like my mental image of a real American cowboy—lean, tight muscles, and too rugged to be perfectly groomed—listened with rapt attention. Under his controlled exterior I knew he was simmering with rage. A muscle in his jaw clenched and unclenched. I felt certain he would come close to dismembering anyone who attempted to come near Angela, and I also knew that under the loose jacket he wore, he carried the ultimate threat of a loaded pistol.

I told him about her parents, and explained that he should stay even after they returned, and, in fact, no matter who came. I told him about Ranjan Michaels, gave him my card, writing Ian's and Lisette's phone numbers on the back in case he couldn't reach me. Then I placed Angela's welfare in his capable hands. I never worried once I had one of the Kent brothers involved; I knew they would rather die than fall down on the job.

As I hesitated before leaving, he said, "Don't worry, Alex. No one will get near her. Geoff'll relieve me in the morning. We'll be with her round the clock."

"Thanks, John. I know you will."

He grunted in response, having taken up his watch.

Once outside, I waved sardonically at the white Ford and started the hike back down to Bedford Square. At least, I thought, they might offer me a ride; we all knew they were going exactly the same place I was. Shaking my head at the ridiculousness of it, I realised that I was exhausted. I briefly considered going back to the Orchard for the night, but quickly rejected the idea. I had several very important things to do—particularly preparing Angela's and my life insurance policy. Max wouldn't question my being gone all night, and he knew that I sometimes spent the night at the Press when I didn't feel like making the trip home. I still had an extra change of clothes stashed there; they would do for the next morning.

I would, however, need to make a stop at the house at some point before catching my flight to Paris on Friday—and even at the hellacious pace of the last few days, that should be possible.

Paris. Friday. Sarah would be waiting. My heart beat a bit faster at the thought. In addition to my cycling gear, I'd be packing the very small box I'd picked up the week before from Garrard, jewellers to the Queen.

I ambled tiredly down Gower Street towards my home

away from home—though if I'd imagined the sort of living hell waiting for me there, I would have turned and run.

The Press was cool and dark when I opened the door. The horrors of Angela's hospital room with its unplugged equipment seemed comfortingly distant. As I mounted the stairs in the peaceful darkness, my mind swam with thoughts of the Illuminati, Frances Macnamara, and my last meeting with Denny, how I'd word my letter to Mike Chelmsford and my solicitor . . . and through it all the thought that my all-important week was coming up with Sarah, and I didn't even know if I should go. What's worse, I hadn't told Sarah what had happened yet.

I stopped short outside Lisette's office, hearing a creak that it seemed to me shouldn't have been. But it was still so remarkably humid that it could have been the old wood expanding in one of a million places. I snapped on the light. To my surprise, someone had put away all the folding chairs from the announcement and the room looked as it always did; Lisette's desk overflowed with a flood of paper that appeared to have no order whatsoever. It hadn't taken me long to learn that she was one of those people who, despite appearances, always knew exactly where everything was in the apparent chaos, and woe befell the man who suggested a more traditional filing system.

I turned off the lights again and walked on down the hall to my office. The smell of construction materials and the inevitable dust involved in any building project seemed stronger than it had earlier in the day, but then I'd just come in from the fresh air. Sighing, I flopped down on the sofa that stretched along the wall opposite my desk without even taking off my shoes.

It was with a sense of unreality that I heard, rather than saw, at first, the lamp on my desk switch on just as I was slipping the glasses off my nose. My eyes flew open, and I pushed the glasses back on. I stared with disbelief at the scene in front of me. A strange man sat at my desk, smiling at me cheerily as if he belonged there.

But that wasn't all; there was a new doorway behind my desk, opening into an area I hadn't known existed. My eyes flicked from the stranger to the door-size hole in the wall and back again. I must have looked a complete idiot.

"Surprise," he said at last in a wry smoker's voice. I guessed that he was sixty, perhaps; prize-winning jowls hung from his fleshy face. He didn't actually seem sinister, but it gave me a bad feeling that he was sitting in my office this late at night, with a fairly ominous black hole in the wall behind him.

"It's unfortunate that we won't have a chance to become better acquainted," he continued pleasantly. "I was a friend of your father's, and I would have perhaps met you socially. I'm a member of Folio B too, you know." He smiled at his conversation and toyed with a pen on my desk. I suspected his fingers were longing for a cigarette.

He followed my eyes as they flew again, involuntarily, to the opening in the wall behind him. "Yes, that must be quite a surprise for you." Again he smiled, as if we shared a secret. "It was Marie-Louise's room; Stonecypher had it closed up after she died there." He must have seen my eyes widen. "Oh, don't worry, she's not there anymore. No, no."

The Room of the Maiden, I thought incredulously. It was the fourth title. It had been inevitable.

"Interesting thought," he continued, "whether your great-great-grandfather Edward knew about the room. I rather suspect he did, though I don't believe anyone knows for sure." He eyed me appraisingly. Then he put the pen down and leaned forward at my desk. "I suspect you're wondering what I'm doing here. You remember the letter you received—the one you disregarded. Unfortunately, Alex, we are going to have to kill you."

At that unpleasant moment, a familiar form appeared outside the door of my office, to my left. It was Rich, if that was in fact his name, of the construction accident and respirator near-disaster. My eyes narrowed as I saw him, and I felt raw hatred as I had rarely felt it before. The man behind my desk was saying, "When principalities and kingdoms fall every man will come to power through knowledge of the written word."

With surprising rapidity Rich brought up a gun with a silencer on it, the likes of which I had seen in a good many films but never in person, and shot me as I began to rise to my feet, from a distance of barely three feet.

The shot knocked me backwards, against the sofa. Immediately I was frozen into an ineffectual stupor, though my mind seemed to be working perfectly well. Despite the searing pain shooting through my body, the awareness that I had been shot was somehow far more traumatic. Rich's bullet had found my upper chest, and as I looked down at the reddening hole in my shirt, absorbing that fact, he fired again. I stared at him in disbelief.

I felt Rich dragging me unceremoniously off of the sofa and across the dust sheet they had prudently spread across the carpet. In future—if there were to be a future—I would turn on the lights in a room before entering. Seeing a dust sheet on the floor that hadn't been there several hours before might have clued me in; I could have turned and run.

I had a curious feeling of being detached from the situation; it seemed that I was watching someone else being dragged across the floor of a second-storey room at Plumtree Press in Bedford Square. Rich's every step seemed to deliberately scrape together the jagged edges of this unfortunate stranger's wounds in the most gratingly painful fashion. My mind, unbidden, worked on the question of how they had known I would be here tonight. Perhaps they had been hiding somewhere in the building earlier, eavesdropping. Had I mentioned to Lisette when I phoned that I would be going back to the Press after visiting Angela?

It slowly sank in that the person I was watching, the person who had been shot, was being dragged into the nether reaches of his own building to die. With effort, I reminded myself that the person was in fact myself, and it occurred to me that I was the only one who could possibly remedy the situation. Rich still had the gun. If I waited until he'd got me into the room, and thought I was unconscious, perhaps I could kick the weapon out of his hand and knock him down—fight him on my own terms, on the floor. Logic told me I didn't stand much of a chance of winning, but I had to try.

We passed through the doorway into what the gentleman had said was Marie-Louise's room. So Stonecypher *had* had something to hide, or hide from, in this room, the casual observer in me said.

The musty smell was overwhelming; it was very much like entering the disused old barn at the Orchard, only ten times more intense. My nostrils inhaled an unpleasant odor that consisted of damp, mold, rotting furniture, something that might have been mouse or rat droppings, and books.

Think, Alex, I ordered myself. Don't worry about the smell—how are you going to stay alive?

He was letting me go, dropping my arms now that he had me far enough into the room. What were they going to do? I wondered. How would they hide me and the room from the others tomorrow morning? Rich stood over me, trying to gauge, I assumed, whether I was still alive. I lay perfectly still, eyes closed, and felt him bending down slightly and shining a torch on my face.

There wouldn't be a better moment. I reached up with both hands to grab the gun out of his hand. But my limbs didn't respond as they should have. It was as if their connection to my brain had shorted out, Rich saw me moving, with the disastrous result that he delivered a vicious kick roughly where he'd placed the bullets.

A horrible, involuntary sound of air escaping from my lungs seemed to satisfy him that his job was finished, and it seemed to me that it probably was too. With a flicker of regret for leaving the world, and my responsibility to Angela, but especially my unfulfilled hopes with Sarah, I drifted off into a daze.

Much, much later, or what seemed to be much, much later, I opened my eyes to utter darkness. My first thought was that I was still alive. I was so grateful for that favour that the burning in my chest that consumed most of my remaining energy and brainpower hardly seemed significant. Difficult to ignore, but not something to grouse about if I still had life and breath.

Next, I noticed that the normal light that should have been coming into the building, even at night, was nonexistent. It was pitch black. The first thing I had to do was get to a telephone and ring for help; maybe George would consider a house call.

Then I heard a noise from behind the wall. Damn! They were still there. It was a strong noise, but muffled. Pounding, but as if from far away. I lay and listened as best I could, desperately trying to think. They must have closed the door on me after getting me safely inside, safe for them meaning dead, of course. I would simply have to wait until they'd gone. If I didn't bleed to death first.

What could they possibly be doing? Why should they be pounding on anything in my office at Plumtree Press?

Puzzled, and still frightened that Rich would blast through the door and wreak havoc with the fragile equilibrium I'd somehow achieved, I had a desperate feeling that if I didn't do something soon, I might slip away again—and it bothered me that I didn't know when, or if, I'd come back.

Raising myself onto one elbow, I fought nausea, always my body's reaction to severe pain. When I had come to terms with that position, I gently, slowly, brought myself onto hands and knees. That was all right, except that when I lifted my head I got the whirlies and had to hang it down again.

Getting that far had been a huge effort, and as I panted there on hands and knees, I was aware that my shirt was stuck to me with what could only be my own blood.

Lifting my head again cautiously, I did better this time. I inched across the floor to where I thought the door was, being careful not to jar my torso, and finally reached the wall. The smell of building materials was very strong; dust, and something chemical-smelling like paint or sealant. I groped along the wall for the line where the door met the wall, and felt none. Moving slowly along the wall, I finally came to a line—but it wasn't a door. Stunned and horrified at what was dawning on me, I groped for the next line, where the other side of the doorway would be, and knew that I was right.

They were entombing me. They were building me into Marie-Louise's room, virtually in my own office. The part of the wall they had cut out to make a doorway had been replaced, fixed solidly in place as a wall. I put my feet against it and pushed with all the strength I had, but it didn't give an inch. My heart sank as I remembered how, when Rich had dragged me through the doorway, I'd seen the incredibly thick wall between the two rooms. There had been layers of wood, metal, plasterboard, and who knew what else—to a thickness of well over a foot.

Now I understood.

I turned round until I was facing away from the wall but tight against it, then sank down on one side and gently flopped back into a sitting position against the wall. The effort required for these simple operations was enormous. I closed my eyes and my mind raced ahead.

Surely I would be able to make someone, somehow, hear me tomorrow. It would be Thursday. Thank God it wasn't Saturday, I thought, when no one would be in. For all I knew, it might already have become Thursday, though the fact that they were still on the other side of the wall indicated that it hadn't been very long since they'd confronted me. For the first time I noticed that my watch didn't have a lighted dial and regretted the fact.

My eyes popped open again when I remembered the bon voyage present Lisette had given me that afternoon for the trip with Sarah. The little three-pronged device should work as well in this hellish situation as it would out on a romantic hillside in French wine country. Feeling pleased with the small but significant victory, I reached into my suit coat with my good arm and pulled it out, feeling for the end that would open as a base. I opened it, flicked the little wheel that made the spark, and *voilà!* I had light.

What I saw, fuzzy as it was in the dim light, was sobering and eerie enough to make me catch my breath. I'd been transported back to the turn of the century, to a maid's room. I squinted and peered about. The room was perhaps ten feet by twelve feet. It was furnished with a single bed, a small desk with a chair, and a minimal cupboard for clothes.

The bed had been slept in, the bedclothes pulled back and rumpled, the dimpled pillow exposed. I shivered. It looked as if Stonecypher had had this room closed off immediately after Marie-Louise's mysterious death. A small table next to the bed had toppled over, as if perhaps there had been a struggle there. I found myself wondering exactly what had happened on the day that Stonecypher's mistress had died.

I noticed a broken crockery candleholder, with the half-candle it had held, on the floor nearby. I could make use of that, I thought gratefully.

As I stared in wonder at my surroundings, I wondered why they had put me in here—they being the Illuminati, I assumed. If they were going to shoot me, why not just dump me in the Thames? Or, perhaps easier yet, push me in front of a train during rush hour? Perhaps they thought it would be the undiscoverable crime, or else someone had a strange sense of irony. I had come back to sleep in my office, and sleep there I would . . . forever. Or so they thought.

The whole lot of them had a collective screw loose, I decided. All of my nuts and bolts were still firmly in place, however, and I wasn't about to let them win this battle. Not only was I going to get out alive, I was going to get Angela's book into the bookshops, deliver my speech in Menceauville, and have my week with Sarah.

Remembering that my reason for going for the candle had been to check the time, I lifted my left wrist too fast, instinctively, and swore, seeing black blotches before my eyes. I closed my eyes and waited for a moment, then took the candle to the watch. Eleven-thirty.

Perhaps it was the shock of the pain when I'd moved my arm, but I'd broken out in a cold sweat and felt very cold indeed. My hand shook slightly as I got on with the business of trying to do what I could to stop the bleeding. Darker, coagulating blood surrounded the wound, but bright red blood still oozed from the centre.

As I removed my tie with my good hand, I realised that I'd scored another victory over Rich. If he'd been aiming at my heart, he'd been inches high and to the left—closer to my shoulder than my chest. He would be horribly disappointed, I thought, if he knew. Blood must have spilled promptly and copiously enough, in roughly the right place, that he'd been satisfied.

I folded the tie neatly again and again until it made a very thick bandage, then pressed it to the wound with my good hand. My shivering was growing worse, the tremors so violent now that my teeth chattered. I knew enough to understand that bodies went into shock when bad things happened. I needed to keep warm.

Holding the improvised bandage against the wound with my chin, I used my good arm to pick up Lisette's candle, flick it off, and put it in my pocket. Then I pushed myself to a standing position. The whirlies came again, but I closed my eyes and fought them. It worked. I shuffled the five feet or so to the edge of the bed, reached over to where I'd seen books on Marie-Louise's desk, grabbed one, and lowered myself onto the bed. Placing the heavy book on the bandage to hold it on the wound, I sighed.

Given the choice, I would have opted for my own bed, and linens that had been laundered once in the last eighty-three years, but Marie-Louise's bed felt like heaven. No snakes or spiders or mice that I could discern crept out of the sheets, though I thought I could feel small clumps of material in piles, as if at some point little creatures had made nests there. I pulled the coarse wool blanket over me and fell asleep before I had a chance to wonder if it would be for the last time.

CHAPTER 14

And out of olde bokes, in good feyth,
Cometh al this newe science that men lere.
—GEOFFREY CHAUCER, *THE PARLIAMENT OF FOWLS*

When I awakened, there was no instant of confusion, no delay in remembering where I was or what had happened to me. Grateful to be alive still, I wiggled my toes and fingers and said "thank you" just to prove it. As long as I didn't move much, I could tolerate the burning in my chest. I even felt warm again.

I had no concept of time, so my next act was to pull out the candle, ignite it, and check my watch. Quarter past four—A.M., I assumed. Plenty of time to plan some means of attracting attention from employees on their way to work at nine.

I extinguished the candle, lay still, and mused; this room was directly above the production department. If I dumped the wardrobe over on the floor, or picked up the bed repeatedly and dropped it to make a thundering noise, surely someone would investigate. Mentally, I shook my head at the bizarre situation; someone might listen, but would they think of ripping out a wall to find the source of the noise? More likely, they would just chalk it up to a construction worker in the alley between the two buildings, and get on with their work.

Harry. Harry, the construction supervisor, would be there.

He would be certain to notice that the noise wasn't from any of the construction he was supervising. And perhaps if people got close enough, I could make my voice heard. Full of hope and optimism, I made my plans, resting and dozing the early morning away. One far-fetched idea had already been rejected: burning my way out of the room with fire started by the candle. I would almost certainly be dead from smoke inhalation by the time anyone saw my smoke signals.

But that desperate idea had given rise to another thought, an unwelcome one: how much oxygen was there in the little room? As I thought about it, it seemed to me that the air was already thin. Feeling the beginnings of panic, I told myself to stop imagining things, and turned my mind to other thoughts.

What had Marie-Louise been working on at her desk? What books had she been reading? And by what sort of accident had Stonecypher killed her—possibly with his wife's assistance, if Angela's book was to be believed? For the first time I thought of a *ménage à trois*, then rejected it as being too fantastic.

When I was tired of these thoughts cycling endlessly, and there was no more sleep in me, I decided to risk disturbing the relative comfort I'd achieved and investigate the desk. At least there wasn't far to go, I thought wryly, lifting the book off my bandage and setting it next to me on the bed.

After I'd pulled out the propane candle and ignited it again, something on the bed caught my eye. It was a peach-coloured satin ribbon embroidered with tiny yellowed pearls, perhaps an inch and a half wide and two feet long, with an open clasp at one end, a hook on the other. It looked, I thought, as if it might have been the belt to a fine lady's dress—but not that of a maid's.

Transferring the candle gingerly to my left hand, I picked up the belt with my good hand and studied it, intrigued. Perhaps this had been something precious of Marie-Louise's, a bit of finery given her by Stonecypher. I quickly dismissed the thought of the sad end of their affair, and of their lives, thinking that I had a fairly desperate situation of my own to be getting on with. As if to drive that point home, an odd vibration shook the floor subtly but continuously beneath my feet. I couldn't think what the vibration meant—it was too early for the building's central heating to have boomed to life. Dismissing the thought, I turned my attention again to the desk.

I won't relate what it cost me to get up, bend over to pick up the wax candle on the floor, and toddle over to Marie-Louise's desk. The bleeding didn't resume, at any rate. When I got there I sat down in her chair and set the candle on the desk in an open inkwell, lighting it with Lisette's propane candle. The desk came to life in front of me as I shut off the propane, and the taller candle illuminated my immediate surroundings.

It was small wonder that Stonecypher had found Marie-Louise intellectually as well as physically attractive. She had owned several small volumes of poems by Charles Baudelaire, which happened to be beautifully bound and gilded, and which I knew for a fact were now very valuable, by virtue of having been bound by Dove's Press. Anything Dove's Press had done was a sensation these days.

It was possible that these had been a personal gift from Stonecypher. I checked the first few pages of each for an inscription; they were there. The first read:

To Marie-Louise with all my love, Marcus.

The second one had been more creative. He had written, in his handsome, looping hand:

Marie-Louise, see page 26. That is how I feel when I think of life without you.

Being human, I flipped to page 26. He had good taste. This was one of my favourite poems; I'd had to recite it in a French competition at school once.

Recueillement
Sois sage, ô ma Douleur, et tiens-toi plus tranquille.
Tu réclamais le Soir, il descend; le voici:
Une atmosphère obscure enveloppe la ville . . .

I closed the little book, feeling oddly comforted, and looked at the others. She had several popular novels of the period, among them, *The Room of the Maiden*. With a shiver at the appropriateness of the title to my current situation, I opened it and read in his hand, *For my darling Marie-Louise. It is all for you.* That made me think for a moment. Was that merely a romantic turn of phrase, or had Stonecypher intended to leave all he had to Marie-Louise?

I considered. The Bloomsbury Group as a whole had a reputation for at least speaking freely to one another of unorthodox romantic relationships—"free love," as members of the group had themselves referred to it in those days, in addition to homosexual love, and still more unusual forms of association. Virginia Woolf, I remembered reading, had complained that this reputation was unjust. After all, she and her sister did eventually marry men, and if one believed her, they did more talking about untraditional relationships than indulging.

Staring at the "it is all for you" inscription, I wondered. Had Stonecypher considered leaving his wife? Marissa Stonecypher had largely escaped notice, having been characterised as a helpless invalid for most of her married life. I knew that she and her nurse had taken over the upper front room that Lisette and Shuna now shared, and I could see why. It had a beautiful view of the gardens and would be refreshing for someone who was bedridden.

More important, the room also happened to put her close to the maid's quarters. If Marissa had sensed something between her husband and the French maid, it must have been awkward to know that Marie-Louise was so close. I could practically feel the electricity crackling down the hallway, as it did when Lisette was having a bad day. What if, snooping in the maid's room one day, she'd seen the inscriptions I'd just read?

I shook my head, marvelling at the fact that I was sitting at a desk that hadn't been touched since before 1914, with two bullet holes in my chest, thinking about—of all things—jealous women. I looked at my watch. Seven fifty-two. Not so very much longer to wait now. At least Harry and his gang would be coming soon, if they weren't there already. I kept an ear out for the air compressor, which had startled MacDougal so successfully, and thought that it really should be on by now—the construction workers usually started at seven-thirty.

Then I had a truly horrific thought. What if the vibration, which hadn't stopped, was the air compressor? With rising panic I carried that thought to its logical conclusion. If I couldn't really hear the compressor, but could only feel it, there was no hope of them hearing me over the blasted thing, not to mention their tools.

I pushed the thought away and decided, for the moment, not to believe what I knew, deep down, was true. Perhaps I would hear the real thing start any moment now, I lied to myself. I looked at the pen and papers on Marie-Louise's desk, forcing myself to focus on them, telling myself that I was the privileged first visitor to a very special museum—or, at the very least, a sort of time capsule. The top sheet of paper was blank, but I looked at the next few sheets just to see. Ah, yes. There was writing on the second page. Marie-Louise and I had something in common. I often did it myself; started journals on page three, or five, or covered private papers on my desk with a newspaper so I'd have time to catch snoopers before they got to the good stuff. I saw, however, that it was a letter from Stonecypher to Marie-Louise:

My dearest,

> *As I leave your room for the last time, I can scarcely believe that our beautiful life together has ended thus. It is unimaginable to me that we should be apart, so that I feel soon I must join you.*
>
> *Everything has fallen apart—Marissa knows about us and has insisted that you must leave, and I know I shall never see you again in this house, in your delightful room where we have spent so many golden, stolen hours.*
>
> *The Bibliati have turned on me, and revile me for objecting to their growing fanaticism and violence. What was once a fascinating philosophical salon has*

*become a group of evil men, and I have lent my books
to it.*

I am desolate.

*All my love,
Marcus*

Bibliati?

I looked at the next sheet and saw that Stonecypher had
written it too. *"I hereby confess to the accidental killing of
Marie-Louise Boudreau in an act of passion."* The letter was
signed Marcus Stonecypher in his characteristic, handsome
handwriting.

But beneath that shocker was a missive that was more
stunning yet. I blinked, realising what I'd found, and how
important it was. Angela had been right. She *had* known
something I hadn't: Stonecypher's wife had been involved
indeed. Numbed by my own disaster, I read, hardly moving
or reacting.

My dear Marie-Louise,

*You were right, my darling, you were right. If only I
could change the fact that I didn't believe you. You are
gone; she has taken you from me forever. I cannot
bring you back, but I will come to join you.*

*I never thought that she could or would do such a
thing, but I see how she has done it—how she left the
marks of the pearls from her belt on your fine white
neck. You are still here, on the bed, next to me. My
heart is breaking, but I shall be with you soon. I have
confessed the crime since I am to die anyway, so
Marissa needn't go to gaol in her state.*

Stunned by what I had found, I read and reread the papers,
finally understanding that the first letter had been written
while Marie-Louise was still alive. The last two had been
written by Stonecypher after her death, probably upon desolate visits to her room. I could only assume that Stonecypher
had for some reason decided against delivering his "confession" to the police, and had left it here with the other letters.

When I made out from my watch that it was eight-thirty, and I still couldn't hear anyone, I knew I was in trouble. Horrified, I felt the onset of panic unlike any I had ever felt before, an uncontrollable rising tide. I restrained myself successfully until nine o'clock. Then I burst into a round of yelling "Help!" and banging on the walls with my good hand.

I would pause, listen, and begin again every three or so minutes at first. By nine-twenty I had gone to every ten minutes, and by eleven o'clock I was so tired and discouraged that it didn't seem to matter anymore. Thoughts of Sarah waiting for me at Orly, and reservations at country inns in Alsace going unused flitted through my head. I would never show up for the Folio B speech, and someone—probably the person who had arranged to have me entombed here—would announce a change in plans due to my failure to appear. They would win—and so easily.

I settled into a lethargy that wasn't entirely unpleasant, because I filled it with thoughts of Sarah. Sarah laughing, Sarah rowing in front of me, Sarah kissing me.

I concentrated on recreating the feel of her kisses from memory.

I drifted through the hours, until roughly three-thirty in the afternoon, when I had what was my final panic. I flailed against the walls and attempted to yell, though by that time my voice came out in a hoarse whisper. When I finally collapsed after the effort, I might have truly given up for good and all, had I not heard a sound.

I held my breath. There it was, the same kind of pounding I'd heard last night before, but louder and deeper. Then there was the clamour of things falling, and finally the best sound of all: "Alex?" The name was spoken with a French accent. It sounded as if it was not far outside the room.

"Here! In here!" I wasn't sure that it was loud enough, so I thumped my foot as best I could, twice, against the wall.

"My God!" I heard Lisette shout in an anguished voice. "You were right—'e *is* in there! 'Urry . . ."

Then, "Alex. Hang on. We'll have you out in no time. . . ." It was Harry, the construction foreman.

Of course I did hang on, then, and heard snippets of conversation. Lisette: "Look at this—a foot's thickness of insulation, metal sheathing—Mr. 'Eppelthwaite, if not for you, we would never 'ave found 'im."

HARRY: "The whole thing was sturdily built, right enough."

MAX: "Who could *do* such a thing?"

Finally there was a knocking on the wall, very close now, and Harry said, "Alex, we're going to knock the wall through. Stand back—" There was a crash, and light exploded into the gloom, along with the business end of a sledgehammer and clouds of dust. I shielded my eyes. Lisette gasped, and Harry broadened the hole. I looked out and saw them all there—Ian too—mouths open, horrified.

I started to crawl out, and Harry offered me his arm. Together he, Max, and Ian pulled me out onto the dark plum-coloured carpeting of my office.

Lisette knelt over me, pushing the hair off my forehead, her eyes drawn to my bloodsoaked shirt and the makeshift bandage. "*Mon Dieu!* What 'ave they *done* to you?" She trailed off, looking up at Ian, who looked worried in the extreme, then at Max, who hurried from the room. Lisette got to her feet. "I'll call an ambulance."

"No," I rasped. My lips were so dry that it was difficult to form words with them. All I wanted to do was lie still and be grateful, and perhaps have a drink of water—after getting whatever medical help I could from Lisette's husband. I had a very important holiday to be ready for, though at this point I doubted that there would be much cycling involved.

"Call George?" I asked economically.

Lisette, angel that she was, instantly understood. She marched over to my desk, skirt swirling, her weight on the high heels making the old floor creak. Picking up the phone, she punched in some numbers, spoke to the receptionist, then told George to get to the Press right away. "It's Alex. 'E's been shot," she said, and rang off.

Max came back into the room, knelt, and held out a cup to me. I sat up and took it with an embarrassingly shaky hand.

"I don't know about the rest of you," Lisette said with barely controlled anger simmering beneath her voice, "but this is the limit. We must ring the police. I've 'eard of 'arassment, even grudges that got out of 'and, like the *imbecile* Rupert Soames. But this is too much."

"Lisette," Ian said. He so rarely spoke that his utterance stopped her in the doorway. She turned to listen. "Alex already has a great deal invested in stopping the people who did this to him." He looked down at me with something between pity and regret. "Even more than he yet realises," he said softly. "No doubt in the end he will inform the authorities. But perhaps we should let him decide."

Lisette looked Ian in the eye. Then she nodded, turned back to join our group, and looked at me, challenging me to ask for help from the police. I started to stand, and Max came and took my arm, helping me up. "I need a moment to think," I said, and there was an awkward silence.

"Well. Time for me to be getting back to work." Harry looked at me with baleful eyes. "I can't tell you how sorry I am that this happened with my materials. It couldn't have been one of my men though, I'm sure of that. I've got an old friend to replace Martin, so that miserable bloke Rich isn't working for me anymore."

"Not your fault, Harry, really. Besides, you got me out. Thanks." As he left, I was aware that Max was still standing next to me, supporting me. It was nice to be able to lean on my brother, for a change. Ian stood near the door like a sentry.

"I should be going too," said gentle Mr. Heppelthwaite from the Historic Buildings Society. "I hope the project goes smoothly for you from now on."

"You should know, Alex," Lisette piped up, "that it was Mr. 'Eppelthwaite 'oo really found you."

I looked at him, not comprehending. Modestly, he lowered his eyes to the floor.

"Do you remember that 'e asked for the original plans before 'e left the other day?" Lisette asked me. "Well, 'e studied them in 'is spare time and found a discrepancy between what 'e'd seen in your office and what was in the plans. Said it didn't line up properly, or something." The man was actually blushing. "And there it is, that extra space—the buffer area, and then your little room." She shuddered.

"I think I owe you my life, Mr. Heppelthwaite," I said, reaching out to shake his hand. "I don't know how to thank you. Best of all, I have a larger office now."

He smiled and laughed, grateful to me for not embarrassing him by gushing my thanks. "Well. I really must leave you now, Mr. Plumtree. Best of luck with your, um, difficulties. See you again soon, I hope."

We all bade him warm good-byes, and Lisette went downstairs with him to the door. I sagged a little against Max, and he and Ian wordlessly guided me over to the sofa, where I sat. Lisette reappeared with George in tow. I knew that he must have practically flown from Harley Street to have arrived so quickly. From the look on his face, he'd expected the worst.

"Let's give the man some quiet," he said by way of asking the others, including Lisette, to leave the room. When they had, he demanded in a rough bluster, "What in God's name have you done now, Plumtree?" Then he began to peel back my shirt.

It took me a moment to think of a smart remark, which told him a thing or two. Eventually, it came, though it wasn't up to snuff.

"Just do your job, Stoneham. If I'm not perfectly fit for this trip with Sarah, and I end up single all my life as a result, I'll hold you fully responsible."

"Going all litigious on me, eh? Sarah's turning you into a true Yank." He tossed my bloody shirt into a rubbish bin with a look of distaste. "Lie down, then, and I'll see what I can do." He took some long swabs out of his bag, dipped them in a container of clear liquid, and set about swabbing the wound. "Sorry if this hurts. It's a topical anaesthetic; it'll relieve some of the pain while I work on it."

It hurt like Hades, but I nodded and said, "Thanks."

"This looks pretty clean," he mumbled thoughtfully. "No infection." He threw away the swabs, reached into his bag, and came out with a long pair of tweezers. Squinting at the wound, he said, "What did you manage here—two shots in one spot?"

"Mmm."

"Never do anything halfway, do you, Plumtree? You do know that I'm ethically bound to report gunshot wounds to the police." I acknowledged this with a nod, briefly imagining the look on the face of any constable unfortunate enough to hear my story. George frowned as he worked. "If you don't mind my asking, why exactly haven't *you* rung the police?"

Grudgingly, I nodded. "I can understand that it must seem strange to you." Translating my instinctive feeling into terms that George would understand, I continued. "It's looking more and more likely that Angela and I have stirred up a secret world-wide political society. If the police believed that, it would be a miracle. I myself didn't believe it until last night. Besides, I think I stand a much better chance of getting to the bottom of it all by travelling to Menceauville and finding out how Folio B is involved than I do sitting in a police station for the next day or so. There's more, but I'm not about to endanger you with it. You'll just have to trust me, George."

He closed his mouth and swallowed. "I trust you, Alex—I just worry about you." More quietly, he mumbled, "After all, I'm not *legally* required to report it.

"Now then," he said, all business. "Let's get this over with, shall we?" After poking about a bit, George rolled me halfway over, somehow knowing how to do it without causing a great deal more pain. "I don't believe it," he exclaimed, shaking his head. "If you don't beat all, Plumtree."

"What now?" I asked, curious.

"You lucky sod. The bullets have gone right the way through—both of them. That's good. It means that the bullet has just damaged a narrow path through you—in this case not through anything more vital than a bit of muscle—and hasn't created a giant crater."

He peered at the wound again. "Even so, I imagine it's rather painful." He didn't know the half of it, I thought. "I don't even like to ask how you got this bruise around the wound," he said, wincing.

I thought of Rich's kick and winced myself. "I've had better days," I said.

"You really don't seem too badly off, considering," George said, looking at me appraisingly as he placed some gauze over the wound in front. "Remarkable." He burrowed in his bag, eventually drawing out a roll of tape, and proceeded to secure the gauze into place.

"But I can't imagine that you would go ahead with the cycling trip," he continued. "Most people would be in bed for a week after a trauma like this." He sighed, tearing another strip of tape off of the roll and half-turning me over to stick a dressing onto my back.

"But I know you," he continued. "So, here." Finished taping, he reached inside his bag and pulled out two bottles of pills. "Standard antibiotics." He handed me a bottle with red-and-white capsules in it. "Painkillers." He handed me another bottle of all-white tablets. "God knows you'll need them," he murmured. "Now. For goodness' sake, Alex, stay still and let this heal as much as possible. If you had to have a gunshot wound—wounds, plural, rather—you could hardly have asked for better. Just don't overdo it, all right?"

"Thanks, George." He kindly helped me sit up, then pulled open the drawers of my desk until he found the clean shirts. He helped me into one, then twisted off the lid of the antibiotics and the painkillers, handing me one of each, and passed me a second glass of water. I loathed and detested the thought of taking pain pills, but even I had to admit that they would be a relief now. As I was taking the pills, he dug in his bag again and produced a long strip of fabric.

"Here," he said, fastening it with a safety pin around my neck. Gently, he slid my left arm into the resulting sling. "You'll be more comfortable this way." When he'd gathered his things back into the bag, he said breezily, "I'll send you my bill." We both knew he wouldn't. "I must pay for my malpractice insurance, you know—in case my friends sue me."

He was halfway out the door when he turned again. "Good luck on the trip. Don't—er—hesitate to go ahead with your plans with Sarah. And you don't have to worry about Angela—I'll check in on her every day for you." He winked and closed the door behind him.

Grateful to him for shouldering some of that burden, I walked over to my desk without mishap and sat down. No sooner had I lowered myself gently into the seat than the phone rang. One ring, an internal call.

"Yes?"

It was Lisette. "Alex, it's Sarah for you. I called 'er when we realised you were missing this morning—I thought she should know. I 'ope you don't mind."

"No, no—thanks, Lisette." Actually, I was filled with fear. What would I say? Was the trip really on? Off? What should I do? "You think of everything," I told her.

"But of course. 'Ere she is."

I gripped the phone with my good right hand—the one not attached to the painful shoulder—and steeled myself.

"Hello—Sarah?"

"Alex!" Sarah's rich, melodic voice vibrated through the receiver, full of worry. "What's going on? Are you all right?"

"Yes, of course, I'm fine. But I'm glad you called. I won't be there tonight as we'd planned, I'm afraid. I'm sorry, Sarah."

I heard an instant of hesitation before she exhaled and said, "It's all right. As long as you're okay." Another pause. "Are you still coming—at all?" Her voice sounded almost wistful. I'd never heard that from her before. I began to think that she actually cared if I came.

"Oh, yes. I'm not about to miss this week." If she had any idea how many waking hours—even sleeping ones—I'd spent dreaming about those precious days with her, she'd be floored. "It's just that I'll be coming in tomorrow morning instead. And—well, this is a bit awkward, but some of my Folio B friends will be less than pleased with me tomorrow, after I've made my speech."

She waited. It was one of the many characteristics I appreciated in Sarah; she wasn't afraid of silences.

"So, though I hear the wine is excellent and the tapestries—um—inspiring at Château Menceau, I think it would be best if I met you somewhere after I've dropped into Menceau's to give my speech Friday morning. We really can't spend the night there."

I found myself doodling on a leftover press release for *The Stonecypher Saga*, and looked down at what I had drawn. It was a long line of interlocking, overlapping A's. Startled at the sight of them, I wondered if I was drawing them for "Alex" or "Angela." Flustered, I quickly started a line of S's.

"Shall I come back to Paris for you, or would you prefer to

meet somewhere near Menceau's?" I asked. "I know you've got the bike to transport . . ." My voice trailed off, the very thought of cycling making me feel weak.

She didn't ask why I would be persona non grata after the speech; I suppose she knew I'd tell her sometime if I could. "I know," she said. "Let's meet at l'Auberge d'Ananas."

Sarah proceeded to describe an auberge, a sort of French country inn, several towns away from Menceauville. She'd been there once with a client, she told me, and it was very pleasant. I immediately wondered why she and her client had found it necessary to visit an auberge so far away from the financial centre of Paris, but just as quickly realised that I had no business being jealous. After all, I'd had an eligible female friend living in my house all summer. We could have lunch at the auberge before we started out, if we wanted, Sarah said.

"Great," I said, hardly believing that I would be having lunch with her the next day, let alone a week together afterwards. I'd built it up so much in my mind that I was half-dreading it—because I had to make it perfect—and half-dying to get on with it. "I'll meet you at the auberge between noon and one, then, all right? I'm not exactly sure what the situation will be at the conference, but I'll do my very best to be there by then."

"Fine," she said. "Don't hurry. Enjoy yourself—if you can, given the, uh, problem. I'll be waiting with a good book."

Uh-oh, I thought. She's bringing a book after all. Not a good sign. I hoped she wasn't planning on long evenings in her room alone.

"Thanks. And thank you for being so understanding about the change in plans. You're a gem, Sarah. No, far better than a gem, you're—" I gave up and laughed. "Now I know why we prefer to write letters."

She laughed too, and we hung up, professing happy anticipation of the next day. But there was no question in my mind; it had been awkward. I was certain she'd felt it too.

As I put down the phone, my eyes scanned the untidy surface of my desk. A newspaper caught my eye. I hadn't seen one in a couple of days, and I picked it up. Unfortunately, my own name was the first thing I saw. It jumped out at me from a short story at the top of page three, the page to which the paper had been folded open.

Publisher sought in hit-and-run accident

Publisher Alexander Plumtree is missing today, according to family and friends, as police search for him in connection with a hit-and-run accident that occurred at 7:20 p.m. near the Bedford Square offices of Plumtree Press. An abandoned automobile belonging to Plumtree was discovered today on Bury Street in Bloomsbury, and is believed to have been used in an accident involving Plumtree Press author Angela Mayfield, now in stable condition at a London hospital.

The dark green Volkswagen Golf was found to have blood matching Mayfield's on the dented front headlight and wing, and matched the reports of witnesses at the scene of the accident.

Ian knocked on the open door. "If you're feeling up to it, Alex, I'd like to have a word. . . ."

Stunned by what I had just read, and wondering if the painkiller might be having an hallucinogenic effect, I held up the paper in a mute question and stared at him.

Ian came into the room, followed by Max, then reached back to close the door—something we rarely did at Plumtree Press. "Ah—yes, that was unfortunate," he said. "But not to worry. Mr. Falke, the wine merchant, called the police and told them you were at his class that evening from seven until eight. The police called to let us know that you're no longer being sought for questioning."

I gave a huff of exasperation as they settled on the sofa opposite my desk. "So it's just the general public that thinks I run down my authors, and not the police. That's something to be grateful for, I guess."

Ian looked sympathetic but worried. His sandy eyebrows nearly met in the middle, where a frown pulled them into a deep V. "You are alive, Alex."

He let those words hang for a moment, then shifted uncomfortably. "Alex, Max, I'm afraid things have come to a point with this Stonecypher affair where I need to give you both some rather disturbing news. I didn't want to tell you before now because there was a chance that you would be left alone—that you'd be safe." He looked at me and shook his head sadly. "But after what Alex has just been through, I think you'll agree that the gloves are off now."

Max frowned at Ian, then looked at me and shrugged as if to say, "I don't know what this is about either."

Ian transferred his gaze from my brother back to me. "You both know about the Stonecypher sentences." We nodded. I for one dreaded hearing what he had to say, and wondered if it would be a repeat of Denny's stunning news. But I was to be surprised yet again.

"Well," he began reluctantly, "evidently Stonecypher had quite a political following. It was his particular slant on things that attracted them." He leaned forward and folded his hands on the table deliberately; the leather chair creaked in the silence. "You see, he had read some Voltaire at university."

He watched us for a reaction, and, seeing none, went on to explain. I could imagine him thinking how far the standard of education had fallen. We didn't even know what Voltaire stood for!

Ian cleared his throat and went on. "Voltaire was a member of a group called the Illuminati, a sort of secret brotherhood founded in the 1760s along Masonic lines." At the mention of the Illuminati, I felt myself go rigid. Mike had been right. "Voltaire and his friends felt that it was through books that people were educated, and through books that people could be empowered to lead themselves, without the need of monarchs, and without need of the church."

I began to see where he was going with the Voltaire business.

"So Voltaire and his friend, Rousseau, helped publish the first 'encyclopaedia,' as they called it. This was still in the eighteenth century; it was meant to make education available to the common man. Part of the Enlightenment, really. Later, people credited—or discredited—Voltaire by saying that the encyclopaedia was one of the catalysts for the French Revolution."

Was Ian saying that Stonecypher had got his anti-Royal attitude from Voltaire?

"Okay. Back to the twentieth century," he said decisively.

"Stonecypher moves to Bloomsbury at roughly the same time as Lady Ottoline Morrell, Virginia Stephen—later Woolf—her sister Vanessa Bell, Maynard Keynes, and various painters and sculptors—the famous Bloomsbury Group. Among them is a literary and well-educated fellow, in fact the Cambridge mate of Maynard Keynes, by the name of Lytton Strachey. Strachey, who made his mark on history with *Eminent Victorians*—a very popular book for a while—is a Voltaire fanatic. Strachey even strives to look like him—pale, sickly, all skin and bones. He also believes every word the man ever wrote. Who is the first person who befriends Stonecypher upon his arrival in this very house?"

Max bit. "Lytton Strachey?"

Ian nodded. "It's not surprising that Stonecypher became inundated in Voltairean philosophy, as in a way he was dependent upon Strachey for membership in the coveted Bloomsbury crowd, at least at first."

Now when Ian met our eyes, no doubt he saw a bit more understanding there. "So Stonecypher put his coded sentences in his books, as an inside joke to the literary crowd. Your great-grandfather Edward, and Virginia and Leonard Woolf, who were small Bloomsbury publishers themselves, you know, at Hogarth Press, loved *The Figure in the Library* and wanted to publish it themselves. But Edward won the contract, and Stonecypher's books were printed."

Ian pursed his lips. "Then things went sour. As the word got out, some of Strachey's more political friends—members of the Illuminati, which lived on—got very serious about it all. A serious group of anti-royalists emerged, and made Stonecypher their secret standard-bearer. It all had to be quite under wraps, you see, because it was treasonable to propose the abolition of royalty.

"This group, which came to base itself solely on the secret Stonecypher sentences, began to branch off from the Illuminati, calling itself the Bibliati. They believed in achieving their political ends through the use of books, just as Voltaire had. The Bibliati adopted the open-book dingbats from Stonecypher's novels as their symbol, and Stonecypher had himself taken it from a part of the symbol associated with the

Illuminati. But it's been a well-kept secret that the Bibliati lives on."

Ian shook his head. "The secret is, in fact, extremely well-kept. Those who find out about it, who aren't members, tend to die rather violent and unpleasant deaths. They—"

"This is unbelievable," Max broke in incredulously, looking from one of us to the other. "How can it be so secret that none of us knows about it? Does Angela know this?" He turned to me for the answer.

"Not that I know of." I thought for a moment, biting my lip. She'd certainly known one secret at the time of her accident that none of the rest of us had: Marissa Godwin Stonecypher had murdered Marie-Louise Boudreau. But I wasn't ready to introduce that issue into the conversation just yet. I had the feeling that Ian had a great deal more to say. "They must *think* she knows."

"Is it some group we've heard of—like the Stonecypher Society?" Max asked, trying to get a handle on it.

"No." Ian shook his head. "The Stonecypher Society is a harmless group of literary scholars, and a few distant relatives of Stonecypher's." He looked grim. "However, the Bibliati does have a membership that overlaps considerably with that of Folio B. Your father, you see, was never invited to join because they knew he was loyal to the Christian faith. This crowd believes that religion merely controls and numbs people." He sighed and scratched his forehead with a long, tanned forefinger. The very thought bothered him; for Ian, I knew, Christianity was a matter for the intellect as much as it was for the spirit. There was no lazy or muddled thinking regarding his faith, and he couldn't understand people who assumed otherwise.

"But your father knew. You can't be an active part of a group and not piece things together after a while." He looked uncomfortable for a moment, and shifted his shoulders inside his tweedy linen jacket. "I was invited to join the group when I was quite young—somehow they weren't aware of my faith. I didn't realise what they were about until I'd already joined, and by then I knew too much to get out. I gradually realised that I had two alternatives: play along or die."

He looked at me, then at Max next to him on the sofa,

meeting our eyes, seeking our understanding and forgiveness. "I hope you don't think less of me. My only hope was to wait for a chance to expose them all. But I've had enough waiting—your father, and now you—I must take action."

It came as a great to surprise to me when stoic Ian covered his eyes with his hand and whispered, "I'm so sorry."

Max, who was much more used to such frank displays of emotion, put a hand on Ian's back. "It's not your fault, Ian," he said kindly in a quiet voice. "You did the only thing you could do."

All *I* could do, meanwhile, was stare. Ian had always been nearly perfect in my eyes; he had become almost like a father to me. Now he was telling me that he was part of some bizarre political group that had killed my parents. I was aware that I should say something, but couldn't seem to choke out the words. My silence was louder than any words; it must have been like a knife in his heart. But I simply couldn't rise to the occasion.

At last I understood, at least through a glass, darkly. But poor Max was still hopelessly confused, and I couldn't blame him. He frowned, shaking his head. "I don't understand why the Bibliati would still exist."

Ian seemed to recover himself somewhat, and shifted to face Max on the sofa, blinking as he regarded him patiently. "They exist for a purpose: to spread their political philosophy throughout the world using books. That part of it is fairly legitimate. But I'm afraid they've made a lot of headway in the 'books are the root of all power' matter, using illegitimate means, namely the rewriting of history. It's no secret, for instance, that Frank Holdsworthy has a stranglehold on history-book publishing in this country." He raised his eyebrows meaningfully.

"Oh, my God," Max breathed. "I see. Revisionist history taken to the extreme."

"Exactly."

It was my turn to sit open-mouthed as the full gravity of the situation sank in at last. The nation's children were conscientiously studying the Bibliati's subtly altered version of history, and had no reason to disbelieve it—nations are bad, religion is bad, kings and queens are bad, the European Union is good.

And I was the new owner of the leading revisionist author's next series. A series sponsored by the Bibliati, one might say.

"But surely they couldn't hope to . . ." I spluttered, faltering.

"To rewrite history?" Ian prompted. "Certainly they do hope to. And they're doing an excellent job of it. Ever so subtly and slowly, you see. Let me show you their latest world-history text, used by eighty-five per cent of the nation's schools." He stood and went to his office to get it.

Max and I looked at each other, stunned. "What have we done, to be involved in this?" he asked softly. "They wanted to kill you." He tilted his head to one side. "And Dad knew. I wonder if he and Ian ever talked about putting a stop to it all."

"I'll bet they did," I said thoughtfully. "They were confidants." I hoped Max wouldn't make the next leap in thought, to the violent and unpleasant death my parents had faced because of our father's knowledge, and his inability to let something evil continue unchecked.

Max was reaching for my arm, saying, "Alex, are you all right?" Just then Ian walked in, saw Max looking at me with concern, and our eyes said what words couldn't, at least in front of Max. I can't explain it, but with the extraordinary understanding Ian and I had, he knew that I understood why my parents had died.

He opened the history book, which contained a number of yellow sticky-note flags jutting out of the top edge. Obviously he'd been studying the book for some time, watching for the Bibliati's slant on the words. "See? Look at this section on World War One, the way it's distorted." He read aloud: "'In the year 1914, during the reign of George V, monarchies began to crumble all over the world. World War I began to expose the absurdity of royalty: royal figureheads had everything to do with privilege, and little to do with the country over which they reigned. How were the royal family of 1914, who were more German than English, to condone the killing of their close relatives in Prussia by their own subjects? George V's parents, Edward III and Queen Mary, both spoke English with a German accent. But fight their subjects did—one of the bloodiest and most gruesome wars in history—because, as Lord Esher said in August 1917, if Britain failed to beat the enemy 'we shall be lucky if we escape a revolution in which the Monarchy, the Church and all our "Victorian" institutions will founder.' "

Max and I stared, and he looked up at us from the book. "And this: 'In an increasingly democratic world, the royal family's close relationship to Tsarist Russia added an embarrassing twist. The royal family could no longer pretend that World War I was merely one of democracy vs. autocracy. In an attempt to curry favour with the public, the British monarchy hurriedly changed its name from Saxe-Coburg to a more English-sounding Windsor. In 1917 George V attempted to make the monarchy seem more English and democratic by announcing that the royal family would be permitted to marry into British families.

" 'In that same year, George V learned that the Tsar of Russia, his cousin, Nicholas II, had been forced to abdicate. Eager as he was to preserve his own monarchy, he refused to grant him asylum, fearful that anti-monarchists would protest. Nicholas II and his family were slaughtered the next year at Ekaterinburg. When it came to preserving the monarchy, national allegiance was thicker than blood.' As if it all happened because of the monarchy. It's done so subtly—the statements aren't exactly untrue—that no one seems to notice." He paused for a moment, apparently having difficulty framing the next sentence. "All we can do now is protect the living." He wiped his eyes with a shaking thumb. "You've got a guard on Angela now, I understand. I wonder if she really did know about the Bibliati."

"I told her about the letter I found in Virginia Holdsworthy's Wodehouse," I whispered. "So we both knew that something was going on within Folio B. They were aware that we knew, because they stole the Wodehouse—with the letter in it—and the Stonecypher too."

"I can't believe any of this," Max protested. "The Wodehouse with the letter and the association copy of the Stonecypher were stolen?"

I nodded.

"Why didn't you tell me, Alex? What's going on here?" I didn't like the fact that the first sentence had ended with a note of suspicion, and that the second had ended in rising anger.

Suddenly I felt weary beyond belief, but there was nothing for it but to tell Max exactly what had happened. "It was Saturday night. There was an intruder in the library." His eyes widened, and I went on. "First I had a strange dream, which I'm still not sure *was* a dream, in which Stonecypher's ghost—yes, ghost—seemed to visit the library, where I was sleeping. Then I heard books being tossed about in the library, and ran down to find it vandalised. The Stonecypher and Wodehouse were gone, and that damned Stonecypher dingbat was sitting on the desk." I tried to smile and said, "I still don't know who took the two books and left the dingbat—the ghost or the intruder." Max simply stared.

"Really, Max. I just didn't want to worry you with it."

His face clouded, and I wondered if he was worrying about whether I'd discovered his absence that night. Max and I didn't have the telepathy that Ian and I did, but I guessed that was probably it. Then he squinted, suddenly indignant, and I understood that what he thought was far worse.

"You think *I* stole them, don't you?" he said. It was half accusation and half hurt. "I saw it when I commented on the worth of the association copy, on the night you bought them. That's why you didn't say anything."

This last twist more than took me by surprise. I let out an incredulous laugh and opened out my right hand innocently. "No! Max, look, it's not that way at all. I just told you that there was an intruder. He took—"

"Don't lie to me. I can see what's going on here. You'll never trust me again; I can understand that. It's my fault, I know, for going against you in that business last year. But I thought . . ." He stood up, flustered, tears in his eyes.

"Max, no, it's not at all what you—" I stood and grabbed his arm as he flew past me, wincing at the jolt that reverberated through my injured shoulder.

He turned and shook me off, starting another shock wave through my body. I bit my lip and concentrated on Max. He looked not so much angry as embarrassed and hurt. His eyes held more pain than I could bear. "Let me go. I don't blame you, Alex."

He stalked off then, and Ian said, "There's nothing you can do now, Alex. Let's hope he can sort through it himself."

I shook my head in frustration and defeat and fell into the chair again. Rubbing my good hand over my face with its two-day beard, I asked the obvious question.

"Who, Ian?"

He sighed. "Holdsworthy. Beasley, against his will, in a way. Pillinghurst. Farquhart. Menceau. Soames. And many others, in different cities and European countries. Most of them have already disposed of their monarchs, you'll notice." He sat forward in his chair. "Look, Alex. I'm not sure how many of these people you know. But let me warn you again: they've never let anyone live who knows, unless they belong. I watched my back for a while after your father died, thinking they might have discovered where my true loyalties lie. But all these years, I've been watching and waiting quietly until I could make a case. Now I can. And I must. But you, Alex, are faced with a decision."

Our eyes met. Ian said, "You risk your life to do away with this once and for all, or you run forever."

I nodded. Even the idea of the letter to Mike Chelmsford and my solicitor, exposing them, was small comfort compared to the thought of incapacitating the Bibliati forever. Ian had known my answer before he'd spoken, as a father would. I thought for a moment about my speech, and the trip with Sarah. "There's a lot at stake with Sarah," I said. "I can't let this ruin my chances with her."

Ian watched me and nodded once, seriously. There was a lot at stake for him in this as well. As Sarah's doting grandfather, and my surrogate father, he wanted us to marry almost as much as I did.

"Here's what I'm going to do," I said, and told him what I had in mind.

"You realise that they want you dead," he said grimly when I'd finished.

"I do. I think I know a way." I looked at him and he nodded at me again, once. "Keep an eye on Angela for me, would you? Max too." My heart sank at the thought. "I hate to leave him like this."

"I'll make sure he's well looked after. No doubt Madeline will be a comfort to him." He smiled, and I almost did too. "I should tell you, Alex, that I think your father might have put something in writing about the Bibliati—he mentioned it once. You know where to find his private papers; you might want to find out what he had to say. And don't worry about anything here at the Press," he added. "We'll take care of things."

I stood to go, feeling wobbly, as if I'd just endured a particularly nasty bout of flu. "Thanks, Ian."

He nodded and stood too. "God go with you, Alex. Can I drive you home?"

I looked in his piercing blue eyes, then shook my head. "No, thanks." I needed to be alone, and it was a short walk to the tube station. My painkillers made all things possible.

Without further discussion I left the conference room, first stopping in my rubble-filled office long enough to collect my ticket for the flight to Paris, extra business cards, and briefcase. Then I guzzled another glass of water and actually rode the construction-ravaged lift down to the ground floor for a change.

As I walked to the station, followed, of course, by the Neck, I felt I was in one of those nightmares in which I ran and ran and never reached my destination. I had actually had a dream, the sort that recurs every few months, not unlike what was happening to me at that moment. In it, I was rushing to meet Sarah at an airport, not only late but unpacked because I couldn't find my luggage, and the cappuccino vendor couldn't find the right change, and then I turned up on the wrong concourse and was stopped by security for running, and locked up in the airport holding pen. Now, on top of it all, one of the people I admired most in the world was part of the group that had not only murdered my parents, and Denny, but nearly Angela and me as well.

Real life was fully as bad as my nightmare—and worse.

Shaking my head, I turned into a small sandwich bar at the corner of Oxford Street and Tottenham Court Road where I sometimes purchased a buttered bun on my way into work.

Neck considerately waited outside, several doors down outside a photo shop. I bought several ham rolls, a Coke, and a big bottle of mineral water. I sank my teeth into a roll hungrily as I hurried toward the tube station, and had polished them all off by the time I sat down to wait for the train. I guzzled the Coke as the end of the lunch hour crowd stared at my unshaven face and otherwise wild appearance, and thought I could feel the rush of caffeine as my thoughts raced from one mind-boggling issue to the next. Staring at me from the wall above the gap, life-size, was Hollywood's answer to the prayers of women everywhere: Jean-Claude Rimbaud. The French movie star was, according to Lisette, every woman's dream of what a man should be. He'd started years before with violent action films, and moved on to more sensitive roles, with the result that he was now perfect: tough, yet gentle. I wasn't about to tell anyone this, but I had viewed two of his most recent films, including the latest, entitled *RESCUE!* as the advertisement opposite me shouted, on the sly to see what Sarah thought I should be like. Jean-Claude was able and willing, I had learned, to discuss his feelings (with a French accent) on celluloid, and did not look the least bit foolish for it. I hoped I could rise to his standard.

Detaching my eyes from Rimbaud's, I took out the mineral water and unscrewed the white plastic cap with my good right arm. I reflected that things seemed to be going from bad to worse. For a change, I couldn't see the Neck on the platform. He had become a part of my life, I thought wryly; I almost felt something was awry when he wasn't around.

Prematurely, I gloated as my eyes darted from one cluster of people to the next. Perhaps I would make it to Paris in one piece after all.

Then a chill crept up my spine. I successfully suppressed an urge to do a double-take, but there was no doubt about it: I'd seen Giles Rutherford, Armand's secretary and quite possibly personal companion, lurking behind a pillar when I'd turned. I tried to relax so he wouldn't know that I'd noticed, staring blankly at Jean-Claude on the opposite side of the track with the handful of other waiting passengers on the platform.

Giles?

He had reacted oddly at Armand's party to the news of

Angela's book. I dithered between thinking that he was in that neighbourhood for the book fair, and this was a logical tube station for him to use, and that he was charged by the Bibliati with disposing of me. Perhaps they'd already got wind of my escape from Marie-Louise's room.

There was no escaping the fact that I was now a hunted man, and I broke out in a cold sweat at the memory of Denny's words, and then Ian's. They were intent on killing me now because I *knew*, not merely because they were trying to prevent the publication of a book.

The train whizzed past then, slowing to a stop. I stood and walked down the platform, away from Giles, as if searching for an uncrowded carriage at the front of the train. With any luck, Giles might think I was overcome with the lemming instinct that strikes people waiting on crowded train platforms. Anyone who habitually rode the tube knew that people always hurried toward either the very first or last carriage in the vain hope of finding a vacant seat. I drifted with the crowd.

Then, I drew even with a stairway off the platform, and bolted, if you could still call it that, given my inhibited motion, up the deserted stairway. I pounded up enough stairs to equal the two giant escalators that normally transported people to street level, and never heard anyone following me. But I didn't take time to turn and check either. The sound of my own breathing was ridiculously loud, and I tried to walk normally through the station exit and onto Tottenham Court Road.

Forcing myself not to look back for several moments, I finally glanced over my shoulder when I had crossed Oxford Street, moving down Bedford Street in the direction of the Press. To my utter horror, I saw Rich ambling nonchalantly across the street behind me in his trainers. I wouldn't have minded the Neck so much, or even Giles; but Rich had shot me twice while looking me in the eye.

Stay calm, Alex, I told myself; you know this neighbourhood better than almost anyone—definitely better than Rich. I proceeded at a respectable pace to the shop where I'd bought the ham rolls barely ten minutes before, nodded at the proprietor, pointed to the rear of his shop, and said, "May I?"

He nodded pleasantly as I moved quickly through the tiny

shop with its several linoleum-covered tables, whacked the loo door shut, and opened the door to the alley. I slipped through and closed it again, fairly certain that Rich couldn't have got into the shop fast enough to see the door close.

Nonetheless I ran for my life to the end of the alley. I was not aware that I was running anywhere in particular, but the alley emptied me out into Great Russell Street. Once there, I glanced back and, miraculously, there was Rich.

Swearing under my breath, I forced my legs to pump like parts of a machine down Great Russell and across Gower Street. My legs were beginning to feel unreliable and shaky, despite the fact that the day before I had been in peak physical condition. It was remarkable how the gunshot wounds had sapped my endurance.

It dawned on me that my subconscious was taking me somewhere familiar, but I couldn't have said where. Running past onlookers and creating a spectacle of myself, I practically staggered into Bury Place, Denny's street, only to realise that they probably already knew about his cellar. Hesitating for a precious instant, expecting to see Rich pounding round the corner behind me, I had an idea.

CHAPTER 15

*As good almost kill a man as kill a good book: who kills
a man kills a reasonable creature, God's image; but he
who destroys a good book kills reason itself.*
                                        —JOHN MILTON, *AREO PAGITICA*

The interior of St. George's was blissfully dark and
cool, as it had been several days before. The doors
were open, and I ran in, not seeing Rich in the street behind
me, where I had turned past a fence bordering Museum
Street. Unless the man had extrasensory perception, which I
very much doubted in Rich's case, he couldn't know that I'd
gone in.

The altar in a small chapel to the side beckoned, covered
as it was in linen to the floor, and I ran into the small alcove at
the side of the church and ducked under the table just as I
heard footsteps inside the church. The footsteps were made
by leather soles though, and not by the trainers that Rich had
sported each time I'd run into him.

The footsteps hesitated, then stopped. I imagined that the
cleric I'd seen in the church the day before was standing still,
considering whether he'd really heard someone run huffing
and puffing into the sanctuary. Hoping that he wouldn't say
something like "Who's there? I know you're there. Come
out at once!" I tried to hold my breath while panting at the
same time.

A moment or two of this sort of dread passed; then I heard the squeak of a rubber-soled shoe making a fast turn into the marble-floored entrance.

"Good morning." The cleric spoke pleasantly, evidently addressing the wearer of the shoes. I thought I knew who the visitor was, and doubted that he would be kneeling to pray. "May I be of assistance?"

There was no answer, but the squeaky rubber soles were silent. I could almost see Rich standing there, casting about for his prey, thrown off by the kindly vicar.

"No. No," Rich's gruff voice said. A pause. "No one here, then?"

As I tried to quiet my breathing, I pictured the vicar looking around the apparently deserted church as if to acknowledge the obvious, perhaps even holding his arms out towards the empty pews to illustrate. Now, perhaps, he was frowning in kindly concern. "Were you expecting someone?"

"No," my hunter said curtly, sounding disgusted. The shoes squeaked back into the distance.

I deemed it safest to stay where I was. To my surprise, the leather soles travelled in my direction. They stopped before the altar, and I heard a rustle of clothes and the popping of a knee. He was kneeling, just on the other side of the linen cloth from me.

In a quiet voice the vicar said, "He's gone."

Astonished, I got painfully to my feet and peered out from behind the altar. His head was bowed, as if in prayer, and I suspected that he was merely trying to camouflage his conversation with me in case Rich returned.

"Thank you," I said. "You knew."

He rose and smiled briefly. "I knew. Come this way; the exit is less conspicuous." He guided me quickly through his office to a side door.

Intrigued, I asked, "Why did you pretend I wasn't there?"

He shrugged. "The church has offered physical sanctuary through the ages. I saw no reason to break that tradition now." Studying me with compassion, he added, "And I saw you here the other day."

"Thank you," I said again. "Very much."

He held the door open for me and I slipped out onto

Bloomsbury Way, a busy street running into Shaftesbury Avenue. Either I was lucky, or the vicar had begun praying for me immediately—I suspect that the latter was the case—because a taxi was cruising my way, heaven sent. I stuck up the index finger of my right hand briefly, ducked in as the driver came to a stop next to me, and darted inside. A hard vinyl taxi seat had never felt so good. I paid the driver to take me all the way to Armand Beasley's house. Watersmeet would be a seventy-pound fare. I had more money at the moment than other commodities, such as energy and an automobile of my own. The driver was well pleased, and chauffeured me in relaxed silence to the end of Armand's drive.

My decision to go there hadn't been well thought out. I considered it now as the taxi pulled away, leaving me at the large shrubs that marked the edge of the property.

At some point, trusting people comes down to instinct, not logic. Even if Armand was involved in the Bibliati and their history-altering activities I simply knew I could trust him. I needed to hear what he would say when I confronted him. I was fairly sure he wouldn't kill me. He would probably be at the book fair most of the day, but it suited me to wait in a quiet place and think things through until he returned. In fact, the very thought of staying alive for another few hours sounded good to me. Who would think to look for me here, skulking about in Armand Beasley's shrubbery?

I lowered myself gently into the leafy hedge, which was conveniently overgrown and gave me a nice layer of protection. Lying still, even on the mossy ground in the midst of branches, was an immense relief after my flight from Rich and the bumpy taxi ride. I relaxed into the greenery, my eyes burning as I closed them.

The next thing I knew, I was blinking aching eyes in dusky light, having been awakened by a car coming slowly up the drive. I stayed where I was, and as it passed I saw that it was a silver Peugeot. The windows of the car reflected tree branches so well that I couldn't tell who was inside, though I thought I saw two heads. Armand and Giles? I would soon find out.

Gathering the courage to move again, I heard another car coming and again stayed motionless. Headlights first, then a

Volvo, steely blue. Doors banged as people got out of the first car at the front door; I heard Armand's voice carry in the twilight silence. A quieter voice answered him. Then the second car crunched to a halt on the pea gravel just behind Armand's, and Michel Menceau got out, along with the birdlike man I'd met at Armand's party. The valet opened the door, or perhaps it was Giles, and they all went in together.

I didn't know how Armand would feel about having an audience for the discussion I was about to have with him, but perhaps he would agree to see me privately. I sat up and got slowly to my feet, closing my eyes against the pain in my shoulder. It was worse after having been still for a long time. The deepening purple of the sky and the foliage swam slightly for a moment. I blinked and things evened out, then made my way towards the front door. No sense in wasting time now they were here, I thought. With all I'd absorbed in the last few days, and all that had happened, I didn't even feel fear. Had I been functioning fully on all levels, and not operating courtesy of painkillers, I would probably have been terrified.

The look on Giles's face when he opened the door and saw me was priceless. He gave the distinct impression that he thought I was back from the dead, judging from the way he stared. I thought that Giles Rutherford had probably only stared open-mouthed several times in his entire life, and it was a sight worth seeing.

"Hello, Giles. Could I have a word with Armand? I see that he has guests, but . . ." I let my voice trail off in an unspoken question.

"Alex," he said finally. "Good to see you. Good. Yes—I'll just tell him. Please, please do come right in." I stepped in at his urging, enjoying seeing him off balance. He closed the door, then left me in the hall as he backed up a step, still looking at me incredulously, then turned and hurried off to find Armand.

I didn't hear the rise and fall of voices anywhere. It occurred to me that perhaps Holdsworthy, Menceau, and the bird man were staying with Armand for the duration of the book fair. Watersmeet was miles better than any London hotel, and they obviously had a great deal to discuss in privacy. Perhaps the men were changing for dinner, or otherwise getting comfortable, and had each gone to his own quarters. I stood looking at the antique maps of Hertfordshire and Buckinghamshire that hung on the wall, and before two minutes had passed, Armand was greeting me, looking pleased but perplexed.

"Alex," he said warmly. "What is it?" His eyes travelled quickly to the sling, then to my face. "What's happened?" He frowned.

"Hello, Armand," I said as naturally as I could. "Oh, nothing, really," I said, referring to my arm. "Sorry to surprise you like this. I need to talk to you for a moment."

"Of course, of course." He was all warmth and solicitude, and it wasn't an act. "We're just about to have a drink—join us?"

"Yes, thanks." It struck me that this would be a convenient time to confront Holdsworthy directly about MacDougal and the doctored history books.

Armand indicated that I should follow him down the hall, and I did so while he chatted. "Frank Holdsworthy, Michel Menceau, and Martin Applebaum are staying here until we leave for the conference at Michel's this weekend, and then the Paris book fair the following week. Nice to have the place filled for a change." He turned into a pleasant study and rubbed his hands together in front of a full bar on a tray. "Please—do sit down." He looked at me with a concerned sort of frown, and I wondered if I looked as if I needed to sit. "What can I get for you?"

"Scotch, thanks," I said.

He nodded and poured two. "Your father's drink."

"Yes." I bit back what I would have liked to say about my father, deciding to begin with the less incendiary matter of the book-stealing ring.

"All right," Armand grunted as he sank back into one of the larger chairs. "What brings you out on the eve of the Folio B conference?" He gazed at me pleasantly, smiling as he brought his drink to his lips.

"It's about Folio B," I began as gently as my anger allowed. "Actually, it's rather disturbing, Armand, and I know that I can trust you to tell me the truth."

His eyes widened at this direct approach, even grew a bit

wild. At that moment Frank Holdsworthy walked through the door, followed immediately by Menceau and the strange little Applebaum.

We both looked up at them as they entered and said civil hellos, obviously surprised to see me. I could sense Armand making an enormous effort to remain calm and handle the situation with good grace. I felt sure he knew what was coming, but was just as sure he didn't know I'd been so near death because of Folio B.

"Excellent," Armand said with emphasis. "We nearly have the full board here—all the better to hear what Alex has to say." He frowned and looked back at me. "Disturbing news though, he says. Help yourself to drinks, everyone," he said, waving a hand towards the bar. Still looking at me, he nodded and said, "Now, please, do go on."

It was going to have to be one of the greatest thespian performances of my life, bringing up the book-stealing and history book issues while pretending I didn't know about the Bibliati—in case it still mattered. I also wasn't about to give any of them the satisfaction of mentioning where I'd been for most of the last day.

"All right." I took a deep breath and looked up from the half-inch of neat Scotch in my glass. "I have reason to believe that I am on the board of an organisation that receives rare library books in excellent condition, and, under the guise of restoring them, removes the library markings with expert care—or forges new pages with authentic ink and paper—and sells them at top price. Bookplates are inserted to make them appear to be legitimate copies belonging to well-known collectors." I didn't mention Virginia Holdsworthy's name; everyone in the room knew what I was talking about.

All were motionless, stunned at either my words, or my audacity in speaking them. "This is done only for books of which there are enough fragments about, or other copies in bad condition, so that a replacement can be sewn together and bound for the library, and restamped to look authentic."

I stopped and waited. Frank Holdsworthy banged his glass down on the silver tray of the bar, where he had mixed gin with something, and started towards me. His eyes never left mine, and he stalked, rather than walked, until he stood directly in front of me.

"How dare you," he began in a low voice. *"How dare you!"* The second one came out in a shout. He was so upset that I felt droplets of saliva flying at me. His eyes were wild, and his hands, clenched in fists, were held away from his body in readiness to fight. "You know very well Diana handles the restoration. You're besmirching her reputation! What grounds do you have for this ridiculous accusation?"

"Physical evidence," I continued calmly, meeting his eyes, "which I came upon while the door of the restoration workshop was open. Boxes of some of the most valuable books in the world, ready to be shipped to Menceau's, presumably to sell at the Paris book fair. Fragments of the very same books stored in a cupboard. And everything that anyone would need to print a forged page, particularly a letterpress that uses polymer plates."

Holdsworthy stared at me for a moment after I'd finished speaking, then let out a short, incredulous laugh and shook his head. Suddenly he was calm and merely derisive, which took me by surprise. He moved off towards the bar to retrieve his drink, then sat down as everyone else looked on.

"You've got some sort of paranoid imagination, Plumtree. That's the most absurd story I've ever heard." He shook his head some more and sipped at his drink, smiling.

Armand spoke next. He looked displeased, and I was growing more uncomfortable by the minute. Had I been wrong?

"Alex, I'm concerned that you would have received that impression. Perhaps you didn't know that Diana teaches some classes to professional book restorers, and shows them her techniques. Thus the materials for printing from scratch. And it might have escaped your notice, but there is a restorationist's book exhibit scheduled for the duration of the Paris book fair. That's why Frank and Diana would have been shipping books there."

He frowned, tipping his head towards me as if he were trying to understand. "What would have made you think that Folio B was behind a book-forging—even stealing, you're saying—operation? You know that's exactly the opposite of what we stand for."

It was my turn to be stunned. They had just made it all look reasonable, and I was the one who looked the fool. I kept my silence, wondering if I should even head into history-book territory. The book-stealing and -doctoring bit had been only the tip of the iceberg.

I nodded sceptically, clinging to the shreds of my dignity.

"All right. Let's assume that what you've just said explains it all," I said, peering down at my drink, trying to sound reasonable. I looked back up into Armand's eyes. "How do you explain a leading history-text author who, for years, has been distorting history so subtly that no one has even noticed—especially the children who are being trained to think the way he does?"

"My God, Plumtree, you need a psychiatrist! Where do you come up with these things? And what does this have to do with Folio B?" It was Holdsworthy who said this, then looked to his friends for corroboration. Menceau looked bored, as if we were wasting his time, and the bird man exhibited a multitude of nervous ticks.

Armand still looked worried. "Who told you this?" he asked. "And who is the author?"

I thought quickly. I wasn't about to let them know that Ian had informed me. "It wasn't difficult to figure out, now that Frank's ex-author is conveniently mine." I looked at Armand and said bluntly, "MacDougal."

To my great surprise, Holdsworthy choked on his drink, laughing. He laughed so hard that he was silent, and the others around the room smiled to see him, normally such a serious man, so overcome with mirth.

I waited, eyes on the rug, humiliated by his reaction but still clinging to what I had seen with Ian in my own conference room. I respected Ian enormously, and might possibly have jumped off a cliff if he told me it was the right thing to do. For a moment the possibility flashed through my mind that Ian was more loyal to the Bibliati than to me, despite his words to the contrary. He was a member, after all.

But MacDougal's insistence on the contract changes supported it too, and it seemed quite clear to me that Frank

Holdsworthy had attempted to distance himself from suspicion by allowing me to recruit MacDougal, and have the obnoxious Scot distort history from under my roof, his distortions bolstered by the "specialists" he approved to review his books.

Eventually the laugh wound down, and Holdsworthy wiped his eyes with a handkerchief. "God, that was great," he said. "Haven't laughed like that in years." He sniffed and looked at me, blinking and still smiling. "So now, Alex. If this wild idea is true—and the news gets out—you're the one responsible, eh? Oh, that's rich." Guffaws burst through his newly restored calm, and he was off into another paroxysm of laughter.

I'd had enough. I wasn't sure what I'd expected when I'd rung the bell, but it wasn't uncontrollable ridicule. Humiliated and confused as I hadn't been since early schoolboy days, I stood and said, "I think I've provided enough entertainment for one night. I'll let myself out." The only bright spot of my visit had been Rupert Soames's absence; at least I hadn't had to face his attacks—verbal or otherwise.

Armand rose, unsmiling but kind, to walk with me to the door. As we were passing through the doorway into the hall, Holdsworthy called after me: "Does this mean that you won't be speaking at the Folio B conference tomorrow, Alex?" It sounded like a dare.

It was at that moment that I realised the brilliance of what he—or they—had done. It was stunning, and must have required months of advance planning.

If I backed out of everything and ran, I would be acknowledging my awareness of the secret society. I either played along or was killed—Ian's set of choices too—and they had done a good job of ensuring that I wouldn't choose a different option. Greed, not to mention impatience and arrogance, had got me into this; I was so eager to expand our academic line that I assumed MacDougal just happened to be available when I wanted him to be. It had never entered my mind, egocentric as I was, that Holdsworthy had made him available to me at a specific time for a specific purpose.

I turned back and looked into his eyes, considering. I

would let them think I was weak, that I would go along with it all to save my skin and my publishing house.

"No, of course not, Frank," I answered pleasantly, surprised at my own equanimity in the face of this unparalleled disaster. "I'll be there as planned." Then I stepped out into the hallway and heard Armand's footsteps behind me.

When we reached the front door, he said, "Well done," and put his hand on my back roughly. I had the feeling he wanted desperately to tell me something. Instead, he merely inquired, "Where's your car?" He looked down the drive, searching for it in vain.

"Never mind. Please, don't let me keep you. Good night, Armand."

"Good night." Sounding bewildered, he closed the door and I trudged down the drive. It would be a very long walk home, but I had a lot to think about. I was so lost in a replay of what had just transpired that it took a moment for me to realise that someone was whispering my name.

"Plumtree! Over here!" It was a stage whisper; I couldn't make out to whom the voice belonged.

A trap? Was I about to meet my end in Armand's drive?

Altering my course slightly towards the source of the voice, I found that I was approaching Giles. I could just barely see him motioning to me from the edge of the drive, near its end, from behind an ancient oak. I walked towards him hesitantly, unsure of his intent. Nothing, I told myself, could surprise me any more than what had already happened.

I was wrong.

"Over here," he said softly as I drew closer. I went warily, half-expecting to receive another bullet for my pains. It might have been my imagination, and admittedly I couldn't see well in the deepening twilight, but out here by the oak Giles had lost his effeminate traits. He somehow looked a different man—more upright, more definite, more decisive. Athletic, almost.

"What an unbelievably excruciating time you had in there." I thought I saw him wince at the memory as he drew me into the greenery with him. So Giles somehow heard what we'd said, then hurried out here to meet me. "What happened to your arm?"

I shook my head, minimising it. Giles folded his arms across his chest. "All right, Plumtree," he said with slight condescension, as if speaking to a child, but not unkindly, and with great interest. "Somehow you've found out about the Bibliati. You know part of it, obviously, but not all—and believe me, you don't want to know it all." He hesitated, letting this sink in. "I can't express to you how careful you must be, now that they know you know."

Abruptly, he laughed, shaking his head. "You've got balls, bringing it up before a whole roomful of people. I thought one or two might croak right then and there." As an afterthought he mumbled, "That would've solved a couple of problems."

I didn't know what to say, so I kept my mouth shut.

Giles sobered quickly. "I can't be gone too long, or they'll wonder." He hesitated, glancing quickly towards the house in the fading light. "It's taken me a year and a half to work myself into a position of trust with Armand Beasley and the rest of them. Armand is innocent of the violence used to prevent interruptions to the work of the Bibliati, but he is a member, and he's brought me in too. Like you, I want to see them stopped, but because of their methods, not their beliefs. I'm not sure that their beliefs could do any real harm."

A car approached on the lane, and we both ducked more deeply behind the oak, into the boxwood. There weren't any other homes nearby, as most of these edifices rested comfortably on forty acres or more. Not much reason for a car to be travelling down this lane after nine o'clock at night. But it passed Armand's drive without slowing, and we both relaxed a bit.

"You almost blew it all to hell in there. Good thing you didn't actually get round to mentioning the society." He said this dispassionately, a critic evaluating a performance.

Finally I felt a need to speak. "How do I know you're not just saying this to make me trust you? Placating me so I won't cause any more trouble until you can dispose of me?"

"If I'd wanted to do that, I could have disposed of you handily the afternoon you and your friends were nosing about in Balfour Mews."

"But—" I looked at him in disbelief and alarm. "There was no one—"

Giles nodded grudgingly. "You may not have seen anyone, but remember, these people are hardly amateurs. Nor am I." He paused, shifting restlessly. "Except that they're getting careless. For instance, it seemed that the police paid an inordinate amount of attention to Virginia Holdsworthy's death. No charges in the end, but really—to kill the poor woman when she was already at death's door?" He looked bitter. "It was cruel and disgusting."

"I have to know something," I said. "Do you know about Virginia Holdsworthy's letter?"

I thought I saw his brow furrow in confusion. "Letter?"

"Hmm," I said. "Then you didn't break into my library and steal the books I got at Armand's party that night?"

"No," he said, taken aback. "The association copy was *stolen*?"

I nodded. "Sorry. Go on."

"All right. Your friend Angela. That was unnecessary and just plain stupid. And I think I know who they recruited to organise that little job." He looked me in the eye. "You guess. Someone who would do anything to be considered part of the inside group within Folio B, someone fairly new who desires Armand Beasley's approval intensely. Someone who despises you and Plumtree Press beyond all reason, and desires not only your business but your personal demise."

"Good God, no," I whispered, horrified. "Not old Rupert!"

He nodded deliberately. "One and the same. He wouldn't actually have done the deed himself, you understand, but he made sure that it happened."

Rupert's obsession with all things related to Plumtrees and Plumtree Press was worsening rapidly. "He could be charged with murder, if she—if she—" The whispered sentence tapered off. I was stunned by Giles's revelation.

"Well, I trust that you can be persuaded not to make any more public statements until we have all we need to lock them all up for a while."

The alarm bells went off. Was this a trick to get me to keep quiet until he could silence me for good? I did my best to look compliant and said, "Who's 'we'? What do you mean?" I wondered if he knew just how confused I was.

"A formidable force of one: me. I'm making audiotapes. In fact, I'm going to Michel Menceau's house party, and the Folio B conference, wearing a hidden tape recorder. That should be enough, especially if I can entice them to say things, or tacitly approve them, through conversation."

I slumped, rubbing my forehead with my right hand, suddenly feeling overwhelmed. My upper chest throbbed viciously. "Hang on." I could scarcely believe we were having this conversation. "First, can you please tell me which of them exactly is doing what? Was I really so wrong about the books? And who is the head of it all—the one who had me built into my building, and who has Rupert arrange for people to be killed?"

Giles leaned forward. I could almost feel his puzzled frown. "What do you mean, built you into your building?"

"Just what I say. They built me into Marie-Louise's charming little room, where, by the way, she also died and left her journals. Stonecypher couldn't resist leaving a confession that he killed her. But it's a long story—someday I'll make sure it all comes out. At any rate, they rebuilt the wall round me, about two feet thick."

His eyes widened and stayed that way. "Oh, my God," he said incredulously. "So he really did kill her."

"No, actually," I replied. "His wife did."

Evidently that meant something to him; he thought about it for a moment. "Remarkable. So that's where you were when they tried to discredit you with that story in the paper . . . inside the walls of your own building. How on earth did you get out?" Either he suddenly seemed to realise the gravity of my own personal circumstances, or he'd had a hand in it and wanted to know how I'd outfoxed him.

"It was a miraculous reprieve." I smiled at the thought of gentle Mr. Heppelthwaite, who knew nothing about secret societies that were twisting the nation's history for the young. "It's a long story—I'll tell you about it sometime. Please go on."

"Okay." Eyes still wide, he glanced round before answering. "Pillinghurst's the real sociopath. I think he arranges to have people silenced, in one way or another. Armand and Frank and the others are naive enough to believe that a lot of people they know are involved in horrible accidents. They honestly don't seem to know."

For a moment I felt so much hatred towards Edward Pillinghurst that everything in front of me turned black, and I felt dangerously calm. Blinking away the blackness, I tried to put it out of my mind that I had met the man who had killed my parents. Focussing on the fact that what Giles had just said jibed with the reactions I'd seen in Armand's house, I managed to say something profound, along the lines of, "Mmmm."

He continued. "But Pillinghurst's got something going with Soames now, and I don't like the look of them when they're together." I thought I saw an expression of distaste come over his face, though it was hard to tell in the gloom— especially with my eyes. "As I say, I think Rupert Soames took care of your friend Angela. Pillinghurst knows he's getting on a bit, needs someone as ruthless as himself to take over. Soames presented himself at an opportune time."

Sighing, he continued. "Most of Folio B has no clue that the Bibliati exists. The vast majority of the members believes that Folio B is devoted solely to the preservation and 'restoration' "—I noticed that he pronounced the word ironically— "of old books." He chuckled humorlessly. "I wanted to throttle you when you launched so fearlessly into that with them in there. I've been trying to keep quiet about the relatively minor book forgeries and thefts until the larger issue of Holdsworthy's history texts was taken care of—not to mention the things you don't know about yet. I didn't want you to blow it wide open and create a lot of questions that would make them more cautious, and harder to expose."

I squinted at him in disbelief. "So I was right?"

He snorted, closing his eyes briefly. "I think I've got it worked out, but I can't tell you yet." He shook his head. "If I'm right, it's an amazing fiddle."

A smile curved up one side of his mouth. "You have style, Plumtree; I commend you. Coming here to talk to them about all of this when you know they've already tried to kill you."

He shook his head in a combination of admiration and disbelief, and checked the luminous numbers on his watch again.

"I must go," he announced. "If you get as far as the speech, do us all a favour and stay out of the way for at least a week afterwards. I hear you're going on holiday—please stay away for a while." He began to walk back towards the house, suddenly looking rushed. Then he stopped again. "And I wouldn't advertise your itinerary."

"Wait a minute." My eyes sought his in the darkness. "What's in this for you?" It had occurred to me that not many people would set their lives aside to observe a gang of rare-book enthusiasts for more than a year. "Are you with the authorities?" The idea sounded absurd the moment the words had left my mouth, even to me.

He laughed bitterly. "Do I look like I work for the police?" He looked at me with something like determination. "No. I'm on my own." With that cryptic remark he began to back away towards the house, adding, "You could say I'm sort of a fanatic myself." With that he was off, and I was left feeling that I'd somehow landed on a different planet.

I shook my head to clear it and began the long walk home, considering what I should do next. Giles seemed to have the situation well in hand, and I didn't want to do anything to ruin his carefully-laid trap.

If I could believe him.

I sighed. The thought of meeting Sarah tomorrow after my speech was of little comfort. Holiday with Sarah, the dream of years now, seemed absurd in the face of what I'd uncovered in the rare-book world, not to mention the threat of unnatural and untimely death. Being virtually inches away from her all day for a week would be like a mirage in the desert of the Bibliati's calculating evil. The whole holiday had, in fact, already taken on a feeling of unreality.

If Giles were for real, the best thing I could do would be to merely stay alive until after his exposé.

And if Giles weren't authentic, I was merely postponing the inevitable.

CHAPTER 16

In nature's infinite book of secrecy
A little I can read.
—SHAKESPEARE, *ANTONY AND CLEOPATRA*

As I approached the narrow lane that led to the Orchard's winding drive, I was surprised to see a dark green Rover parked along it, off to one side in the darkness. I'd been wondering about the white Ford; it seemed a long time since I'd seen it. Had it developed car trouble? Had they traded it for a green Rover, or was this a new batch of hunters? There were no heads visible inside, and for all I knew they might be up at the house, waiting for me.

If it was the white Ford crowd, did they still think I was dead? Was that why they dared to park in my driveway?

Without slowing, though my pace could be described as plodding at best, I took a detour through the neighbouring farm. Elderly Mrs. Wickford lived alone on her twenty acres now, in a very old and modest home near the road, but she and her cattle wouldn't mind. A public footpath went through her property, and I climbed carefully over the stile and onto the path.

The evening was quiet and warm, a gentle breeze blowing the occasional grasshopper chirp across the pasture. It was a comfort on that night fraught with danger and uncertainty to be on the quiet footpath, hearing the animal sounds emanating from Mrs. Wickford's cows. This was a safe place, a sane place, and I hoped that the Orchard would one day return to its safer and saner past as well. What's more, I hoped that I would still be there to enjoy it.

Diverging from the footpath, I wound to the left up a small rise. From years of childhood exploring, I knew that this route would bring me out even with the tall pines along the edge of our property, behind the rose garden. It was a strategic position from which I could observe my domain with impunity.

What my enemies did not know was that I had a secret weapon in my advantage; I had spent countless weekend and summer days playing secret agent in these fields with my friends. If they were foolish enough to think that they could outwit me on my own turf, they would be very surprised.

I slowed, panting, as I climbed a thick hedge and stepped onto a carpet of pine needles on Plumtree land. There was roughly half a moon, and I could see passably well. I sat between two of the ancient and massive conifers and waited, watching and listening. An owl was running through its repertoire. Normally I found them irritating, as I couldn't resist listening for the next set of hoots, and counting how many there were each time. Besides, it was often three in the morning when they gave voice. But at that moment I thought of the bird as my friend, my accomplice, and a reminder of how insignificant the small inconveniences of life really were. I longed for a time when there would be so little to worry about that I could actually be irritated by an owl.

As I watched, the muted flashing of torches shone from within the house. They were there, looking for me. For all I knew, Giles or one of the others at Armand's had radioed the green Rover and said I was on my way home. There was no sign that Max was inside with Madeline. I hoped that they would be all right; surely the Bibliati wouldn't assume that Max knew merely because I did. They couldn't have known about our conversation with Ian that afternoon, though they had probably been watching from the white Ford when Max entered the Press.

I watched their ridiculous lights, so stupid and obvious,

yet so deadly. The green Rover was a puzzle . . . had the occupants of the Ford had a change of heart as well as a change of vehicle? They had watched me for so long that I had almost reached the conclusion that they were harmless. Were the Neck and Rich the ones now hunting me in my own house? I wondered.

A thought niggled at my brain as I watched, and I knew that I had half-realised something important but didn't yet know what it was. Frustrated, I noticed that the owl was heading into the fourth set of hoots of the overall pattern of five. This was his third time through. By the time the fourth round began, I would be familiar with the pattern, would know what was coming next . . . for over time, I had learned that they did always follow a pattern.

That was it! The Bibliati had a pattern to its activities. And I had an uncomfortably certain feeling that it was planning something, something that Angela and I had threatened— poor Denny too. I felt it. Knew it, in fact.

I concentrated as the lights, two of them, flashed through the bedrooms and down the stairs. Look for lessons in the past, I told myself; that was the single most valuable lesson of having read history. What was the pattern? What had they done in the past?

Way back, depending on how one looked at it, the Illuminati had helped to foment the French Revolution. They had worked to bring the people round to their political point of view, supporting Voltaire and his encyclopaedia. Ultimately, it had led to the death of Louis XIV and Marie Antoinette. It was not an insignificant mark to have left on history.

To my dismay, I heard the tasteful roar of Max's BMW coming up the drive. I was at the back of the house, so I couldn't see it, but I would recognise its sound anywhere. The lights had been turned off now. I moved round behind the rose garden and the gazebo, behind a line of rhododendrons that ran in a semicircle eight feet or so in front of the tall pines, and stopped when I could hear voices by the garage.

"What do you mean, an accident?" Max's worried voice drifted across the lawn on the breeze. Madeline made a small sound of alarm. "Not *another* one?" There was incredulity in his voice as well. Good on, Max, I thought. He knew instinctively not to trust them. His new-found sensitivity was serving him well.

The voice that answered made my skin crawl. It was the man I'd found seated at my desk, who had chatted with me so sociably before instructing Rich to shoot me.

"It's not serious, you understand, Mr. Plumtree." So kind and pleasant. "It's just that we wanted to let him know." A pause. "You have no idea where he is, then?"

"No," Max said slowly, thoughtfully. "He's often at his office, you know. You might try there, especially during the week of the book fair. We've been so busy with the fair that we haven't had much time to talk." Another pause. "There's also the chance that he's left for Paris—he's speaking at a conference there tomorrow. He might have gone tonight; I don't know his travel plans."

"I see. Well, you might ring me at this number if you find out where he is. I'd like to break the news in person if possible, you know, lessen the shock."

Who were they saying had been in an accident? I wondered. I had missed that part of the conversation, creeping through the bushes.

Max asked doubtfully, "You think Ian will be all right, then?" I froze. Ian. Had they really done something to him, or were they merely trying every dirty trick in the book to get to me?

"Yes, the doctors say he'll be all right. It's just that he asked for your brother when he was brought into hospital."

"Well, thank you. If I see him, I'll be certain to let him know."

They all said sober good-byes and I heard Max pull into the garage, then close the automatic door. I heard the oh-so-kind man swear and then mumble something irritably to his companion. Then I heard the pair crunch purposefully off across the gravel, towards the Rover, which was now parked in our drive. I crept round a bit further so I could see them, and it was indeed the gentleman from my office. I wasn't sure about the other man.

They got in and zoomed off, possibly in the hope of a reunion in my office at the Press, but I thought they might be back. I didn't want to endanger or bother Max and Madeline with knowledge of my presence, but I did need to retrieve those papers of my father's that Ian had mentioned. They would be in his private safe in the library. I would let Max and Madeline settle in upstairs before going inside to find the papers, then spend the night somewhere on the grounds.

As I walked cautiously towards the house, I debated what Max and Madeline would do that night. Sometimes, if they thought I wouldn't be home, they took the candelabra into my parents' old bathroom, ran a warm, deep, and scented tub, and spent hours in there. On other occasions they took a more direct route to Max's bedroom and stayed there.

I took out my key and went to the French doors of the library. The curtains were open again; Emily, our old family friend who did the cleaning and shopping, had come on Wednesday. As I stood just outside the door, inserting my key into the lock, I could see lights blinking on in the hall to the library. Max entered the room and turned on the sconces. Fascinated by this new perspective on my own home, I withdrew my key from the lock and stood motionless at the glass doors, watching.

What I saw next made my skin crawl. My brother walked straight to what I would have called one of the top ten books in our collection, the seventeenth-century Indian Bible, by John Eliot. It was worth at least a hundred thousand pounds if it was worth a penny. He gently plucked it out of its spot on the shelf, briefly turned it over in his hands, opened it, and checked the first few pages for the information which I knew by memory. He had a conniving smirk on his face which I hadn't seen in a long time, and then he turned to look at me.

There was no way he could have seen me. There were lights on inside, and the light of the half-moon was no match for their incandescent splendour. But perhaps he had felt my eyes on him. I had sensed people watching me before, and I supposed he could too. Surprised, I ducked further into the leaves and continued to watch him. His smile faded, to be replaced by a look of confusion and worry. Then he turned decisively towards the doorway and turned out the lights as he went, book in hand.

Next I saw the lights blaze in the dining room, and knew

there was a good chance he was fetching the candelabra.
I was not only sorry that Max was messing about with the
most valuable books from our library, which I was certain he
wasn't foolish enough to read in the bath, but even as I suspected him of being up to no good, I felt sorry that he had to
slink around with Madeline on nights when I wasn't there.
We were rapidly approaching the time when we would have
to establish separate households, and by the tradition of pri-
mogeniture he had first rights to the house.

Chiding myself for having done so much fantasising about
living out my life at the Orchard with Sarah and a full household of children, I felt at an all-time low. What possible
reason could Max have for removing these books from the
library? And how on earth was I going to get out of the mess I
was in?

The light went out in the dining room. I stepped back to
get a better view of the house, and saw the lights go on in my
parents' suite. All clear. They'd be in there for hours.

I unlocked the door, swung it open, and heard the roar of
the plumbing in the old house as they filled their bath. That
was helpful; they were unlikely to hear me—unless Max came
down to pilfer more books. Telling myself not to be nasty, I
moved across the room in the dark to the desk and picked up
the phone, dialling Ian's home number from memory.

"Hello," he answered gravely as if he were expecting
a call.

"Ian, it's Alex. Are you all right?"

There was a pause. "Of course. Don't worry about me,
Alex; I can take care of myself. It's you I'm worried about."

"All right; just checking." I thought of all the things I
should say: that I cared about him, that I was sorry, that I
understood why he found himself a member of the Bibliati.
Instead, I merely said, "Good night, Ian," and hung up again
before he could say anything more.

I was becoming positively brutal, I thought, shaking my
head. Crossing to the section of library shelving that looked
exactly like the rest of the room's walls to everyone but Max
and me, I pulled on the top of the shelf of books. It opened
outward, the door of a simple cupboard. To make things easy
on myself, I grabbed the entire sizeable stack of manila

envelopes and closed the safe again. I was learning how to function quite well with the use of just one arm, though it was awkward. Clutching the stack of envelopes between my right arm and body, I went to the French doors, leaned down to push the handle to open the door with my right hand, stepped outside, and set the whole pile on the brick walk. Re-entering the library, I closed the doors behind me, and tiptoed through the room into the downstairs hall.

While Max and Madeline were occupied, I would have to gather what I needed for the coming week with Sarah. I knew I had everything I needed, from weeks of planning; I'd even bought some new white athletic socks. After all, if I wanted her to marry me, I didn't want her to think I was a slob. The problem now, besides the fact that I didn't know if I could cycle half a mile—let alone over hill and dale through half of France—was that everything was upstairs in my wardrobe, including the duffel bag in which I intended to carry it all.

I listened at the bottom of the stairs in the dark. Giggling and murmuring travelled down the hall, and still the sound of running water. It took a long time to fill the old bath, I knew, but with any luck they'd already have climbed in. I used the cover of the roaring water to climb the stairs and dart into my room. It was at the opposite end of the upstairs hall from my parents' room, and the bathroom was at the far end of their suite. I wasn't too worried about Max and Madeline detecting my presence; they had other things on their minds.

Gathering up first the duffel bag, which I put on the bed, I then threw into it biking shorts, two well-worn pairs; one bona fide biking shirt—a present from Sarah; and five T-shirts. Then I tossed in the new socks, all the clean underwear in my drawer, my two casual pairs of shorts, and several polo shirts. I was about to gather it all up and move on to the bathroom for my shaving kit, when I remembered I would need clothes for the Folio B conference and the Paris book fair. Not many speakers in the history of Folio B conferences had shown up in their bike shorts, I'd be willing to wager.

I took my suiter down from where it was hanging in the wardrobe and hung several clean shirts and my two favourite ties in it, then my best navy blue suit. Fortunately I remembered dark socks and dress shoes, which I stowed in some of the many pockets of the bag, along with a belt as an after-thought. I didn't do much travelling anymore, and this wasn't as automatic as it had been at one point.

Finally, I grabbed another change of clothes; I would put them on after the sponge bath I'd be taking in lieu of a shower. Max and Madeline would hear if I turned on the shower and stood under that deliciously warm stream of water; it seemed an eternity since I'd had a relatively normal—and clean—existence.

I crept along the hall to the bathroom, carrying duffel and suiter, and took off the clothes that had seen me through one of the worst times of my life. I cleaned up as best I could, and thankfully donned the clean clothes. After brushing my teeth, I dropped the toothbrush and toothpaste into the shaving kit, and threw the whole thing into my duffel bag. I was ready.

On the way out the door I grabbed a fleece sweatshirt along with my waterproof trousers and hooded jacket, and I thought that was everything. I had it all on the brick walk outside the library doors before I remembered the bike gloves, which were in the garage, and my panniers.

I trudged back into the house yet again, and through the kitchen to the garage in the dark. Once in the garage I turned on the light, went quickly to my bicycle, and grabbed the gloves off the seat. I also snatched the helmet off the handle-bars, where it hung by its strap, and at the last moment grabbed a torch that we kept by the garage stairs just in case.

When I turned out the garage light and opened the door into the kitchen, I got the surprise of my life. Max and Madeline were standing stark naked in front of the refrigerator, gig-gling over a bottle of chocolate sauce that they were obviously planning to take upstairs with them. It was quite a sight. They looked at me, stunned, and I am sorry to say I did the same.

Gathering my wits, I said something like "Pretend you never saw me. I know about Ian's supposed 'accident'—don't call the gent who was here, I've taken care of it. I'm just off for France, sorry, no time to talk. Remember, if any-body asks, I wasn't here, okay? Bye."

It said it all in what I hoped was a friendly, absent-minded tone of voice, and whisked off through the hall into the library again. It would have been better to go out through the garage, but I couldn't take the chance of anyone seeing me from the lane or the drive. I hoped they were wrapped up enough in themselves to laugh off my odd behaviour. As I walked past the desk, on impulse I snatched up the portable phone and added it to the load borne by my one useful arm.

Exiting through the French doors in the library as quickly as I could, I walked past the pile of envelopes sitting on the walk and carried my things to an overgrown corner of the perennial garden. A stand of three-foot-high yarrow made a nice screen; if anyone came looking, they'd never spot my bags behind the browning lacy blooms and their fern-like foliage.

Grabbing the torch, with switch firmly in the off position, I retraced my steps, picked up the envelopes, and retreated with them to the gazebo. The gazebo was near the back of the garden, almost at the point where the pasture began, and afforded some amount of privacy. The octagonal building was about fifteen feet in diameter, with windows all the way round except for a set of French doors. We kept cushions under the built-in benches in the summer, and I thought I would be quite comfortable there for the night. I'd be able to hear what was going on round me if I left the door open, and Max and Madeline could quite honestly say I'd gone to France and wasn't in the house if anyone got heavy-handed with them.

I situated myself with green and white striped cloth cushions on the wooden floor, in a place where the weak moonlight shone, and sifted through the thick envelopes. Cruelly, a gentle breeze carried the scent of the roses to me through the open door. A beautiful night, and a disastrous situation.

The envelopes bore various titles, written in thick black ink on the front, such as "Alexandra," my mother's name, and "Artwork valuations." I was vitally interested in each of them, but shuffled through them quickly, looking for something that would have a bearing on Folio B or Stonecypher or the Bibliati.

On reaching the bottom of the stack, I stopped cold. There on the front of an A4-sized foolscap envelope was a small black insignia. Even in the pale moonlight there was no question; it was the Stonecypher dingbat. With a sense of foreboding mixed with fascination, I gently tore the envelope open and tipped the contents out onto the floor.

It was a small stack of papers and envelopes, held together with an elastic band. The old, hardened band broke when I stretched it, and I picked up the top piece of paper. It was a simple note scrawled in black ink on a piece of my father's engraved stationery. I gazed at the note with fascination, then reached for the torch and switched it on low, letting a cushion rest atop it and my hand. The bright, direct light made it possible to read; I had to take the risk of creating a glow within the gazebo.

To Max, Alex, or whomever it might concern,

This will be a very odd message, but bear with me. I cannot express strongly enough how important it is that you follow these instructions precisely; your life may be in danger.

Open the enclosed envelope if, and only if, you feel you understand the *full significance* of the symbol on the front of this envelope and if you feel it is a matter of life and death. If you are in any doubt whatsoever whether these conditions are satisfied, put the contents of the envelope back in the original envelope and replace it in the safe. Do not speak of this to *anyone*.

MP

"MP," for Maximilian Plumtree, was the way my father had often signed informal correspondence. It brought back a flood of affectionate memories of him, but I thrust them away for the moment and refocussed on the note. There was no doubt in my mind that I did understand the significance of the Stonecypher dingbat; I only wished that I didn't. I also felt that for Virginia Holdsworthy, and Angela, and me, and several other people I could think of, this was most certainly a matter of life and death. For all of our sakes, I hoped it wouldn't turn out to be the latter.

Slowly, I opened the envelope and unfolded another note scrawled in my father's messy but beloved handwriting.

Max, Alex—

    I regret that you've had to get this far. Please be aware that, incredible as it may seem, there are people who will kill you for what you now know, and what you are about to learn. I implore you to be careful with this knowledge.

    You will find more information on the subject where stars shine in the darkness and the doors are all closed, in something that the Earl has rejected.

                        MP

I knew exactly what he meant. Turning off the torch, I got to my feet again, hurried back down the path to the library doors, opened them silently, and pushed the door closed again just as quietly. Then I took two steps backwards and looked up.

In a long-untouched corner of the library, up near the ceiling on the short side wall that adjoined the French doors, was a book that my father, mother, grandfather, and I had found on a holiday to Dartmouth in the West Country when I was twelve. My mother had wanted to see the small coastal town of Dartmouth, as her father and brother had gone to Dartmouth College in the States, and she had designs for her boys to go there as well. As I came to know well during my days in New Hampshire at that small but well-loved college, the Earl of Dartmouth had funded its establishment for the purpose of educating Native Americans in the region.

We'd visited one of the local bookshops and my father had found a rather offbeat treasure: a book that had once been the Earl of Dartmouth's that sought to reconcile a Christian view of the universe, including all of its stars and planets, with a scientific one. It had been published in 1769 with uncut signatures, as all books were published then. Part of owning a book used to be slitting open the pages.

Someone had put a brown paper dust wrapper on the volume, which was entitled *A Scientific Treatise on God's*

Own Creation, and when my father had gently slipped the wrapper off to expose the book itself, we saw that the front cover was a gorgeous deep blue leather embossed with gold stars. My mother had drawn in her breath and exclaimed, "Maximilian, look!" My father had bought it to please her.

Later, at tea in our hotel, my grandfather had taken out his pen-knife and begun to cut the pages for her. They were closed across the bottom only. I remembered saying rather rudely, with adolescent intensity, "No! Stop, Grandfather! You'll ruin it!"

They'd all looked at me with surprise over their teacups, and then my father had nodded slowly and said, "You know, Alex may have a point. This is the book's original condition, and one never sees uncut signatures in the bookshops anymore. One day all the uncut books will be cut, and this will be a rarity. Shall we save it? Leave its doors closed as a mystery for the future?"

With sparkling eyes my mother had looked at us for a long while across the clotted cream and scones, then suddenly hugged my father, winked at me, and smilingly agreed. It was the binding that had caught her eye anyway. My grandfather was a bit confused over the whole thing, having cut countless books over his seventy-some years, but he shrugged and put his knife away again. Why would someone buy a book and then not read it? Remembering it all now, I marvelled at their tolerance for the wishes of an obnoxious adolescent boy, and was grateful.

Pulling the rolling library steps over to that section of wall where the less valuable books were stored, I mounted the ladder. I was searching for a brown paper spine—the one that the Earl of Dartmouth or his descendants had sold, or "rejected," with the golden stars shining in the darkness beneath it, with all but one of its "doors closed," or pages uncut.

I spotted the book on the very top shelf, reached up on my toes from the top step of the ladder, and carefully pushed in the books on either side of it, so that it stood out enough for me to grasp it halfway down with thumb and forefinger. I'd seen too many people tear the spines off old books by pulling out on the top of the spine with a careless forefinger, and wasn't about to subject this lovely old specimen to that kind of torture. Gently I carried it down, off the ladder, then slipped off the dust wrapper as I walked to the doors to catch the moonlight.

The stars were there, beautiful as ever, and I turned the book so that the fore-edge was facing me. Only one cut signature, then a number of folded sections that looked rather like envelopes. I felt a small flush of pride that though in my life I had done many foolish things, I had done this one good thing. The book was rare, more so for its uncut pages, and valuable. Besides, it had been well preserved over the years and was quite readable with the bottoms of its pages fused.

Opening the cover, I flipped through the first few pages. I noted with pleasure the attractive, rather large font and the as-new condition. Then I saw that one of the sets of folded pages bulged slightly. Gently, I pried it open with my fingers and peeked in. A small sheaf of very thin papers, air mail weight, had been folded into a square and sat snugly in the pocket created by the closed bottom of the uncut signature.

Fascinated, I turned out the lights, closed the door, and sneaked back to the gazebo. Then I smoothed out the papers on the floor and read.

Dear Max, Alex, or your descendants,

I am very sorry that it has become necessary for you to read this. As you will see when you read the accompanying papers, not only I but your grandfather and great-grandfather have had to cope with the dangers of the powerful political society camouflaged in the ranks of the Society for the Preservation of Rare and Antique Books—about to be renamed Folio B, if they ever actually get around to changing it.

I must state again that it is of the utmost importance that you never speak of this to anyone. If you do, you will almost certainly lose your life, though even at the moment you are in danger if you are reading this.

I will be concise: ever since Stonecypher published his first "dingbat" novel in 1910, a fanatical political society committed to the abolition of the monarchy,

*and indeed any remnants of national identity, has been
alive and at work within the Society. At no time is the
political society openly discussed, except within
private meetings. These meetings coincide with major
book fairs, and are called by symbols cleverly placed
in catalogues of member book dealers. I have stumbled
across this knowledge by coincidence during the many
years of my involvement in SPRAB, and have spoken of
it only to Ian.*

*I know that this bunch is deadly not only because I
have evidence that they have been involved in terrorist
acts threatening the Royals, with the help of the IRA,
but they once killed a friend of mine who had
discovered their secret and made the mistake of talking
about it. You remember Anthony Bywater, don't you?
It was made to look like an accident, but it was all too
clear to me what had happened.*

*If you can, stay away from them; avoid involvement
in the Board, because the kingpins are there. If it's too
late for that, be absolutely sure that you never give a
hint of recognition of what they are doing—unless you
are willing to sacrifice your life to the cause.*

*I am committed to finding a way to expose the group
while remaining alive to provide for and enjoy my
family; perhaps if you are reading this, I am dead and
they have found me out. I simply can't ignore their
horrible deeds, and suspect that you will feel the same
way if I've done my job as a father. But please—your
life is precious. Be careful.*

*By the way, the Stonecypher Society itself seems to
be strangely free from this secret organisation; it
seems to have infected only SPRAB.*

Your loving father,
Dad

I stared at the page for a moment, my mind numb. My
father had known that he might be in danger for what he
knew about the Bibliati. If only he had found a way . . .

I had to read on.

The next page was written in what I recognised to be my grandfather's hand, in a very small, tight script. It made me sad to think of my father gathering this disastrous correspondence, and a tingling at the back of my neck told me that I already knew what it would say.

My son,

> *My heart aches that I should have to pass this burden to you; I thought that I could save you from it. But your grandfather Edward wrote me a letter like this, which I now pass on to you, and hope that you will never have to do the same for your children.*
>
> *If you are reading this letter, you already know that the author Marcus Stonecypher and his readers established a secret society called the Bibliati, a book-based branch of the Illuminati. The group believes in the principle of world government, and the triumph of human reason through education. They believe that the people should govern, not elected officials of any sort. They stand against all forms of nationalism, including royalty. As a long-standing member of the Society for the Preservation of Rare and Antique Books, I came to suspect the existence of this rather academic and idealistic secret society only after years of observation and interaction with these people. I myself was never invited to join; they knew of my involvement as a deacon in the church, and my friendship with the Prince of Wales. Then, upon my father's death, I received the enclosed letter and knew for certain.*
>
> *I am disturbed to note that these men are becoming more determined to achieve true political goals rather than enjoying some quiet political dissidence, and if I am not mistaken, they have been communicating of late with the Irish Republican Army.*
>
> *I want to urge you to have nothing to do with them, because I fear for the direction in which they are heading, and also I feel it might be dangerous for you.*
>
> *My son, your grandfather's association with Marcus Stonecypher should cause you no shame. He*

*published the misprints for his friend as a rather
naughty but intriguing joke, never imagining that it
would turn into something like this.*
                            Father

I found myself reading the letter over and over again. This was a fascinating, if disturbing, glimpse into family history. So my whole family had been involved, for three generations, in one way or another. And now Folio B had a Plumtree on its board. My ego had been so overgrown, as Pillinghurst had intimated, that I had thought they were honouring me.

Cursing myself for having got into this mess, I allowed myself to slump down against the cushions. I looked at the octagonal pattern of the boards in the bleached wood floor of the gazebo, holding the papers loosely in my good hand. Shaking my head in disbelief, I was drawn irresistibly to the next letter, that of my great-grandfather Edward. It was his inscribed copy of the Stonecypher that had been stolen on the first night of the entire ordeal.

Dear Charles,

*I am leaving this letter to be opened by you upon my
death on the assumption that you will choose to
continue to run Plumtree Press as I have taught you.
Should the matter ever come into question, I want you
to have this proof that I willingly and knowingly went
along with a set of misprints that Marcus Stonecypher
asked me to allow in his works as a condition of signing
with us. I do not understand their significance, but he
has assured me that in time I will be glad of it, that it is
a sort of "poetry of the mind," as he put it, that will be
understood in the fullness of time. Intrigued, I agreed to
publish his books with those minor "mistakes" intact
and, as you know, his books have been so successful
that it was well worth my while to do so.*
                            *Your
                            Father*

Woodenly, I put the papers back into the signature, then rose uncomfortably and went to the library door, unlocking it. I climbed the ladder, put the book back where I'd found it, and returned all the manila envelopes to their place in the bookshelf safe.

All the while I'd been growing up, and for the three years I'd been running Plumtree Press, this disaster had lain dormant in a wall of old books. It was a high price we would all have paid for my great-grandfather's good-natured agreement to go along with the whims of a politically-minded author.

I took a large envelope ever so quietly from the drawer of the big desk and wandered outside again in a daze, automatically locking the doors behind me. Out of nowhere came another association, something I was doing that was similar to what my great-grandfather had done. I stopped and stood in the darkness.

MacDougal. I had wooed him for Plumtree Press, in my endless desire for expansion and improvement, on the condition that I would agree to publish his historical novel—which was, there was no denying it, not up to snuff by our usual editorial criteria. I, too, had compromised my own publishing standards for the sake of greed. Why hadn't I seen it?

I knew that I was still missing an important piece of the puzzle, and it was an uncomfortable feeling. The next set of hoots in the owl's pattern . . . the next step on the Bibliati's agenda . . . what was it?

I knew that I stood a good chance of suffering the same consequences that my great-grandfather, grandfather, and father had, and trudged back to the gazebo to do the only thing I could.

Poor Max. I wrote him a letter explaining everything I knew about Folio B, from Virginia Holdsworthy's letter to what Giles had said about Rupert Soames. I explained who the Illuminati were and how the Bibliati had hoped to further their political goals by altering history books and doing away with the Royals. Then I told him cryptically where to find the other letters in the book in the library. Finally, I asked him to please try to make sure that Mike Chelmsford put it all into a story for *The Tempus*. Then I wrote the whole thing all over again to Mike, per our agreement at the press conference.

I folded Max's letter and put it with my father's note and

letter to me, and stuffed it all into the fresh envelope, addressing it to my solicitor with a melodramatic but, I judged, effective, message across the lower front:

IMPORTANT: THIS LETTER TO BE KEPT SECURE AND UNOPENED BY YOU, TO BE OPENED ONLY ON THE OCCASION OF MY UNNATURAL OR SUSPICIOUS DEATH.

I then did the same with Mike Chelmsford's letter, except that I addressed it to him, and signed beneath the message on both. Then I pulled two postage stamps out of my wallet and stuck them on the letters. I would post them on the way to Waterloo Station and the Eurostar train in the morning.

CHAPTER 17

In first novels the hero is usually the publisher.
—ANONYMOUS

When dawn came, I'd had at least three hours of sleep, which seemed a great luxury. I opened my eyes, saw the rosy glow, slowly picked myself up and dusted myself off. If all went well, I'd see Sarah that very day.

Gingerly, I walked down the path to the neglected patch of yarrow and retrieved my bags, one over my right shoulder and one in my right hand. Then, as I hiked down Mrs. Wickford's footpath to the bottom of the lane, I assessed the general state of things and realised that I felt reasonably adequate to face the day. My wound never let me forget that it was there, but it was manageable, and I felt stronger and more myself than yesterday. I was still taking antibiotics, but had abandoned the painkillers; they took the edge off my senses, and I had a feeling I'd be needing all of them over the next few days.

My sense of well-being didn't extend far enough to cover the walk to Chorleywood tube station and possible straphanging on the way into London, so when I reached the street that intersected the lane from the east, I crossed it and knocked on the door of one in a line of tiny cottages. This one was pink and impeccably neat, with white lace curtains at the front windows. A small white-painted sign above the door announced that it was QUEEN ANNE'S COTTAGE.

"Morning, Alex." A small, wiry man with bright eyes and a bald pate looked me up and down unabashedly as I stood on his doorstep—bags, wrinkled trousers, overnight beard and all. "Heathrow, is it?"

"Waterloo Station, Lacey. The Eurostar train. Sorry I didn't give you notice this time, seven twenty-three departure. Can you do it?"

"Fetch my keys, be right out." He was as good as his word, and when he emerged seconds later, he was wearing his driving cap. Lacey was the only independent driver in town, and I liked to use him whenever I could. He didn't have a fancy dispatch service, but to me, being able to walk up and knock on his door without a booking in emergencies was a far greater convenience. Normally, of course, I gave him a good deal more notice than this. "Waterloo, you said?"

I confirmed the destination, got in with my bags, and we were off.

He was silent the whole way, nearly an hour, for which I was grateful. When we reached the station, he said, "Have a pleasant journey, Alex." I knew I would receive his bill precisely two weeks later, like clockwork.

"Thanks, Lacey. Bye."

He was off with a wave, and I was safely at the station.

The three-hour-long voyage was uneventful except for the superb coffee and ham-filled baguette. In Paris I hired a car for the drive to Château Menceau, and before long I was speeding eastward on the French motorway, aware that I was in the same country as Sarah, and even in the same one-hundred-mile region.

I had a letter from Menceau, passed on from Armand through the post a week or so before his fateful books party, providing directions. I had another forty-five minutes to drive, I estimated, which was perfect—I'd be at the château at precisely noon, when my keynote speech was due to begin, giving them no time to do away with me before I had my say in front of the membership. And they couldn't do away with me in front of the entire membership—could they?

I knew that all the others were already there; the key members of Folio B, and the Bibliati, I presumed, had been flown out last night, latish, in Menceau's private jet. At Armand's party I'd heard that he kept it at Denham Aerodrome when he came for Folio B meetings and book acquisition trips, in order to be convenient to Watersmeet. The other conference attendees would already be at Menceau's too, settling in for the day's speeches, educational sessions, and fine meals. For a moment I had the feeling that I was driving to meet my doom, with all of them waiting in a silent, cavernous room— waiting to do me in. But for every one of the sinister Bibliati members in attendance, I knew there would be at least a score of normal members—mainly from England and France, but a few from other European countries. They certainly wouldn't gun me down as I stood at the podium, and I hoped that what I had to say would keep me alive for many years to come. I would find out all too soon whether my plan would work.

As the congestion of Paris faded and I emerged into the true countryside, I felt immense regret that Sarah and I hadn't been able to cycle this route together as we'd first planned. If we'd been able to carry out our original plan, I would have spent the night at her flat, I wouldn't have a half-crippled arm, and we would have cycled this route to Menceauville that very day.

It was just possible, though, that we might still be able to have some remnant of the holiday I'd planned, even if it was a sort of pretend escape with a changed life stretching before me on our return.

Grateful that I'd had the good sense to protect Sarah by suggesting that she meet me away from Menceauville, I drove confidently on through the vineyards. I was doing the right thing, in fact the only thing I could do.

I followed Menceau's directions until I arrived at a crossroads. Even the knowledge that I was close to Menceauville did not prepare me for the castle I saw on a hill, surrounded by what must have been hundreds of acres of vineyards. I counted five turrets, all in whitish-yellow stone. A small sign bearing the words CHÂTEAU MENCEAU in medieval script pointed to the left, and I drove on in awe, uphill on the winding road, between trees lining both sides of the macadam.

As I drove under the protective arch of the porte-cochère, I slipped off the sling that had helped keep my arm immobile, not wanting to call attention to my injury in front of the crowd. A short, bulky man in uniform welcomed me with a lopsided smile. "*Bienvenue,* Monsieur Plumtree. We have been awaiting you."

He started to take my bags and keys, and I said, "If you would just leave the bags in the car, please—I'll get them later."

"*Oui,* Monsieur, but I will need your keys to park the car."

I thanked him, handing them over, and as he hopped into my car and drove off, I heard a woman's voice behind me. "Monsieur Plumtree." I wheeled to see a petite woman with extremely short, jet-black hair who wore a white Chanel suit. She stretched out a hand with a dazzling smile, and I took it, brushing my lips to it. Her tan was dark brown, and against it her teeth, and the suit, were remarkable.

"Thérèse Menceau. I am so happy to meet you. Please come with me." With a hand under my elbow, she ushered me towards the front door. Menceau's wife? I wondered. Sister? Daughter? The woman had an ageless sophistication that made it impossible to tell.

If she was about to have me thrown into the moat, she showed no outward sign of her intention. We stepped into an awe-inspiring entrance hall, at least two stories high, all creamy stone and heavy wood. Despite the rustic surroundings, deep rugs with a design of tan on cream cushioned our feet. Château Menceau had obviously been standing for a very long time. Menceau hurried forward to meet us.

"I didn't expect you to be the last-minute sort," he said, smiling as he checked his watch with exaggerated interest, "but you are punctual. Welcome to Château Menceau."

He could not have been more cordial, more casually welcoming. Returning his smile and trying to hide my surprise, I began to wonder if the contretemps with Holdsworthy in front of him had ever taken place. But then I remembered that they all thought I was capitulating, that I had too much to lose *not* go along with them.

"What an extraordinary place, Menceau. It's magnificent," I said as we passed through the hall on our way to what I could see was a large, fully-inhabited meeting room with its doors open.

"Thank you," he said with a smug smile. "The château was standing for several centuries before the Revolution. Many interesting events to do with the history of France have taken place here—but that is a story for another time. Now it is time for *your* story, yes?"

I looked at him and wondered if he knew what I was about to do, but received only an enigmatic smile in return. I could only hope that I had managed to achieve the same neutrality in my expression.

A chiming clock started the long haul to twelve bells, and we arrived behind a podium at the front of a huge ballroom that was anything but rustic. No doubt this had been the "great hall" at one point in history, where feasts and banquets and festivals had taken place. Now the room bore the mark of pre-revolutionary France, with gold-encrusted murals of cherubs flying about in the clouds, and dozens of chandeliers that would, in the evening, hold hundreds of candles.

Round tables covered with pristine white tablecloths filled every last corner of the room, with a collection of mostly men standing, sitting, and finishing what looked like croissants and coffee. A comfortable rumble of their voices filled the room.

Menceau indicated that I should take a seat near the podium as he stepped up to the microphone, tapping it once. "If you would all take your seats, please." Looking out over the room, I saw an audience that I estimated at about one hundred and fifty men and—no estimation required—exactly six women, of whom Diana Boillot was one, and the white-toothed Thérèse Menceau was another.

"Ladies. Gentlemen." He paused while they scooted their chairs in at the tables, clinked Limoges coffee cups, coughed, shuffled papers, and generally got settled. "It is my great pleasure to have you all here in my home, and I extend to you a most sincere welcome. We have much to be pleased about at this point in Folio B's existence, and much to look ahead to as well, but I will leave that to Mr. Farquhart and the president's speech, scheduled for just after lunch."

He beamed at Farquhart, who nodded and smiled self-deprecatingly in return. I did a double-take at Farquhart, who

I could have sworn hadn't shaved a large section of the left side of his face. His right eye was twitching in a tic, and he looked like a different man from the dapper, civilised man I had seen five days before at Armand's. What was going on with him?

"It is my privilege as host to introduce our keynote speaker, Mr. Alex Plumtree. He has undergone great difficulty to be here with us, and we are very grateful to him."

I looked at Menceau sharply, but he merely regarded me with something like encouragement and admiration. So this was the public face they were going to put on things . . . he was referring openly to their attempt at doing away with me, and I was to stand up and smile, and act as if everything were all right. I was amazed. But I had done more difficult things in my life.

"We're very glad you could be here, Alex." I nodded at him in acknowledgement and thanks. Out in the audience Rupert Soames, Giles, Pillinghurst, Farquhart, Diana Boillot, and Holdsworthy stared at me with intensity from one of the front tables; I smiled back at them.

"We are delighted to have Alex here today to tell us about the well-known and unusual Plumtree Collection, one of the finest and most closely held private collections in England. I understand that Alex will also share with us some of his thoughts on the rare-book world. Alex, as many of you may already know, runs Plumtree Press, following in the footsteps of his father, Maximilian, whom we fondly remember as our friend and past president of Folio B."

Menceau paused before the next sentence, and I was stunned to see and hear the room rise and break out in a standing ovation for my father. It was a moving moment, and I wished he could have seen it; for the thousandth time I lamented the fact that people are usually appreciated and recognised for what they've done only after they're dead. I joined them in the applause.

When it had died down to a dull roar, Menceau gestured to indicate that the floor was mine, and said, "Alex."

"Thank you, Michel. And thank *you*." I nodded to the audience, and as my eyes swept the crowd, I froze, amazed to see Ian at one of the rear tables. Despite my phone call of the night before, it was a relief to see him alive and well. He acknowledged me calmly with a nod, and I went on, trying to take it in my stride, greatly encouraged by his presence. I was becoming accustomed to the fact that Ian seemed to appear miraculously at my moments of most dire need. I'd even come close to deciding there was something supernatural about the man. It was small wonder that such a man was responsible, through his daughter, of producing a woman like Sarah.

"I'm delighted to be here, and look forward to sharing the Plumtree Collection with you as well as what I hope will be a pleasant journey into one of the little-discussed aspects of the world of rare books." Fortunately, it didn't matter that I had never actually finished writing the speech; it would be easy for me to improvise on this subject now.

Since Armand had, weeks ago, specifically requested that I include the Plumtree Collection in my speech, I began with a description of the collection that I knew would practically have them salivating—the Malconbury Chronicles, *Pilgrim's Progress*, the Tyndale Bible, the Stonecyphers. Several listeners sat up a bit straighter at the mention of Marcus Stonecypher's name, I thought, and Ian, it seemed, tried to telegraph me a warning, shaking his head ever so slightly. I described the haphazard way in which the collection had grown, each generation of Plumtrees purchasing and adding their favourites to the library. Not what they were *supposed* to like, but what genuinely pleased them. As a result, there were many unusual books that no one would have expected to mature in value at all, but many of them had become priceless treasures.

The Malconbury Chronicles, for instance. "Many generations back, in the reign of Elizabeth I, one of the Plumtrees flirted briefly with Catholicism and developed a fascination with the Malconbury set of monks, who had lived a couple of centuries before. They were known for their colourful illuminations of the Scriptures, and there is a Malconbury Bible in the collection as well.

"My ancestor travelled to East Anglia, to the ruins of their friary, and was welcomed to tea with the rector of the Malconbury Anglican Church. At that time, of course, Elizabeth I had made Catholicism a crime, so the word 'Catholic' was never mentioned. The rector, however, had in a different political climate been Catholic himself, and the two men had an understanding. 'Please,' he said to his visitor asking about the Malconbury Friars, 'do me the favour to wait while I search for something that will interest you.'

"An hour later he emerged with dust on his vestments, carrying the volumes now known as the Malconbury Chronicles, and handed them to my relative, ten generations back. Successive clergymen had hidden them, to prevent them from being burned, hoping that one day Catholicism would no longer be a crime and people would again be interested in records about the amount of grain stored, vellum made, and so forth at an obscure monastery. 'No one else cares about these but those of us who lead the church here in Malconbury,' he told my ancestor. "They were almost burned last year. I thought some of the illumination was rather attractive, and saved them. Disgraceful, of course,' he said, winking, 'but rather attractive. Why don't you take them and keep them safe for us?'

"And now the Chronicles are the only surviving record we have of what life was like for those monks, and the books did prove to be treasures of illumination. Not only did they have a particular style of painting, using many objects of nature in their work as well as an uncommon number of wheatsheaves, but the root of a plant in the area used in making their paints had an unusual deep blue hue that experts deemed unique." The crowd murmured, enjoying the romp through the serendipitous joys of old books.

Describing these precious books to this audience was akin to letting them into a bakery to smell the goods but not touch or taste them. I could practically feel their fingers twitching to feel the fine old goatskin.

"Now. How far would you go personally to get your hands on some of these books? To acquire them for practically nothing, and have them in your own library to peruse at your leisure or sell for unbelievable gain?"

Their eyes glinted. They were really listening. It was a roomful of respectable people, except for the Bibliati, but all bibliophiles and collectors—and all were human.

"That's what I thought," I said, smiling, and momentarily

transferred my gaze to Holdsworthy's table for maximum effect on that crowd. Nearly everyone chuckled with the exception of Holdsworthy's table. But when they heard the audience's response, they tried to fit in, smirking and sipping coffee to recover.

"The little-known tale of bibliophile crime may be entertaining in some respects, but tragic in others. One thing is for certain: bibliophiles show more creativity in their crime than any other group of criminals." More laughter, strained at the table in front. I glanced briefly at Ian. He nodded at me bravely, chin held high, as if we were entered upon a suicide mission together.

I was going to have a lot of fun with this speech, I could tell, even if it was slightly suicidal. It felt like careering down a single-track lane on a motorcycle at high speed, sans helmet.

"As long as people have found books valuable, which has been practically as long as books have existed, there has been an unending series of misrepresentations, forgeries, and scams perpetrated by the unscrupulous. I'd like to chronicle several of these for you."

I proceeded to tell my audience about the forged-pamphlet scam that Carter and Pollard had exposed, then the Larrovitch farce, and the Blumberg robberies. The Blumberg story made them furious; I could feel their indignation in the air.

"Finally, a more modern example." I paused and enjoyed the moment of suspense. Did they suspect what I was about to do? Smiling at the front table, I fancied I could feel the heat radiating from their collective brows. Edward Pillinghurst looked as if he were focussing all his energy on burning a hole right through me with his laser-beam eyes. Soames, meanwhile, scowled and muttered something hostile but unintelligible when I met his eyes. "This is perhaps the most nefarious scheme of all, as it affects books that are the public property of Britain. Would you believe that a well-respected organisation in England, which claims to restore books, actually spirits them away, carefully exchanging perfect copies for imperfect partial ones?"

There were murmurings in the audience, and I could tell

what they were saying. It sounds like Folio B, they were whispering, just like us. How remarkable.

"This organisation restores the imperfect copies," I continued, "putting bits and pieces together into reasonable facsimiles of the original books. It then sells the perfect copies to fund its fanatical and violent political activities."

I had to pause for more conversation in hushed, incredulous tones. To my great surprise, Giles was the only one at the Folio B table who looked truly upset, though he was trying to hide it. Farquhart simply sat with his mouth open. The others, Menceau, Soames, Holdsworthy, and Boillot included, now looked merely stunned and rather confused. From their reactions, I would have guessed that it was Giles who had something to hide—as indeed he did, if he'd been telling the truth the night before.

Giles looked as if he were trying to tell me to keep quiet about it without the others seeing, but I charged forward. I couldn't take the chance of not exposing them in this way, while I still could. Besides, I still didn't know if I could trust him.

"You would think that one audacious fraud would be enough. But there's more. Much, much more. As I said, bibliophiles never disappoint in their creativity." The atmosphere lightened, except for the table in front, where a major thunderstorm was imminent, and I continued.

"Not content to use priceless national treasures to fund their acts of terrorism, they use books in another, more insidious way. I won't blame you if you find this difficult to believe, but it is true: certain members of this same group have contracted with authors, who have deliberately twisted history to their political advantage. It is this twisted history that hundreds of thousands of Britain's schoolchildren have learned over the last decade in their schools."

More gasps, and I saw Holdsworthy tense as if ready to spring to the podium and garrotte me with his twisted table napkin in one motion. Armand looked alarmingly florid. His face was frozen in a careful mask of neutrality. "And I must say, for a crime of this nature, it has been executed with a remarkable degree of taste and style." Incredulous laughter in the audience.

"It all began with a message left in a book." I watched

the front table again for an involuntary flicker of recognition from the person who had my Wodehouse containing the letter from Virginia Holdsworthy. To my great surprise, it came from William Farquhart. We held each other's gaze for a pregnant fraction of a second. There was no mistaking it; he had something to do with the letter that the others hadn't. I filed away Farquhart's reaction for future use.

But the real "message in the book" that I planned to discuss was Stonecypher's message, his code, not the letter from Virginia Holdsworthy.

"As you may know, one of our authors at Plumtree Press has written a novel based on her discovery of a secret code within the works of Marcus Stonecypher, the famous Bloomsbury author. The code reveals that Stonecypher believed in abolishing the monarchy, and in using books and knowledge to empower people to rule themselves. He was a member of a secret society called the Illuminati, which worked to further these goals."

I looked round the room, making eye contact with these people who needed to hear my message. "But, sadly, some of Stonecypher's followers became fanatical about these beliefs, and in essence used him as a symbol for a splinter group of the Illuminati, appropriately named the Bibliati." A lump formed in my throat at the thought of Angela.

"These people, the Bibliati, not only run the book scam I told you about, and not only alter the history textbooks, and not only seek to abolish the monarchy through terrorism"— eyes went wide—"but they repeatedly threatened and very nearly killed my author, Angela Mayfield, barely three days ago." Murmurs and stunned looks were exchanged among the audience.

"So as you can see, this group is very much alive, and threatened by what Angela Mayfield's book reveals. I would entreat you all to stand with me against this group and its activities, not because of its political beliefs, but because of its violent means of—"

I heard an unnatural gurgling and choking noise, and fell silent. Armand was doubled over in pain. My first instinct was to run to him, but others were closer, and probably knew better how to care for him. I, on the other hand, was temporarily in charge of maintaining calm in this roomful of people, since I had the floor.

A rare date with Sarah flashed through my mind; we'd been at a concert at the Barbican in London, and the conductor had keeled over with a heart attack in mid-symphony. In that case, as with this, there was no way to continue with the program as if nothing had happened; the room was intimate enough that it was impossible not to acknowledge it.

Michel Menceau quickly but calmly rose from the table to telephone for help, and Giles slipped out of the room at the same time. Frank Holdsworthy bent over Armand, lowered him to the eighteenth-century carpet, and started unbuttoning his shirt collar. I heard a man at the next table say to Holdsworthy with a French accent, "It's all right. I am a *médecin*, a doctor."

Taking all this in, I thought the best I could do as the one unfortunate enough to be at the podium in such a situation would be to attempt to keep everyone calm. I opened my mouth to say something like, "We have a medical emergency, but it's under control. Perhaps the best thing we can do is stay where we are until Armand is safely taken care of."

But of course Rupert Soames was there, and somehow in his sixty or so years he had escaped any training whatsoever in what my father had simply called "doing the right thing." He rose from the table, where he was unfortunately positioned next to Armand on the other side from Holdsworthy. Looking around wildly, he blurted out, "My God! He's having a heart attack! He's dying! Somebody help him!"

At that, the members of Folio B International stood and attempted to catch a glimpse of the action. People from tables surrounding Armand's crowded in to see if they could "help." The doctor who had come to Armand's rescue ordered that Armand be carried to a quiet room until an ambulance came to take him to the hospital in the next town. I did my best to get people to clear the way as Soames, Holdsworthy, Giles, and Farquhart carried his considerable bulk out of the room. The room was bedlam.

Armand was gone with remarkable speed, and I found Menceau reclaiming the microphone and taking charge as host. He put his hand on my back amiably and said, "Sorry, everyone; we'll do our best to take good care of him. Fortunately, one of our members is a fine physician. He has told me that he will stay with Armand to the hospital."

He turned to me. "Alex, we thank you for an informative and entertaining morning. Whoever would have thought that the refined world of books would hold such diabolical secrets, *hein*? It is fortunate for all of us that you say these people have been apprehended . . . but it makes one wonder what the next creative crime will be, doesn't it?"

He joked, but tightened the clasp of his hand on my left shoulder—the side that had been shot—and gave it a friendly little shake. I breathed in sharply, involuntarily, and caught a chill blast of enmity from the man. Recovering as quickly as I could, I raised my eyebrows as if in mutual consideration of that question, and smiled. I could feel a cool layer of sweat on my face.

"And now, in view of what has happened this morning," Menceau said, "I would suggest that we all go in to luncheon. We will drink to Armand's health, *n'est-ce pas?*"

The crowd quieted and solemnly agreed, no doubt subtly cheered at some level by the thought of the fine wine Armand had told me would be uncorked for the occasion. Servants began ushering people out through the same door they had entered to the banquet hall, and Menceau turned off the switch on the mike.

Digging in his thumb with surprising accuracy in another parting squeeze, Menceau released me. I broke out in a fresh cold sweat. It wasn't just the pain; it was the menace I felt emanating from him.

"A very creative job, Alex." I couldn't tell if he sneered or smiled. "You are leaving on holiday, I understand, but you will at least stay to lunch with us, won't you?"

I thought quickly. A small tidal wave of Folio B members surged towards us with questions and comments, and I was glad. There was safety in numbers.

"Thanks, Michel, but I really can't. Someone's expecting me." I smiled and lowered my voice, inclining my head towards the much shorter Menceau confidentially. "By the way, I'm glad we have this moment to chat—I wanted to talk to you about the safeguard I mentioned in my speech. Obviously, the word is out now, and as you can see, no individual members have been identified. I have, however, sent a detailed letter to my solicitor. It shall remain unopened, and specific members of the Bibliati will continue to be anonymous . . . as long as I remain in good health and the terrorist activities stop. Fair enough?"

He studied me, his eyes slightly wider than normal but otherwise showing no emotion, and said evenly, "I believe you are mistaken, Alex Plumtree. I believe it is too late for such arrangements." I thought I caught a hint of doubtfulness, or hesitancy, which gave me some small amount of hope. I had reached him.

The people waiting to speak to us occupied themselves by chattering quietly in a semicircle around us, waiting their turn. Trying to appear normal, I reassured him again. There could certainly be no arguing about it here, now. "Thanks again for the opportunity to speak, and I assure you, the arrangement I mentioned will be successful. There really is no other option, is there?"

Menceau looked down and rubbed his nose with a smoothly manicured forefinger and came up smiling—rather smugly, I thought. Perhaps he thought I was bluffing. I continued. "And thanks for the offer of staying here at the château, Michel. I hate to miss your famous hospitality."

"Oh, no, no; I understand. The ladies come first." He nodded to emphasise this, with a glance at Thérèse. Then he put his head to one side thoughtfully, and raised the same elegant forefinger in the air as if to make a point. "But somehow, Alex, I think you will enjoy my hospitality one day soon—perhaps *with* the lady." With a sour grin he turned away and was sucked immediately into the half-dozen people waiting to speak to him.

With my mind very much on getting out of the château to meet Sarah, I did my best to deal with my own small crowd of would-be conversation partners. Not wanting to be rude, I drifted in the midst of them out towards the front hallway, which led to the dining room, answering their questions all the while.

"Is it necessary to have a humidity monitor for a private collection? Do you have one?"

"Have you had the Malconbury Chronicles appraised?"

"Hello, I sell insurance for rare . . ."

If I could just get to my car . . .

When I was within sight of the front door, I excused myself ruefully, glancing at my watch, and said my good-byes. As I made a subtle beeline for the door through the hungry crowd, I wondered. Had I made my point clearly enough to Menceau? Did he understand that I would protect all of them as long as their unethical and violent attempts to influence politics stopped, and as long as I was alive and well?

For a moment I really thought I was going to make it. Then the woman in white, Thérèse, stood suddenly before me, blocking my path. "You're not leaving us so soon, Mr. Plumtree?"

Her dazzling smile told me one thing; her painful grip on my arm, made to look friendly enough to a casual observer, another. She began to walk, pulling me with her, away from the crowd. "Michel wanted me to be sure to show you the wine cellar before lunch. This way."

We went back inside, down the hall in the opposite direction of the happy crowd. I would have wriggled free and made a dash for it, but we had been joined almost immediately by two solidly built men, the one with the lopsided smile who had parked my car, and another, who was not in uniform but was just as clearly an employee of Monsieur Menceau's. They pressed close behind me and nuzzled twin muzzles in the region of my kidneys. I can't say that I was surprised; I knew too well by then that book people were anything but civilised.

They marched me down a long stone hallway with no windows until we came to steep, curving stairs. They had dropped the pretense of conversation altogether and made me go first down the stairway. I had to step carefully; my size twelves were twice as long as the steps themselves. It felt as if I were walking on my heels.

The air here was cool, even in the stairway, ideal for a cellar. I speculated that this was Menceau's personal cellar; surely the bulk of his stock would be stored at the winery itself, another handsome building I'd seen in the grounds as I'd approached the château.

The little steps went round and round, spiralling downward, until I began to feel dizzy. When the length of the passage down the stairs came to seem ridiculous, Thérèse stopped in front of me and I could see that the steps had come to an end at last. Thérèse pressed a switch that illuminated the room, courtesy of a number of electrified fixtures placed at four-foot intervals along the walls.

The two men shoved me forward into a long, narrow room. Its stone walls were rough; it appeared that the room had been hewn, literally, from the rock beneath the château. Running the length of the room was a primitive-looking iron grille, with a door at our end that boasted an ancient and formidable lock. Three feet behind the grille was an entire wall full of diamond-shaped shelves for holding wine bottles, from the floor to shoulder height, with ancient calligraphed signs interspersed occasionally.

Above the diamond-shaped cubbyholes was a series of recessed arches with statues in them—roughly two feet deep and five feet tall. The eight or so arches held statues of knights holding shields, anemic-looking men looking straight ahead, a fleur-de-lis, a woman looking similarly militant, who I assumed was Joan of Arc, and an unhappy-looking gargoyle.

So I was to be imprisoned in Menceau's personal wine cellar, behind bars with the wine. There were worse fates, I thought.

But that was before I noticed, by the light of the weak light fixtures, that there appeared to be someone lying on the floor behind the grille. Someone had already been locked in, and something was badly wrong with him—or her.

One of my escorts remained behind me with the woman, gun still pressed against me, while Lopsided Grin pushed roughly past me and unlocked the lock with a giant skeleton key. He then reached round, grabbed my arm, and shoved me inside.

"Tombez pas," he said sarcastically as he banged the door closed. "Don't fall."

"Thank you for your concern," I replied pleasantly as the three of them retreated without further speech, their footsteps echoing hollowly up and down the stairwell.

Immediately I went to the form on the ground, kneeling

next to it in the cramped space. The first thing I made out in the dim light was the shiny ponytail.

"Giles!"

He was lying on his side on the hard stone, and I gently took his shoulder and rolled him over. He moaned, and I heard him draw a raspy breath. To my horror, I saw that a dark pool of blood had collected beneath him. Without help I knew he couldn't be long for this world, and there would be no help for him here other than what I could provide.

I leaned over him, hoping he would know that I was there. "Giles, it's Alex." With shaking hands, unable to think of anything else to do for him, I gently loosened his tie. Then I held his shoulder so that he would know I was with him.

He whispered something in the darkness that I couldn't hear.

"Sorry?" I said, leaning closer to his mouth, my ear nearly touching his lips.

"Save . . ." Another tortured breath, and a momentary burst of strength. "Save . . . family," he said definitely, then went limp. A sort of wheeze emanated from him, and I knew it was the end.

Anguish at seeing him die, and an awareness that my fate was unlikely to be much different, filled me with despair. "I'm so sorry," I said uselessly. "I'm so very sorry." Then, still kneeling at his side, I prayed for him. Finally I took off my suit jacket, draping it gently over his pitifully lifeless form.

I stayed there for some moments, unable quite to grasp the instantaneous transition from life to death, marvelling at the spark that I had just seen extinguished. Giles was here, his body still warm, but in a very definite sense he was gone. It was eerie. If the part of him that had been alive wasn't here anymore, where exactly was it? What had happened to it?

Often I had felt my father's presence after his death, and my mother's too, in such a real way that I couldn't minimise it, couldn't tell myself it was a result of my overactive imagination. Now I wondered if Giles was watching me as I knelt over him, but most of all I hoped his worries were over.

Save family. I got up and paced the length of the room behind the grille, which I estimated was nearly twenty feet long, though only six or so wide—three feet of that behind the cage, three more outside it. My footsteps sounded loud on the stone. Giles hadn't struck me as the type to make pithy admonishments about family life in his last moments, particularly as he hadn't had a family, to my knowledge.

Then I began to wonder in earnest. Who exactly was Giles? Of course he had a family somewhere, wherever he had come from. Where *had* Giles come from? What had he done before becoming a secret agent in Armand's household? Why did he care so much what happened in the Bibliati cleverly camouflaged with Folio B—so much that he would give years of his life to solving the mystery? In the end he had given his whole life to it, I thought, grieving.

I sat down on the cold, dusty floor, knees to chest, and wrapped my arms around my legs. Then I put my head down. Refusing to think about the moment when the two men I'd seen earlier would come down the stairs and train their weapons on me as they had on Giles, I told myself that if they'd waited this long, they must have a reason to let me live. Otherwise I'd have been disposed of immediately to save them another trip down those treacherous stairs.

Already certain what I'd say if given a chance to speak to the Folio B board again, I decided to think instead of Sarah. At least she was safe and not locked in the dungeon with me and Giles. I thought of my plans to give her her ring, and propose to her in a way that I knew she would like. Not that I had actually rehearsed it.

Feeling guilty, I glanced over at Giles, who lay not three feet from me. Among bits of broken glass and the wine labels of broken bottles on the floor, my eyes caught sight of one of the wire frameworks that keeps corks in champagne bottles. My fingers caught at it and I twisted at it absent-mindedly as I realised, still looking at Giles, that the moment had come. He had made the transition to dead body and had ceased to be my companion. Suddenly it was unpleasant to be so close to him, not to mention eerie, so I walked over and sat down on some stacked cases of wine with "Folio B" stamped on the side, leaning my head back against the stone wall.

"Sarah." My voice sounded strange and lonely as it broke the tomblike silence. "Will you marry me?" Very ordinary, that version, but there was no doubting its effectiveness.

A vision of Angela, unconscious in her bed, drifted into

my mind. I shook the guilt away, feeling absolutely confident that it was right and good for me to think of Sarah at that moment.

"Sarah, will you be my wife?" Too possessive . . .

"Sarah, would you stay with me forever?" Definitely not; it sounded as if I were proposing a life-long affair instead of marriage. Not at all what I had in mind.

"Sarah, will you live with me and . . ." No, that made it sound as if I were interested in one thing only. I realised for the first time that if I ever did get the chance to propose to Sarah, it would be far more difficult than I had anticipated. Frustrated, I looked down at the piece of metal in my hands. I had twisted it into a ring.

CHAPTER 18

Man builds no structure which outlives a book.
—EUGENE FITCH WARE

W hen I heard the endless echoing of footsteps
coming down the narrow stairs, I jumped to my
feet. I had been dozing, and my heart beat fast with the sudden awakening, not to mention fear. Looking over at Giles, I
glanced at my watch and saw that it was ten o'clock—P.M.,
surely. In the wine cellar, time seemed to stand still without
natural light to indicate the time of day.

Once again I reminded myself that they had let me live
this long, so perhaps they were coming to talk and not to kill.
Perhaps they had left me here with Giles, with the ineffective
lights on for full effect, so that I could rethink my decision
not to capitulate. The echoing of the footsteps was so chaotic
that the very sound of it seemed a bizarre and ancient method
of torture. There was, however, a different sound to this collection of steps; one had a different sound from the others. It
seemed quieter, gentler.

I was standing like an animal in the zoo, fingers laced
through the grille, watching and waiting, when I saw her.

Sarah. Menceau's words from earlier that day came back

to me: *"But somehow, Alex, I think you will enjoy my hospitality one day soon—perhaps* with *the lady."*

Stunned, I watched the sarcastic man who had spoken to me earlier unlock the door again, sneering in my face.

"Ça va?" he asked nastily. I didn't bother to answer.

My eyes were riveted to her face. I went almost blind with anger when I saw that there was a dribble of blood under her nose. "Sarah," I said, my voice quavering with fury. "What have they done to you?"

I saw the look of astonishment on the faces of the hired guns. Clearly they had been unaware that they were uniting lovers in the dungeon. Idiot, I scolded myself. Now they'll take her and put her elsewhere. I restrained myself until they'd made what sounded like a lewd joke in French, from their guffaws afterwards, and pushed her in. I didn't move until they were gone, echoing their way back up to the world, laughing raucously.

Then silently, I took her in my arms and held her, rocking her gently back and forth. I buried my nose in her long, dark hair. She smelled like Sarah, heaven in my arms, and I didn't let go for a long time. She hugged me as if she were glad to see me too, in fact as if I were the mast of a sinking ship. I thought I felt a sob or two, but couldn't be sure.

When at long last I could let go, I took her head in my hands and looked over her face. I looked at the long, noble nose they had mistreated but apparently not broken, her almond-shaped eyes, her heavy, dark eyebrows, and the curves of her moist lips. Then back into her eyes. She was calm, she was smart, she was brave, she was stunningly beautiful. Throwing caution to the winds, I kissed her and held her again.

Then I said a remarkably stupid thing, a habit I had whenever I was with her. "What are you doing here?"

"What am *I* . . . ?" She laughed in spite of the circumstances and said, "I came to save you, Alex. But I'm afraid I didn't succeed." Stunned, I stared at her. In my self-centredness, and with my male ego, I had assumed that she'd been found and thrown in the dungeon as a way to get to me, to bargain with me. I still hadn't learned.

She glanced around her for the first time, and gasped when

she saw Giles's legs sticking out from under my jacket. Fortunately the cellar was cool enough that his body hadn't ripened much.

"That's Giles Rutherford. He was on my side of this whole thing—or at least I think he was." I sighed. "I'd better tell you what's going on." Even in that situation, from which it was doubtful that one or either of us would emerge alive, I hesitated to tell her about the Bibliati. But it wouldn't all make sense otherwise, and she deserved to know, coming after me like this and risking her own life.

"But first, Sarah, you simply can't imagine how good it is to see you. I—I care for you more than you would ever believe." I looked at her, and tears stung my eyes at the thought that she had put herself in this desperate position for me. "How did you know . . . ?"

She was holding my arms, which were clasped around her firm waist, just above the elbow. For the first time in days, I didn't feel the pain in my chest as I used my arm. "I know you," she said simply. "You wouldn't have been late to meet me."

"Wow," I said.

"And," she went on, "I could tell that things were bad for you when you didn't write." She raised her left eyebrow at me, a habit which I always found disconcerting. "Also, when I spoke to you yesterday, you were vague. I knew then that you were trying to hide something from me. And that meant that whatever it was had to be really awful."

She was referring to the "vagueness issue," or what she had seen as my habit of hiding my feelings from her. In fact, many of our recent letters had dealt with the subject of honesty, and sharing our feelings. There had come a point some months ago when she had said that if I was never going to open up to her, we would never grow closer than we were at that moment. It was exactly what Max was always going on about, and I recognised it for what it was: an ultimatum of the gentlest and kindest sort.

By return fax I'd explained that it wasn't a conscious effort to hide my feelings from her; rather, it was a lifetime of training in keeping such things to myself. I would try, I'd promised.

And try I did. Before sending each fax, I would read

through it to see if I'd really told her anything she'd want to know. She seemed to want to know mostly about me—including fears and problems I was facing—and how I saw things, like Davy abandoning her career in *A Severe Mercy*. If I hadn't included information of that kind, even if she hadn't explicitly asked, I'd go back and add to the letter. In our phone call the other day, such niceties had fallen away and left the bare bones, and she'd cared enough to notice the difference. She was amazing.

"How did you get here?"

She shrugged and smiled slightly, as if she had a secret. "My client brought me."

"The one you've been staying with?"

"Mmm-hmmm."

"That was nice of him."

"Very. Also, he knows Michel Menceau, so I knew I wouldn't have any trouble getting into the château with him along."

"Ah. Well, that was convenient . . . but unfortunate." I felt a frown line crease my brow as I listened to her talk about the client. There was an odd note in her voice—of elation, or something. I would have worried more about him, but after all, she had risked her life to come here and get me, so she must still have cared for me.

"Yes," she said brightly. "Also, I explained that the situation might be a bit awkward, and asked him to come back for us if he didn't see us at his cottage—I left the bicycle there for safekeeping—by dinnertime." She wilted a little, shoulders sagging as she looked at her watch. She sighed, and my heart galloped in response. Her every motion and breath was endearing and exciting to me at the same time, even in a situation like this. I would have done anything for her. Anything.

"I don't know what's keeping him," she said, a frown creasing her normally smooth and creamy forehead. "He really should have been here long ago. Perhaps they've persuaded him that we've left, in your car."

I nodded and continued the inquisition. "What happened to you after you got here? What time did you come?"

"I came around four, because you said you'd meet me at

the inn by two. I knew you wouldn't be that late, certainly not without phoning. My client's cottage isn't far from here, and he's very kind—I knew he'd want to help. After Menceau welcomed me inside and smiled and waved at my client as he drove away, I asked where you were." She let out an incredulous laugh. "I thought I'd be rescuing you from an embarrassing social situation—nothing more—but I quickly realised it was a bit more serious." She paused, and I saw in her face some of the fear she must have felt. It was still difficult to believe that I was talking to, and looking at, Sarah. I ran my hand up and down her arm. "They took me to a room alone and asked me questions."

"Who?"

"Menceau and a woman; I was never introduced to her. Menceau didn't like it that I had brought my client into things, and slapped me across the face. It wasn't really that bad." My heart ached at the note of false bravado in her voice. She had probably been terrified, and all this was because of me. What had happened to Denny and Angela was horrible, but these were the ultimate stakes. Now it was Sarah I was worried about.

I heard her take a deep breath. "Now. Do you know what we're waiting for? What's happening?"

"Sort of." I pulled her gently away from the door with me, well away from Giles, returning to the small seat made by the stacked cases of Folio B chardonnay. My arm around her, I began. "To make a long story short, by coming here I led them to believe that I was going to play along with them, promising not to make trouble. But then in my speech I let them know that I knew all about their book-stealing ring and revisionist history, and their forays into terrorism."

"Terrorism!" She pulled back from me and looked into my face, stunned. "This book group you've been talking about?" She made Folio B sound like a ladies' book club.

I nodded soberly. "I found a letter from my father, telling me about some of their international efforts, and you know what happened to Angela." I didn't go into what had happened to me.

"At any rate, I let Menceau know that I had not publicised any of it." I turned and faced her squarely, gripping her upper arm. "You are the only one who knows," I whispered. "You must let them think that I haven't told you."

She nodded.

"And I think he was listening when I said that I had posted everything I did know to my solicitor, specifying that by law the letter must not be opened unless I—" I hesitated to mention my death; Sarah had already lost one husband at an early age. Not that I was her husband, of course, but I did hope to be someday.

". . . unless I'm found in concrete overshoes."

Looking down, she nodded again. "I understand. You have to hold them at bay for the rest of your life."

"That's it. Not ideal, but so much better than the alternative."

She smiled a sad little smile that travelled up only one side of her mouth.

I sighed. "So if I were to guess, I would say that Menceau and a few of his cronies would like to iron out that agreement with me—one way or another—tonight." I looked at my watch—it was just after midnight. "Or maybe tomorrow."

Sarah frowned. "Why did they kill Giles? Do you know?"

"No. They're a ruthless lot. I do know that he'd been living among them as a spy for the last year or so. Perhaps they found him out. That would be enough for them."

She shuddered and leaned close. "Oh, Alex, I'm so sorry this has happened to you."

I looked down at her and pulled her close, squeezing her tightly. No point in clarifying that it had happened to both of us now. Of the two of us, she was the one I was worried about.

"We'll be all right," I said with as much conviction as I could muster.

There was an interval of silence. I don't know what she was thinking, but I was pondering the fact that I would do anything to get her out of there alive. I didn't want to go on without her if they accepted my bargain but killed Sarah for what I'd "shared" with her.

It was then that I had the idea. I must have turned and looked at her abruptly, because she sat up straighter and demanded, "What? What is it?"

My eyes were drawn to the scrap of wire I'd twisted into a ring earlier. It was lying not far from the door in the grille. This might be the only chance we'd ever have, if the worst happened. . . .

Quickly I reached for it, then knelt in front of Sarah, taking her hand. I felt an adrenaline surge a hundred times more powerful than I had in the most important regatta of my rowing career, and two hundred times more powerful than when Plumtree Press's first trade book had hit *The Tempus* bestsellers list.

"Sarah," I said. My hand shook slightly as I held the thing up in front of her. "Will you . . . ?"

To my astonishment, at that very moment we heard the distinct sound of clanking keys, evidently opening the door at the top of the cellar stairs. Sarah and I jumped to our feet, and she said, "Yes," urgently, as my jaw dropped, and I saw her fiddle with the scrap of metal in the grille door. She'd thought I was asking her to try to unlock the door with the piece of metal, and bent it straight, into an improvised lock pick. Almost frantic, she seemed to assume that whoever was coming through the door was going to give us the same treatment Giles had received. As she tried to turn the mechanism inside the heavy old wrought iron lock, we heard the door at the top of the stairway far above us swing open.

The familiar sound of footsteps echoed down the stairs, along with the voices of our captors, ratcheting up our suspense and fear with each moment. Sarah looked at me beseechingly and rattled at the door, desperately trying to shake it open. I thought her instinct might be accurate, and I couldn't let her stand floundering, rattling the door in desperation. I had already worked on the door myself and had found it hopeless, and it wouldn't have done us much good anyway to run up the stairs towards our attackers. I looked at her and took the scrap of metal from her shaking fingers. "I'll jam this into the lock—delay them a bit." She nodded. At least, I thought, we could postpone the inevitable for several seconds more.

The unpleasant characters charged with our care were chatting, making their way carelessly down the stairs. More raucous laughter erupted, echoing on the stairway. It sounded to me as if they'd been imbibing, dipping into the master's abundant stores. Perhaps that would give us an advantage.

"It's no good just standing here waiting for them," I said, gripping her shoulder with my right hand. She was trembling. "Let's at least hide in the gloom back there; it will buy us some time," I whispered. She nodded, and came willingly as I hurried her towards the far end of the enclosed section and the pitch darkness I'd investigated with my hands earlier. We covered the twenty or so feet in no time to the opposite end of the long, narrow room, running beneath the statues of Joan of Arc and her compatriots. "It sounds as if they've been drinking," I said into Sarah's ear. Even at such a desperate moment, I enjoyed having her so close, having my nose in her hair and smelling the light scent of her shampoo. "Maybe we can overcome them back here." I felt her nod next to me, her hair moving against my cheek. It did feel better to be less exposed in the darkness, and we were further from the threat, even if we were up against the proverbial wall.

Sarah and I crouched against the rear wall, listening to the echoing steps as they came nearer. Sarah's head was turned towards the wall and down; I didn't know if she was in the depths of despair, or studying something.

"Alex!" she whispered. "There's something here!"

"What is it? I—" I had almost said, "I can't see," but the words were too horrible to utter.

She was bending over, speaking with excitement into the wall of rock that I had been so certain was our final, unbreachable barrier. "I don't know, a kind of iron ring—Alex, there's a *door* here!" She was alternately pushing and tugging at the ring. "Help me push it open!" The loud voices and footsteps were still descending the stairway, and I remembered with gratitude how long it seemed to take for them to reach our little prison at the bottom.

I reached out to take her hand. Finding the warmth of her fingers and grasping them, I felt beneath them. The ring was large and metallic, probably wrought iron, I thought. A centuries-old version of a doorknob. It was attached to a solid, smooth slab of wood—I couldn't see it, but there was the pattern of a grain running through the smoothness, and it was markedly different from the rough, cold stone. Hurriedly I ran my hand over to the edge of the door to get an idea of its size, and as I followed the barely perceptible crevice between the door and the wall in an arc, I found that the door was roughly five feet tall and two feet across. People certainly had been smaller centuries ago.

Sarah and I battered at the door, first her hip and then mine, over and over, as the voices and the footsteps sounded ever closer, echoing in a cacophony that effectively prevented them hearing us. "Warped shut," I mumbled, panting. She stopped, and I could feel her panic rising. We glanced back towards the stairway as Lopsided Grin and cohort caught our eyes, coming at last into the weak light of the cellar. There was an eruption of swear words in passionate Gallic style as the men stood staring for a fraction of a second as we worked frantically at the door, then rushed with their keys to the door in the grille. I was grateful for the idea of jamming it; that temporary barrier would buy us valuable time. I doubted it would be enough.

Sarah turned back to the door and jerked at the ring hard, sort of shook at it, and to her surprise it fell off in her hands. A desperate, sob-like sound escaped from her, and then I really set to work. The only reason I could think of for the door grating open several inches after eight full-body blows, requiring roughly the force it had taken me to win Threepwood's ergometer contest, was that Sarah's panic had turned me into an animal of sorts.

The swearing and rattling at the grille lock grew louder and angrier. Sarah gasped and leaned against the door, helping me to push it open far enough for us to slide through. We stumbled under the low arch of the doorway practically bent double, and stopped, blinking in sudden light. Large floodlights were mounted on the ceiling of a very modern, commercial-looking wine-production room; the pungent smell of fermenting grape juice was almost overwhelming.

"I don't believe it," Sarah breathed as she gripped my arm and pulled me into motion, away from our prison. "We're in Menceau's winery." She let out a little chuckle at the improbability of it as we began to run. Huge vats of wine in process stood in rows; roughly half were the oak casks favoured by traditional purists, and the rest were rounded, closed stainless steel tubs on stilts.

At full speed we made for the rows of vats as our would-be pursuers remained stranded at the grille, but I thought I heard one of them turn back and run up the stairs. We would have to be quick. The room was two storeys high and we both saw the door up several flights of stairs, against the far wall. We had roughly half an American football field to run across to get to it, and I was grateful that at this hour—after midnight, I guessed—there was no one working there.

Evidently Menceau's people gave tours through here; there was a sort of grim humour to running along the red-painted footsteps that showed groups of visitors where to walk. In moments we had arrived at the foot of the steps in the deserted winery, and I took time to glance back at the tiny door through which we had escaped. Lopsided Grin was scrambling through the doorway, and, to my profound dismay, was hoisting his snub-nosed automatic weapon in our general direction. Needless to say, he was no longer grinning.

"Arretez!" he shouted as the first of the shots rang out, bouncing off the metal railing of the staircase. I started to say to Sarah, "We'll just have to run for it," but before I could make a sound she had taken off ahead of me like a rabbit, mounting the stairs in threes. I followed her, marvelling at her, delighted with her, and the seconds passed like hours. Three flights of cement stairs seemed endless, and the "ping" of ricocheting shots rang in our ears.

He never stopped shooting—apparently there was an endless supply of ammunition in his horrible little machine. All we could do was blindly head for the door and hope that he would miss. Time after time, every time, he did miss us too, and I couldn't imagine how except that he was far away, and probably drunk, and also on the run. At any rate, ears ringing from the shots, we made it to the top and through the door to the outside, with Sarah in the lead.

As we paused in the warm summer air and deafening quiet, trying to assess our position, I looked briefly up at the stars and said, "We'll try to find my car—the valet took it; the keys may still be in the ignition."

"Mmm." Sarah had, at last, recognised the usefulness of

that conveniently brief English response. I would have to remember to tease her about it—if we ever had the chance.

Then, again, we ran, our feet crunching in the gravel of the drive and the fertile smell of Menceau's vineyards assaulting our nostrils. It seemed odd that there was no wailing alarm upon our exit from the winery; no blinding spotlights shone down on us from above. Quite possibly, I knew, there would be a silent alarm, and we had no time to lose. It was tempting to try to disappear among the vines, but smarter to try to reach the car. This patch of French countryside was owned by someone who would track us down on his own land in no time, much as I could have found anyone on the grounds of the Orchard.

Of course they would know that we would try for the car, but we hoped we could get there first. We ran round the north side of the château, sticking close to the building; I'd seen a branch of the extensive drive heading in that direction, and thought it might be logical that the cars would be parked there, out of the way, where they wouldn't ruin the view of the surrounding countryside.

Unfortunately, I'd not had much time to inspect the layout of the place before I'd been locked up. It came as a surprise when we ran into a bunch of late-night revellers on a stone patio, seated at tables lit with chubby citronella candles. It was too late to go back, so we ran through them, the car park area in view past them under a shingled shelter.

"What are you . . ."

"Mon Dieu!"

"I say! Look here now . . ."

But we kept running, leaving them standing gawping in our wake, so sated with good food and wine that they couldn't be bothered to run after us. We ran off the patio onto a gravel turnabout, and then into the vehicle shelter. My car was at the far end—a result of having arrived so late in the morning, no doubt—and we breathlessly sprinted towards it.

As we raced, reaching for the car doors, shoes skidding on gravel as we turned between the cars, I saw too late that the driver's side door was open. I slid to a belated stop.

It was Menceau, sitting in my car. He looked up at me pleasantly as I stared at him with an odd feeling in my stomach, and one of the henchmen moved forward from the back of the shelter, his weapon held loosely in front of him, as Lopsided Grin ran up, panting, behind us.

"You did not like my hospitality? Not enough oak in the chardonnay? A touch too much lemon, perhaps?" Menceau laughed briefly. "Yes, I've heard it before. Well. I am not offended. Please. Come inside with me, have some coffee and we will talk. I promise—my coffee will be better."

He stood and we followed his dark, compact form as he strutted across the gravel yard, the patio, and through a door that led into the meeting room. His two henchmen followed us. I took Sarah's hand and squeezed it as we walked hesitantly into whatever Menceau had planned for us. Guilt and a determination to do whatever it took to keep Sarah safe overrode all else as the men closed and locked the door firmly behind us.

Menceau led us through the meeting room to a door which he opened onto a remarkable scene. Armand Beasley, pale but otherwise apparently well, sat in a deep leather chair surrounded by Holdsworthy, Boillot, Farquhart, Pillinghurst, Rupert Soames, and Applebaum in what was evidently Menceau's private study. The room was octagonal, and less formal than the others I'd seen. Half the walls in the room were covered in velvet draperies of deep blue, and I guessed that the view of the surrounding countryside would be awe-inspiring during the day.

I saw by the chiming clock in the corner that it was one o'clock in the morning, and was astounded that they would all be assembled at that hour.

"Please—sit." Menceau was civil enough as he sank into a chair of his own behind a huge desk, and indicated with his arm that we should take two that were obviously intended for us. The group was seated roughly in a circle round the room, and the gathering had the eerie feeling of a tribunal. No one looked at us with the exception of Armand. He looked uncomfortable, a film of sweat over his pallid skin. I wondered if he'd really had some sort of heart problem and was all right now, or if the whole thing had been staged. He quickly nodded and attempted a smile at me, but it looked sickly.

"The time has come for some discussion about exactly

what we should do about Mr. Plumtree—and his friend here—since he seems bent on the ruin of Folio B's reputation."

I was struck not only by the ambiguity of his words—did "what we should do" mean remove me from the board, or from the face of the earth?—but by the fact that he was the one in charge. Menceau was clearly the driving force behind the Bibliati.

There was a light knock on the door, and a uniformed man appeared, nodding to Menceau. He turned his back to us and wheeled in a serving cart on which was a large urn of coffee and a number of cups with saucers. "Good. Please serve us now, Henri." There was the most awkward of silences while the poor man made the rounds of the room, sugaring and creaming as he went. Sarah and I refused.

I looked at her as she sat proudly, perfectly straight, calm, and lovely despite her bloodied face. A sort of strength radiated from her that strengthened me as well. I would be the most fortunate of men to belong to her. When we were through this, I told myself, nothing would stop me from asking her to marry me. Nothing.

When Henri had left, I cleared my throat. "I have a few questions."

Pillinghurst laughed like a maniac, starting high and ending low, and I felt Sarah shiver. Menceau snapped, "For God's sake, shut up, Pillinghurst." For some reason the old man actually listened to Menceau. He looked chastened as the horrible sound died in his throat.

Menceau opened a cigar box, took out a cigar, and guillotined it as we watched. Deliberately, he puffed it to life, then scrutinised me through the smoke. He smiled slightly, then waved the cigar in a gesture of largess and said, "Why on earth not? We've got all night."

"Thank you. What, exactly, is Giles Rutherford doing dead in your wine cellar?"

"Ah, that. Yes, I thought you might want to know. Well, you can understand that as a prominent political figure, I must have strict security at the château."

I thought "security" was rather a euphemism for what he had there, but kept quiet.

"So when my guards found him snooping about in my

study just after Armand fell ill, and he turned quickly as if to shoot them"—he shrugged—"they shot first." He made a tongue-in-cheek sad face. "Imagine their regret when they realised it was a Montblanc pen he held in his hand instead of a weapon.

Yes, just imagine, I thought. My contempt for him was immense.

"You've rung the *gendarmes*, then," I said, challenging him.

He gave a snort of derisive laughter. "You do not understand how things work in rural France, my dear boy. I *am* the law here." He took a puff of his cigar. "So, you see," he added as an afterthought, "you really are quite safe."

The threat running beneath these innocuous words was so sinister that my blood ran cold. I could hear Armand breathing stertorously across the room, and worried that he would have another heart attack.

"You should be grateful that I have taken care of Giles for you—accidentally, of course. I'm afraid you were rather taken in by Mr. 'Rutherford.'" Menceau pronounced the name sarcastically as he stuck an index finger in the air and wagged it at me. "Always remember, Alex, that things are almost never what they appear."

He left us to dwell on that enigmatic statement as he puffed on the cigar for a moment. Then, sitting forward at his desk, he said in a confidential sort of way, "You see, Giles Rutherford was, in actual fact, Giles Stonecypher."

He paused to let this sink in. I frowned in confusion as Menceau continued.

"And Giles Stonecypher was obsessed with his great-grandfather. You've heard about all those ridiculous sightings of the 'supernatural being' that appears to offer wisdom in Stonecypher's books? 'The figure in the library?' That it was Marcus Stonecypher's ghost?" I thought of my own experience in my library and recalled how very realistic it had been. Now I could almost imagine that it had been Giles, who, in retrospect, did resemble Marcus Stonecypher in a way. I'd always been plagued by the feeling that I'd seen Giles somewhere before; now I knew it had been in the portraits of Stonecypher in my literature books.

"Giles loved dressing up, keeping that 'supernatural being' alive. What's more, of course, he collected all the royalties from the Stonecypher books sold today, so keeping the legend alive made sense." Menceau sighed. "Delusional. But his obsession with preserving the legend also drove him to prevent Angela Mayfield sullying his famous ancestor's reputation with stories of radical politics and unnatural deaths at 54 Bedford Square."

If what he said was true, it had been Giles who had visited my library, though Farquhart seemed to have stolen the Wodehouse and the Stonecypher. (Had there been two intruders that night?) Then it had also been Giles who had issued the dingbats and the letters, Giles who had hired Rich, Giles who had had me followed by the white Ford and the Neck, Giles who had run down Angela, Giles who had had me shot and buried in my building, Giles who had had the warehouse burnt in Oxford, and Giles who'd had the printer's ransacked in Singapore.

That explained nearly everything that had happened to me in the last week—except the harassment over the building renovation, and the Malconbury Chronicles and other books going missing from the library and reappearing.

It was too pat. I didn't believe him.

"No. I don't think so," I said, rising to my feet, suddenly angry. "Giles wasn't responsible for all that. You are the ones who are delusional, you and *your* obsession with Stonecypher."

I felt Sarah's eyes on me. They were very wide.

"I know about your sick, anachronistic, Voltairean Bibliati group. And I know, too, that my father died because he knew." My eyes burned into the eyes of each person in the room one by one, fleetingly. There were tears flowing from Armand's and Farquhart's. "I know about the other people you've murdered because they knew. If you think anyone in his right mind could let all that go, you are utterly insane.

"Now. I don't have anything against your benign—if unrealistic—political philosophy. People are free to think what they like. But if you don't stop the killing, the book crimes, the political terrorism, the diabolical altering of history, I will slowly, as I demonstrated today, begin to strip off layers of your anonymity. Over time, your reputations will be shattered. If anything ever happens to me, my solicitor has instructions to open a letter that I posted some time ago, stating exactly what you have done, and who you are. You would be berated by everyone you know and damned by history."

"I don't think so." Menceau settled back in his chair and smiled.

I looked at him and swallowed, feeling suddenly very exposed and vulnerable. I had just played my best—and last—card. If it hadn't worked, I was finished. And so, I feared, was Sarah.

What had I forgotten?

He must have seen the horror in my face. This time it was he, not Pillinghurst, who emitted the bloodcurdling laugh. There was something so thoroughly sinister—and triumphant—about it that at that moment I knew I had lost.

"Oh, why is it that a Plumtree always thinks he can change history?" He emitted the last few chuckles of laughter, winding down, shaking his head. His mouth twisted downwards in an ugly sneer. "I don't know who in God's name you think you are." With that he waved his hand subtly at the subhuman beasts holding the weapons, and everything happened very quickly.

The goons lifted the automatics as Armand bellowed, "No!" and pulled out a tiny gun of his own, aiming it at Menceau. As soon as I saw the firearms in play, I threw myself on top of Sarah, which would have been very pleasant under different circumstances, so I didn't see exactly what happened after that.

There was one distinct shot fired, which I assumed was Armand's, and then continuous bursts of the little automatic weapons. I think I knew that they were aiming at Armand; I had suspected all along, somehow, that he'd been on my side.

To add to the confusion, at that moment the door burst open. Still spread-eagled over Sarah on the carpet, I was afraid to attract attention by turning my head. Slowly, though, I turned for a peek out of the corner of my eye, and to my astonishment there in the doorway stood France's—and possibly the world's—most popular movie star, Jean-Claude Rimbaud, in the flesh.

An angry voice boomed, *"Qu'est-ce qui se passe ici?!"* Stunned as I was by his sudden appearance, I couldn't help but notice that Rimbaud looked exactly as he had in his films—and the flashing green eyes were every bit as stunning in person as they'd been in the cinema, and in the tube station poster. Rimbaud was just short of musclebound, and was even more of a freakish height than I was, poor man, at six foot seven—an almost unheard of distinction for a Frenchman. He possessed a certain unmistakably French grace of movement that I had never seen in other males of the species. He stood now with his arms slightly away from his sides, poised for action.

When the goons saw him filling the doorway, they hesitated, gaping, for a split second before raising their guns, during which he boomed authoritatively, *"Mettez-les là!* Put those down!"

To my astonishment, they actually did put them down, glancing uncertainly at their employer, who lay unconscious, head down on his desk. Behind Rimbaud there were two bodyguards who had unlikely bulges in their jackets, which they were allowing us to see.

"Let's get on with it," he said disgustedly in French. "Someone call for help—these people are injured!" We all remained immobile for a split second, stunned at the turn of events, then I picked myself up and went to the phone.

I punched 999, only to be stunned into silence as Rimbaud said, *"Sarah! Mon trésor!"* and ran to her, taking her in his arms.

"Qu'est-ce qu'ils ont fait de ma Sarah!" He took her head in his hands exactly as I had—at least, I thought, I had done that right—and gazed at her nose tragically. "What have they done to my Sarah?"

I dropped the phone, staring, and fumbled to pick it up again. Someone was already squawking impatiently on the other end. I told them where we were and what we needed in my basic French, and hung up again, still staring in disbelief. Sarah and *Jean-Claude Rimbaud*? How? Why?

Then I thought of her desire to get a flat in Paris, to take the job there with her client, running his foundation. What an idiot I'd been! Somehow she'd met Jean-Claude, and of course they were smitten with each other. I couldn't blame either of them, but that didn't mean I was happy about it. Sarah was taking this vacation with me as a gesture of sympathy, and would no doubt tell me along the way that we were through. Shaken, I felt relief that I hadn't actually got round to popping the question to her. Perhaps she hadn't noticed the scrap of metal—trash, for heaven's sake—that I had been holding in my hand in the wine cellar. At least I was to be saved that humiliation.

I longed to skulk away to lick my wounds, but there was Armand, lying on the floor barely eight feet away from me. From the greyish pallor of his face I wasn't certain he would live. He seemed to be having difficulty breathing, and I prayed that the ambulance would arrive quickly.

I knelt next to him and his eyes flickered open. "It's all . . . yours . . . now." He gasped, and the air wheezing into his lungs made a frightening sound. He was very badly off indeed. I wondered if he meant that looking after Folio B, and keeping it honest, was my responsibility now. Perhaps he had been trying for some time to root out the offending branch of the society.

"Armand," I said. "It'll be all right." It might have been a lie, but I always appreciated those words when disaster struck. "Please don't try to speak."

"The royals . . ."

His eyes closed again, and I felt for a pulse on the side of his neck. It was there. Poor man; he had been looking forward to meeting the Princess of Wales the next day when she appeared to kick off the Paris book fair, in honour of the European Year of the Book. He may even have been invited to a reception of some sort in her honour.

For lack of anything else I could do to help, I took a serviette from Henri's serving cart and mopped at his brow with the thick burgundy jacquard linen.

"Plumtree." The voice came from above and behind me. I looked up, turning. It was Holdsworthy, looking stricken, with Diana Boillot hanging on him like a second skin. "I—er—I am sorry."

Not quite up to a "Not at all," I acknowledged him with a stiff nod, and looked back down at Armand, who was still breathing. Just. I wondered what exactly Holdsworthy was sorry about.

"I had no idea, you see." There was actually a touch of emotion in his voice, and I looked up to see his lip quiver as he fought for composure, standing over us. "After what you said about your father, I began to wonder if perhaps they'd killed my wife. Virginia acted so strangely, and rather suspiciously, for the last weeks of her life. Perhaps she'd found out about the society somehow, and . . ." His voice trailed off and he shook his head, blinking.

"Don't, darling," Diana breathed into his ear.

"Yes—yes, I must." He licked his lips and went on. "Your parents, and your author, and *you*—God, you've been through hell. You've got to believe me, Plumtree, I had no idea the other members were going that far. I was part of it, and I did allow MacDougal to present the facts in a certain way and then engineered his defection to you. But Voltaire did the same thing, you see, and it looked to me . . ." He took a ragged breath. "I didn't know they were hurting people— not *physically*. Please, you can't think that I . . ."

At that moment, thankfully, the doctor who had appeared earlier in the day came into the room in a dressing gown, having been summoned by Henri or someone from his comfortable bed in the château. He looked at Menceau, pronounced him dead, and took over with Armand. Moments after he had begun to work on him, the ambulance arrived, and the doctor left the room with Armand when the attendants rolled him out.

The *gendarmes* arrived next—it seemed that there were real police in rural France after all—and it was hours before they released us. They found it difficult to believe that the dead and injured parties had shot each other, and that no one else had been involved. Most of all, they found it difficult to believe that the famous Jean-Claude Rimbaud was in the room with them.

Not being entirely sure who was who within the Bibliati, I kept my mouth shut as to why they might have wanted to kill each other and offered only factual details, such as what I had seen when the shooting began. With Menceau gone, perhaps the danger was over, but I couldn't be sure. Holdsworthy and

Boillot did not come forward with further details, but Holdsworthy did let it slip that Pillinghurst had sneaked off sometime just after the shooting, and was a rather suspicious character. He might have had something to do with it, Holdsworthy said.

During our little chat I sat on one side of Sarah, Jean-Claude Rimbaud on the other, and was keenly aware of her body language. She seemed just as comfortable brushing against his massive side as she did mine. She didn't lean against either of us. By this time the irony of his *RESCUE!* had sunk in, and I could only marvel at the twisted humour of it.

It was towards the end of our interview with the police that they enquired about the reason for Rimbaud's presence there. "My investment banker," the actor said in French, indicating Sarah, "was joining him"—he jerked a thumb at me—"for a holiday." He looked none too pleased about the standard of his banker's company, and after an assessing look at me, turned away again.

I reeled. The client? Jean-Claude Rimbaud was her *client*?

Rimbaud went on. "She came to meet him here. She said if they weren't back at my house by a certain time, to come after them; that there could be some sort of awkward situation." He shrugged the shoulders that made women swoon. "So I came back and found . . . this."

My mind raced as the police continued their interminable questions. So it was Rimbaud's foundation that she'd been invited to run. And I'd imagined some sort of wealthy geriatric ex-industrialist, with an ample belly and double chin. That'd teach me to let down my guard.

When they finally let us go, Sarah introduced us officially. Jean-Claude seemed civil enough as he shook my hand, and told me that he wished we could have met under more pleasant circumstances.

"Let's get out of here," he said. "We can go to my house and"—he looked at his watch—"have breakfast." We walked outside. There was a moment of supreme awkwardness when we all realised that Sarah would have to decide which car to ride in—his or mine.

To my immense relief, she said, "I'll ride with Alex. If we

lose you on the way, Jean-Claude, I can help him find the house."

She had chosen me—for the ride home, at least. I would have to wait to see which of us she would choose for the rest of her life.

CHAPTER 19

If well used, books are the best of all things; if abused, among the worst.

—RALPH WALDO EMERSON

Jean-Claude's house—that one, at any rate; he might have had a dozen or so tucked away in various exotic locations for all I knew—turned out to be a refreshingly modest two-bedroom home dating from the 1920s, rustic down to the cloth curtain which hung to the floor beneath the kitchen sink.

With the hands that had slain a thousand villains, and more recently massaged a thousand shoulders, Jean-Claude had made an omelette. Sarah and I had bathed as he did so—separately, unfortunately—taking turns in the ancient metal tub that dominated the house's only bathroom.

As we sat over second and third bowls of coffee, having disposed of the superb omelette, I decided that I liked Jean-Claude. In fact, I liked him very much. At least if Sarah chose him, I knew she would be in good hands.

I had decided something else that morning, with which I was about to break the friendly silence that ensconced the little pine table: having come so far and gone through so much, I was oddly compelled to go to the Paris book fair that day. The original plan for the holiday had been to skip the fair and cycle onward to Alsace. Now I only hoped that Sarah would forgive me for ruining yet another day of our long-awaited vacation.

Putting my giant coffee bowl in its saucer, I cleared my throat. "I'm afraid this is not going to be a very popular suggestion, but considering all that's happened, I really feel I must go to the book fair. If nothing else, I want to see if Diana Boillot is actually conducting her restoration demonstration with the books I saw in Farquhart's studio." I wrinkled my nose and said, "Sorry," looking at Sarah, expecting the worst. "It'll mean one less day in Alsace."

My announcement provoked nothing more than a smile over her café au lait. "That's all right. I'd quite like to see a book fair—I've never been to one." Jean-Claude stood and began clearing the dishes. "When are you thinking of leaving?" she asked me.

Being married to Sarah would be almost too good to be true, I decided. Would she never be upset if I had to come home late from work? Had an unexpected business dinner in town on a Friday night? Would she never mind if I forgot to empty the dustbins, or bring her breakfast in bed on her birthday?

I raised my eyebrows at her and smiled naughtily. "Er—soon?"

"Mmm." She took a final sip and put down her coffee. "I'll just finish getting ready—be right back." She rose, but at the doorway she turned. "Great breakfast, Jean-Claude—thanks."

I realised that they probably spoke in French normally, and that she said this in English as a courtesy to me. I did speak and write French, but wasn't nearly as fluent as Sarah. The realisation that they had their own private language was deeply disturbing.

Jean-Claude, his back to me as he did the dishes by hand in the tiny sink, looked round quickly before speaking to make sure that Sarah was out of earshot. I could smell the lemony essence of his washing-up liquid. Turning back to the dishes, he said, "I would be blind, Plumtree, if I did not see that you have plans for Sarah."

I was quite certain that he wasn't referring merely to the book fair.

"You knew her first, I realise, and the two of you have a— a history." Here he turned to face me, holding a dripping handful of cutlery. It occurred to me that this was how a man of the nineties got his hands to look weather-beaten for the close-up shots. He did dishes.

"But I am, by my own admission, competitive by nature." He waved the knives and forks for emphasis. "As she has not yet promised to marry you—as far as I can tell—I feel it is only fair that I stay in the running. I hope this does not upset you." He watched my face, still holding the cutlery aloft.

"No, of course not," I lied. "Sarah should choose." The latter statement was true, at any rate; I wanted her to be happy, and if she preferred Jean-Claude and the life he could offer, she should have it. Part of me almost wanted her to have the life he could offer. The travel, the endless funds, the people she'd meet . . .

Rotten luck, though, for me.

He nodded slowly, meeting my eyes, and I knew that we had an understanding. We would do what was best for Sarah.

"Thanks," I said. "Splendid omelette."

"Take my car and driver if you like—Sarah knows how to call them from the town. Parking in Paris is such a pain in the neck." This from the man who supposedly drove his own stunts, wrecking dozens of police cars in a single scene.

I smiled and thanked him again, then went to put on my suit and tie, gather my wallet, and don my shoes. While I was doing so, Sarah emerged from the bathroom and summoned the driver, so that a grey Renault was waiting for us when we were ready to go.

On the way from the tiny town of Ville-en-Tardenois, where Jean-Claude had his retreat, to Paris, we mostly watched the scenery go by, holding hands and enjoying being together. At least I hoped she enjoyed being with me. I hope I'll be forgiven for paying so much attention to her appearance, but she is stunning, and I am human. She is one of those women who glows, on the outside as well as the inside. In fact, her outward beauty sort of reflects what's inside, because she's more than conventionally beautiful.

What's more, she has the rare gift of wearing clothing that suits her. On that day she was wearing a navy blue, crepe-y, shortish spaghetti-strap dress that showed just how stunning she really was. Evidently, in addition to a smooth summer tan, she had acquired the French habit of wearing high heels on a daily basis, which made her long legs look endless. Jean-Claude and I had exchanged a glance at the door as Sarah walked to the car, as if acknowledging how much was really at stake in our gentlemanly race.

In the Renault I wanted to stare at her bare, smooth arms and legs, but restrained myself. I was aided in this by a recurring half-thought; something that preoccupied me, though I couldn't have said what it was. Something I had forgotten that was important—the same thing I'd felt rather than understood in the grounds of the Orchard the night before last.

The driver let us out at the door to the exhibition hall, and I paid for the catalogue of exhibitors which allowed us entry. We took a moment to check the timing of the Princess's appearance—I wasn't immune to the world-wide fascination with the rumour-inspiring royal—and saw that it was in an hour, at ten o'clock. "I've been to a few royal appearances in my time," I told Sarah. "We should go to that room in half an hour at the latest if we even want standing room."

"Yes," she said. "I'd hate to miss seeing her."

The half-hour flew by; we went first to the Folio B restoration exhibit Armand had described in answer to my accusation of theft merely two days before, and I explained its significance to her. Diana Boillot was there, giving dispassionate explanations of her trade to anyone who asked. Interestingly enough, there was no sign of any of the extremely rare and valuable books I had seen being shipped from Farquhart's workshop anywhere around the restoration exhibit.

When Diana was free, I introduced her to Sarah, whom she greeted with a curt nod, exactly as I remembered her greeting me when we'd been introduced at Armand's. I asked her specifically about several of the titles I'd seen in the boxes shipped to Menceauville, and Diana shook her head, saying she hadn't restored any of those books, and they were not in her exhibit. She added that some of those books were very rarely on the market, and that no complete copies were known to exist—exactly my thoughts when I'd seen them the Sunday before.

While my mind started working on who was shipping the books, and who had restored them if she hadn't, Sarah spoke with Diana at length about the art of restoration and watched her demonstrate the tools of the trade, and in the end I had to tear her away to see the Princess.

By nine-thirty the room where the Princess was to appear was already jammed. "Come on," I told Sarah. "We won't give up so easily. Maybe we can get a spot behind them, or to the side—somewhere closer than this anyway." We fought our way back out of the room and searched for another door that would let us in closer to the stage. Someone was just locking such a door as we hurried up to it. I saw that he was wearing the badge of an official of the book fair.

"Please, do you think we could just sneak in before you lock up?" Sarah asked it in her best French, looking at the man conspiratorially.

Ready to turn down the request, he looked at her, smiled, said, *"Vite, vite!"* and shooed us in. We were behind the platform they had set up to accommodate the Princess and her entourage.

In awe of the security required for an appearance like this, I looked round and saw a huddle of police officers surrounding the platform. They scanned the crowd nervously, sweating in their uniforms. The heat and noise in the room were unbelievable. Sarah and I slowly jostled our way to the front corner of the platform, but we were still at the very edge, not far from the door through which we'd come.

At last they filed in, right past us, to Sarah's delight. And it wasn't the Princess alone; to the delighted surprise of the crowd, the Princess's two sons, the first heirs to the throne after their father, had joined her as a surprise. A sort of "ooooh" emanated from the crowd, and applause broke out. I'd heard of the Princess doing this before, surprising crowds with an impromptu appearance of the young princes, never announcing her plans, for security reasons, to bring the children. They seated themselves on the chairs on the platform, the boys remarkably at ease before the huge crowd. The head of the committee for the European Year of the Book, of which Armand was a member, stood to give the inevitable welcome. He spoke in English first, in honour of the Princess, though he himself was French.

"Ladies and gentlemen," he intoned with a heavy accent, and I looked away, not expecting him to say anything worth listening to. As I gazed at the elder prince, thinking about his turbulent family life and how difficult it would be to have any semblance of a normal family life as a royal, something caught my eye behind him. The door we had come through was opening, and a police officer was coming through it.

But something was wrong . . . his face, looking down . . . something in his hand. It was a plastic carrier bag from one of the book vendors at the fair, with something heavy in the bottom of it. Puzzled, I recognised him as the Irish bookseller from the Hotel Russell. He'd looked down in just that same way when he'd passed Rupert Soames a note.

It was only then that Giles's words, and Armand's, made sense to me. In a flash I knew this was the next step I'd half-realised, the logical progression of events that the owl's song had suggested two nights before.

"Save . . . family . . .

"The royals . . ."

Armand and Giles hadn't meant what I thought they had at all. They had known that the princes were joining their mother. This was it; this had been the long-term goal of the Bibliati. *"When principalities and kingdoms fall, every man will come to power through knowledge of the written word."* They were going to systematically eliminate the direct heirs to the throne. My father had even mentioned this in his note, and I'd been blind not to see it all sooner—but I hadn't known that the children were coming.

"Sarah." She turned to look at me, and her face fell when she saw my expression. "There's a problem. I can't explain now, but please, get to the edge of the room and make your way out through that far door."

"Now?" She looked nonplussed.

"Now," I said definitely, moving away. "Please. I'll explain later."

I made my way gently through the crowd, forcing myself to stay calm and move slowly. If I attracted too much attention from the police, the police would think I was the one causing the trouble and would nobble me. Then I wouldn't be able to get to the Irishman, and the police would never believe me that one of their own was about to plant a bomb beneath the royals.

If I yelled, "It's a bomb! Everybody run!" there would be mass panic and all would be lost. That would be nearly as ridiculous as Rupert yelling about Armand's heart attack. There was only one thing to do: get the device from him and dispose of it.

Keeping my eyes on the man, I tried to give the impression of casually drifting across the fifteen or so feet I had to go. Given the throng, it was no easy feat. I thought about what I should do. Let him place it, watching all the while, then retrieve it when he turned away? Or try to disable him, grab the bag, and run before the police could catch me?

The speaker finished and the Princess stood, saying something about her mother-in-law being willing to read everything but the Budgie the Helicopter books to her grandchildren. The crowd roared at the joke about the relationship between the Queen and her ex–daughter-in-law, the Duchess, who had written the Budgie series. I pushed on, still not knowing exactly what I was going to do with him until, suddenly, he was a mere three feet away from me.

It was instinct, not logic, that told me to stomp my heel on the man's foot, hit him hard between the legs with my good hand, and then apply so much pressure to his wrist that he had to momentarily release the grip on the carrier bag. I had surprised him, and he groaned in agony at the all-consuming pain between his legs. Still, I saw the flash of a knife as it flicked out from his sleeve. As I grabbed his wrist, the knife sliced into the palm of my hand, but it didn't matter. I wrested the bag from him as he was doubled over, incapable of fighting back.

Almost stunned at my success, I bolted for the door Sarah and I had come through, clutching the bag. I heard gasps from the people around us, and saw one of the policemen catch sight of the crumpled Irishman in the uniform of his colleagues, and then of me as I headed for the door. I knew how it looked; I had assaulted a policeman and was fleeing. Already I sensed the righteous anger that would suffuse the copper as he came after me.

Praying that the Irishman had counted on getting away through that same door and had left it unlocked, I hurled myself into it and crashed it open, running through the thin crowd in the hallway until I saw a policeman ahead.

"Can you help me?" I yelled, running wildly towards him as I held the bag out in front of me. "I've got a bomb!"

It was a stupid thing to say, and to this day I don't blame the man for what he did. Seeing that I wasn't going to stop for a chat, he tripped me. I saw the carrier bag go flying through space in front of me as if in slow motion, turning over in the air. Then I hit the ground, and a second later the policeman's truncheon hit me squarely in the back of the head.

"More ice?" Sarah asked again as I began to doze off. The doctor had told her to keep me awake for twelve hours, owing to the force with which the good officer had hit me on the head, and it was getting harder for her to do so now that it was ten o'clock at night.

She came and sat next to me on the edge of the denim sofa, leaning over me to check the bag of ice beneath my head as I reclined on Jean-Claude's cushions. That woke me up a bit—parts of me, at least—and from across the room I felt as much as saw a resentful look from our host.

The newspaper sat on the coffee table, its pages ruffled by the evening breeze. It had been left open to pages two and three, where I could see photos of the two experts who had been killed as they attempted to defuse the bomb. According to the article that surrounded their pictures, the bomb had been enough to do away with the entire roomful of people. We had received a phone call from the Princess herself, thanking me, and cryptically saying that soon she would thank me properly. Great, I thought; the Princess of Wales would be some measure of comfort when Sarah left me for Jean-Claude Rimbaud.

I had placed a call home and, not finding Max in, phoned Lisette.

"Angela is doing fine, Alex—she even spoke today. It is as

if the switch 'as been turned back on. Dr. Michaels says that some swelling 'as gone down in her brain.

"I know what you're thinking," Lisette bubbled on. "You're wondering if you should come back. It would be a big mistake, Alex," she said firmly. "You're there, Sarah's there—'ow often does either of you get a 'oliday, let alone together?" She dropped her voice conspiratorially. "Now, listen to me, Alex. I know about these things. If you want Sarah to marry you, you must spend some time with 'er—time that will draw you closer together. You must not let this chance pass."

"I'm not sure . . ."

A mild scream of exasperation came down the line. "All right, that's it. I want to speak to Sarah! Good-bye, you!"

Suspicion crept into my voice as I heard myself ask, "Why? What are you . . ."

"Put 'er *on*, I said!"

Wincing at the very thought of Lisette's wrath, I'd called Sarah to the phone and been treated to such rapid bursts of French that I could hardly follow them. Jean-Claude tried not to look as if he was listening, but from time to time he smacked his hand on the armchair, without expression, or fiddled with his magazine.

Jean-Claude had been irritated all afternoon that I had come home the hero—to his house, with his woman, in his car. To give him credit, however, he had tried to conceal his frustration and had even been solicitous, offering cups of tea and various comforts—such as his favourite place to sit in the room. I had decided to retire soon and let the two of them have some time together: I was keenly aware of how I would feel if he were in my favourite chair in the sitting room at the Orchard. With Sarah. It would be almost too much to bear.

"Oh! The news," Sarah exclaimed, and got up to turn on the television. Her leggings, as she stood, revealed her rippling leg muscles. I knew Jean-Claude was watching too. "We can't miss this." I could almost hear Jean-Claude groan, but I was intrigued at the thought of seeing how it would be presented on French television.

My French was not good enough to catch the rapid-fire narration by the newscaster, but I had no trouble recognising the now-familiar faces of the two dead bomb experts, and of the Princess and her sons as they sat on the stage, looking pleasant. Next, they showed a mug shot of the Irish bookseller, and then him being taken away by the police in handcuffs. Next, to my horror, they showed me being led stumbling from the building, looking half-crazed.

"How embarrassing," I said. "I look like a maniac."

"No," Sarah said, still watching and listening to the report. "They're saying you're a hero, that you risked your life to save all those people." They aired a statement from the Princess, and I could hear her deliberate words beneath the translation of the newscaster. It was a formal one-sentence statement thanking the French police and me for having foiled the terrorists. Finally a commercial came on for Euro-Disney, and I heard a shuffling noise from the corner.

Jean-Claude was standing. "Well," he said abruptly. "I think I'll go to bed." It was as much as he could take, I thought, and I was sorry. "You know that you are welcome to stay here, Alex, for as long as you like. At least you should stay for a few days to get over the head injury, yes?" I admired him; he was even able to smile. What a gifted actor.

He looked at Sarah longingly as he came over to the sofa, where she now sat next to me. Standing in front of me to reach her, which was incredibly awkward, he satisfied himself with a lingering hug. I heard him murmur something in her ear in French before he detached himself.

"I feel terrible about this," I managed after he disappeared. "If we're going to go on our holiday, I think we should leave tomorrow."

Sarah looked at me as if she thought the blow on the head must have been harder than any of us thought. Then she laughed incredulously. "Alex, what about your head? And your hand?" I was glad she didn't know about my shoulder.

"I'm fine. And if I have a headache tomorrow, well, I'd rather have it on a bike than here in Jean-Claude's way. You can ride in front and do the hand brake." Secretly, I was pleased about that; I would get to ride behind her and feast my eyes all the way to Alsace.

"I see." She looked down at me speculatively, her brown eyes bright as she considered. Her breath smelled of the hazelnut coffee Jean-Claude had served us after dinner. "You're very persuasive, you know." She brushed a persistent lock of hair back off my forehead, and a thrill travelled through my body from head to toe. "All right. But you have to promise me that you won't overdo it." I nodded, and, looking at me suspiciously sideways, she stuck out a hand for an American-style agreement. I lifted my bandaged right hand and she took it tenderly as I laughed at her insistence. She put it back down on the sofa next to me gently, even lovingly, using both hands to cradle it.

"One more thing," she said.

"Hmm?"

"If you find anything to be heroic about on the French country roads, just let it go, all right?"

"Mmm," I said, shaking my head hesitantly and frowning. "Can't agree to that. You see, there's a woman about whom I care very deeply. I'm afraid that if anything ever happened to her . . ."

She smiled. "Someone needs to start looking after *you*," she said. That sounded like a promising start, but to my disappointment she checked her watch. "Speaking of that, it's okay for you to go to sleep now."

"Well, thank you very much," I said, laughing. To my surprise, she blushed and became super-efficient, standing and walking over to the bookshelf against the wall.

"I'll take a look at the map before bed, and we can go over our route tomorrow, all right?" I nodded, watching her. It wasn't often that she blushed like that; when she did, it left her cheeks cherry-red for several minutes afterwards. "And we don't need to get a terribly early start—let's sleep until we feel like getting up."

"Sounds good."

She had picked up her clear plastic map case and was going to take it with her into the spare bedroom. "Good night, Alex," she said, and was about to leave the room. At the last moment she turned, ran back to me where I still sat on the sofa—somewhat bewildered by her behaviour—and gave me a luscious, loose-lipped hazelnut kiss on the mouth. Then, as quickly as she had come, she was gone, hurrying off to her solitary bed.

I felt like crying and laughing simultaneously. At least I still had time with her to come, time alone with her, away from time pressures and everyday worries.

Or so I thought.

Morning came, and I could detect the strain on Jean-Claude's chiselled face as we sat at the breakfast table. Sarah had stirred up waffles for us, with blackberries layered on top, and a syrup she'd made from more blackberries. She made light conversation, doing her best to dispel the awkwardness but not obsessing about it, and Jean-Claude reminded us of several places we might enjoy along the way—his aunt's bakery here, a café there, and his favorite wine bar in Ribeauvillé, finally a place I'd heard of. Ribeauvillé was the Alsatian town that was famous as the home of the wine festival.

We were all glad, I think, when breakfast was over, the dishes done, and it was time for us to leave. It took forty-five minutes to get all our things together, panniers packed, helmets and gloves at the ready, water bottles filled, and so forth. I took some aspirin for a raging headache, along with that morning's antibiotic.

Then we said our good-byes. Jean-Claude looked half-sick as he shook my hand, then gave Sarah a hug. I left them to say further farewells and went outside, carrying my saddlebag, to check over the bike, which had been waiting patiently in Jean-Claude's garden shed. I tried not to think of him pressing her close in precisely the black cotton-and-spandex cycling top I'd dreamed of her wearing. It was difficult. She was so fit that her well-tanned skin didn't bulge out even the least little bit below the top.

Think of the bike, Alex, the bike, I told myself as I rolled the vehicle out of the shed. Sarah had rented a racy metallic purple tandem. It had mountain bike-like shocks, wide tires for touring, and ten speeds. This had been a dream of mine for so long—not riding this particular bike, but riding it with Sarah—that I could scarcely believe it was finally coming to pass. I only hoped that my now-battered body would be capable of living the dream.

With the bike leaning against the shed, I strapped on my

pannier behind the front seat. Next I tried out the seat height, and decided to adjust it upward two inches. I loosened the bolt holding the seat in place, moved it up, and by the time I was done tightening the bolt again, Sarah had still not come outside. What were they doing in there?

Checking the tire pressure on each of the tires, I found them just right. Then I checked the brake pads and cables, and was about to give up and sit down next to the bike, when Sarah emerged.

"Sorry to keep you waiting." She offered no explanation for the delay.

I waved off the apology. "The bike looks great," I told her. "You really found a beauty."

"Lovely, isn't it? It's brand new. This will be its maiden voyage." She looked supremely happy, all energy and enthusiasm. "They said if I want to buy it after the trip, they'll give me a special price."

We set off down the lane from Jean-Claude's, with Sarah in front to handle the brakes. It was an odd feeling, balancing a bicycle with someone else, but we got the hang of it before we'd reached the end of his road. Cautiously, we turned onto the road that would take us on our way eastward, towards Alsace. It was level for the better part of a mile, then started a gradual uphill slope that seemed to go on forever . . . the length of the uphill stretch was, however, distorted by some very strong feelings, which I am unlikely to ever forget.

Pumping the bike together, and watching Sarah's legs and shoulders move in front of me, was one of the most erotic experiences of my life. It was almost the way I imagined that the real thing would be with her, though of course I had only my dreams to go on. For a while I indulged myself in the sensations that swept over me, but before long my legs were weak. I had to put my mind to work on something else.

The route . . . that was it. I had to concentrate on where we were going. I tried to visualise the web of roads in my mind.

"All right?" Sarah turned around briefly and glanced at me as she asked the question. I was glad that I'd got myself under control before she'd turned.

"Great!" I shouted, and meant it.

We were on the D1 from Champillon, in the heart of the

Champagne district. At Châlons-sur-Marne we would turn on the N77 briefly to get to the D2. Our original itinerary had taken us a different route as far as Châlons-sur-Marne, because we hadn't banked on setting out from Ville-en-Tardenois, where Jean-Claude lived, instead of Menceauville. But at Châlons we would take up our original route eastward for two hundred miles, following the Marne on the smallest roads possible as far as the city of Nancy. Then we would pick up the Moselle, all the way to Kaysersberg in Alsace, and finally head north to Ribeauvillé.

We were staying with our original plan for inns for the rest of the trip, so that meant we were staying in a tiny village called Sainte Geneviève for the first night at Domaine de l'Abbaye.

It had been described to me as one of the most romantic hostelries in France, a fourteenth-century abbey now decorated with fresh flowers, its stone cool on hot days, and the Marne burbling past in the quiet evenings. It even had a first-class restaurant. Because of the nature of our relationship, I had reserved two rooms, not wanting to pressure her in any way. But as I pumped along on the bike, I began to wonder if perhaps I didn't need to be a bit pushier.

If I didn't ask her to marry me soon, at a particularly good moment such as during dinner at Domaine de l'Abbaye, with candles, champagne, and medieval tapestries to my advantage, Jean-Claude would . . . if he hadn't already. I simply could not allow Sarah, the one part of my life that I really cared about—far more than the Press, far more than anything—to be lost for lack of planning and effort.

I would do it, I decided. I would do it that night.

It had been nearly an hour since we'd left Jean-Claude's. There was no doubt that Sarah was enjoying herself, and I couldn't have been more pleased. The weather was cooperating too; huge, fluffy white clouds drifted in a deep blue autumn sky, and the air was cool.

The more I thought about it, the trip had been a fantastic idea; we were building camaraderie and shared experience without any of the pitfalls that continuous conversation might have held. And it was, as I have mentioned, a powerful experience, riding together. In addition to which, the countryside seemed vast and fertile and full of expectation—as if it had been waiting for us and that very moment.

I shouted up to Sarah, "Coming up on Châlons already." She turned back briefly, then round again. "Tour de France next year, I reckon."

A joyous burst of laughter, followed by "Right!" drifted back to me, and I was supremely happy.

"Want to keep going?"

"Yes."

I smiled to myself and kept pedalling. There was a bit of traffic to deal with at Châlons, and we kept our heads down and concentrated on catching the right stretch of highway that would take us back to the quiet country roads we'd enjoyed so far. We were through it all in fifteen minutes, and were happily continuing southward on the D2 along the Marne towards a hamlet by the name of Vitry-le-François, when I first saw the car.

It was one of those things that one notices without noticing, a car stopped in a turnabout by the side of the road. This was a grey Peugeot, unremarkable but for the fact that it was of the very latest model. I had just seen an article in a car magazine that rated it.

I couldn't help but notice it again when it passed us several minutes later. A sneaking dread replaced the euphoria I'd felt earlier. It wasn't logical to react so strongly to a car passing us more than once, but after what I'd been through that week, my awareness of danger was instinctive and seemed absolutely essential.

I didn't want to stop and talk; they might suspect that I was on to them, if there still was a "them."

"Sarah, I think someone is—well—circling us."

"Circling?"

"Yes, I've seen a couple of cars, apparently scouting for us. I think we should get off the road."

"All right," she said with significantly less euphoria than she had earlier. Her shoulders slumped.

She braked hard, and we rolled to a stop. "Let's push the bike and take it over there into the woods," I told her. "I'm so sorry about this." We were already moving fast away from the road, through a flat pasture that would afford us no protection from view.

"You wouldn't be Alex if these things didn't happen," she said philosophically, and kindly, and my heart ached.

As I ran sweating toward the wood, maybe ten yards away now, I swore inwardly. Damn! There went the candlelight at l'Abbaye, the tapestries, the champagne, and yet another chance. How could they still be after me? Would this never come to an end?

Sarah was doing a great job of propelling her end of the bike, and if anything, she was pulling me as we ran. With gratitude I noted that my left side was holding up all right, but I could certainly feel it as we bumped across the field. A number of cars passed on the road behind us while we were crossing the field, and I didn't see either of our potential pursuers among them. But that didn't mean they wouldn't find out that we had left the road, and where.

"Damn! What a mess," I grumbled irritably as we dragged the bike into the thicket that signalled the start of the woods, desperate to have the branches close behind us. It wouldn't be easy to get the bike through those woods, and we'd have to move—we couldn't just sit there and wait for them to come looking for us.

Sarah was silent as we remained on a course perpendicular to the road, ducking under branches and dodging saplings. I couldn't blame her. We could both see that the bike was acquiring the first few scratches that it was never meant to have, from branches scraping its purple paint.

And we both knew that at that very moment she could have been enjoying the company of France's most famous movie star in the comfort of his own home.

The more I thought about it, the more mortified I became. It seemed clear that this time I had well and truly blown it with Sarah—and it had all been going so well. I'd been wrong; the trip had been a bad idea.

"Shall we check the map?" she asked. At last we were hidden from view, or so it seemed, by a thick screen of trees and brush. I won't say that she seemed happy, but she did seem resigned to get through this new ordeal without unpleasantness.

"I suppose so," I replied, almost too discouraged to speak. Unfastening the clip that kept the helmet strapped to my head, I half-shook and half-pulled it off.

"Okay." We stopped then, and I waited for her to open her pannier and get out the clear plastic map case.

She was studying the map, her finger pursuing the likely area where we had left the road, when I said, "*Damn!* That's it—I told them." I put both hands in my hair and pulled.

She looked at me and frowned. "What do you mean?"

"At Armand's party, Menceau and Armand and I were chatting about our trip. They asked about our route, and I told them. They know *exactly* where we're going."

"Well, it doesn't do us any good to worry about it now. We've got to think of a place they won't suspect." Her eyes roved the map, and I came back and stood next to her, still holding up the bike. "It looks like we might be here," she murmured thoughtfully, pointing to a spot with her well-trimmed nail. "There aren't any other roads but the main ones around here." She let the map drop slightly and looked at me. "We could hide the bike and run, but sooner or later we'd have to cross a road, and they might be watching. Or we could just hole up and hope they don't find us."

I shook my head. "I can't do that—just wait like a rabbit for the hunter." Sighing, I looked again at the map. "What *won't* they expect?" I thought for a moment, then turned to look at her. "How about a very busy road—a super-highway—where cyclists are illegal? The police might even pick us up." Feeling uncomfortable, I remembered Michel Menceau's statement about the rural police. They couldn't all belong to the Bibliati, I thought. But I didn't convince myself.

Sarah chewed her lip as she studied the map, considering the possibilities. "It'll take us hours to get to the A26, but we could do it. It would mean just that one road to cross before we got there—the N77 again." She looked at me for a response.

"Mmm." I was disgusted. Ten miles of hiking with the bike on our idyllic holiday. I could barely raise my eyes to meet hers. "I'm so sorry, Sarah. I don't see anything else we can do."

She nodded and tucked the map away again, heaving to on the bike without another look at me. She looked as if she were thinking, which I didn't like very much at all. If I had been Sarah at that moment, I know what I would have been thinking. I would have been thinking what a twit Alex Plumtree was and what a welcome relief Jean-Claude Rimbaud would be.

He'd have some way out of this—some solution that wouldn't have forced her to snag her new bike clothes in the woods on a three-hour hike. He would have summoned a helicopter, or called for support on a radio, or they'd have seen the villain's car blow up mysteriously from a charge he'd managed to set much earlier. They would then walk arm in arm through the lush countryside into the sunset.

At some point I stopped torturing myself and merely slogged. It was very hard going through those thick woods, and I admired Sarah for not complaining. It seemed terrifically hot and humid as well, in contrast to the cool breeze that had caressed us on the bike. But I don't know what I should have expected—running for one's life probably never takes place under pleasant circumstances. From time to time I felt just annoyingly weak enough that I would suggest we stop to drink from our water bottles. It wasn't entirely an excuse to rest; I knew that I had to keep the water flowing if I wanted my body to keep going after all it had been through. Also, I had come to the conclusion that it would be a physical impossibility to continue without the painkillers, much as I hated them, as we hiked in double-time, pushing the bike through trees and scrub over rough terrain. It was not a task I could believably perform with one arm hanging at my side. So when Sarah drank from her water bottle and surveyed the countryside, I surreptitiously slipped two pills—one antibiotic capsule and one painkiller—from the pack round my waist and stuffed them into my mouth. I hoped the act was hidden successfully by a swipe I took at my mouth with the side of my hand between gulps of water.

Three hours and twenty minutes later we had covered the ten miles and stood in a valley below the A26, a major six-lane highway. I shook my head and speculated that when

Lisette had encouraged me to spend time with Sarah, it was probably not this precise scenario she'd had in mind.

So ashamed that I could barely face Sarah, I squeezed her shoulder with my right hand as we stared at the roaring horde of vehicles in mutual distaste.

"We've done it," I said. "You're fantastic."

"Thanks," she said, bending down to lift her water bottle out of its holder. She took a long swig, then wiped a drip from her chin. "You too." I thought she said it a little sceptically. Holding her water bottle out to me, she added, "Here, go ahead. I'll get out the map."

We both looked at the map and saw that we could take the A26 all the way to another super-highway, if necessary, which would take us eastward again. Perhaps the law enforcement authorities would pick us up before nightfall, roughly six hours away now, for cycling on the highway.

Suddenly I was struck with the hopelessness of it. Letting out an exasperated sigh, I said, "Look, Sarah. I've thought of about a million different ways we could handle this. One would be to get to the nearest reasonably-sized town and ride straight to the police station. But then I think about what they'll say. They'll ask, 'Did someone threaten you?' I'd have to say, 'Well, no, not this person, exactly. But I have been threatened in the past.' 'Who exactly was it that you saw in the car?' I'd have to say, 'I'm sorry, I don't know.' Then they'll laugh at me and say, 'If you don't know who it is, we can't stop him.'

"Or we can just keep cycling on the most major roads we can to Alsace, but what kind of a holiday will it be if we have to look out for these mysterious cars?

"Finally, we can simply find transportation back to Jean-Claude's for you—or to your flat in Paris—and to London for me. Forget the whole blasted thing."

She eyed me thoughtfully. "You know, Alex, I humoured you, trekking all this way through the woods, because I respect your judgement and intuition. But let's face it. We're not really even sure that there is anyone looking for us. What if that car belonged to someone who had forgotten something at home, or happened to be turning round anyway?"

Looking at me as if she were trying to determine how sane

I was, she continued. "Besides, you've got your agreement with them. You should be protected, unless they're totally out of their minds, like Menceau. We've done what we could to lose the suspicious car. Now I say we get on with our holiday, try to forget about any possibility of being followed, and get on to Alsace. Besides, if they're going to find you, they'll find you wherever you are, for the rest of your life. Maybe they just intend to follow you for a while. Anyway, we might as well go there as anywhere else."

My natural defenses rose, and I was momentarily offended that she questioned the sinister nature of the car. Perhaps she still didn't understand—even after Giles in the wine cellar, and the scene in Menceau's study—exactly how dangerous and ruthless these people could be. And she didn't know yet about my parents having been killed by them or about the shootings and imprisonment in Marie-Louise's room. She also hadn't seen Angela since her accident.

Then I realised: maybe it was better this way. I felt confident, considering my devotion to her, that I could protect her from harm at least as well as Jean-Claude Rimbaud might. I would certainly give my life for her. Why not let her think that everything was fine, and allow her to enjoy the trip? It seemed a bit patronising, but I *had* tried to tell her the seriousness of the situation.

"All right," I said, cheering slightly. "We'll just get on with it, then."

She smiled and we stowed things again for the hike up to the highway.

"Will you agree," she asked, "to get back on the smaller roads again once we reach the A31 if we don't see the car up there?" She tipped her head towards the roaring motorway as she spoke.

I nodded. "Fair enough."

With that agreement we trudged up to the verge, hopped on the bike, and got it rolling again. I felt sorry about it as soon as we'd begun, that I'd brought us there. Eighteen-wheeled, multi-ton juggernauts screamed past, flinging gravel and clouds of dust in our faces, not to mention hot blasts of wind. Their aerodynamic force was something to be reckoned with as well; each time one passed, we had to struggle for equilibrium.

Twenty minutes passed, my mind racing all the while about whether this was even feasible. The road had been fairly flat so far, but I could see that we were approaching a long, uphill climb, and we'd already been through a lot. Another horrible idea, Plumtree, I told myself. You are a disaster. Bringing Sarah on a super-highway! With paranoia I scanned the traffic continuously for the car at every moment, and didn't see it. Just as I had made the decision to hold up my hand for the stop signal to Sarah, I saw, to my horror and disbelief, the new grey Peugeot.

It was in the far lane, coming from the opposite direction, slinking down the long, gentle slope ahead of us like some sort of animal. The driver was erratic, using the slow lane to overtake, and going faster than any of the other cars on the road.

With a sick feeling I shouted, "Car!" to Sarah. When she glanced back, I pointed in the direction of the oncoming vehicle.

The car suddenly swerved, as if perhaps the driver had seen us. Then, to my surprise, it began to thread its way across the lanes, back to the fast lane, closest to us. I didn't like its drawing closer to our side of the road, but speculated that whoever was following was merely trying to get a better look at us—or use the proper lane to overtake for a change. But when I saw the Peugeot crash through the median barrier and enter the traffic moving in our direction, I knew that my worst fears had been justified.

Horns hooted, and over-inflated tires squealed in the Indian-summer heat as cars tried to avoid the maniacal driver and one another. I remember thinking that whoever was driving that car was irrefutably, positively, beyond the shadow of a doubt, revoltingly, dangerously mad.

"Turn round! Turn round!" I bellowed to Sarah, and jerked my handlebars and wheel round towards the edge of the verge as Sarah did the same. There was the horrifying sound of multiple crashes as we struggled through the tight turn, nearly toppling over, and coming dangerously close to the edge of the verge, from which we would have rolled down a steep hill into a sort of gully below. Now we were going the wrong way, against the speeding traffic, pedalling like mad. In an adrenaline rush I yelled, "Go, go!" though I doubt if Sarah needed any encouragement.

Suddenly a car was coming towards us on the verge, as it tried to avoid the pile-up ahead. Sarah screamed, and I yelled, "Down the hill!" She turned immediately, and we careered downward to safety, away from the traffic. I heard an odd sound behind me, and a fraction of a second later, stunned, I saw the grey Peugeot come literally flying past us, its nose gradually falling downwards until it hit the ground. The car bounced, flipping upside down, then hit the ground and bounced twice more. Then it came to rest on its roof in the gully at the bottom of the hill.

Sarah and I were jolting wildly down the hill, nearly thrown off our seats by the rough terrain, braking desperately and trying to stay aboard the bike as the big car went through its death throes ahead of us.

Staring at the unfolding drama, we flew down the hill towards it, the brakes finally having some effect as the slope flattened out slightly. We coasted, bumping, toward the gully, and eventually manhandled the bike to a stop about twenty feet from the Peugeot.

"Please—let me," I said breathlessly to Sarah, and ran towards the overturned car. Even if someone had been trying to kill us, they deserved my help now—if they could possibly still be alive. The Peugeot was sizzling ominously, and my first thought was of fire. It was a serious risk, but I had to remove any passengers before they were incinerated.

I got to the car and fell to my knees, looking in the window. With complete confusion I saw that I was looking at the body of Frances Macnamara, in the driver's seat, and the still-groaning Edward Pillinghurst on the passenger side. Frances Macnamara's head hung at a truly impossible angle from her neck. There was no way that she could have been alive. On an impulse I grabbed the locket that swung on a chain from her neck and ripped it free, tucking it into the pocket of my cycling shirt.

Struggling to wrest the door open, I heard a "whoomph!" and knew instantly what it was. I felt the searing blast of heat as I abandoned the door, turning, and flung myself as far as I could away from the burning car.

Stunned by the explosion and the heat which seemed to be melting the clothes off me, I heard Sarah scream as she ran towards me, and pulled me, grunting and sobbing with the effort, to safety.

"Alex! Alex!" She was kneeling, looking at my face. "Are you all right?"

I heard my own voice say, quite reasonably, "Am I on fire?" I was, for some reason I couldn't fathom, unable to move.

She made a little sound of near-hysterical horror. "N-no! You're not on fire!" As she knelt sobbing by my head, stroking my hair off my face, we became aware of the first of the people from the motorway who had come down to help. "Does it feel like you're on fire?" she asked, crying.

"Yes," I said. "On the left side—my chest, below the shoulder."

She looked, then gasped. "Just a second!" She ran away and came back a moment later with the water bottles from the bike, which she proceeded to pour over me. When I got over the surprise, she said, struggling for calm, "Your bike shirt has melted there—I'm not sure . . ." I could feel her pulling on the shirt tentatively, ever so gently, and then she stopped.

"Alex, I can't tell if it's melted onto your skin." She paused. So much for form-fitting, Lycra-blend biking shirts, I thought. I'd have been better off with an old-fashioned cotton T-shirt. "We'll have to wait for help," Sarah said, wringing her hands.

The crowd swarmed, in awe of the fire, but no one was really able to help. They milled about until we heard the whine of a siren, by which time I felt somewhat more myself and was sitting up. A phalanx of emergency workers descended from the highway to us; a team of firemen made for the fire as one team of paramedics made for me, the other for the car.

There was an uncomfortable moment as a paramedic cut my shirt apart, near the gunshot wound, and said something rapidly in French, looking at me. Sarah translated, "He says, what do you have under the bandage?"

"Gunshot wounds," I said.

Her eyes opened wide, and she stared at me as she told him, *"Coup de feu."* Then she addressed me. "Alex, what—"

"I'll tell you some other time," I said.

The paramedic let loose with a long string of sentences. He spoke to Sarah, realising that she was the only person of sufficient taste in our twosome to speak decent French, and she nodded, her eyes still unnaturally wide. They looked deep and hollow, I saw, and she seemed to be shaking slightly. She was so beautiful, with her naturally red cheeks glowing next to her very dark hair, and at that moment she looked delicate in a way that I hadn't seen before. Because she was tall, and well-proportioned, she had what I thought of as a strong beauty about her. But there was something about her eyes . . . was it vulnerability? Was that why she seemed so uncharacteristically delicate?

Sarah seemed to be fighting for calm as she translated the string of sentences. "He says you have some second-degree burns, especially where the tape that was securing your bandage was melted. He says you need to go to the hospital in Bar-le-Duc to see a burn specialist."

I nodded. "Are you all right?"

She looked at me for a moment, then began to shake in uncontrollable sobs, covering her face with her hands. The paramedics said something to one another, and one put an arm around her and gently guided her up the hill towards the ambulance parked on the verge of the motorway. I started to protest when they loaded me on a stretcher, but then decided I felt very peculiar indeed and allowed them to proceed. As the ambulance rolled along, sleep overcame me, and I drifted off.

When I woke, there was an IV in my arm, and Sarah was sitting by my side.

"Oh, for goodness' sake," I mumbled, sitting up and looking at the contraption.

"Don't worry," Sarah said. "It's just a precaution. They're going to let you go. There's a nice place for us to stay nearby, they said, if they have room."

"Great," I said, pining for our forsaken rooms and meal at Domaine de l'Abbaye. There was a moment of silence while I dealt with the disappointment, as I watched her rub something in the palm of her hand and over and over, almost lovingly. "What's that?"

"Oh. It's the locket you took from the woman in the car. It fell out of one of the pockets of your shirt." She passed it to me, with the deeply hand-engraved monogram on the top. FMG. Frances G. Macnamara. "That was thoughtful of you, Alex. It'll mean a lot to her family." She hesitated, and a shiver shook her from head to toe. I speculated that she might have remembered Frances G. Macnamara had wanted to kill us very badly, and had too nearly succeeded. "Did you know her?"

I nodded, inspecting the golden oval. "Frances Macnamara," I said thoughtfully. "The backbone of the Stonecypher Society. I never thought that she—or the society—had anything to do with the Bibliati."

Carefully, without moving my left arm or shoulder, I stuck my thumbnail in the edge of the locket and opened it. As I stared at the photo inside, understanding hit me in waves, one realisation leading to another. I had certainly stumbled into a complicated maze, and I could only hope that my discovery about Frances had now put me at the end of it.

Sarah watched me, her head cocked to one side in the pose I loved so well. "What is it?"

I turned the locket towards her so she could see the photo, roughly an inch tall by half an inch wide.

"It's incredible," I said softly. "It must have been Frances all along . . . that was what Angela knew that I didn't."

Sarah waited patiently while I let my thoughts run their course, and gradually organised them for speech. Finally I shook my head in disbelief and began, passing the locket back to her. "Do you see the belt this woman is wearing?"

"The belt? Mmm—" She pulled it close to her face and studied it intently. "It's a tiny photo, but it looks as if perhaps there are pearls on the belt, sewn into a design." She looked at me, waiting for more information.

"I can tell you more about this later, but there's been a spare room at Plumtree Press all these years, right behind the wall of my office. It was the maid's room, Marie-Louise's— Stonecypher's mistress. Some intruders at the Press shut me up in the room, and while I was there I found the belt that woman is wearing in the photo. It was on the bed. There had been a struggle there; the bedside table had been knocked over, the candleholder lay broken on the floor. Stonecypher had obviously had the room closed off very shortly after her death, without bothering to clean anything up."

Still Sarah waited; I hadn't really explained anything yet.

"On Marie-Louise's desk were papers . . . a letter from Stonecypher to Marie-Louise, after her death, which confused me because it referred to 'her' and 'she'—his wife, Marissa Godwin Stonecypher. He never thought that 'she' would do such a thing." I glanced at Sarah, and I could see she was beginning to sense where I was going. Her lips, rosy without the aid of cosmetics, like her cheeks, parted slightly. I wanted desperately to kiss them.

"Among the papers was a confession from Stonecypher that he had killed Marie-Louise, accidentally of course, in case the police should think her death suspicious. He didn't kill her; he wrote the letter to protect his wife. His wife strangled her with the belt. But the police never even looked into it, because Marie-Louise was a maid, and they believed exactly what her master told them—that a mysterious intruder was responsible for the death."

"And I'll bet you're going to tell me," Sarah said, "that Frances Macnamara's maiden name was Godwin."

I nodded and smiled at her perceptiveness. In my experience, women were much better than men at the mysteries of human relationships. Like Angela, she had known. "Spot on."

"And," she continued, enjoying the moment, "somehow Angela sussed it out and proposed it in her book. Frances Macnamara couldn't bear the disgrace of having her great-grandmother revealed for the jealous murderess she really was, the family name maligned."

Sadly, I nodded again, thinking about the strong influence of ancestors long gone—for Frances, for Giles, and for me. "Angela was the first female scholar to publish about Stonecypher. She saw the possibility first." I thought then about the way Angela had so skilfully suggested, in *The Stonecypher Saga*, three possibilities for Marie-Louise's killer: a mysterious intruder, which was the official story the police were told: Stonecypher's wife, which no one seriously considered because Marissa had been an invalid; and Stonecypher himself, through accident. Angela had allowed the reader to decide for himself, but that was too close to the truth for Frances Godwin Macnamara.

The doctor came in then, followed by a nurse, and engaged in a rapid-fire volley of French with Sarah. He smiled as he gave me a little bow of acknowledgement and then left, nodding to the nurse to release me from the drip.

"We can go," Sarah told me. "While you were asleep I took care of signing the papers they needed, and the bill. I'll go out and see if I can get a car to take us to the inn they mentioned."

An hour later, at seven o'clock in the evening, a taxi deposited us at the door of a timbered inn.

"Why don't you wait here," she said, getting out of the car. "I'll see if they have rooms."

I waited, feeling numbed by the turn of events, and trying to be a good sport about the ruin of my carefully laid plans, until she came back to the car. Her face appeared at the window. "You're not going to believe this," she said, smiling and looking slightly awed. "They already have a booking for us."

"What?" I asked, confused. "Where are we?"

"Domaine de l'Abbaye, in a town called Sainte-Geneviève."

I broke into a grin, then a chuckle, then a full-fledged belly laugh as Sarah looked on, then joined in. Things, I decided, had a way of working out for the best.

CHAPTER 20

A blending of all beauties—streams and dells,
Fruit, foliage, crag, wood, corn-field, mountain, vine,
And chiefless castles breathing stern farewells.
                                    —LORD BYRON ON ALSACE

S o," Sarah said, twirling her champagne glass, seeming to be more affected by the wine than usual. She was drinking the bottle virtually alone, as I'd been instructed to drink nothing stronger than tea. I'd had half a glass nonetheless, just to be companionable, but it was dessert time now and the bottle was very nearly gone. I was delighted that she was able to relax after what she'd been through. "Tell me about the gunshot wounds," she said, then paused, raising her eyebrows. "Not just one, I understand—two."

"Ah. That." I stalled for a moment by deliberately placing the calligraphed dessert card on the table in front of me. "There's not much to tell, really. I came into my office one evening, stretched out on my sofa after visiting Angela, and suddenly the light went on at my desk. There was a man sitting there, and we chatted briefly, then another man pulled out a gun and shot me." I shrugged, picked up my water glass and took a long drink.

"Oh—so that's that," she said, amused. "All right—what about the second shot?"

I nodded. "He just . . . did it. Right after the first one."

She looked at me with a mock matter-of-fact attitude that made me want to laugh. "Oh. Mmm-hmmm. Well, let's see . . . he shot you, and earlier you said he shut you up in the room. How did you break your way out? Pick the lock?"

"Not exactly. There wasn't a door or a lock."

She frowned. "How could there not be a door?"

I said, "Oh, there used to be, but they decided to plaster me right in and soundproof the room while they were at it. They put a couple of feet of wall between Marie-Louise's room and my office. They didn't think I was ever coming back out, you see; they thought I was out of the way for good. And if it weren't for Mr. Heppelthwaite of the Historic Buildings Society finding a discrepancy in the plans and coming round to show them to me, they would have been right."

"But you . . ." Her voice trailed off. She looked horrified. "Oh, no." She seemed to be looking for something in my eyes. "For how long? When did you get out?"

"Um—let's see. I was in there for fourteen hours and twelve minutes, and I got out on Thursday at about three-thirty. Harry, the construction foreman, chipped through the wall. He got me out."

She shook her head. "And all this goes back to Angela's book?"

"Mmm-hmmm." I took the final sip of my half-glass of champagne, knowing that any more than those few sips would compete disastrously with the painkillers. The waiter appeared at the table to take our orders for dessert.

"Crême brulée, s'il vous plaît," Sarah said.

"Mousse au chocolat," I said, ordering my favorite.

The waiter thanked us and departed, and Sarah shook her head again. "You know, Alex, you keep getting burned by this publishing business." The double-entendre didn't strike her until the sentence was out, and she giggled. "Sorry." We both laughed some more, with not a little giddiness.

"How about a career in banking?" she suggested. "Or literary criticism? Or something—anything—else?" At this I saw tears glistening in her eyes. She was tired, and had had quite a lot of wine, but I knew she really meant it. I couldn't blame her. Who would want to be attached to a person who got shot at, and run down across six lanes of French motor-way, and built into hidden rooms?

"No, I'm sorry," she said, putting both hands out in front of her as if to push back what she'd just said. "You need to do what you want to do. And Plumtree Press is—well, it's in your blood." She sighed, and we watched silently as the waiter glided over with our dessert plates and deposited them in front of us.

"Sarah," I said when he'd left, praying for the right words. "What if I could make my life a bit less exciting? You know," I said, opting for honesty, "I'd do anything for you."

She looked alert now, like a deer preparing to run. I hoped I was misinterpreting her body language. I had to try, had to know . . .

"Would you please," I said, pulling the small blue-velvet-covered box from my pocket, "marry me?" I opened the box towards her.

The ring was gold, with a large, square Dartmouth-green emerald flanked on both sides by slender baguette diamonds. Her mouth fell open and she let slip a tiny, opened-ended "oh." She went very pale, and for a moment I worried that I'd shocked her with the suddenness of it all.

"Are you all right?"

She nodded mutely, still staring at the ring but making no move to take it. Finally she looked up at me, put both hands in her lap, and said, "Oh, Alex. I can't." Then she seemed to recover herself, and said, "I mean, thank you—really, thank you very much—but I can't." Then, very quietly, she added, "Not just now anyway."

I tried to keep my sense of humour as I put the little velvet box down on the table. It seemed ungracious to take it back and put it in my pocket again, as if I had offered a chocolate and then withdrawn it, so I left it there. " 'Not now' . . . does that mean there's hope?"

Her eyes were full of sympathy and kindness as she reached across the table and took my hand. "Of course." She smiled. "You know how I care for you. Look what we've been through together." At that she gave a short laugh, and shook her head once.

She paused, then put her head slightly to one side. If I were ever to have her portrait done, I'd want it done that way.

"I should have told you about this sooner," she said. "Jean-Claude has asked me to manage his charitable foundation. I do know how to set them up, and I would know just how to invest his money. And the best part is that I would get to suggest to him where the donations could be used to best advantage within the areas of children's sports and literacy, his pet interests.

"Alex . . . in case you're wondering, it has nothing to do with any romantic ties between us—to me, he will only ever be a very sweet friend. He knows how I feel, and if you're thinking that he seems affectionate towards me, well, that's just the way he is. He's an affectionate person."

"You don't have to—"

"No, no, I want to explain," she said. "We've discussed the job; it would be nine months on, three months off each year. Jean-Claude believes in holidays, and enjoying life. And it would be on a strictly professional basis—no favours tied to the job. He knows I'd quit immediately if it were any other way. But here's the real meat of it, Alex."

I sat forward, everything in me straining to know what she would say next. She was still holding my hand, and her fingers began to fidget slightly. "I won't be young and free forever. I want to enjoy living in Paris for a while, travelling, covering France in Jean-Claude's private jet, maybe even learning how to fly. When I decide to get married, I will want to be near my husband, not living in a different country. And then there would probably be children"—my heart stopped. She did want children, then—"and I couldn't live in Paris and live all of those dreams."

Ah, I thought. The Davy question from *A Severe Mercy*: career vs. marriage. Now I understood.

Her eyes seemed to grow misty. "Do you see, Alex? I have just a few more years to enjoy my freedom, just being me, and I've already been married once. I want to do this. So, no, I'm sorry, I can't marry you *now*. I can hardly dare to hope that you would still be free when I'm ready, and I would never ask you to wait. But if you—if you still want me when I'm ready, I hope you'll ask again."

She looked embarrassed. I said, "Thank you for being honest with me. And believe it or not, I'm genuinely happy for your opportunity with Jean-Claude's foundation." Especially since you think of him as nothing more than a friend, I thought. I even managed a smile. Things could have come out worse. And now we had this out of the way—we could enjoy the rest of the trip together without worrying about it.

My eyes fell on the ring on the table. "Would you keep this . . . anyway?" I held it out to her and shrugged. "If you like it, you could wear it sometimes—on your right hand, or something. No commitment implied. I bought it for you, and I'd love you to have it. Regardless of whether we are ever engaged to be married."

"Thank you, Alex. It's stunning. You—you're so—" As she gingerly picked up the box and lifted out the ring, the tears came and her words faltered. She slipped it on her long, tapered ring finger—on the right hand. It suited her perfectly.

"Please. You don't need to say anything more." I sat up straight, realising that I had allowed my shoulders to slump. In defeat, I thought. Or partial defeat. Not all hope was gone. "Would you care for a brandy, or shall we call it a day?"

She nodded at the latter, gratefully, it seemed to me, and murmured, "I am tired." We slowly made our way through the inn up to the rooms. "How are you feeling?" she asked. Then she blushed and said, "Your shoulder, I mean."

"It's fine," I lied. "I'm just glad it's over." Then I blushed and said, "The Folio B mess, I mean." We stopped outside her door and by mutual agreement held each other in a long, tired embrace.

"Good night," I finally said, disengaging myself. I could have stood in the hall with her all night without difficulty.

"Good night, Alex," she said softly, looking at me with a great deal of tenderness. "And thank you."

I walked on down the hall and thought that things could be much, much worse. All I had to do was to wait for a few years—and for a lifetime with Sarah, and our children, that would be no problem.

Provided, I thought, that publishing didn't do me in in the meantime.

•   •   •

The rest of the week passed in a delightful blur of the train journey to Alsace (we decided to forego the tandem), phone calls to England, and restful time with Sarah. We hiked during the days and sampled wines during the evening, enjoying the festive atmosphere, and I enjoyed seeing the ring on Sarah's finger far more than the spectacular mountain scenery. She wore it all the time. We rested a lot too; I think we were both exhausted, inside and out, by the events of the weekend.

One of the high points of the trip occurred on an evening when Sarah and I were back at our inn—a castle, actually—in Ribeauvillé, looking at the wine festival brochure to plan for the next day. Sarah fell asleep with her head on my shoulder late in the evening on the next-to-last night of the week. We were sitting on a comfortable sofa in the inn's crowded and cozy bar area, in front of a fire. It was early September, and in the mountains it was pleasantly chilly at night.

I wouldn't have moved for the world, and spent the next half-hour pretending that this was a normal night in our lives, that it was always like this in the sitting room—the "family room," she would call it—at the Orchard. As I felt the warmth of her body against me, and smelled the soft scent of her hair, I realised that something earthshaking had happened in the course of our five days in Alsace. We were comfortable together, more like sister and brother than anything else. I smiled. Perhaps the failed proposal had been the best thing that could have happened: there was no longer anything for us to be afraid of.

When she awakened, we went upstairs to bed. It was only when I was in my room, alone in my bed in the dark, that I remembered change was brewing at home. Max and Madeline had dibs on the Orchard. I would have to find another place to make my home and prepare for Sarah.

As my train sighed into Waterloo station on Sunday evening just after six o'clock, I was thinking about the way Sarah had kissed me good-bye. She'd insisted on going with me to the

Gare du Nord to catch the Chunnel train and we had stood looking at each other unabashedly, through new eyes, while people hurried by and children howled in the inevitable travel scenes. I held her hand on top of mine, palm to palm, and brushed the top of the emerald with my other hand.

"You won't forget me, then?"

She smiled and shook her head.

"Not even when Jean-Claude flies you to the Caribbean for a quick weekend getaway?"

She closed her eyes, still smiling, and shook her head more emphatically.

"Don't do anything impulsive, all right? Call me before you form any entangling alliances." I was aware that I was speaking to her as a friend, or a brother, and it was fine. The rest of it was there, but on hold.

"The same goes for you," she said, one side of her mouth turning up in a delicious smile. Her creamy skin creased into deep smile lines, which made her look cheerful and pleasant, even in repose. I loved them, wanted to trace them with my finger. On an impulse I did; she seemed to like it, and her upper lip quivered involuntarily.

"Will Angela be staying with you indefinitely?"

Now it was my turn to laugh. "She's going up to Cambridge as soon as they release her from hospital, according to Lisette. She's going to be far too wrapped up in television interviews and meetings with film producers to bother with me."

"Let's keep writing," Sarah said, slipping her arm around me and holding me tightly. She was careful to choose my right side in deference to the still-tender wounds on the left.

"Yes, let's," I said. "Do I get to choose the book this time?"

She nodded agreeably.

"I don't suppose you'd care to read some P. G. Wodehouse . . ." I offered, holding out little hope.

"What a good idea," she said brightly. "How much tragedy and catharsis do people need, when they've been through what you have? It would be wonderful to simply smile through an entire book, with nothing more to worry about than when I had to stop reading."

"It's settled, then," I said. "*The Crime Wave at Blandings.* Nothing more demanding than Lord Emsworth and his pig."

"I like it already," she said. "We'll relax and enjoy ourselves for a while—enjoy living."

And that was the note on which we parted—presumably until October, when I'd been invited to return to Paris. She had reached up, taken my face in both of her hands, and given me what I can describe only as a strong, determined, convincing kiss. It was more than a passing peck. Perhaps she really would come to me in the end.

"Thank you, Alex, for caring enough to want me to be happy."

"Of course," I said softly. "If you ever need anything, anytime—a cup of water in the night—"

We both smiled at the thought of me speeding under the English Channel to fetch a cup of water from her bathroom to her bedside. "A cup of water in the night" was something that Davy and Van had done for each other in *A Severe Mercy*; it was a way of saying, your smallest need is important to me, and I would *like* to sacrifice for you.

We hugged again, a long hug as if we could become part of each other and stay that way even after we had parted, but it was the kiss that lingered in my memory.

I was still in my reverie about the kiss when I saw Max and Madeline smiling and waving at me at Waterloo station. As I walked towards them, I was struck by the enormity of Max's change in personality. Not only had he come to fetch me, an unheard-of kindness in former years, but he looked so healthy, confident, happy, and generally positive that no one would ever believe he was the same man who'd conspired to ruin both my business and my person last year.

"Alex! You made it in one piece." They greeted me with gentle hugs and concern, and I allowed myself to be pampered, cosseted, enquired after, and tsk-tsked about as they drove me straight to Angela in hospital. Over the phone, from France, I had told them about Frances, and Armand, and Menceau. But I hadn't heard their news to speak of, and I soon learned that there was plenty.

As we left the car park, Madeline, in the front passenger seat, twisted round to face me in the back. "We have a surprise—or two, or three—for you," she said with a Mona Lisa smile.

I had come to dislike surprises, but I suppressed my dread and merely asked, "Really?" If she was smiling, it couldn't be too horrible. I tried to relax against the taupe leather upholstery of Max's BMW. This was the first time I could remember riding as my brother's passenger, in his car.

"Mmm-hmm," Max said, not about to relieve the suspense. In the rear-view mirror, I could see the anticipation in his face. "Mostly good too. We'll tell you all about it at home." He reached over and patted Madeline's hand as he drove. "Madeline's made us a wonderful dinner. I thought we'd have it in the sitting room, by the fire."

"Sounds wonderful," I said, meaning it, and sighed as I stared out at the light traffic of an early Sunday evening as we travelled north along Whitehall. "It will be so good to be home."

We drove in relaxed silence, and I sincerely looked forward to kicking off my shoes in front of the fire at the Orchard. But I also felt the mild sensation of anticlimax I always felt after arriving back in London after travelling abroad. Many of my problems were solved, it was true. But Sarah was far away again, there was a dampness approaching misty rain in the air, mingling with the coal smoke, and my holiday was over. It would be back to the grind, back to guilt over Angela, back to MacDougal, back to the building protesters, back to my suspicions about Max and the Plumtree Collection, and—perhaps worst of all—back to wondering whether I was obliged to leave the Orchard.

We reached the hospital in roughly half an hour, and though I was eager to see for myself how Angela was doing, I dreaded walking through the doors into the antiseptic smell. But I had got her into the vile mess, I reminded myself, and I would see her through it. I took a deep breath of misty city air before entering, and put one foot in front of the other until, followed by Max and Madeline, I found myself at Angela's door.

"Surprise number one," Max said, smiling. "We'll wait down the hall."

I stepped through the doorway and looked with trepidation

towards the bed. Since the first victorious Monday morning when I'd phoned Lisette from Jean-Claude's and learned that Angela was speaking, Lisette had brushed off all my enquiries with "She's doing fine, just fine." She always moved the conversation briskly back to Sarah and our holiday in an effort to keep me from dwelling too much on Angela. As a result, I didn't know quite what to expect, and when I saw her I felt my face split into a grin.

"Well, look who's here," she said at full volume, waggling her fingers in a little wave. "Back from the bicycle wars, are we?"

I went straight to her and kissed her forehead briefly before stepping back to get a better look. "Angela, you look marvellous," I said in wonder, and sat down in a chair at her bedside to study her further.

It was true—in relative terms, of course. All her features were visible again, not hideously muddled from swelling. She had lost the black eyes, and the merest shading of yellow remained. There was a bandage on her head, still, but it didn't cover the whole head, just the right rear quadrant. With a pang of regret I realised that they would have had to shave that part of her head; she'd start her new job at Cambridge wearing hats. In a way, that would suit her: she'd be a trend-setter, the first ever Stonecypher lecturer in modern times to wear hats to all her classes and meetings.

"Did you have a nice holiday?" she asked, tongue in cheek not only because Max and Lisette had reported our adventures in France to her, I knew, but also because I'd been with Sarah.

"Very nice indeed, thank you," I said, smiling. "I presume Lisette told you that Frances Macnamara proved to be a wolf in sheep's clothing."

She nodded, but not too vigorously, I noticed. No doubt she still had a fair amount of pain from the accident. "To think that one elderly woman with a family name to protect could have been more deadly than the Bibliati and the IRA together! When I found out that Frances had been with Pillinghurst in the accident in France, I knew it had been Pillinghurst who ran me down with your car. I saw him behind the wheel, you know; it was the white-haired, eccentric old man at Armand's party that night."

I nodded. We'd had it all wrong; the white Ford and the Neck had been innocent. Perhaps the Bibliati had hired them to simply keep an eye on me; Armand might have arranged it for my own protection. Frances had printed the dingbats, I was sure; it seemed something the Stonecypher Society would have on hand, or be able to produce. Rich had worked for Frances, and the man who'd been sitting behind my desk that night had pretended right up to the end that they were working on behalf of Folio B. Folio B and the Bibliati had proved extraordinarily convenient for Frances Macnamara.

I speculated that Frances had, possibly, been romantically involved with Pillinghurst—or else her goals had so neatly coincided with his that he decided to join her in eliminating Angela's book, Angela, and me.

Angela sighed. "I only wish I'd known in time to put it all in *The Stonecypher Saga*, secret room and all. What a sensational surprise ending it would have made."

"May I remind you that you really did suggest the correct ending? You were the first one who understood their relationships well enough to figure it out. That's why Frances was so upset."

"Well," she said in her characteristically wry tone, "we've lived to tell, at any rate." We both knew that after all she'd been through, the book would do fantastically well, and she'd be in great demand on the speaking circuit. Her job at Cambridge would just be a hobby, a lark, compared to the rest of it.

"I want to thank you, Alex," she said, reaching for my hand. Something about the way she did it was comfortable, and friendly, and made me think that perhaps she had come to peace with the nature of our relationship. "Thank you for the opportunity to write the book, and thank you for bearing with me this summer at the Orchard."

"Not at all," I murmured, but she was already speaking again, looking down at her pale blue cotton hospital gown.

"I can't imagine what you must have thought of me," she went on, expelling a long breath. "But you were always kind. Always. I hope you'll still think of me as a friend—we've been through enough together. Maybe you'll even publish my next book." She smiled a cunning little smile then, and I laughed.

The next book idea was never far from my mind, and as I said, "Let's hope we'll never have to go through this for another book again," it came to me. I would publish a book about publishing *The Stonecypher Saga*, a sort of "epi-book"—a book written about a book. It would be like the books about making movies: Behind the Making of So-and-So; The Untold Story of Blah-Blah . . .

With utmost seriousness she said, "Most of all, Alex, thanks for putting my family back together." A tear slipped down her cheek, and she let it be. "They didn't like my pursuit of academia—and a real job for a Mayfield, heaven forbid—but when I needed them, they came. If this hadn't happened, we may never have . . . I might never . . ."

"I know," I said, eager to relieve her tortured attempts at self-expression. She'd been reared with a stiff upper lip too, and we weren't very good at coming out with our feelings. She didn't know that I knew about her leukaemia, and therefore understood why it was so important for her to settle things with her family.

As if on cue, her dignified, elderly parents stepped into the room, and expressed satisfaction at meeting their daughter's publisher. I, in turn, was gratified to meet not only Angela's father, but the man who had made his family's name a household word for scents of all sorts—everything from perfume to potpourri to air freshener. We had our own little decorator pots of May Fields potpourri in various nooks and crannies of the Orchard to combat musty smells.

We exchanged pleasantries and they thanked me with what were no doubt mixed feelings; for while I had made sure their daughter was well cared for, I had also nearly got her killed. Angela looked tired but happy at seeing us all there together, and after a while I promised them I'd be seeing them the next day, and toddled out to meet Max and Madeline.

They were holding hands in the waiting area down the hall, and didn't even see me until I was on top of them. As I looked at their clasped hands, I saw that Madeline's left ring finger bore a huge diamond ring, guarded by a wide wedding band. Evidently this was the season for rings, I thought. Something ached inside me; jealousy, I decided, and longing. But at the same time, I was thrilled for them, and for myself because I now had a happy family.

"Are congratulations in order?" I asked, gazing pointedly at the rings.

They looked up, startled, then their faces lit up. Madeline's stunning white smile practically exploded in my face. "Isn't it super?" she bubbled. "I wondered if you'd ever notice."

"Surprise number two," Max announced proudly, putting his arm around his wife.

"It's wonderful!" I cheered, and there were more hugs. We were becoming positively sappy, I thought, with all this affection and joy, but I realised how little of it there normally is in the day-to-day. I decided to store it up against a rainy fortnight. Besides, Max had gone the long way round to find his happiness. He deserved every last bit of rejoicing.

They told me about it on the way home; on the Wednesday I was gone they could wait no longer, and asked a registrar to marry them. They couldn't wait, they said, for the banns of marriage to be read at the local church for weeks and weeks, giving people time to come forward if they objected to the union.

I smiled to myself in the back seat, a little sadly, thinking that I, too, didn't want to wait—but would, for an indefinite period, for just the ghost of a chance. As Max piloted the car away from the hospital and turned northwards, I had a fleeting sense of having left something undone in London.

In the next second, it came to me. Farquhart. Before I could put it all behind me, I would have to confront him about having stolen the Stonecypher and the Wodehouse from the library.

Madeline was just beginning to elaborate on the mannerisms of the "odd little man" who had married them, when I rudely placed a hand on her shoulder and said as mildly as I could, "Sorry, Madeline, just thought of something . . ." She looked at me without offense and nodded. "Max, would you mind very much turning left there and going back to May-fair—near Grosvenor Square? I'll tell you exactly where when we get closer."

He glanced at me in the rear-view mirror, then quickly indicated for the turn, nimbly entering the left-turn lane. "Of course I don't mind. But what . . . ?"

"Just one last matter to be settled about Folio B—I really shouldn't let it go." I saw the apprehension in his eyes as his glance flicked back to me via the mirror again. "No," I laughed, "you don't have to worry. Honest. Nothing danger-ous this time. I just want to have a quick word, in person, with William Farquhart—you know, the president of Folio B." Max's shoulders and brow relaxed at that. He knew of Farqu-hart's stylish shop in Sackville Street, and his reputation as a prestigious book dealer.

"Oh." Max seemed a bit nonplussed, and I hurried to explain.

"I don't want anyone else to know this," I explained, "but Farquhart was our burglar in the library on the night of Armand's party."

Appropriate exclamations of shock and disbelief emanated from both sides of the front seat.

"I know—it is hard to believe, but he virtually admitted it during the Folio B conference. So—if it's all right with you, Max—I'll make a deal with him. If he puts an end to acquiring his stock through theft, and gives my books back, I will agree not to prosecute him."

"Sounds extremely fair." Max nodded approvingly. "But why would William Farquhart stoop to thievery when he has so much going for him? I mean, his shop is nearly as famous as Quarritch's, and he's the president of Folio B." He shook his head. "It doesn't make sense."

I put my head on one side, considering. Like Sarah, I realised with a smile. "I don't understand it either, unless he's in serious financial straits. He did say something at Armand's party about not being able to afford to stay away from the Antiquarian Booksellers' Association conference, but I didn't think much of it at the time—just assumed it was a figure of speech." I shook my head. "Money, or the lack thereof, has a strange way of making men desperate."

"Don't I know it," Max said sadly. Just last year he had sold his own brother down the river to profit financially. The memory was probably all too clear in his mind. Madeline put a hand on his arm and squeezed. He looked at her, caught her smile, and nodded. "Right. That's behind us now." A pause. "Do you want me to come in with you?"

"Thanks, but no—it might be easier on him if it's just the two of us."

"Right." He drove in silence then, down Tottenham Court Road, then skirting Oxford Street until he could turn south down Park Lane. From there I directed him to Farquhart's house, and Max found a place to park across the street.

Farquhart's house was a tall, narrow structure of white stone. In the way that buildings do often wear expressions, his looked like a silent scream. The windows looked blankly out on the street, and the door, painted black, looked like a wide-open mouth. His wife had left him some years ago, I knew, and the house bore the cold, unlived-in look that came from an absence of the female influence.

"It looks as if he may be in his workshop," I said to Max and Madeline. "I saw a light on in the mews building as we drove past." In many areas of London, the mews houses themselves, once the alley-facing homes of servants who cared for the master's horses and grounds, had become pricey dwellings. Farquhart's home was in a neighbourhood where some of the mews flats had remained with the main house, making for a sort of guest house in the back, or workshop, as in Farquhart's case.

The mews building was, I speculated, where he'd printed the BBFA book fair's program, inserting all the suitable miniature Stonecypher dingbats to signify when and where the annual Bibliati meeting would be held. It was also where he did his own restoration work—something I had become increasingly curious about. If my unconscious musings on the subject over the course of the last week were valid, Holdsworthy and Diana Boillot were completely innocent of wrongdoing as far as the book-stealing ring was concerned.

I'd had a wild idea, while on holiday with Sarah, that perhaps Farquhart had copied one of Virginia Holdsworthy's bookplates and made a stack of them, on appropriately yellowed paper, to stick inside the new books he had made out of scraps and bound together so artfully. The idea had come to seem less wild to me over time, and I had virtually convinced myself that it had been Farquhart's fakes that we had seen the men loading into their van. It had only been my suspicion of Holdsworthy, planted by his wife's letter, and augmented by the apparently advanced nature of his relationship with Diana Boillot, that had made me sure it was Holdsworthy's and Boillot's fiddle.

Now I could see that Diana Boillot's restoration exhibit, and courses, were a very convenient front for Farquhart's less ethical restoration projects—just as Folio B and the Bibliati had been useful to Frances Macnamara. What a remarkably tangled web, I thought, shaking my head.

"I should be back within ten minutes; he won't want to sit and chat, I shouldn't think." I opened the door of the BMW and stepped out into the street. Dusk had finally turned to darkness, and I could see a glow of light from inside Farquhart's workshop behind the utterly dark house.

"All right. We'll be here," Max said. "No hurry."

Madeline smiled cheerfully as she leaned over, entwining her arm with Max's. "No—no hurry," she said, winking as I looked into the car. I winked back, then headed across the quiet street. The air bore the slight chill of early autumn; it seemed to me that the scent and feel of the air had changed from summer to autumn while I'd been away with Sarah. I strode up the path that ran past the side of the house, next to a wrought iron fence separating Farquhart's property from its neighbours, and advanced towards the workshop. Heavy, lined curtains prevented me from seeing into the smaller building as I approached, but it was clear that Farquhart, or someone, was there. The clatter of a small hand press was audible, and I recognised it well from our own small museum of printing gear in the Orchard's shed. Farquhart was printing something. More counterfeit manuscript pages, I thought cynically.

I waited until the gentle, rhythmic clacking stopped, then knocked firmly on the varnished oak door of the workshop. Silence. I waited several moments, then several more. No answer. I knocked again. "Farquhart, it's Alex Plumtree. I'd like to speak with you."

To my surprise, the lights went off. The door drifted ajar with nothing more than a small click as the latch slid out of the jamb. "Farquhart?" I queried, gently pushing the door open. "Are you there?"

Silence.

Something was badly amiss. It was dark; I couldn't see a thing. The logical course of action seemed to be to put the lights on again, so I stepped in through the doorway and groped along the well to the left of the door for a switch, feeling the usual aversion to fumbling in the dark as a precursor to a future of permanent darkness. As I stepped out of the arc of the door's swing, it closed quietly behind me. I whipped round, sensing him there, then, feeling the heat of him, but still he didn't speak.

"What is it, Farquhart? What do you want?"

When his voice came, it was far back in the room. It was amazing that he could move so soundlessly through the room; no scraping, feet, no clicking ankles, no swish of clothing—nothing.

"You just couldn't leave it alone, could you, Plumtree." It wasn't a question. The voice was the same, it was the William Farquhart I knew, but there was a peculiar detached quality to it that I hadn't heard before. "And I was willing to stand by you, you know. I had agreed with Armand that we would prepare you to lead a new Folio B, an organisation that would have nothing to do with the Bibliati. You would have chosen your own board members as we dropped off by attrition, and it all would have worked out beautifully." A long pause. "But you just wouldn't stop. You're very like your father that way, you know, Alex."

As he spoke, I was aware that the wisest thing to do would be to find my way back out of his little trap and back to the safety of Max's car. But we had something to settle, and I felt the least I could do would be to hear him out. So, as he prattled, I continued to search for the light switch with my hand, hoping it was where it ought to be, just inside the door. It had all taken just a few moments, and with relief I had found the switch and was pressing it on, when I heard, or felt, something coming in my direction via the air. The lights had gone on, but I'd ducked and covered my head with my arms, so what I saw when I opened my eyes and stood erect was astonishing.

William Farquhart stood before me, bloodshot eyes unnaturally wide, with nearly black hollows beneath his eyes. His face was ashen. He looked like an entirely different man from the self-respecting and respectable book dealer I had once known. He wore a rumpled and soiled grey sweatsuit, which looked as if he'd slept in it several nights in a row, and his mouth hung open slackly, as if in astonishment. In his hands was a glass jar, the kind I'd seen in the workshop the Sunday before, only then it had been stoppered. All round us there was a pungent chemical smell. When I twisted slowly to see what I was hearing on the door just inches behind me, I saw that varnish was bubbling off the oak door, actually smoking and hissing.

William Farquhart had thrown a frighteningly effective acid of some sort, probably the kind he used to etch copper printing plates. He'd sent it in the general direction of my face, hoping to get me out of publishing and Folio B forever. When he saw that he had not succeeded, he collapsed into a mound of trembling flesh, not five feet away. I could smell him from where I stood, and guessed that he had been surviving in some sort of broken-down condition in the sweatsuit for more than a week. The acid-throwing had been the desperate, irrational act of a man in the throes of a nervous breakdown. I didn't think he had any other tricks up his sleeve.

"Farquhart," I said gently, "it's not so bad. Look. Give me my books back, and stop switching and selling the restored books, and it'll be all right. All is forgiven."

"Go away!" he cried, still crumpled into a messy pile on the floor. "Just go away and leave me alone." He sobbed, his entire body shaking, and my mind raced. I couldn't just leave him there; he might do harm to himself. But how could I help him?

His daughter, I thought. I knew he had a daughter in London, and there couldn't be too many Farquharts listed in London. I'd try her from Max's car. Slowly, reluctantly, I left, hoping I was doing the right thing, and closed the door behind me. With luck, he would be all right before long and I would be able to speak to him rationally again. I knew from my own circumstances last year what havoc financial ruin can wreak on a soul.

Max and Madeline looked at me inquiringly when I opened the car door. I sat down heavily and pulled the door closed. "How did it go?" Max asked.

"Not very well, I'm afraid. He's—um—he's unwell. Could I use your mobile phone to ring his daughter? I think he'll need some looking after."

Before I'd finished the sentence, Max was passing the phone back to me. I got the number from directory enquiries and reached the daughter, who was disturbed to hear that her father was emotionally unwell and said she'd call his doctor and get right over to his workshop. After I hung up, we rode home in a subdued but not unpleasant manner. Max and Madeline seemed to sense the seriousness of my encounter with Farquhart and kindly refrained from drawing me into idle conversation.

Ten minutes or so after I'd rung off with Farquhart's daughter, it struck me how close I'd come that night to experiencing my ultimate nightmare of blindness. The maiming of my face I wouldn't have minded so much, but my eyes were precious. Even with my glasses on, I had a feeling that some portion of the jar full of acid would have drizzled down into my eyes before I could have stopped it.

My body began to shake from head to toe, some sort of delayed reaction from fear, I supposed. I clenched my teeth and crossed my arms to still the involuntary tremors, and longed for home. When I was home at the Orchard, I would know that it was over at last.

Back at the Orchard, we had scarcely got the fire going in the sitting room, when the front doorbell rang. Max went, insisting that I stay and relax by the fire with my new sister-in-law—no difficult task—and returned with Ian.

I stood up, surprised. Ian was something of a recluse. He normally avoided social gatherings involving more than one person, even with us, his adoptive family.

"Ian," I exclaimed. "What a pleasure." I went to him, delighted, and ushered him to a seat near the fire, beaming at Max along the way. He smiled back almost tentatively, wondering, I suppose, if my doubts about him and his involvement in the Bibliati had been resolved.

As Max passed behind me to a table to get us drinks, he whispered, "Surprises three and four, coming up." My brother seemed somewhat more serious about these, and again I fought back a feeling of dread.

"I'll be back," Madeline told us. "I need to check a few things in the kitchen."

The glow of the flames before us burnished Ian's face. "Alex," he began with what seemed to be reluctance. "I'm here to celebrate your safe return, and the elimination of the malignant elements of Folio B." He smiled a sober little smile. "But there are a few things you need to know, and we thought it was best to wait until now to tell you."

My dread had been justified, I could tell; I braced myself for another in the apparently endless stream of disasters that had become my life.

"Armand Beasley died in hospital in France on Friday, and was sent back here for burial. It was done quietly, just as he specified." He let this sink in, and Max quietly deposited rather hefty tumblers of whiskey on the table at our elbows.

"I'll just see if Madeline needs some help," he said, and left us.

Ian continued, turning to focus his bright blue eyes on mine. "I hope you're not angry, Alex. At times there seems to be so little respite in life, and you seemed to be having a rather pleasant time with Sarah. We all discussed it—Lisette, George, Max, Angela, Madeline, and I—and decided to leave you your few days with Sarah. We've arranged for a memorial service next week."

I reflected that Ian had special reason to leave us undisturbed; he cared perhaps as much as I did about Sarah's happiness, as her dedicated grandfather, and also cared for me as a father would a son. More than anything, I speculated, he would have liked to see us become husband and wife.

After a momentary flash of anger at having things taken out of my hands, I understood that they had all wanted what was best for me, and for Sarah. "Thank you," I said rather stiffly, leaving the remainder of my thoughts unexpressed. "That was kind."

He closed his eyes briefly, acknowledging my true feelings. "I'm afraid there's more. . . . Alex, there's been a fire at Watersmeet."

"Oh, no," I breathed, thinking of Armand's beloved and priceless books. It was the final insult to the man, who, at least, was now beyond caring.

"It could have been much worse. Evidently Armand had had an alarm installed, and they caught the fire before it was too far along. A neighbour persuaded them not to hose down the library with water." He shifted in his chair, as if uncomfortable at the thought. "The structure is intact, but there is some smoke damage."

The very thought of inundating the books in Armand's library with a flood of water, their arch-enemy, was horrifying. I had a mental image of all those priceless books, dripping wet, the leather covers of the older volumes warping, and the dust jackets of the more modern books disintegrating into pulpy puddles on the shelves.

He saw the look on my face. "Alex, Armand has left Watersmeet to you, along with all of his books."

My mouth dropped open, and I stared at Ian. "Me!" I gaped. "Why me?"

He looked down for a moment, as if considering how best to present what he had to say. "Do you remember the night you were asked to join the board of Folio B?"

I nodded dumbly. How could I ever forget that night? It seemed decades ago, though, a part of the distant past.

"Armand had made a decision to groom you for the position of a new, untarnished head of Folio B, to move us away from the Bibliati and rejuvenate the organisation. He felt that as your father's son, you would have the respect of the others. He also knew you would never allow the Bibliati to flourish in your organisation. Armand had tremendous respect for you, Alex—and faith in you." He focussed on me again, and my eyes were drawn to his. "So do I."

I stared, hardly able to take it all in.

"As Armand lay slipping away in hospital, he asked me

to write down his wishes, and to help him sign them. He trusted you to take care of his things, and do what was right for Folio B."

The fire crackled and popped as I absorbed what he had said. I was tremendously honoured. Armand's words in Menceau's study came back to me: *"It's all . . . yours . . . now."* At last I understood all of it.

I thought of Giles, and realised that he had been working for good, and had somehow found out about the plot against the Princess and her sons. He'd probably been trying to make sure that his ancestor's name carried on untainted; after all, as I'd learned from Stonecypher's letter in Marie-Louise's room, the unfortunate author had been used by the radicals within the Bibliati. Why, exactly, Giles had been snooping in my library the night of the party, I still wasn't sure—though considering his shocked reaction to the news of Angela's book at Armand's party, he may have been looking for information she had on the meaning behind the misprints.

It was Farquhart who had printed the elegant dingbats on his letter press, just as he had printed the beautifully typeset and designed programs for the BBFA fair with their tiny code of dingbats. No doubt he'd provided them to the Stonecypher Society for a special occasion, or at Frances's request, as a favour. Pillinghurst, or Frances herself, I speculated, had delivered them, and written the letters Angela and I had received. The odd man Frances had had appear behind my desk, claiming to have been a friend of my father's, was simply to throw me off—just in case. I knew now that it hadn't been Folio B or the Bibliati who wanted me shot and entombed in the room; it had been Frances. Rich had been employed by Frances.

I sighed and looked at Ian, who, kindly, was staring into the fire, allowing me time to absorb all that he had said. Ian had succeeded in absolving himself from guilt in ever having been a member of the Bibliati; he had cooperated with Armand to make sure the organisation would be purified and strengthened—surprisingly, under my leadership.

I shook my head and sank back in the chair as Max strode into the room. "Hors d'oeuvres, anyone? Stuffed mushroom caps?" He knew that I loved stuffed mushroom caps more than anything, except perhaps potted prawns, so no doubt he wondered why I stared at him as if seeing him for the first time as he stood proffering the steaming plate.

The idea had hit me suddenly when Max entered: Madeline and Max needed a home. The Plumtree brothers now had two homes. The Orchard, of course, rightfully belonged to Max, though he'd been good enough to let me live there. Would he and Madeline mind, I wondered . . . ?

I shook myself and managed to say, "Thanks, Max," and took the cocktail serviette he offered, along with two of the small round delicacies. He set the plate down between us and left again, slightly nonplussed. I nibbled a mushroom and reached for my glass of Glenfiddich, noticing that Ian did the same. The peaty-smelling drink was warm, earthy, and comforting.

"I might as well let you have it all at once," Ian said, having swallowed a stiff mouthful.

"Not more!" I goggled, incredulous.

"Just a bit. I had a chat with MacDougal."

"Oh." I'd almost forgotten about the strange man and his even stranger history books.

"Mmm. He's agreed that in exchange for keeping him on, he'll revise his history texts—which are basically excellent, aside from the anti-royalty distortions—until experts of our choice approve their accuracy. We'll give them an entirely new cover design and format, and add a foreword about the dangers of letting politics influence textbooks. I think we can turn the whole thing into a marketing and publicity advantage. MacDougal claims that he is eager to get away from writing unfairly slanted books, no matter what the pay, and is hoping for a fresh start with us."

I thought back to my meeting with him, and remembered his words about starting "a new career." Perhaps he was an honest man after all. His preoccupation with reviewers of his own choice may well have had something to do with his remarkable sensitivity about his work; perhaps he planned to have his friends do the reviewing.

"And"—Ian beamed a victorious smile at me—"Mac-Dougal is so grateful to us for not turning him out into the street as a tainted author that he is releasing us from our commitment to publish *The Storms of Time*."

"Thank God for that!" I exclaimed, feeling slightly overwhelmed. In the same breath, Ian had both reminded me of a disastrous problem and relieved me of it. We sat in comfortable silence for a moment, reflecting. In the background I was vaguely aware that the doorbell had rung again, but some combination of the Scotch, relief, and weariness conspired to make me leave it for someone else to deal with.

Ian tucked into a mushroom cap, and I thought perhaps Madeline had got hold of peyote buttons by mistake, that I was hallucinating as I heard three familiar voices in the hallway. Max's elated greeting rang out, and then there was no doubt.

I jumped up and ran out of the room, all lethargy gone. There with Max, standing in the tall, creamy fabric-tented vestibule my mother had created for warmth and intimacy, stood a tearful, laughing Sarah, along with Lisette and George. They were tangled in a bundle of greetings and incredulous exclamations.

Moving towards them in a fog of surprise, I heard Lisette say, "She pulled into the drive just ahead of us! I don't know . . ."

As I passed Lisette and George, Lisette gave me an affectionate peck on the cheek and a hug. "Welcome 'ome, you."

George clapped me on the back and whispered in my ear, "Looks like you've done it, you old devil!"

Then they all evaporated, just like that, into the sitting room, and we were alone in the front hall.

Sarah seemed to be laughing and crying at the same time. I willed myself not to say anything foolish this time, and went to her, taking her in my arms. Having her there, in my arms, in my warm, beloved home, was surely not far from heaven. Perhaps this was heaven. Hardly daring to wonder exactly what her appearance here meant, I closed my eyes and merely enjoyed burying my nose in her hair as she wrapped her arms more tightly round me.

We stayed that way for several moments, drinking each other in. I had never, I thought, been so happy in my life. She had come back. To me.

Finally, it tumbled out. "You came back," I said, nearly choking on the words.

She turned her face towards my neck, still not pulling away, and breathed into my shirt collar, "Life is short, Alex. I realised it would have been a mistake to stay away." She was silent for a moment, then dug her face into my shoulder—the right one—more deeply. Her voice was muffled when she spoke again. "I never even left the Gare du Nord. I watched you go, and thought of Davy and Van. I bought a ticket for the next train."

Again, I wondered if I was dreaming, but I heard heels tapping on the parquet-floored hallway. We both looked round, and saw Madeline standing in anticipation. "Sarah?"

Sarah pulled away then, and crossed to greet the woman who, I hoped, would soon be her sister-in-law. "Yes," she smiled, wiping away tears. "You must be Madeline."

"I'm so glad you're here," Madeline said warmly, and embraced her. Ian could restrain himself no longer apparently, and appeared in the vestibule. "Grandfather!" Sarah said, going immediately to him. As they, too, embraced, I realised that we were all a family. I had never dared even to dream of such a moment, such a conclusion to the disaster that had been that autumn.

" 'Ey! Come on, you lot—the party's in 'ere!" Lisette was peeking around the edge of the doorway, waving her glass of wine at us.

No, I thought as we went laughing to sit round the fire, the party—and life—is wherever Sarah is. They all arranged themselves in the semicircle of chairs and sofas that ranged in front of the huge fireplace, and pointedly left two spaces together in the center love seat. Sarah and I sat in our allotted places and I put my arm round her, utterly contented.

Lisette said, leaning forward in her chair with anticipation, "I want to 'ear about the bicycle chase first!"

And so began that first blissful evening of the rest of our life together.

It was some hours later, after a dinner and claret that had us sprawling like rag dolls on the chairs and sofas in the library, that Max looked at me with what I can call only a mysterious smile. He then glanced at his wife, apparently for her approval to proceed.

"Er, since this seems to be the night for surprises, I would like to present you, Alex, with a small token of my appreciation—and Madeline's—for, well, for all that you've done for me."

I felt myself shake my head slightly and blink, astounded that this could be my brother Max speaking. Keeping my arm round Sarah, I sat up a bit straighter, curious about what he had done.

He reached into the drawer of the Pembroke table next to his voluminous chair and pulled out a large envelope. "I know I haven't always been the most responsible of older brothers, and I hope you'll consider this a start." He handed me the envelope, and I lifted my arm over Sarah's head to take it. I could feel the warmth of her next to me, and was aware of her every move. She was watching me with a smile curving up her lips, eyes dancing, and I gave her a quick glance that said "What can it be?" She inclined her head slightly and raised her eyebrows in a facial shrug.

It was heavy. I undid the clasp and lifted out a spiral-bound album half an inch thick, with the Christie's crest on it. A boldly typeset title read "A Catalogue of the Plumtree Collection," with the month and year below.

Once again, relief and astonishment swept over me as I realised what Max's presentation meant. He hadn't been stealing books from the Plumtree Collection; he'd been taking them to experts—most likely Madeline—for evaluation, wanting to surprise me by taking charge of some aspect of the giant responsibility we now carried towards all aspects of the Plumtree estate.

"Max, you're a marvel." I beamed at him. "Thank you so much. This is a great weight off my mind." I flipped through it, seeing the names of our precious volumes, including the Malconbury Chronicles, flash by, with corresponding paragraphs commenting on their rarity and history, with a column of values on the right. Now we could have the collection insured for its true worth. "I'm going to enjoy studying this. Really, thank you so much, Max." No doubt he could hear the delight in my voice, and knew that I understood what the gift meant.

We gabbled on for half an hour or so more, with me reading snippets about some of the more interesting books, until at last Lisette rose to her feet, sighing. "Come on, George," she said, ruffling his hair. "They are going to kick us out soon." Ian stood then, too, and after issuing more thanks and congratulations, they left. Finally just Max, Madeline, Sarah, and I remained, closely grouped in sets of two, not wanting the night to end.

"It occurs to me," Max said thoughtfully, staring at the fire, "that between us we now own two houses." He transferred his gaze to me. "Technically, I own this one, and you own Watersmeet."

I nodded.

"But it's always seemed to me that this house is more— well, it's almost a part of you." He sighed. "I spent some horrible years here—my own fault, of course. Poor Mum and Dad." Shaking his head, he closed his eyes briefly. Madeline stroked his hair for a moment in silence. "Anyway," he said, looking back at me, "I don't know what your wishes are. But if you and Sarah would rather have the Orchard, and if Madeline and I would have your permission to live at Watersmeet . . ."

He let the sentence trail off, and I found myself looking at him with wide eyes and tremendous enthusiasm.

"You wouldn't mind, Max? Really?"

He shook his head, pursing his lips. "It would be a fresh start for me," he answered. "This house has too many ghosts."

I nodded at him. I understood: ghosts of all the arguments he'd had with my father, ghosts of all the loutish things he'd said to my mother when she'd tried to redirect him from his disastrous course, and ghosts of the injuries he'd inflicted upon his younger brother in the name of sibling rivalry.

I looked at Sarah for her approval. She nodded, grinning broadly. "This is your home," she told me. "I love it here."

That was all I needed to hear.

"Max, I hardly know how to thank you. I should be

thanking you for all you've done for me, not the other way round."

He was pleased to hear it, I could tell, though he waved it off. "Just promise you'll see us occasionally, and we'll do the same."

"Done," I replied, and reflected that there was not a single thing I would have changed about that moment. Mere hours before, virtually every aspect of my life had seemed disastrous—or, at the very least, unsettled. Now Sarah was by my side and we were at the Orchard. What could possibly stand in our way now?

Max and Madeline said good night and climbed the stairs, and Sarah and I relaxed still further into each other's arms. Our heads were touching as we watched the remains of the fire flickering in the grate.

"Have you ever thought," Sarah said softly, "that Plumtree Press might need an American office? In, say, Boston?"

The tumblers fell and locked into place. I turned and smiled at her, then reached up and touched her glossy dark hair, playing with it. "Yes," I said slowly, nodding. "I have often thought that we do need an American office, and rather urgently too. It shouldn't be too far from the alma mater, definitely not in New York, and not too far from some very special people who live on Nantucket. Yes, Boston would do nicely."

It had been my turn to provide the cup of water in the night, and I was honoured. We would find a way to merge our two lives into one without either of us asking more of the other than they could give.

I disengaged myself from Sarah's embrace and knelt on the rug in front of her. Her eyes sparkled; she knew what was coming. It hadn't been done properly yet.

"Sarah," I said, sliding the emerald off her right hand, "will you marry me?"

"Yes, Alex. I will." She smiled at me, her eyes moist.

I slid the ring onto her left ring finger, and thought of the scrap of metal in Menceau's wine cellar that I had nearly presented to her.

A hilarious, carefree laugh rose in my throat, and it emerged full-blown in a roar of joy. And with the laughter came release of all the worry and fear I had carried for so long, and Sarah joined me, laughing at *me* laughing, until the tears came. I pulled her down onto the soft flokati rug in front of the sofa, and, still crying from the laughter, we sank into a repeat of the good-bye kiss at the Gare du Nord.

Unfortunately, what Michel Menceau had said in his château was true: things are rarely what they seem, even happy endings. But even if I had known what the future held for us, it would not have marred the joy of that evening.

Nor could it change the fact that from that moment on, Sarah and I were one, and we would never really be apart again.

CONCLUDING NOTE

For readers who think it the product of my imagination that textbooks could be skewed to purposefully serve a political agenda, I offer the following information from Gary Kah's book, *En Route to Global Occupation,* which I used while researching the Illuminati. Kah falls squarely into the category of conspiracy theorists. For those of us who don't believe in that sort of thing, the mere possibility of textbook influence—by anyone—is intriguing nonetheless.

Kah writes that Gary Allen claimed, in a book called *The Rockefeller File*:

> Since America's public school system was decentralized, the [charitable] foundations had concentrated on influencing schools of education (particularly Columbia, the spawning ground for Deweyism), and on financing the writing of textbooks which were subsequently adopted nationwide.

Kah continues:

> The Rockefellers not only used their money to seize control of America's centers of teacher training, they also spent millions of dollars on rewriting history books and creating textbooks that undermined patriotism and free enterprise. Among the series of public school textbooks produced by Rockefeller grants was one called *Building America*. These books promoted Marxist propaganda to the extent that the California legislature refused to appropriate money for them.
>
> Rene Wormser concluded, "It is difficult to believe the The Rockefeller Foundation and the National Edu-

cation Association could have supported these text-books. But the fact is that Rockefeller financed them and the NEA promoted them very widely."

Hmmm. Did you hear that clicking on the phone line? And what was that noise outside the window just now?

I'm sure it's . . . only the wind.

ABOUT THE AUTHOR

Julie Wallin Kaewert, a graduate of Dartmouth and Harvard, worked for book publishers in Boston and Bedford Square before beginning her writing career with a London magazine. She now lives near Boulder, Colorado, with her husband and two daughters. She is the author of UNSOLICITED and UNBOUND and is currently at work on her third Alex Plumtree novel.

If you enjoyed UNBOUND, you will not want to miss UNPRINTABLE, the latest entry in the Booklover's Mystery series featuring Alex Plumtree and the Plumtree Press.

Look for Julie Kaewert's UNPRINTABLE at your favorite bookstore in October 1998.

And in the meantime, turn the page for an exciting preview!

UNPRINTABLE

A Booklover's Mystery

by

JULIE KAEWERT

When the prime minister's henchman rang, asking me to publish the political novel of a bestselling author, he added confidentially that I would be doing the nation a great favour. "This election could be a near thing, Plumtree," he said in hushed tones. "We need every last bit of help to win it." Terrific, I thought. A bestselling novel for us, and I would be helping my father's old school friend, the PM, at the same time. My only reservation was the novel itself, the first chapter of which had already been published by a serial publisher. Its overtones of class- and race-hatred were distasteful to me in the extreme, but I couldn't sneeze at having a bestselling literary author like Nigel Charford-Cheney in the Plumtree Press stable. Besides, being part of the PM's inner circle was quite flattering.

I couldn't have known that once again, tendencies toward vanity and greed would wreak havoc—not just for me, but for all of England. For when I published Nigel Charford-Cheney's novel this spring, it was not unlike dropping a match into a sea of petrol. Political volatility had built inexorably over the preceding years, fueled by fearful speculation over the consequences of Britain joining the European Union. Charford-Cheney's novel, fiction though it was, seemed to give xenophobics, paranoiacs, and the racially prejudiced long-awaited permission to come out of the closet. Bizarre political groups came crawling out of the woodwork. The whole tragic mess not only changed the history of Europe, it nearly made *me* history.

It was in the calm before this storm that I walked down Clerkenwell Green with my newly hired editor of Plumtree Press Trade Editions. We had just met with our printer about Charford-Cheney's novel, which even at that point was proving problematic. It was a deceptively balmy March day, and I'd suggested that we stop at the Farringdon Road bookcarts on our way from Clerkenwell back to Bloomsbury.

"All right," I said as we walked, eyeing young Nicola Beauchamp with mock suspicion. "Here's one that might stump you. What, I ask you, is the literary significance of the Farringdon Road bookstalls?"

Nicola smiled at me, eyes narrowed, ever in control. Since I'd interviewed her for the job a month ago, I'd been stunned not only by her knowledge of literature but by her poise. "Surely you don't think I'd apply for a job in Bedford Square without having read my Dickens?"

There. She'd done it again, made me feel ridiculous. She was twenty-eight, ex-editor of a literary magazine, and never caught off-guard. I was thirty-four, a book publisher, her boss—and frequently caught off-guard. I knew I was incredibly fortunate to have hired her: from our first meeting it was clear that she was the product of the best family and schools, and her subtlety and tact were exceeded only by the Queen's.

She went on as we strolled toward busy Farringdon Road. "Oliver Twist was set up by Artful Dodger, who had stolen the wallet of a Mr. Brownlow as he browsed for books in the Farringdon Road bookstalls. Clerkenwell was the site of Fagin's den, as I recall."

She was exactly right. I'd have to brush up on my lit to keep pace with her.

"Bravo," I said. "Changed a bit since then, hasn't it? I read the other day that houses here in Clerkenwell go for more than three hundred thousand pounds." Clerkenwell, after several centuries of ecclesiastical splendour as the home of the Order of St. John and numerous churches, had slid into infamy in the nineteenth century as the home of London's worst thieves, jails and slums. But over the last decade it had enjoyed one of those renewals that sometimes takes a neighbourhood by surprise, and now housed our trendy, pricey printer of fine editions, whose offices we had just left.

As we arrived at the huge wooden bookcart, which had undoubtedly been drawn into Farringdon Road by horsepower at some point in its history, I couldn't help but notice the way Nicola caught the eye of every passing male. Journalists walking from the

Watch newspaper offices to Farringdon tube station couldn't resist a glance at the well-sculpted leg muscles rising out of her high heels, and then did a double-take to fully absorb the wonder of her upper half, loosely cloaked in an expensive-looking taupe linen suit. I wondered how they'd react if they knew that her appearance was only excelled by her mind.

Nicola delicately touched several spines of the books on the cart, then plucked one out. *"Riceyman Steps,"* she exclaimed. "A rare find." I looked at her, my own rare find for Plumtree Press, and saw the intent, wistful faces of men passing behind her on the pavement as she spoke. "This one was set here in Clerkenwell, you know—Arnold Bennett, 1928."

"No moss on you," I said, laughing. "I thought Plumtree Press employees were the only people who'd heard of it."

She looked at me, puzzled. "Why's that?"

"Nicola, you must admit it's one of the world's most obscure novels. The only reason I know about it is because a friend, the book restorer Diana Boillot, told me about it. She asked me to publish several commemorative editions of Clerkenwell-based works—*Riceyman Steps* being one of them—for the Clerkenwell Neighbourhood Association fete. And she suggested that I work with Amanda—her protégée—to print them. Didn't I tell you about the boxed set we did for the occasion?"

She shook her head.

"*Riceyman Steps*, *Oliver Twist*, and *The Collected Writings of William Morris*."

Nicola's face lit up, as if she were pleasantly surprised by this folly of Plumtree Press. "Really," she exclaimed. "But what does William Morris have to do with Clerkenwell? He was a printer, I know, and designer, but . . ."

"Aha! Finally, something you don't know. I was getting worried—it's nearly the end of your first day on the job. Just up there, across from Amanda's Printshop on Clerkenwell Green, is the Marx Memorial Library. But before its incarnation as a library, it was the first Socialist publishing house—founded by William Morris. He published *Commonweal* there, the newsletter of his Socialist party."

She raised her eyebrows, and with a "Well, well," turned her bright gaze away from me and back to the book. "I'll buy it," she said, flipping over the weathered cover to check for a pencilled price inside. "Just for the privilege of reading it from yellowed paper."

"I'll give you a boxed set when we get back to the Press. Amanda did a fine job on it."

The very thought of Amanda Pitkin, and her eponymous printing business, made my stomach churn. Nicola and I had been to visit her because of a troublesome novel that seemed—for one reason or another—virtually unprintable. I groaned at the very thought of that book and its knotty problems.

Nicola's smile of thanks was chasing that particular cloud away when I was startled by the pounding of running feet on the pavement behind us. I wheeled at the same instant that a winded young man, who was turning to look behind him, crashed into Nicola and me. *Riceyman Steps* flew into the carbon monoxide cloud over Farringdon Road, and my tailbone slammed into the base of the bookcart.

For the next few moments I seemed to see through a lens which showed everything in slow motion. I caught a glimpse of the boy, and his thick shock of long, kinky black hair, as he stumbled at our feet. Going down, he grasped the strap of Nicola's shoulder bag, hanging from it to recover his balance. Nicola, already struggling for equilibrium after his impact, fell backwards, graceful arms flailing.

The boy, his balance restored, crouched next to me for a fraction of a second as if hiding. Terror in his eyes, he cast a panicked glance toward the way he'd come. Then, breathing hard, he looked up at me. In that moment, the boy's face imprinted itself clearly on my mind. His eyes were wide with fear.

The next moment he had scrambled under the bookcart, which stood at about waist height, passed Nicola on the ground, and with great daring escaped into the traffic on Farringdon Road.

The world miraculously came out from behind the lens and returned to normal speed.

"Hey!" I called angrily, watching his fleeing form dart between the cars. As the shout resounded, people turned to look.

Nicola. With churning stomach, I recalled hearing the thud of her head against the edge of the heavy wooden cart. Momentarily torn between helping her and chasing after the boy, who was already halfway across the snarl of rush-hour traffic on the road, I opted for Nicola. But I was stopped short again as a pack of half a dozen young urchins raced past noisily, issuing catcalls and obviously pursuing the terror-stricken boy. As their leering faces flew past, not three feet away, one of them caught my eye. He looked familiar—a blonde-haired, blue-eyed version of an adult I knew. By this time the first boy was making a getaway up Clerkenwell Road opposite us, having made it alive through the tangle of cars.

"Nicola! Are you all right?"

She had pushed herself up into a half-sitting position, but her face was in a shadow beneath the cart. As I focussed on it, I saw her blink. I gently lifted her up and out from underneath the cart.

"Yes, fine," she said, standing next to me on the pavement. I kept my arm around her because she looked exceedingly pale, and it was a good thing I did. In the next moment her legs buckled and she sagged. "Sorry, sorry," she said weakly, as I supported her, as if the spirit were willing but not so the flesh. "I . . ." To my horror, she went limp, and her eyes fell shut.

"Dear God," I breathed, gently letting her down onto the pavement, supporting her head with one hand and then the other as I shook my jacket off one arm at a time. Hurriedly I pulled my cellphone out of a pocket before rolling up the jacket and shoving it under her head as a makeshift pillow, and punched 999. The answer was immediate, and I watched Nicola's inert face as I spoke. "Yes, I need an ambulance in Farringdon Road, Clerkenwell, just north of the *Watch* offices."

As the bookstand owner came at a run, I felt a flash of fear, or dread, that once again I had endangered someone near me. It seemed to happen all too often as I went about my business at the Press—not at all what I'd expected when I'd been called upon to take over my father's sedate academic publishing business.

By this time the great British public was reacting to the disturbance—in an orderly manner, of course. Someone had flagged down a police car, and I was aware of the bookstall owner directing constables on foot up Clerkenwell Road after the boys. I saw someone with a notepad approach, his step quickening as he drew near. Of course. The hordes of journalists employed by the *Watch* just up Farringdon road were all on their way to Farringdon tube station, just around the corner, on their way home—or, more likely, en route to the pub.

Another policeman was kneeling next to me, looking at Nicola. Reaching for his radio, he said, "I'll call for an ambulance, shall I?"

"I've done it. Thanks."

"What happened here?" Bystanders started telling the story to both the policeman and the journalist before I could turn away from Nicola. They told it with a twist, claiming that the first boy had attacked Nicola for her handbag—they had seen him clinging to it—and then run off. The bystanders pointed at me. "He—yeah, the one in the white shirt—he yelled, and the bloke ran off. But by that time a pack of kids chased after him, up there." More fingers, pointing up Clerkenwell Road opposite.

The policeman radioed this information to his colleagues, and Nicola's eyes fluttered, then opened.

She blinked, then seemed to grasp what had happened. She rolled her eyes at me, wordlessly apologising for her inability to cope but unable to do anything about it.

"It's all right," I said. "Don't worry about a thing. He gave you quite a bashing." Even as I said it, I was aware that the bystanders had told the wrong story; the boy hadn't intentionally bashed her. In fact, his grab at her handbag hadn't been deliberate. I was quite sure he'd been reaching for a handhold in the panicky effort to regain his balance and flee from the gang of boys chasing him. They had been chasing him, I was sure, long before he'd run into us.

With paternal feeling, I brushed a wisp of hair off of Nicola's face. The journalist chose that moment to approach, and I felt myself stiffen. The fourth estate had proved to be far from friendly in the past.

"Your name, sir?"

I didn't look up. The young journalist was trying the oldest trick in the book—trying to make me feel as if he were an official on the scene, who deserved my cooperation in the fulfillment of his duties. I knew better; my older brother, Max, had been with this journalist's paper for years, and had told me all the tricks.

"None of your business," I mumbled, wishing—but doubting—that he'd take the cue and bugger off.

"Pardon me?"

As he bent down to get a closer look at Nicola, I stood abruptly and—how clumsy of me—knocked him right over.

"Oy!" he exclaimed, in high dudgeon. "Mind who

you're. . . ." Having got himself upright, he began to dust himself off, then caught my eye. Seeing that I was not effusive with my apologies, he stopped and glared at me.

"I'm going to find out just who the bloody hell you are," he said quietly, forefinger in my face. The accompanying threat of unflattering journalistic coverage went unspoken as he stalked off to find more cooperative witnesses.

Some time later, as the paramedics urged a now ambulatory but embarrassed Nicola to come into the ambulance with them "just for a check," I heard my name spoken. With consternation, I turned to see a bystander speaking to the sneering journalist. The writer caught my eye again and held it as he smirked. "Alex Plumtree. Right. I've heard of him."

Sighing, I turned away. My face had been in the papers too many times since I'd been with Plumtree Press. I couldn't seem to avoid it. First it had been success over an unsolicited, anonymous manuscript that had made the Press, and me, news. Then it was an author of mine who'd uncovered a secret about one of Britain's favourite authors. Suffice it to say that it's been one thing after another.

At least this time, I thought, they couldn't say anything bad about me, justified or not.

But there I was wrong.

BANTAM OFFERS THE FINEST IN CLASSIC AND MODERN BRITISH MURDER MYSTERIES

DOROTHY CANNELL

____56951-1	HOW TO MURDER YOUR MOTHER-IN-LAW	$5.50/$7.50
____29195-5	THE THIN WOMAN	$5.50/$7.50
____27794-4	THE WIDOWS CLUB	$5.50/$7.50
____29684-1	FEMMES FATAL	$4.99/$5.99
____28686-2	MUM'S THE WORD	$4.99/$5.99

COLIN DEXTER

____29120-3	THE WENCH IS DEAD	$5.99/NCR
____28003-1	LAST SEEN WEARING	$5.99/NCR
____27363-9	THE RIDDLE OF THE THIRD MILE	$5.99/NCR
____27238-1	THE SILENT WORLD OF NICHOLAS QUINN	$5.99/NCR
____27549-6	THE SECRET OF ANNEXE 3	$5.99/NCR

CHRISTINE GREEN

____56931-7	DEATH IN THE COUNTRY	$4.99/NCR
____56932-5	DIE IN MY DREAMS	$4.99/NCR

Ask for these books at your local bookstore or use this page to order.

Please send me the books I have checked above. I am enclosing $____ (add $2.50 to cover postage and handling). Send check or money order, no cash or C.O.D.'s, please.

Name _____

Address _____

City/State/Zip _____

Send order to: Bantam Books, Dept. MC 6, 2451 S. Wolf Rd., Des Plaines, IL 60018
Allow four to six weeks for delivery.
Prices and availability subject to change without notice.   MC 6 2/96

R. D. Wingfield's

Jack Frost Mysteries

Jack Frost, Denton Division, is not beloved by his superiors. In fact, he's something of a pain in the brass: unkempt and unruly, with a taste for crude humor and a tendency to cut corners. They'd like nothing better than to bounce him from the department. The only problem is, Frost's the one D.I. who, by hook or by crook, always seems to find a way to get the job done . . . .

Hard Frost
___57170-2 $5.99

A Touch of Frost
___57169-9 $5.99

Night Frost
___57167-2 $5.99

Frost at Christmas
___57168-0 $5.99